Praise for *Protest:*

'A kaleidoscopic feast... A great gathering of voices, a dispersal of perspectives' – *The Skinny*

'The variety of voices and subjects create a series of ever moving perspectives, but they unite around one focal point: our collective experiences of oppressions and our political responses to them. The book largely ignores leaders and icons and instead looks to the people, engaging in a bottom-up myth-making that is about the collective rather than the individual.'
– *Glasgow Review of Books*

'When right-wing populism is seemingly sweeping the west this whistle-stop tour demonstrates the power of people and provides a glimmer of hope and inspiration.' – *Big Issue North*

'Britain has a proud radical history of challenging injustice, and the eminently readable short stories in *Protest: Stories of Resistance* cover 600 years of uprising. Each story is followed by a brief essay explaining the historical context, revealing how tactics and philosophies have flowed to and enriched subsequent movements.' – *New Internationalist*

'The whole anthology is a fine memorial to those tens of thousands of ordinary people who, over the past 600 years, fought against injustice and class rule and for a better world of peace and equality. And long may we continue doing so.'
– *Socialist Review*

'The variety of storytelling ensures that the protests don't feel indistinct or hopeless, yet the injustices described feel depressingly familiar.' – *New Statesman*

'It would be heartening to see more works of historical fiction inspired by Comma Press's approach, serving both to educate and entertain by giving voice once again to people who struggled to make their voices heard in challenging circumstances.'
– *Disclaimer Magazine*

'*Protest* is an important collection highlighting the history of dissenting voices in the UK. It teaches rather than preaches and should be required reading for many of our current politicians.'
– *bookoxygen*

'*Protest* is an illuminating and essential read. The perfect inter-generational birthday or Christmas present, it joins up the dots and gives context, which is invariably missing from disdainful, market-led Media narratives, and rote-learning history ordained by successive governments. Buy it and read it!' – *Bookblast*

'A valuable treasury of reminders of earlier struggles and a persuasive call for us to have courage in our current ones with a ruthless class enemy.' – *Morning Star*

# PROTEST

## Stories of Resistance

Edited by
Ra Page

First published in Great Britain in 2017 by Comma Press.
This paperback edition published in 2018.
www.commapress.co.uk

A CIP catalogue record of this book is available from the British Library.

ISBN:     1905583737
ISBN-13:   9781910974438

Lines from the ancient folk tale of LLYN Y FAN FACH (pp.281-282)
are taken from the version published on www.sacred-texts.com.


This project has been developed with the support of the
Amiel and Melburn Trust and the Lipman Milliband Trust.

BarryAmiel&
NormanMelburntrust

The Lipman-Miliband Trust

The publisher gratefully acknowledges assistance from Arts Council England.

Supported using public funding by
ARTS COUNCIL
ENGLAND

*'The only interest in history is that it is not yet finally wrapped up. Another history is always possible, another turning is waiting to happen.'*

Stuart Hall

# Contents

# Introduction

So you've joined a march. A demo. A protest. You've decided, like Howard Beale, the unhinged news anchor in *Network*, that you're 'mad as hell and you're not going to take it anymore'. You've made a date with the masses and here you are, falling in step with a great throng of humanity snaking its way through the streets.

But something's not right. You're new to this. Something feels wrong.

It isn't immediately obvious where to walk, which banner to march besides, or, more worryingly, what you have in common with any of those around you. You remind yourself that you came here with a purpose, to protest a burning issue or cause you feel strongly about. Yet, within chanting distance, you see people appropriating the occasion for other, unrelated issues. What's worse, everyone looks so utterly different to you. The oddest thoughts start to plague you: I don't belong here; these people don't speak for me; this isn't me.

There's something about this discomfort that ought to trouble you. Why should the harmless customs of more seasoned protestors (the songs, the chants, the familiarity with basic circus skills) somehow upstage the ideological affinity that brought you all together? Keep walking, you tell yourself, eventually it will come to you. As you walk, you begin to realise that you're only accustomed to being places where you 'fit', where your externally worn 'identity' matches those around you – an identity that can be measured in the signifiers you surround yourself with, in your shopping history.

The march comes to a temporary halt; the crowd bunches up.

What happened to ideology? you wonder, in this momentary standstill. Why is it one of the few things people don't outwardly display in everyday life? You try a couple of hypotheses for size. Maybe it's your education, the way history is taught – less and less as a set of skills for questioning sources (which require qualitative understanding of ideologies), and more as a list of dates and names to simply learn by rote. Or maybe, you consider, it's because of the way politics is covered by the media – not as something to investigate or 'get to the bottom of', but as a kind of sport to merely commentate on, where performance is all, arguments are *ad hominem*, and potential leaders are passed over solely because they fail us as *entertainers*.

Whatever the reason, ideology wasn't the first thing you look for when you seek familiarity in strangers. Not even here. It's like you came with it tucked away in your breast pocket, a secret.

Those holding banners set them down for a moment to rest their arms. Others strain their necks to see if there's any movement up ahead.

When identity, as something that can be scanned externally, invades and dominates your political life (as ethnic identity has been accused of doing in the US), it shouldn't surprise you that phrases like 'post-truth' also enter the vocabulary. Truth has no currency in the markets that trade in news – the media – nor is there an 'invisible hand', or some consumer rights mechanism, to steer that market back towards the truth. This is simply because, in every media transaction, you, the user, *aren't* the consumer. In advertiser-funded media (including online media), the primary consumer is the advertiser. *You*, on the other hand, are the *product*, the thing being sold, the audience being shipped by the truckload to the doorsteps of the advertisers. What's more, your chemical addiction to the drug that is news means you really don't care what it's cut with, you'll keep queuing up for it, keep filling those trucks for the advertisers. (Meanwhile, with licence-fee funded media, the only real customer capable of removing their custom is the government.)

Up ahead of you, a protester starts shouting a new chant. You can't make it out.

But if you, the user, really don't have any rights, then you really should be 'mad as hell'. We all should be, you think. And we are. Our distrust of the media is eroding it from both sides. In the US, a new president has found purchase among the electorate by pitching himself directly against the 'mainstream media', even though he is, himself, a construct of it (or reality TV at least). Whilst in the UK, the BBC's quest for 'balance' is sometimes adhered to at the expense of other criteria. On its own, 'balance zeal' can take us to some strange places: 'balance' between experts and non-experts, 'balance' between extremists and non-extremists, etc.[1]

The words of the protester chanting up ahead grow louder.

*Kick the habit*, you think to yourself. The news doesn't make us do anything, except parrot the blame game, or spread the same gossip. *Kick the habit*, you think. Let's go back to looking at the wider picture, at the wider structures. *Kick the habit*, you start to chant. Let's wean ourselves off 'balance' and try other criteria instead: expertise, research, listening to people who've spent years studying a subject irrespective of how rich or popular it makes them.

The march starts moving again.

It was this impulse – to go cold turkey on the news – that inspired the commission that follows. The impulse was coupled with a hunch: that, rather than a series of discrete identity struggles, British protests form a continuum; one where ideas, tactics and philosophies can be seen flowing between movements, triggering new conversations, inspiring and shaping new methods.

# INTRODUCTION

The relevance of short stories to this project was obvious. When a 'world event' occurs, we generally experience it, and respond to it, as an individual; the most abiding sensation is of our own helplessness towards it. But quickly that event gets rewritten. In the media or in the official histories, it becomes a narrative full of agency, full of characters taking decisive actions, determining their and others' destinies. Our own, personal experience of the event – as it unfolded live in front of us – gets over-written, overlain with any narrative available that complies with Thomas Carlyle's 'Great Man' theory, that 'history is but the biography of great men', that the rest of us, the 'bystanders', aren't part of history.

The short story rejects this version of events because, as a form, it has evolved to prioritise the non-heroes – the bystanders, the disenfranchised, the 'submerged' (as Frank O'Connor would say). And when it comes to 'world events', none are more suited to the short story than the protest. In a protest, we're all bystanders, we're all there because of some attempt to marginalise us; the bystanders are the people making history.

In commissioning these stories, we encouraged authors to steer clear of political leaders, the 'heroes' of the history books. But beyond that, we didn't say whose point of view to take up. Some, like Matthew Holness and Martyn Bedford, deliberately chose unsympathetic characters to tell the story. Others, like Kit de Waal, Jacob Ross and Francesca Rhydderch, focused more on the context or climate that led up to the protest.

What we did insist on was that, once the authors had chosen their protest, they then worked with an expert – a historian, sociologist, crowd scientist, or indeed eye-witness – to maximise their story's background verisimilitude. The protests they chose covered a range of different strategies: traditional marches, strikes, pickets, hunger strikes, occupations, acts of industrial and media sabotage, even pub crawls.

Despite this diversity, certain commonalities did indeed start to emerge. Steve Hindle, in his afterword to Holly Pester's story, offers a checklist of common features that you can almost tick off when reading these stories:

– the moral outrage of the dispossessed;

– the use of symbolic violence against property rather than persons;

– the desire to remind the crown (or government) of its legal obligations;

– the importance of oral and especially proverbial culture in spreading word of discontent;

– the self-sacrifice of ringleaders in the interest of the greater economic good;

– the partial success of the protest in forcing the crown (or government), once the insurrection had been suppressed, to redress the grievances that provoked it.

Add to this list, the following more modern ingredients, and you have a fairly comprehensive recipe for a classic British protest:

– police heavy-handedness (Grosvenor Square, the Battle of Orgreave, the Poll Tax riot, etc.)

– government infiltration (Pentrich Rising, onwards).

If the stories commissioned here don't display every ingredient, they certainly boast most of them.

Threads can clearly be traced from one movement to another, supporting the idea of a continuum not just across British movements but internationally. Ned Thomas, in his afterword to Francesca Rhydderch's story, talks about the influence of Martin Luther King's strategy of direct, non-violent action on the Welsh language movement of the 1970s. But incredibly Michael Randle, in an earlier afterword, notes that Martin Luther King was himself influenced by the Aldermaston marches in Britain, via Bayard Rustin (one of the organisers of the 1963 march on Washington, who had been on the Aldermaston-inspired Sahara nuclear testing demo). Likewise, in many of these stories, prior protests loom large over present ones: Peterloo casts a dark shadow over the Radical War; the Suffragettes' achievements act as inspiration for the National League of the

Blind's 1920 march on London, which in turn inspires the Jarrow March 16 years later. When there is a common enemy involved across several protests (for instance, a particular prime minister or police force), there is also evidence of later protests 'settling scores' from previous ones (see pp.405–421).

Protests also appear to cluster around certain historical conditions. In some cases, for instance between 1979 and 1985, there is such a concentration of different protests that they begin to overlap (p281). In general though, the conditions that trigger these protests seem to fall into five types: economic decline, unwanted military escalation, the threat of new industrial technologies, and the introduction of new laws or practices that further marginalise an already marginalised part of society (or the refusal to introduce new laws to protect them). There even seems to be a particular time of year that protests tend to take place in. Excluding those actions that take place over several years, 80 per cent of the protests featured here occur between the months of March and June.

Crowd scientists Stephen Reicher and John Drury offer further conditions that are capable of transforming a peaceful demonstration into a full-scale riot: a shared definition of identity, a sense of the illegitimacy of 'the system', and a feeling of empowerment inspired by the strength of the crowd. Sometimes overzealous policing *on its own* can provide the first two of these.

While there is a temptation to dismiss riots as purely criminal acts that require no more than additional policing and harsher punishments, it's difficult to ignore the fact that riots get noticed. They succeed in lifting the conditions that triggered them up in the political agenda, and often have beneficial long-term legacies (the quiet abandonment of a policy, for example, or the equally quiet dropping of a particular police tactic). Those riots that fail to achieve anything particularly positive, long-term, are the ones that fail to tick the second box on Hindle's checklist: a specific focus on symbolic property.

In the aftermath of Trump and Brexit, it might feel like the UK and US have taken two giant electoral leaps backwards, reversing decades of progress. But, as these stories suggest, the wider, underlying picture must be seen as a positive, inspiring one. The higher concentration of protests after the Second World War is not simply a bias towards modernity, but reflective of what Ned Thomas calls 'rising post-Second World War expectations.' From 1945 to 1979, there does indeed seem to have been an 'awakening', as Thomas calls it, in the way Western governments widened, as well as improved, the protection they offered their citizens. In this sense, the cluster of protests that followed 1979, should be seen in exactly the same light as the recent flurry of protests following Trump's election, namely as a consequence of raised expectations being (temporarily) frustrated.

The march comes to a halt now and again. That's what it does.

In the wider analysis, one particular type of event provides a greater catalyst for progress than any other: War. When soldiers returned from the Second World War, for example, they brought with them an expectation that the nation they fought for, and many of their comrades died for, ought to *deserve* them. They also brought back the rewards of an intense six-year education in how things were being done elsewhere in the world, and how things might be done differently here. Glimpses of life, not just in communist Russia, but Sweden, Germany, France – where welfare states were already partly established – gave the returning soldiers a language for demanding more of the State back home. The construction of the NHS by the 1945-51 Attlee government, the formation of the United Nations in 1945, and the Universal Declaration of Human Rights in 1948 all became things for future generations of protestors to protect, and defend the spirit of. In this sense, contemporary protesters should take heart. They have history on their side.

*Ra Page,*
*Manchester, May, 2017*

# Notes

1. In October 2009, BBC One's flagship politics programme Question Time received more than three times its normal number of viewers when it controversially featured the leader of the far-right BNP, Nick Griffin. This was followed, over next seven years, by a total of 20 appearances by UKIP leader Nigel Farage up until the Brexit vote (compared to a total of ten appearances by the corresponding Green Party leaders, Natalie Bennett, Caroline Lucas and Jonathan Bartley, over the same period).

# The Pardon List

## Sara Maitland

'Why would I do that?' she asked him.

'To be safe,' he wanted to answer. He wanted her to be safe. He knew she had frightened people with the wild gleefulness of her dancing and laughing when they ambushed the manorial clerks and burned the court rolls. He knew in his own dark and, he feared, cowardly heart that they might need to punish her, if not now then sometime. One day, because they had all stepped outside their known space and abused the king's officials, because they had rioted, they might need to punish someone. One day they might look for someone who was theirs to pay for their sins — a scapegoat. Someone like her, who was theirs but whom they did not love.

They did not love her.

It is hard to love someone whose very existence makes you feel guilty.

Of course she does not remember now. For five nights she had wailed in the cottage — the first night fearfully, the second night angrily, the third night desperately and the last two reduced to periods of plaintive mewling; she was fifteen-months old and of course she does not remember. For five days, in the terror of the pestilence, in the horror of the deaths and confusions, no-one had thought to go and see what might be happening in the small cottage beyond the village. On the morning of the sixth day, her mother's brother, nervy and cross,

1

anxious and guilty, had walked up the hill, pushed through the doorway into the living space and seen the carnage. Her mother, her father, her two brothers and the baby were all dead: their fingers and feet blackened and the sickly sweet smell of putrefaction filling the air in the cramped room, making it poisonous, making it dangerous. And the child with her face turned to the wall was huddled in the corner barely able to turn her head for weakness, but alive and untouched by the pestilence.

He was not a wicked man, just a harried and guilt-ridden one. He scooped her up and carried her as quickly as he could out into the sunshine. He knew he should have remembered to come sooner. It was too easy to feel that if she had died too, it would not have mattered that he had not gone sooner and he would not have had to endure his own guilt. His wife, pregnant and panicked, could not bear to have the child near her. They gave her a place by the fireside, fed her as they might have fed a dog, but no-one held her, or consoled her or comforted her. And yet it did them no good; her uncle's wife took the pestilence, the buboes swelled in her groin, her fingers turned black and the child in her belly died with its mother. Her uncle blamed her, spared her no kindness and made her work too hard from too young. Before she was three years old she had heard him trying too often to hand her into the care of someone else. But no someone else wanted the task. She seemed tainted – both too lucky in living and too unlucky in her fate. No-one hurt her or beat her or starved her. But it was cold charity.

Cold charity, but she survived more or less and grew; never sweet, never pretty, never charming and even just to see her walking down the street was to remember they had left her forgotten in the charnel house of hell for five whole days.

She grew up before us like a root out of dry land. She had no form or comeliness, no beauty that we should desire her. She was despised and rejected by us, a woman of sorrows and acquainted with grief, as one from whom people hide their faces.

To be fair to them all, it was a very hard time. Half the people, five in every ten inhabitants of the small rural community died within a few weeks, died fast, inexplicably and horribly. Five in ten — and the fields unweeded, the harvest not fully gathered, the weather unfavourable and the fear palpable, nasty, guilt inducing. Their Lord, away in Scotland with the king's army, offered them no succour, still demanding full rents and later clamping down hard on anyone who wanted to take to the road and find a better service. His Reeve required full serf labour though there were not the villagers to provide it and their own fields needed every hand they could find.

But everyone in the village knew they had left her in that cottage for five days wailing for help and just to see her outside her hovel scattering seed for her hens, or to watch her walk across the fields spinning rhythmically as she walked, or doing her share of the field work... just seeing her reminded them all that they were proved mean-hearted and un-neighbourly. So it was hard to love her. She had to get by without.

Now, more than thirty years later, she stood leaning against the jamb of her door, her spindle in her hand but her head uncovered. She looked up at Sir Matthew with an oddly quizzical expression.

'Why would I do that?' she asked.

Sir Matthew was a priest. Just, he had little Latin and no preferment. He was slightly older than her and markedly less chaste, and through that restless spring and fierce summer he had stirred up communities of protest across Essex. He knew that Wycliffe's teaching was convenient to him, served his own small greeds and ambitions, but he also believed that the fact that it suited his interests did not make it untrue.

So he taught that the new poll tax was contrary to the traditions of the kingdom and the will of God. That taxing married couples as two separate individuals was contrary to the one flesh that God had ordained they should become. That the failures of the war in France demonstrated God's displeasure and proved that the tax was unjust — its endless repetition impoverished the people even while it profited the powerful. That, when the King's fancy tax collectors came knocking, failing to declare individuals or lying about one's true prosperity was justified, even graced. That the hard earned pence of the poor was wasted in corruption and indulgence and mismanagement by the great. And that to refuse to pay such taxes was holiness in the eyes of Christ.

He declared that the clergy should abjure all wealth, hold no office of state and preach the scriptures to the people in English. That the monks in their gated luxury, their Latin singing and their cruel exercise of power over their own unfree labour force were an abomination. With John Wycliffe he believed that, 'Englishmen learn Christ's law best in English. Moses heard God's law in his own tongue; so did Christ's apostles.'

He opened the scriptures to her and to anyone else who would hear him. He taught her that God had no tolerance for serfdom:

'By the law of Christ, every man is bound to love his neighbour as himself; but every servant is a neighbour of every civil lord; therefore every civil lord must love any of his servants as himself; but by natural instinct, every lord abhors slavery; therefore, by the law of charity, he is bound not to impose slavery on any brother in Christ.'

Or sister. Her freedom was guaranteed by God. In her he found a willing student.

Somewhere in the heady months behind them, while the roses flowered in the hedgerows, she and he had become allies, companions, perhaps friends. Today he had come down several miles to see her and she knew it and was grateful. But now the bright full green of June was darkening, fading towards autumn and the hawthorn berries were showing their first streaks of blood red ripeness.

'Why would I do that?' she asked him.

His eyes dropped and were caught by the spinning whorl

that weighted her spindle, dancing in response to the twitch of her elbow that kept it on the move; he realised that she was never perfectly still. He watched the smooth balanced block of wood that span and span, because he found he could not look straight into her face, into the new bright boldness of her eyes. He did not know how to answer her.

The rhythm of her spindle did not waver.

'Look,' she said, 'I did not assault the tax official. I did not burn the court rolls. But you taught me it was right to do so. Was it right? Are you saying now it was not right?'

He could feel the heat of her rage. He shook his head.

'I did not go into the Tower and kill the Chancellor. I wish I had, but I did not.'

After a pause she added, 'I did not kill any of the Flemish weavers.'

He looked at her now, almost nervously.

'So,' she went on, 'what do you want me to seek a pardon for?'

After another pause she added, 'They cancelled the promises the boy King gave us; they took away the freedoms he promised us, just like that. I hear they are executing people – just like we did – only more of them. Are they seeking pardons? Are they putting themselves on the pardon lists?'

The smooth balanced block of her spindle weight span and span, holding the line of thread taut; and suddenly it looked to him like a body on a gibbet – and then, as he watched, it jerked, jumped from the true spin; her yarn tangled, but she ignored it. She said, very quietly, but clearly, calmly,

'They killed Wat. They killed him during a parlay. That is a sin. Do they seek pardon?'

Abruptly she looked down, saw the knotted mess of her spinning, gathered it in, licked her fingers, spliced the frayed thread back onto the loose yarn bundle, let the spindle drop, rolled it against her thigh and started the rhythmic process again. He could taste his own jealousy in his mouth. They were all like this about Wat Tyler – not just the women, the men as well.

There was something about him; people loved him, followed him, honoured him. He was, he had been, a big rough man, not smooth or polite... but something, Wat Tyler had something Sir Matthew did not have and, of a sudden, he minded.

Once her weight was once more dancing smoothly she asked, 'So, Sir Matthew, why would I want to put my name on a pardon list?'

There was something bold about her, some high-handed flourish in her stance, something that had not been there before. Briefly he wondered what she had got up to and with whom in that wild fortnight, after she had danced so gleefully – so wantonly he now thought – round the fire in the Manor Courtyard and had disappeared into the night and, he learned later, journeyed to London in that strange mixed movement, part mob part army, singing and marching and praying, sermon-ed over by braver priests than he; burning and looting and killing, opening the prisons, killing the law officers, but also obedient to Wat Tyler and ordered and fearsome. He was, unexpectedly, frightened of her as well as for her. He found he could not look straight into her face, into the new bright knowingness of her eyes. He fidgeted with the knotted cord at his waist, looking sideways across her small barren yard.

'They say...' he began, then lowered his voice, almost muttering, 'they say you were... were you, were you at... the sacking... the burning... the Savoy Palace?'

'Oh they do, do they? Whoever "they" may be.'

There was a clarion note, half laughter, half pride in her voice and she was mocking him. He looked up and she seemed alight with a fierce joy, a strange triumphant fire. He looked away again.

'No Matthew we did not sack or loot the Savoy Palace, we cleansed it as the Lord Jesus cleansed the Temple. We were zealots for truth and justice, not thieves and robbers.'

There was a silence, and still he fixed his eye on the ground and watched as though counting one by one each blade of grass at her feet.

'Sir Matthew,' she said, reinserting the title of respect, 'You go around and about, you have been all over the land, I am sure you have seen many things, but I haven't. I have just stayed here – I thought our own Lord was grand and rich – and I did not know anything. Look at me, Sir Matthew, look at me.' She waited until he looked up; she smiled a smile of great sweetness and went on: 'I did not know there were so many beautiful things in the whole world as there were in the Savoy Palace. I do not mean just the rich things – the silver and the gold and the parcel-gilt and the jewels. There was lots of that stuff and very nice too for those who have it. Cart loads of treasure, and – as the Book warns us it makes them proud and mean, it gives them power and swagger. But it wasn't that. It was all the lovely things, the truly beautiful things.

There were books with pictures in them, shining big letters and pictures of Our Lord, a little baby, and his blessed mother and angels with wings of gold and trumpets raised – and all in colours so bright, and so tiny and so lovely. But there were not just beautiful things for God; there were beautiful things for Lords and Ladies. I went into a bedchamber, a huge room with a painted ceiling and a great bed all carved and coloured and curtained with hangings and on it, just thrown on it were great billowing cushions of goose feather down – more geese than we have in the whole village – just to make beautiful cushions for some Lady's beautiful head. The bed had a covering that was the softest thing I have ever touched, woven out of softness, made from some thread I do not know, like spiders' webs. And an embroidery on the wall that was sewn with flowers, more real, more lovely than the flowers in the fields in May – with tiny, tiny golden stitches and colours and all sparkled with jewels, with pearls and... and...You know, Sir Matthew, I am counted a good enough needlewoman – not just a decent spinster, who turns good sturdy yarn – but for needleworking also, nice straight little stitches, tidy, firm, but I cannot sew like that, so skilful and lovely and... I do not even know the words... I did not know there was sewing like that in the whole world. I did not know there were all these beautiful things – I did not know it even in my dreams. And now I know.

And I know too that I am more powerful than all those beautiful things.

I found a cup, a beaker made of glass, like the window in the Abbey, a little larger perhaps than my hand and with deep coloured lights in it. The light went into it and came out in sparkled colours. It danced for me and I wanted it, I wanted it so much. It was the finest, the loveliest thing I have ever seen. I almost thought I would keep it, tuck it into my tunic and no-one would know. But we were not there as thieves and robbers. We were there for justice and truth.

So I threw it at the wall. And it smashed, it smashed into a thousand pieces and they lay on the floor and they sparkled like the stars. The floor was dark, there was light coming in the window and the shards of that beautiful precious glass were sparkling on the floor like Our Blessed Lady's Highway does every night in the heavens. I made the stars dance in glory. Nothing, nothing in my life has been beautiful... until those little fragments of glass all the colours of heaven danced on the floor of that lovely, lovely bed chamber.

So then I was a little crazy and it was glorious. We smashed up that palace, we broke all the things, or we tossed them into the river – ripping and breaking and singing and laughing. We were laughing. Hot, powerful, strong. We threw all those things into the river. And then we burned it down – and those hot red flames and black smoke rising matched the heat in me. I tell you, Sir Matthew, I believe that after all those years of meekness and gentleness and goodness the Lord Jesus must have enjoyed smashing up the tables of the money lenders in the Temple. I hope he had as much joy of it as we did when we burned the palace. We were the vengeance of God and it was fun.

Do you know something? When we broke into the Savoy Palace we found this little gaggle of grand ladies, and they were trying to hide, but squeaking like mice, and weeping and moaning and carrying on. Pissing themselves like as not, from fear. And we, the women I mean, were flighting them a bit, not very kind, but light hearted, ragging like children do. But the men... well you know what men are. You could see they knew these women were beautiful, and they were beautiful, but so silly. And I dare say no better than they ought to be. But the men were... they were kissing their hands, all respectful and proper, and offering them safe passage, offering to be their escort, assuring them of their safety. And at first I felt small and dirty and envious, greedy towards them; I felt that they deserved the good treatment they were getting. But afterwards, after we had destroyed the beautiful things and set the palace aflame, I saw some more ladies like that out on the street, looking all frightened and foolish and I thought differently. I thought, 'Well, the only difference between them and me is that they are cleaner. They get to have a bath as often as they want one. That's all. We had this song that Wat and Sir John Ball taught us. It goes, 'When Adam delved and Eve span who was then the gentleman?' And I knew then that those fancy ladies are nothing. Nothing more than I am. I have changed.

So they took back the promises of freedom that the boy King gave us; they killed Wat in front of our very faces and we did not save him; we slunk back home like whipped curs and they will say nothing has changed, nothing has changed, nothing has changed. But they are wrong. They will always be wrong, because all over this realm of England there are serfs, cottagers, poor men, villeins, women even who know the power of their own anger and know how good it feels to use it. Who have changed in themselves. Who know that we did not loot or rob the Savoy Palace the way they rob us. Who know that the only difference between serf and Lord is that they get to have baths. And to own beautiful things. We frightened them and they did not frighten us. So do not try to frighten me now, Sir Matthew.'

He was shaken, shaken by her strength, her bell-like clarity. He did not know what to say. He wanted to warn her, tell her to be careful – to keep her head down and not shout out her crazy triumph. He did not dare. He did not dare to confront her high, hot courage.

She dropped her hand, stopped the steady whirl of her spindle weight, grasped the long straight stick and poked him in the shoulder with it, hard enough to hurt. A more impertinent gesture would be difficult to imagine. He looked straight at her, taken aback, shocked by her unexpected cheek. She laughed at him, loudly, boldly and entirely without respect.

And then, her laughter sinking down, she returned his stare, smiled with an unexpected kindliness and said, 'I thank you for your care of me. But having committed no offence I need no pardon. And anyway I have never had so much fun in my life. I'll not be putting my name on any pardon list. Not now, not ever.'

# Afterword: Wat Tyler and the Great Rising, 1381

## Prof. Jane Whittle
University of Exeter

IN 1348 AND 1349 THE Black Death swept across England, killing an estimated 40 per cent of the population in the most deadly epidemic in the country's documented history. The government's immediate reaction was to pass labour laws setting maximum wage rates. This aimed to prevent ordinary people from profiting from the resulting labour shortage and benefitted manorial lords who were the main employers of labour. Just over thirty years later the Peasants' Revolt shook the ruling classes to the core. It was the first mass movement of ordinary people to challenge England's political system. The rebellion was sparked by the Poll Tax of 1381. Poll taxes were a new form of taxation introduced in 1377, which taxed individuals rather than households or communities. Levied to fund the war with France, poll taxes were collected in 1377, 1379 and 1381. The government was disappointed with the tax assessment completed in 1380, and a reassessment was ordered. It was this process of reassessment that led to the revolt. In Essex, some of the men responsible for village-level assessment, who were ordinary villagers, banded together to resist the demands of the gentlemen tax assessors responsible for the county.

From a very early stage of the revolt the rebels in Essex were in communication with those in Kent, and the actions in the two counties mirrored each other. They targeted tax collectors, lawyers and government officials, destroyed property and documents but rarely killed anyone. They took control of local towns, captured castles and released prisoners from gaol. Then they marched to London, converging on the capital on Thursday 13th June. Wat Tyler emerged as a rebel leader in Kent but was rumoured to come from Colchester in Essex. Very little is known about his background: it is likely he was, as his surname suggests, a tiler. The rebels encountered surprisingly little resistance. There was no standing army in this period. Armed forces consisted of gentlemen leading their tenants or paid retainers. With the ordinary people up in rebellion, gentlemen found they had few people they could command. The government was weak, led by the boy King Richard II, who was only fourteen at the time of the revolt. It was also unpopular, as a result of not only heavy taxation and the oppressive labour laws, but also lack of success in the war with France.

No petition listing the rebels' demands survives from the revolt. However, descriptions of the revolt in medieval chronicles tell us that petitions were created and demands presented to the King, in writing and in person. Between the 11th and 15th of June, each iteration of these demands became more radical. On the 11th, when the King sent his first message to the rebels asking why they had risen up, they replied that they wished to save him from his treacherous advisors. On the 13th June, the rebels sent a list of written demands to the King. They repeated their intention to punish members of the government they considered traitors, but added a more significant social demand for 'charters to free them from all manner of serfdom'. Later that day the rebels entered and took control of London. There the King met with the rebels twice. On the 14th June at Mile End, Wat Tyler presented him with another petition. This repeated the demand for freedom from serfdom, requested that all dues to manorial lords be restricted to a payment of 4d per acre, and that 'no-one should serve any man except by his will', a demand for free wage labour in opposition to the labour laws. The King had little choice but to agree to these demands. The rebels asserted their dominant position later that day by taking the Tower of London by force, and beheading two of the most important figures in the government, the chancellor Simon Sudbury and the treasurer Robert Hales. The next day Wat Tyler and King Richard met one more time. At this point the rebels requested nothing less than a transformation of society: not just the abolition of serfdom, but the abolition of all lordship apart from the King's, a complete reform of the legal system, and that the church should be stripped of its worldly wealth and its elaborate hierarchy, leaving only a single bishop. This meeting did not end well for the rebels. A scuffle broke out and one of the king's guards stabbed and killed Wat Tyler. With Tyler's death the momentum of the rebellion ebbed away. The King rescinded all the concessions he had made and the gentry gradually regained control.

However, just as the movement was coming to an end in London, other parts of England were rising in revolt. The rebellion took a different form in different regions, depending on the particular grievances and leaders. The town of St. Albans was dominated by a great Benedictine Abbey, which was also an oppressive manorial lord. There the townspeople had a long running dispute with their lord over milling rights, which had resulted in their hand mills being confiscated and cemented into the floor of the abbot's parlour earlier in the fourteenth century. During the rebellion these were torn up and symbolically returned to the people. Here the rebellion was at its height on the weekend of 15th and 16th of June, just as it was collapsing in London. Similarly, rebels in Cambridgeshire, who had been active in the previous week, spent that weekend destroying records belonging to Cambridge University. In Suffolk the rebels were particularly violent, beheading Sir John Cavendish on 14th June, and the prior of Bury St. Edmunds on 15th June. While in Norfolk at this time the rebellion was only just beginning. There the rebels gathered and took control of

Norwich (the second largest city in the kingdom) on Monday 17th June and set up an alternative government, remaining in control there until the following week. Across Norfolk rebels attacked the houses of the gentry and burned manorial court rolls that contained records of serfdom.

As well as hostility to the government, to lawyers and the legal system, and to manorial lords, a current of radical Christianity ran through the revolt. The rebels were clearly hostile to the Church in its role as a manorial lord, as the attacks on the great abbeys of St Albans and Bury St. Edmunds demonstrate. But they had amongst their ranks the lower ranking clergy. For instance in Suffolk, the rebels were led by John Wrawe, a parish priest. One of the most enigmatic figures of the rebellion was John Ball, an itinerant priest, who famously preached a doctrine of social equality:

> When Adam delved and Eve span
> Who was then the gentleman?

Ball had spent time in Yorkshire and Essex, before being imprisoned in Kent for preaching against the pope. He was released from gaol by the rebels and joined them, preaching to the assembled crowds at Blackheath. The chronicle accounts of the rebellion linked Ball's views to the more intellectual strand of late medieval religious unorthodoxy promoted by John Wycliffe, but Wycliffe overtly dissociated himself from the rebels and their views.

Historical debates about the Peasants' Revolt have revolved around its causes and consequences. Some see the rebellion as a form of class struggle, with deep rooted economic and social causes in the feudal economic system which relied on manorial lords exploiting their unfree peasant tenants, and viewed the revolt as a key moment in the weakening of serfdom and feudalism. Others argue that the causes were short-term failures in government and that the rebellion had few long-term consequences and little to do with serfdom. Both viewpoints have weaknesses. If the rebellion is seen primarily as a movement against serfdom, it is hard to explain why one of its epicentres was the county of Kent which, unlike most other parts of England, had very little serfdom in the medieval period. Short-term political problems – particularly taxation and the unsuccessful war with France – were clearly important. Members of the government such as Sudbury and Hales, and tax collectors and documents were all targets of the rebels. Yet on the other hand, if the rebels' demands were correctly recorded in the chronicles, they were certainly radical. They wished to keep the monarchy but do away with the rest of the ruling class. Nor should the long-term consequences of the rebellion be dismissed lightly. A parliament held in 1382 effectively conceded that many of the rebels' complaints were justified. And after 1381 the ruling classes lived in fear of another rebellion and moderated their actions accordingly. Unlike most European countries, England remained relatively lightly taxed, and a country that taxed the wealthy more heavily than the poor, for centuries after the rebellion.

We will never know exactly what motivated particular people to take part in the rebellion. Despite the fact it took place over 600 years ago the events are surprisingly well-documented. There are numerous court records and chronicle accounts. Pardon rolls record those who sought to be excused for their actions after the revolt. All these documents record the rebellion from the perspective of the literate male elite who were uniformly hostile to the rebellion. However, it is possible to recapture elements of rebel motivations by 'reading against the grain' and interpreting the rebels' actions, which were notable in being uniformly disciplined and carefully targeted. For instance when they were in control of London they did not ransack and loot the city. They attacked certain properties, such as John of Gaunt's Savoy Palace in central London. John of Gaunt was the King's uncle, and particularly disliked for his important role in the government. The rebels did not loot his palace, but instead destroyed it; those who tried to steal were punished. In London and in the countryside the rebels more often burned documents than took lives. For instance at the Temple in London, which trained and housed lawyers, they burned books, charters and records but allowed the lawyers to flee. They did not kill all the gentlemen who fell into their hands, and in fact surprisingly few people were killed by the rebels. They targeted particular individuals as a result of specific grievances. The only social group who appear to have been attacked indiscriminately were the Flemings: immigrants from the southern Low Countries (modern Belgium), possibly because of competition in the cloth industry.

The careful reconstruction of the backgrounds of those who took part in the rebellion reveals that the rebels were not a desperate mob with nothing to lose. Many were older men with families and property, although these are the people for whom evidence is most likely to survive, and it is also true that many rebels must have gone completely undocumented. Even the description of the rebels as 'peasants' seems inappropriate as many of the participants were craftsmen, wage earners and town-dwellers (like Wat Tyler), rather than small farmers. As the anthropologist James Scott has argued, rebellions are extraordinary moments when the 'hidden transcript' of oppressed and dominated groups emerges into the limelight: customary deference is abandoned and long-held discontents are openly expressed in actions as well as words. It is the historian's role to interpret these messages, refracted through the prism of hostile chronicle narratives and official legal documents. Fiction, however, can go a step further, and imagine the lived experience of the rebellion.

# Heavy Clay Soil

## Holly Pester

'DISORDERLY RABBLE! YOU WILL all be prison ghosts. I will trample you!'

The boy, who was a skilled thief, neighed like a horse and pointed a stolen axe at his friends. They jeered and called out, 'Nuddygate Nuddygate! Knock down his horse! Gut it. Kill his law!'

They pulled the boy to the dirt, threw his axe and boots into the stream then thumped his arms. Before the joke beating became too rough, he raised his head and shouted, 'I am not Jack Nuddygate, I am the starving farmer, Rebel Commotion!'

He smiled into his game.

'Wreck the fences!'

The group of children turned around, set eyes on a fallen fern, screeched and charged at it. After thrashing its branches the boy and the girl who had brought rope organised the torn up pieces into six bundles of fuel. They tied the bundles to the back of the oldest girl who bled each month. She made donkey sounds and butted her smaller companions to make them laugh. So went their routine as they walked through the woodland towards their squatted cottages; play, scavenging, and labour, wandering in and out of private acreage.

A rogue glance from a sly girl made her brothers dash at a bordering hawthorn, where they coordinated their hands and tools to uproot the bush. Once it was fully ripped out they dug

17

into the earth like a machine to bury it. Upturning the soil disturbed the stuff and habits underground; a culture of ants passed over the children's arms, onto their necks and into their hair. Woodlice ran in panicked circles like citizens of a collapsing empire. A girl who was fond of bugs and beasts ducked down to collect an exposed worm. She sang her sister's cradlesong to it, kissed it gently in the middle, then rested the worm on top of a molehill.

A decision was made to tear another hawthorn from its bedding and burn it. A flame was created inside a huddle of small backs and a prayer was whispered as a lit leaf was passed to the shrub. Some bracken was added to the flames, then the dried-up body of a dead vole. The smell of burning animal fur inspired the chant, 'All things in common, all kynde in kindling.' The fire lasted a few minutes. Three of the youngest jumped away from the smoke down to the edge of the stream and crouched. They scratched lines into the ground with sticks that marked out an imaginary plot of land. A boy with lice hair lifted his stick to the sky and shouted, 'Go riot!' Two girls shoved their hands through the dirt, grabbing fistfuls to fling into the air cheering, 'The Earth answers…,' then listened to the plod of material hitting the ground.

The rough covey navigated the woodland like one creature; multiple arms plucking chickweed and goosegrass, garnering berries and smoking bark. As they moved through the trees they spread the seeds of cornflower, pollinating-insects rested on their loot sacks, while blood-sucking insects fed from their boney ankles. They chased rabbits, joked, raided nests, farted, called each other 'ketch', and whipped the backs of each other's knees with limp branches; cried, comforted, then carried on along their route. The offspring of Chrouchley and Smythe were in charge of collecting firewood, the Lambe girls gathered medicinal herbs, while Miller's daughter held tight to the lead of a castrated goat. Some children passed the time by listing their mothers' maiden names, their skills at the whetstone and talents with a scythe. They listed the mothers with pregnant tums and those with pustule diseases. The youngest was a boy called Geoffrey who was lame in one leg. His brother taught him to plant a tiny pause between each step; he kept pace with the others but with a measure of pain coded into his movements.

They headed to the wastes to collect sods of turf and maybe scavenge a goose. They began to sing a song, a mutation of a ballad they'd heard repeated at the alehouse. They muddled and changed the lyrics as they walked,

'Where did the corn tillage go?
Turned to pasture for pigs and weathers.
And where did the commons go?
Turned to brass pie, separated by hedges.
Reap, steal, manfully dye.
What shall we eat today and what tomorrow?
Milk the stinking encroachers who landed our sorrow.
Reap, steal, fill the dykes.
Only God can paint lines from house to houses,
Pull down the pales in the parks and chases!
Reap, steal, manfully dye.
Honey from the bees and greasy ointment from the trees,
It's all ours and Nobodies!
Reap, steal, fill the dykes.
Who inspires this revolt in thee?'

All children screamed the final line.
'Captain Pouch has the authority!'

'That Captain Tinker will not save you.' The surprise voice had a pitch somewhere between a dog's growl and the moan of a plough. The children believed it had come from the mouth of an ancient tree. It silenced them for a moment before they moved to challenge the stranger's speech.

'The Captain has magic rocks in his pouch to throw in the militia's eyes!' spoke the girl most talented at catching fowl. The retort was quick to follow,

'There's nothing in his pouch except mouldy cheese.'

A head peered round from behind the tree; it was hooded, draped in fine, but tatty and stained cloths. The figure was cutting liquorice root into sellable lengths, surrounded by a collection of embroidered sacks. One bag was patterned with weird animals with many limbs, another with lines of poetry in unrecognisable languages, another seemed to show the designs for a complicated machine. The young group moved a few steps towards the stranger, whispering, '*Vagabond, witch, demander for glimmer.*'

'No, it is sacred matter he carries! Captain Pouch is in league with the Lord Almighty and also our Lord, James the King.' said the boy, who trained the dogs and had yesterday eaten a rat.

Looking down at the task of sticks and not the motley audience, the wanderer spoke with a regretful voice.

'King James does not care about you. I have seen this story to its end. I see a bloody battle where amateur mercenaries slay the bodies of rebels. I see many of your fathers hanging by the neck like fish tails under the next moon.'

The stranger, who they decided was an elderly woman, held up one of her embroidered bags. 'Precious truths in here. Precious truths. The sort only your kind could see if I showed them to you.'

A hasty boy threw a clump of mud at the stranger's head. She brushed it off and set to untying the knot that fastened her bag.

'Are you a seer? Or are you mad, or are you…?'

The questions stopped as the group shifted nearer. From a shorter distance they saw an odd looking scar on the stranger's ear, and as the children at the front leant forward they could see a thick layer of dark curly hair down her neck and shoulders.

'The riots are coming to these parts aren't they, friends?'

The children hummed and nodded.

'And all the women and all the men, the angry folk of your community, your kin and carers, they will march tomorrow to a piece of land to rage?'

Many eager answers were thrown at the hairy person, speaking of a good insurrection and godly fight. As the last slogan was yelled, the vagabond woman shrugged and spat a glob of phlegm into some camomile.

'Come and sit with me, I want to show you something about the lines and borders that extend way beyond the ones your elders are battling in the fields.'

The children did not pause before gathering into a half-moon around the tree. They sank into each other's folded legs like puppies.

'Look at the ground, what plots for commotion do you see there? Look at its shallows and ridges, at the mulching leaves and crawling roots, at that red bug dropping miniature pools of vomit. There is more to *this* war than your parents' one that debates logics of property and labour. Look at you, you lovely fragments. Why become literate in adults' arguments of work that makes rent and rent that makes work.'

A boy's head jolted up, 'It is sinful not to work!'

In mock disgrace the elderly woman said, 'Put God into your acts of rest why don't you, and your friends' rest. You know how to feed each other don't you? You know where to shit and where to cook? Don't become your names. You know what your dreams mean, don't you?'

The children paused and then buzzed with reaction:

'I dreamt the clouds in the sky were copulating lovers. They made babies that dropped from above and exploded into flames, falling on every manor house of the gentry.'

'I dreamt an army of hogs wearing emeralds rampaged through Dunchurch village and transformed the well-water into swine blood'

'In my dream every human tongue grew another tongue, and another one extended from that tongue, until the city square was a lacework of tongues, where the people could neither move nor talk.'

'There's nothing holier than that.' The stranger nodded then pointed her long-nailed finger at her spectators, fixing their attention on her next move. She opened up her larger embroidered bag and turned it upside down. A cluster of live earthworms fell out. The pinkish deposit landed on the ground as one twisting mass that gradually separated into hundreds of individual efforts to bury and gorge the soil. The children jumped onto all fours, forming dancing bridges over the worms, laughing at any accidental squishing.

'Look at the worms, friends, look at their versatility and resistance. They move through the land in their own dimension. The worms make the categories of *here and there* that your folk live by seem ridiculous. Now look here…'

The next sack was overturned and out poured some dark grey lumps the size of pebbles. A smell like rank beer and coal emanated from them.

'These are the turds of an extinct ape.' She scattered them to mix with the worms.

'There is information in this dirty content – it explains where we are from and what we still are.'

She muttered her next phrases as if it were an incantation, 'Produce and expression, production and creation.'

The children joined in, changing the words to 'progression and excretion, potion and exhibition'.

To the turd and worm mix the woman added two pearls, a collection of figurines in shapes of wide and fertile bodies, some whale bones and a bag of salt. She looked up with the expression of someone making a great political speech.

Another bag yielded a dark black sludge that subsumed the other things into its gelatinous membrane. 'This is the planet telling us a story from millions of years ago. It tells us to move history forward and to undo relations that become rotten, to make new ones.'

The final offering came from a small leather purse hanging around her neck, which she sprinkled over the mixture. A dozen tiny moths fell out, landed on the ground then took off, growing wide and luminous with every flap.

'These are a future species, not yet in existence.'

The children looked up as the moths flew away, then looked back to the storyteller.

'All these substances are the details of heritage. They are stories we should tell. What are they telling you?'

The children stared back.

'Invent justices. You will need them. Be like the worms in the soil. Be in revolt with every bit of your fleshy bodies. Think like the sludge that melts boundaries, turning everything into slime. Radiate; like excrement, like moths.'

While she spoke the children felt themselves merge with the strange compost. Their limbs felt attached differently and then fused together into tails and wings. They felt connected like one organism then divided and scattered into many different gestures. They felt heavy like rocks and then light like floating ash. Everything moved, time dissolved but the old woman's voice carried on.

'To trouble all forms of class and subjection, embody this slime. Take it with you into your battles against possession.' Her voice took on a deep scratchy echo that seemed to come from another time.

'And with you, I pollute time. Be well.'

The moment held still until a breeze passed through the trees. The children sat up and blinked, their bodies feeling fully distinct and apart. The old woman was cutting up her roots and whistling as if alone. They spoke to her though she wasn't listening.

'We must go back now. There are many jobs we have to do and materials to deliver home.'

The first to rise to their feet were Geoffrey and his brother. The others stood up and followed in groups of twos and threes. The last to leave was the girl who was fond of bugs. She stared at the strange stuff on the ground and thought she saw in the muddle the map of a city that would be interesting to live in. Her cuff was tugged on by her friend and she joined the rest.

It was late. The twilight birds were shrieking. Between the wastes and the cottages the children reached an alehouse. From inside they could hear barrels scraping along the floor and fists banging on tables. Once the goat was tied to a hook, the group snuck in through a narrow door into a stink of piss and hops, and a dim light. The women were sat together at one end of the room and the men at the other. No single voice was distinguishable. The children marched towards the men with their clods and a stolen goose, then dumped them on a table. The loot was quickly hidden away while documents and coins were handed about over the children's heads. Quick moving boys and girls grabbed hold of tankards and necked some ale before their faces were pinched or slapped. The Chrouchleys found a cat to chase while the Smythes tormented a man who was braiding a drum. Eventually they were pushed outside and led back to their homes where they would be put to work on the stove. The girl who was fond of bugs wandered slowly behind. As she passed the men stacking pitchforks and billhooks for the next day's leveling march, she wondered who out of those bearded men would be hewed into lumps by the amateur army, and who would hang at the gallows. She felt a worm slip down her back underneath her dress; it wriggled round to her belly and dropped.

# Afterword: Enclosures and Captain Pouch, 1607

## Prof. Steve Hindle
The Huntington Library

THE 'RISING' WHICH PROVIDES the context for Holly Pester's short story is the insurrection which spread across the Midland counties of England in May, June and July of 1607.

The social fabric of Leicestershire, Northamptonshire and Warwickshire had been flammable for over a decade, not least since the parliament of 1593 had repealed the statutes which prevented landlords from transforming their arable land into pasture. Given this ability to replace the growing of corn with the rearing of sheep, landlords whose estates sat on the heavy clay soils of the midlands rapidly expanded their sheep runs and increased their flocks. Fields which had once been farmed collectively according to customs enforced by manorial courts were now enclosed and the common property rights that had been exercised within them were extinguished. Commons had been critical to poor households, since they offered significant resources of wood for fuel and turf for the grazing of livestock, which in turn provided them with dairy produce that could be consumed at home or sold at market. Without these resources, commoners were struggling to make ends meet, and were often either forced through eviction or chose through desperation to leave. Although the crown argued otherwise, enclosure often led to depopulation.

The hedging, ditching and fencing of common land

which had been so central to the survival strategies of the labouring poor and their families was hugely controversial and contested. Sheep, and the hedges which now bounded the meadows in which they grazed, were hated as symbols of landlordly oppression: as the contemporary proverb had it, 'horn (sheep horns) and thorn (hawthorn) had made England forlorn'. In turn, the elimination of arable agriculture diminished the food supply and drove up the cost of grain, and poorer people were convinced that enclosure and high prices were inextricably linked: in the idiom of a proverb circulating widely in the midlands 'the more the sheep, the dearer the corn'. Indeed, the spark which set the social fabric alight was the rising price of grain in the winter of 1606–1607. The grumbling in the stomachs of hungry children was far louder than the injunction to deference and obedience voiced by the clergy in their weekly sermons.

Throughout the early summer of 1607, the commoners and labourers of the midlands started to attack enclosures, and specifically to smash fences, level ditches and bury hedges. Known as 'levellers' and 'diggers', terms of opprobrium which were to become badges of honour during the English Revolution of the 1640s, the protesters took profoundly symbolic action against hawthorn hedges in particular, often digging them up, burying them in ditches and setting them ablaze. Anti-enclosure protest took place in an acrid haze of flame, ashes, soil and sweat.

The principal targets of protest were those estates where enclosure had been most extensive and the hit-list was apparently coordinated by one John Reynolds, reputedly a tinker from Desborough in Northamptonshire, who took on the figurative name 'Captain Pouch', after his leather satchel which (he claimed) contained the King's commission to destroy all enclosures between the cities of Northampton and York. Reynolds' rhetoric was simultaneously populist and egalitarian, but it was also infused with both popular legalism (derived from royal proclamations) and scriptural radicalism (influenced by the

Book of Isaiah). Fueled by hatred of those who 'ground the faces of the poor on the whetstone of poverty' and convinced that he could enforce royal policy against enclosure better than those magistrates who were often themselves guilty of depopulation, Reynolds mobilised very large crowds (reputedly numbering thousands) at such contested sites as Cotesbach (Leicestershire), Newton (Northamptonshire) and Withybrook (Warwickshire).

Reynolds himself was apprehended at Withybrook on 1st June and sent to London where he almost certainly died under interrogation. Despite his arrest, the insurrection bubbled on and was only suppressed on 8th July after a bloody pitched battle at Newton when fifty diggers were slaughtered at the hands of the Northamptonshire militia. At a subsequent trial in Northampton on 28th July, dozens of those captured on the battlefield were arraigned and convicted of felony-riot and levying war against the crown, and were accordingly subject to the full judicial penalty for treason: hanging, drawing and quartering. Their quartered carcasses were then dispatched to be exhibited at the city gates of the towns where the rising had enjoyed most support – to the terror of all other likely offenders.

The crown nonetheless had to concede that repression of the rising and retribution against its ringleaders did not in and of itself solve the enclosure problem, and before long King James and his advisors (especially Solicitor-General Sir Francis Bacon) turned their attention to redressing the grievances which had provoked such discontent. Encouraged by the ambivalent rhetoric of royal chaplain Robert Wilkinson who blamed the insurrection not only on the labouring poor who had lacked the patience and fortitude to bear their suffering quietly, but also on the landlords who had behaved so greedily, the crown began to collect evidence against enclosers and depopulators, ultimately prosecuting, convicting and fining them in the court of star chamber. To this extent, those who were cut down at Newton or butchered at Northampton did not die in vain. The progress of enclosure across the midlands slowed considerably, and it was not until the sanction of parliamentary statute was brought into play in the mid-eighteenth century that the remaining common fields were finally enclosed on midland estates.

The Midland Rising therefore shares many characteristics with the overall pattern of popular protest in British history: the moral outrage of the dispossessed; the use of symbolic violence against property rather than persons; the desire to remind the crown of its legal obligations; the importance of oral and especially proverbial culture in spreading word of discontent; the self-sacrifice of ringleaders in the interest of the greater economic good; and the partial success of the protest in forcing the crown, once the insurrection had been suppressed, to redress the grievances that had provoked it. Like generations of protesters before and after them, the rebels of 1607 might not have prevented political, legal or economic 'innovation', but they did mitigate its worst rigors. They were, in E. P. Thompson's famous phrase, 'ever baffled, ever resistant.'

Many of these features are prominent in Holly Pester's narrative, in particular in its emphasis on the rhyme and rhythm of proverb and prophecy, and the ghostliness and other-worldliness of the encounter with the witch or sorceress. The rich foregrounding of the texture of the earth (soil, worms, wood, decay), and the closing allusion to the alehouse as the milieu in which plans were made and resolve stiffened, are also highly appropriate. Above all, however, it is the children's perspective which is most powerful and resonant. Popular culture was invariably rebellious, and it was usually rebellious in defence of custom. Although that defensive instinct might seem nostalgic and conservative, those who resisted enclosure were seeking both to preserve and to perpetuate custom, and they did so because they wanted to protect the moral economy not just for their own posterity but for generations of children to come.

# The Mastiff

## Matthew Holness

*'The old World… is running up like parchment in the fire.'*
*— Gerrard Winstanley, 1649*

I ALONE STOOD FOR Colonel Bulwer's company, such had it been at Marston. Then there was the Parson and ten men or more that joined with us at Cobham. So did we journey together for the heath, with much talk to me of the mastiff. Though none about me sought close company with the brute, for it was in truth the largest those others had seen, yet was there great discussion concerning it. Much of this being but youthful swagger, strengthened, no doubt had I, by the good Colonel's cask, yet was there, to my mind, awe in their speech, such as us soldiers had felt before Prince Rupert's Boye, that devil's familiar, for so had we deemed that dog in those dark and terrible days.

The mastiff was mine, though it were property of the Colonel in name, and did surpass Boye greatly in strength, for it was a baiting dog, bred for purpose, and had lost no contest in all its years. Nor did it suffer greatly with injury, so fierce was its deportment. Much renown had it won for our Colonel, yet I alone, a soldier of Cromwell no more, was the dog's true master. For no man's call would it heed save my own, and in all its years left not my side but to fight, and was in truth my lost eye returned, for by the company of that dog alone did I forget my

29

ruin'd sight, and cause men to mark again my former strength.

I starved it often, and beat it with a leather crop I won from a corporal of Prince Rupert's troop, whose horse I did force down in an early engagement by the cutting of its nose, and brought its rider down, whereat I slew him with my pistol to his temple, as occurred often in those cruel and bloody days.

I roped tight that mastiff's jaw and chained it to the post by night, otherwise was the brute tied to my good arm, which I did protect from injury by way of my riding glove, leaving my ruined hand to daunt those affronted by the grim spectre of my visage. Yet never once did the cur turn on me, though in sport it were savage, the like of which many men had not before seen, and travelled far distance to behold.

It was not the ring we journeyed to now, but onward, toward Little Heath. Yet the mastiff sensed our true purpose and strained more than was custom, leaping at those in my company, so that the Parson bade me calm the creature, or else return it to the Colonel's lodging. Thus did I pull hard on the brute, to choke it, and force its head downward 'gainst the earth, whereat it gored the very rock under it. Through which action did I appease Parson Platt, for it was supposed this settlement of Diggers were but God-loving farmers. Yea, though they lived as pigs even and starved for all their talk of treasury.

So had they preached at my Colonel's hearing and in his own manor even, two weeks back, without removal of their hats in defiance of his honour. Which want of respect did offend me greatly and cause me to strike out at them, whereupon they did speak only of my injuries and bade me join them in such brotherly toil and labour as they were about. Which was grave insult to me, as was such talk of common treasury in the taking of wood and cattle from my Colonel's land. This did these Diggers naturally dispute, and 'twas for them most fortunate that I had not the mastiff by me then, yet were such cold reckoning but delayed.

On we marched. When the dog was grown quiet, summoned I the younger of those Cobham men to my side, who would look not once at my ruined eye, nor face me even, but instead drew near with floundering step, for in truth he was afeared.

'Come,' says I, beckoning thus with my free hand, that had but a single finger remaining. ''Tis safe, I promise thee.'

Then did I stroke the dog in demonstration, which reared not at my touch, but when the youth made forward to perform the like, pressed in that part of my glove that was lined full with nails, which did compel the brute to leap at the boy and bare its teeth, whereat he turned from me and ran.

'Now will thou watch me,' says I after him, with no mark of jest. But no sooner had I shown the measure of my worth, than the Parson did condemn my action before all, causing great offence to me, for in truth he held no rank with me, and to command thus was poor treatment indeed, that did serve but the Colonel's interest. And when I recalled how great had been his own condemnation of those Diggers, decrying them from the pulpit as enemies of the Lord, so did I consider more fully what private gains might be had for him in the courting of our Colonel's favour. And thus were it made plain to me that Parson Platt were against me, for though my cruelties were well spoken of, yet there was no business any man there could name that did surpass what I had acted upon Marston Moor.

Being but a mile or less from the settlement we had cause to displace, I positioned those Cobham men full in line as though pikemen they were, yet with cheeks nigh rosy from drink, who did expect sport and promise of fight, though battle of the truest sort had long escaped these younglings. Then did I signal with my ruined hand those trees o'ershadowing the heath to our front, and thus ordered our advance. Upon which I pressed once more that nailed glove hard into the mastiff's back, causing it to tear itself near free from my grasp, whereat I found I had drawn blood from it in my ardour.

Then did the Parson walk close with me and repeat his warning, whereof I recalled to him our charge and duty, mindful that of all men summoned for this day's work, it were I above all other that had full right to see honoured the will and word of our paymaster.

'To prevent such calamity that our Colonel fears may disrupt his cause,' says he, with speech greatly softened, so to make himself unheard by those marching, 'it were well that I keep charge about these boys, who are not men as we, and restrain such riotous passion as youth and folly may let loose. For no blood must be spilled this day, Robert Newton, so to strengthen the Colonel's cause the more fully in court.'

'I act for the Colonel,' says I.

'Thy mastiff?'

'What of it?'

'I am well content it should be feared, that we may with haste reclaim this contested ground. Yet let it prove no dogge of warre.'

'It is well you recall my former triumph,' says I.

'It is for that I make care, for though ye hath fought the Devil once, yet do His agents walk among us still.'

Then did he clap a hand to my ravaged arm, bearing such smile that did carry, to my eye, little of friendship in it.

'A Godly man yet, are ye not, Robert Newton?'

Then did he cross the rye grass away from me and leave the mastiff and I to march with that poor company, as if such rabble were fit brotherhood for an old Ironside. And of a sudden did that dog pull hard and bark as though it were cast down in the ring, whereat I saw well my glove's cruel work upon it, yet felt not the movement of my hand.

We continued through the trees in poor procession, a ragged band such as our army had been before Cromwell taught it the ways of discipline and victory. And yet those true brothers of mine, for such had we called ourselves in former days, rode west of me with God's army through Ireland, while I langoured here, with little cause or pay or strength to fight, with the Parson conversing in whispers about me, so that I who walked behind him, might not hear his speech. Yet did I perceive talk of my lost eye and rotten carriage, for such sport was about me all since that day, and poor exchange for slaying the Devil's agent, with those Godly brothers of mine all unmarked.

Thus did I reflect as we neared the heath, and marked what common treasury it were to dig and live as one upon that slimy earth, wherein lieth but the dead God's judgment hath buried there.

'Boy,' says I to that frighted lad I had earlier scorned, who would face me now, though no closer would he stand. 'Draw close by my side,' says I, 'for I would fain speak with thee.'

He stumbled in his approach, and I had cause to drag the mastiff to my far side, which in truth caused me to struggle, so keenly did that brute sense the sport that lay close by. Yet thus did I afford the boy some comfort, and freedom to calm himself.

''Tis a baiting dog,' says I. 'In the pit, there are those that take it for the Devil's own.'

'Well can I believe,' says he, both eyes of his fixed upon that mastiff's snout, which did sense at once his stare and rear back for him, so that I had need to press my glove hard into it again, whereat I drew a fair deal of blood.

'A damned cur,' says I, and thought again of Boye, that had caused such fright to those that fought on the moor. Aye, and us that met with it.

'I have heard,' says the boy, for I were grown quiet, 'that you were at Marston.'

'Aye,' says I, 'and many men did I know that were lost.' Then marked I how small hardship it were for him now to look full upon me, and so did I pull hard on that dog to force it onward, ahead of us, calling aloud to those Cobham boys for to speed them forward through the trees.

'I have heard,' says the lad again, working to keep step with me, 'you caught Prince Rupert sleeping.'

'Aye,' says I, 'at meat, he was.' Though saw I little of joy in that, for in truth it were a terrible hour to fight, with a summer hailstorm above our heads and the dark of night falling fast around. Thus did Cromwell press our advantage with brutal strength, though t'was little comfort to us that faced the charge.

'An Ironside,' says the boy then. 'So sayeth the Colonel.'

'Aye,' says I, though hardly to be heard. For in truth I lost my horse early in that first clash, run through by a straggler, and spent the rest of that fight on foot. Thus caught was I between both cavalry as Rupert led his own charge to our front and flank, and at the mercy of both did I stand and shout unheeded as they fought at the swords point a pretty while. And 'twere only when the Scots came to our assistance that such tide of dying men and horse did part, and I alone were left on that bloodied plain, with ruined sight and my right arm broken. Aye, alone but for that which I feared above all men.

For though dashed in my sight, yet did I see, running for me across that bloody earth, none but the Devil's dog, coming for me alone, in all that wretched work, to drag my soul with it down to the infernal realm. Boye, Prince Rupert's own, and I alone did face it.

'Take your leave, lad,' says I, and harsh with it, for my mood was grown sour. ''Twas man's business, and should remain so.'

But stay he did, for gone was his fear of the mastiff, that marked him little now, so keen did it sense that which lay ahead.

Then did I recall again the look of death upon that demon's mask as it leaped at me, up from that stained earth, to force its teeth against my good eye. Which drove me to that hellish ground to shield my face, where I did choke on my own life's blood that flowed dark and heavy from that ravaged socket. I felt then not the mouth of death close upon me, as I feared, but hands that did pull me to my feet and hold me steadfast. And when I dared open my good eye, there saw I my honest brothers, that had come for to deliver me from that ungodly ground, yet busy at the beast with sword and blade, in frenzy or fear it were not known to me.

Upon which I did retrieve my own sword from the earth with my good hand, that had fallen from me in the horror of it, and advanced upon the creature, calling for those Ironsides to make room so that I might look too upon the dreaded Boye. Then did I join with them and tear apart that which I saw, drawing the belly of the animal full open, parting flesh from fur, driving the hot bones from that miserable carcass. Then did I sever the head from its neck with a single stroke and draw both eyes from its skull, one after the other, and slash them full open with my blade. Till I grew weary of such hellish sport, and lay down my arms before me, eyeing that bloody pool with awful knowledge.

'Twas but a dog.

'Get thee from me, boy,' says I again, as if waking from the dream of it, 'or set him at you, I will.' Then I pulled the mastiff hard across the front of me, forcing the dog up at the lad, causing both of them to lose footing in the wet clay. At this, he departed from me with wounded pride, yet no mark was there upon him. Thus did I spare him from death.

Then, with the sun falling behind the trees, the Parson gave us signal to halt, causing much relief among those that were weary of our approach.

'Conceal your company among the trees,' says he, passing down that line of men and so delivering his command to each. 'Then upon my signal, advance upon the heath.'

Parting the branches before me, I observed that mean settlement ahead which did cause such affront and quarrel to our Colonel. A wretched clearing it was, with little to commend it but mud, huts and swine. Among the dwellings I saw but a score of Diggers, with their grimy babes at play in the clearing, though more infants were found later when we fired the huts, and 'twere plain to me that this were a dwelling poorly chosen, with no defence against enemies in all that place, nor sentry even to signal warning.

'Stay thy hand, Robert Newton.'

The voice was close by me, and did sound to me like a serpent in the marsh.

'Stay thy mastiff…'

'Twas the Parson, though not as I had heard or seen him afore now.

'The mark of God is upon you,' says he then, 'and He hath condemn'd thy soul.'

No further word did he speak, but drew back from me, as if I did carry the scent of corruption about me. Then were my own thoughts cause of great fright to me, as if that untouched eye did stare inward, to confront my very soul.

And thus did I reflect upon my ruin'd state, and the cause I was upon, and how I was parted from my brother soldiers so cruelly, and thought I then of Boye again, and what that beast were in truth. And thought I also on the Parson's speech, and those Diggers ahead, that were all for me joining with them.

And I saw all before me with sight renewed, my gloved hand firm on that mastiff's neck still, as the Parson betook himself further along that line of men, and raised one hand above his head to motion our advance. And methought I met his eyes once more, before my vision grew dark with the shadow of moving men.

Little do I recall of that charge, for great was the alarm as we advanced upon the heath, the younger of our company crying out with violent oaths, so maddened were they with drink. And while several of those Diggers before us ran to gather up their children, so did many flee into the woods across the way, which did aggrieve me much, for they had not yet looked upon the great mastiff at my command.

At length did I spy a group of men moving to meet with us, so as to prevent our reaching their wives, and in kind did we gather our own pace, that some of our strength did fall about us across the uneven ground. Yet those men ahead, being but common farmers, were soon knocked down as under cannon, and greatly the women ran crying after their husbands and children in all direction, so torn were they between the requirements of escape and protection of their kin.

No sooner had I reached the settlement, then the mastiff barked frightfully and let fly at those around it, biting at them, and in truth I had great difficulty in preventing its running from me. But in little time it had cornered its prey, that were one of those fallen men, and much blood did that dog draw from his arm, and would have torn it clean off had not the Parson pulled the brute back by its leash and helped him away.

At this, Parson Platt cried unto me again to stay my hand, which in all that clash of screaming I could but hardly hear, for in truth wild had I become.

Then I saw that same lad that had accompanied me through the trees behind. Still stood he amid the rush, afeared it seemed, as if facing the charge himself, while those around him fired the huts, from which a great many children ran in fear.

I made for him alone, the mastiff tearing at all around it. And at length he did observe my approach, and retreat from that beast in great fright, that leapt at him and near broke free from me in its fury.

Then did I laugh and chide at him, that he was but a child to play at man's work, and bade him head for home to his hearth and milk.

Till one of their women, greatly fair, caught the eye of the mastiff also, causing it to leap at her, till she cried out and lay upon the muddy earth. Flee she could not, so stricken was she, that it were mean work, in truth, to force that dog upon her still. Yet force it I did, and pushed that brute at her face, which she did turn from, as was natural, and thus stained herself so with the muddy ground that it were hard to know if it were blood or not as she turned back to face me, though greatly frighted, to implore the whereabouts of her children.

Then it grew hard for me to hold back that beast from the grim work it was set upon, and the Parson's hand alone did stay the completion of its task, for he had been watching me all that time, I do believe, and did curse me with such fervour that I had small choice but to yield.

Upon which he drew that woman to her feet and instructed others to care for her safety, and called out aloud to prevent those Cobham boys from killing the swine which ran wild among us and shrieked pitifully when they were run through.

Till at length I observed him disappear into the burning hut, his intention plainly to remove those babes that were trapped within, and so I followed, with that mastiff tearing on my weakened arm, toward the opening of that mean dwelling. And there I saw him within, calming those children, and then did it occur to me that it were hellish work indeed to let that brute fly within at that company with no way of escape, and so did it enter my mind also, from whence I know not, that though Boye were beaten, that I had killed him with my own hand, yet were this mastiff beside me the true Devil's agent. And how cunning and base were the strategy of the Fiend, that had come thus to reckon with me at last, and drag me down with Him to what did await me.

Yet helpless was I to stay my hand, that worked most cruelly in spite of me, and pressed deep down on that mastiff's back, causing it to writhe in agony and fury. And knew I then that it were the Devil working in me also, for my ruined hand moved down to complete the task its other was upon, and so did I hear that lad from Cobham scream at me that there were children afore me, but heed him I did not, or would not, and thus did I set free the rope from that great mastiff's neck.

Then hell ran loose about me, as the mastiff went not for those children, nor the Parson even, but for myself alone. And 'twas as if all the years behind me were as dust, and I were back on that bloody plain, with Boye about me, yet no brother now to pull me free from the horror of it. Then did that brute force me to the ground and tear the flesh from my face, as I had done to Boye, and bite at my throat, till once more I choked on that life's blood of mine, and see, as 'twere still that field of death, the dark figure standing above me, black against the setting sun.

'The Devil take me,' says I, though little could my voice sound it, so torn was my throat, that hung in part from that brute's mouth to mock me.

'Parson...' cries I. And seemed it to me that Platt read well my meaning, yet acted not. For so he smiled most cruelly, and stood back from the dog that were now both life and death to me.

And darkness fell about as that brute tore out my good eye, and nothing could I see more, but heard with only greater suffering my own cries of dread and torment. Thus did I fall into that black eternal depth, till, at long last, I felt the weight of that brute depart, pulled from my chest by that goodly lad that were so afeared of it, who dragged me free by his own hands, I hear, and suffered, as they tell me, such injury that cannot be put right. Thus did that boy deliver me from death, and 'twere courage so rare I would fain call him brother, and ride with him against my many enemies.

And now I walk in darkness, though not, in truth, alone. For in spite of my great cruelties, yet do I keep company of kind, that I could not forsee before the losing of my sight. And though I can spy no path before me, yet am I led by one both straight and true. Aye, and by those I did seek to displace. For so I am fed, and granted warmth like the child, and tended with such care and kindness that only a brother may provide. And their words are in truth my sight returned, for they talk to me of God's land, and bid me stand, or sit, or lie as doth fit my broken body. And 'tis a wondrous land indeed they speak of, with bountiful riches before and around me, for each man, woman and child, the lowly in equal measure. For 'tis a common treasury, they say, and I believe it so, for in spite of this eternal dark of blindness, yet do I see the sun.

And my mastiff, the brute that took my sight for all I won from it, is by me still, within my humble prayers. For in truth 'twas but a dog, yet company beyond words, and rarest warmth for this ruined shell. For know not I where the Devil walk, yet gone is he from me.

# Afterword: St. George's Hill, Cobham Heath and the Fear of Witchcraft, 1649–1650

## Dr. John Rees
Goldsmiths, University of London

## & Prof. Mark Stoyle
University of Southampton

*Dr. John Rees:*

The Diggers emerged from the English Revolution of the 1640s, the most explosive decade of social change that England has ever seen, with the possible exception of the 1940s. Two civil wars had killed, proportionately, more people than any war in British history, including the First and Second World Wars. The King was driven from his capital in 1642 by mass protests at Westminster. People who had never moved beyond their parish joined armies on both sides and slaughtered or were slaughtered in every corner of the four countries of these islands. The authority of the national church dissolved and the Archbishop of Canterbury was executed. The parliamentary army as a whole mutinied when the Parliament that created it tried to disband it. It elected its own 'agitators' who contested its political direction. Finally, in the last year of the decade the King was put on trial, found guilty of treason against the people and executed on a platform built outside the Banqueting House in Whitehall. The House of Lords was abolished as 'useless and dangerous' and the country became a Republic.

The world had indeed been 'turned upside down', as the much-used contemporary phrase put it. But in 1649 the revolutionary momentum of the previous decade had reached a temporary resting point in the Republic headed by Oliver Cromwell. The most numerous and effective of the radical groups that emerged during the revolution, The Levellers led by John Lilburne, were made sacrifice by Cromwell in order to stabilise his rule. Cromwell and his troopers crushed a series of Leveller-led mutinies at Bishopsgate in London, at Burford in Oxfordshire, and in Oxford itself in the course of the year. The Leveller leaders were imprisoned in the Tower of London and Lilburne was put on trial for his life. He was freed by the jury, but only to be driven into exile in the Netherlands.

With the defeat of the Levellers the radical impetus of the revolution splintered into brilliant fragments. The Ranters demanded sexual, as well as political, liberation. The Fifth Monarchist group saw in the dramatic events of the revolution the precursor of the last coming of Christ. Quakers added their distinctive egalitarian reading of the Bible to the already proliferating dissenting churches rebelling against the national church settlement.

And then there were the Diggers.

Their leader, Gerrard Winstanley, was born in Wigan and had come to London, like many others (including many radicals), to be apprenticed into the cloth trade. He had become his own master but his business was ruined, again like many others, by the war. In debt, he left London to live on property he owned in Cobham, Surrey. In an age when radical politics and dissenting religion overlapped to a considerable degree, Winstanley probably became a Baptist before developing his own individual brand of millennial belief.

In early 1649, just as the peak of revolutionary energy was passing, a small group led by Winstanley began to build a settlement on common land on St George's Hill near Cobham. Some other groups followed their example in Wellingborough, Northamptonshire, and Iver, Buckinghamshire.

*Prof. Mark Stoyle:*

In April 1649 Winstanley, an ex-Parliamentarian soldier named William Everard and a group of between 20 and 30 local labourers occupied a piece of common land on St George's Hill near Walton, and set about turning it over to cultivation. Their actions caused outrage among the neighbouring landowners, and soon afterwards Winstanley and Everard were summoned to appear before Sir Thomas Fairfax, the commander of Parliament's New Model Army. During the interview which followed, Winstanley and Everard omitted to doff their hats in Fairfax's presence, thus displaying that principled refusal to adopt traditional forms of deferential behaviour which so outraged many of the Diggers' critics.[1] Fairfax told the two men to bring their activities on St George's Hill to an end. The Diggers ignored these instructions, however, and over the following weeks their local opponents launched a series of violent attacks upon them. Eventually, a formal action for trespass was brought against the Diggers: an action which resulted in several of the squatters being ordered to pay the very substantial fine of £10 apiece, in addition to damages.[2] Some time before August 1649, the Diggers abandoned their original settlement at St George's Hill, and moved to a new site at Cobham Heath, just a couple of miles away.

Exasperated by the Diggers' stubborn refusal to disperse, Francis Drake, MP, the lord of the manor of St George's Hill, and Parson John Platt, the lord of the manor of Cobham, now made plans to rid themselves of their unwelcome neighbours once and for all.[3] In November 1649, troops from the New Model Army were brought to Cobham in order to keep the Diggers in awe, and, while the soldiers looked on, a group of men who had been recruited by the local landowners pulled down one of the Diggers' makeshift houses.[4] At Easter in the following year, Parson Platt returned with a group of around 50 men and set about ejecting the Diggers from Cobham Heath by force. The squatters' houses were burnt down, several of the Diggers themselves were beaten and imprisoned, and in the wake of this affair the camp at Cobham was abandoned.[5] Other similar groups were dispersed at around the same time and by the end of 1650 the Digger movement had effectively run its course. Yet the name of the Diggers was to live on for centuries to come – and to haunt later generations of historians, social reformers and political activists with a mystical vision of an egalitarian world that might have been.

Little is known of the men whom the local landowners recruited to intimidate, harass and eventually eject the Diggers in 1649-50, but it does not seem too far-fetched to suggest that among them might have been several former soldiers who had fought for the Parliament during the Civil War. Hardened veterans of the recent conflict would have been ideal men to act as the landlords' enforcers. Whatever their previous history may have been, these individuals were clearly drawn from the same rural communities as the Diggers themselves. Winstanley himself later wrote that those who assailed the squatters at Cobham had been 'fearefull tenants': men who had done their landlords' bidding 'for fear they should be turned out ... of their livings'. Nevertheless, he went on to declare, 'in their hearts they are Diggers [too]'.[6] Nor can we doubt that most of those who took part in the stirring events at Cobham Heath in 1649-50 would have believed themselves to be living in a world in which witches were a very real threat. During the Civil War, the effusions of the rival propagandists had served to ramp up fear of witches to new heights and tales of 'Boy' – the 'devil dog' who was alleged to protect Charles I's cavalry commander, Prince Rupert of the Rhine, from harm through occult means – had been in a thousand mouths until the beast was killed by Parliamentarian troops at the battle of Marston Moor in 1644.[7] When the Diggers first occupied St George's Hill in 1649, moreover, it was less than two years since the end of the great English witch-hunt of 1645-47: the tragic episode which had witnessed the execution of at least 100 alleged 'witches' across the South-East of England.[8] All in all, it would hardly have been surprising if a former Parliamentarian soldier like Robert

Newton – traumatised by his wartime experiences, fearful of the power of witches and now called upon to eject a peaceable group of men, women and children from the homes which they had built with such high hopes on Cobham Heath – might have found himself oppressed by the darkest thoughts during the turbulent Easter season of 1650.

*Dr John Rees:*

The Diggers did not alter the course of events but they did leave a powerful legacy of ideas expressing the egalitarian impulse of the lowest ranks of those fighting for the Parliamentary cause. Winstanley was certainly religiously inspired and he drew on Biblical expression to highlight social injustice. He also drew on a strain of agrarian egalitarianism stretching back to the Peasants' Revolt when John Ball said that 'Things will not go well in England until all things are held in common'. So, when Winstanley wrote that 'The earth should be a common treasury for all,' he was simultaneously drawing on deep wells on English popular radicalism, millennial religious inspiration, and social disaffection with the lot of many who had fought for Parliament in the civil war.

Some have thought that the title of one Digger pamphlet *The True Levellers Standard Advanced* was intended as a critique of the Levellers in the sense that they merely wanted political democracy while the Diggers aimed at levelling all property. Perhaps this was an element of their thinking. Some Diggers had been Levellers. But as likely is that Winstanley was making a radically religious point: that Christ is the true leveller. The opening of the pamphlet reads:

'In the beginning of Time, the great Creator Reason, made the Earth to be a Common Treasury…but not one word was spoken in the beginning, That one branch of mankind should rule over another.'[9]

The Diggers relied on the 'Lord of Hosts' rather than the 'sword or weapons' to bring about change. But whatever the exact mixture of religious, social and political motivation for their thoughts and actions, the Diggers did highlight the question of property ownership in a way that no other group in the English Revolution did. In thought and deed they posed point blank the question of whether or not a good society, even a tolerably democratic society, can be achieved without economic equality. The Diggers are still remembered because the question they asked has not been answered.

## Notes

1. Manning, B. *1649: The Crisis of the English Revolution* (London, Bookmarks, 1992), p.121.
2. Hill, C. (ed.), *Winstanley: The Law of Freedom and other Writings* (London, Penguin, 1973), p.28.
3. Ibid., pp.28-29; and Manning, *1649*, p.125.
4. Winstanley, G. *A New-yeers Gift for the Parliament* (January 1650), p.17.
5. Manning, *1649*, pp.128-30.
6. Winstanley, *A New-yeers Gift*, p.17.
7. Stoyle, M. *The Black Legend of Prince Rupert's Dog: Witchcraft and Propaganda during the English Civil War* (Liverpool, Liverpool University Press, 2011).
8. Gaskill, M. *Witchfinders: A Seventeenth-Century English Tragedy* (London, John Murray, 2005); and M. Braddick, *God's Fury, England's Fire: A New History of the English Civil Wars* (London, Penguin, 2008), p.428.
9. Winstanley, G. et al, *The True Levellers Standard Advanced* (London, 1649), p.1.

# A Fiery Flag Unfurled in Coleman Street

## Frank Cottrell-Boyce

*September 7th 1666*

*My Lord,*

 *I purpose this day to remove my household across the river to Southwark until the fires in London be quenched. On waking this morning I found my bed linen bespattered with ash, and the house timbers too warm to rest upon. I am sending by my man such silver and furnitures as can be transported with despatch, also papers relating to the matter of Judith Squibb. My Lord, I implore you read them. It is noised about that it may be these fires were started by mutinous hand, protesting the Restoration of the King's Majestie. I have been hourly assailed by doubts but that the testimony of the woman Squibb might be material to the mystery of London's disaster.*

*Jos. Early.*

To Lord Clarendon
December 10th 1660

My Lord,

This morning His Majestie paused in his progress through Whitehall to inquire if I was that same Josiah who was secretary to Lord Clarendon, viz. yourself, saying you had bid him question me on a private matter. He drew me aside and I told him that we had a prisoner – viz. Judith Squibb – who had done murder and that I begged that he might think it politic for her to be presented to His Majestie.

His Majestie asked why he should wish to see a murderess?

I told him it was on account of he who she said she had murdered.

'Who is this that she says he has murdered?'

'She says, Your Majestie, that she murdered you.'

I gave His Majestie fair copies of the accounts she delivered to me of the murder, appending a request in my own hand.

Taking the papers he said he would come and see the woman tomorrow.

*A Discourse with Judith Squibb of Swan Alley*

An officer brought me this morning a woman whose hands and shawl were spotted with blood. He had found her ranting on Whitehall saying that she had a message for the Great Ones therein. Being wary of taking her in to any great personage, but unwilling to let her continue in the road, he brought her to me. I am his cousin.

The woman announced herself as Judith Squibb, prophetess, of Swan Alley off Coleman Street. She might have saved herself the breath of naming her address. As fins proclaim the watery dwelling of the fish, so her manner of speech and her bloody hands proclaimed her address. Coleman Street and its tributaries are a pestilential maze of dissenters and sectaries, together with Antinomians, Quakers, Mortalists, Fifth Monarchists and I wot not what. Button-makers, apprentices, printers and women alike all make free to preach in its chapels and taverns. Coleman Street is a sewer and Swan Alley its cess pit. There are dissenting presses hidden there, and there Thomas Venner, John Canne and the Monarchy Men have their seditious meetings.

I asked after her business. She said that all the Great Ones would be best to leave Whitehall now this very day as His Majestie was departed his life and a new king was coming who would break their bones like a lion.

I asked her what new king? She said, 'None but King Jesus.' Here she expounded upon the Book of Daniel (I believe that if she were asked so much as if she wanted a piss, she would begin her answer by expounding the second chapter of the Book of Daniel). She proposes that in Nebuchadnezzar's dream of the great statue, the head of the great statue was made of gold and this was to represent the empire and age of King Nebuchadnezzar. The arms and chest were of silver, its belly and thighs of brass and its great legs of iron. Each material represents a different worldly monarchy, the last being the kings so-called of so-called Britain. 'Now those worldly monarchies are all destroy'd...' she saith, 'for I have unfurled his banner of flame on Coleman Street and He will burn the city with it.'

I asked her what was to become of His Majestie King Charles?

'He is dead,' she said. 'Killed him myself this morning with these hands.' At this she held up her hands, which were bloody and the which I shuddered to see.

At this I was disconsolate and struck dumb. She then described her murder of the King in such a rapture of precision that I almost voided my stomach. It was this revulsion that finally roused me from my amazement and at last I could speak. I called for my man and sent to inquire after His Majestie's person. My heart gladdened at hearing that both he and His Grace the Duke were safe returned from Rye.

When I told her this she did but laugh and throw the lie into my face.

'It matters not,' said I. 'You have admitted to murder and you will swing for it, though it be regicide or not.'

'It matters not to me neither,' saith she, 'for King Jesus is coming and will break the gibbet under me if He wishes. If He does not wish, then that is all the same to me. Besides,' she saith, 'If I have murdered someone, where is the body?'

Your Majestie, be assured I sent to Rye to enquire if any had been murdered there or along the way. But none had heard so much as a rumour of such work in that direction.

Lacking a body, more lacking an accusation, I cannot in conscience detain her much longer.

Yet, sir, if I give her liberty, she will straight to Coleman Street and proclaim Your Majestie's death, showing her bloody hands as proof. Hearing this, Coleman Street will disgorge its half-digested noxious stew of dissenters and seditionaries into the streets of London. It matters nowt that this rumour be not true. Rumour moves like fire.

Majestie, it seems to me sir that our only safety is to bring her to the Truth. For, if we have the Truth, then surely we can bring her to it. If we say we cannot bring her to it, then we are saying it is not the Truth for all, but only for ourselves and that is no Truth at all, but only Opinion.

It may be, Your Majestie thinks it matters not what a button-maker believes in Swan Alley. I say it matters more than anything. Though her fiery banner be not Truth yet it is hot and must be extinguish'd.

For it is not enough to imprison or even to kill the person: We must seek to kill Error itself.

Therefore I earnestly entreat that you may permit her to see Your Majestie's living person, alive, that the light of your grace might disperse the fog of her unreason.

# A FIERY FLAG UNFURLED IN COLEMAN STREET

*A Report of the Encounter Between the King's Majestie and one Judith Squibb*

The woman Squibb was brought to a closet in the palace at Whitehall. The King's Majestie sat in the next room. Desirous of gaining what intelligences we could from her conversation I commanded a listening hole be drilled into the plaster, with the intention of having my man installed on the other side of this same wall. His Majestie however graciously bid me let him hide himself in the closet, saying it would amuse him to hear an account of his own death.

You must know that Squibb spoke with many digressions and erroneous expositions which I here leave out. It was known, saith she, in every corner of Coleman Street that the King was gone to Newmarket races with his brother James and that they were coming back upon a certain day. It was whispered that there were plots to ambush and kill both him and his brother on their return. I asked her how she came by this intelligence, which was treasonous. She would say only that these things were brought before her own inner light by the Holy Spirit. She asked if I would regard the Holy Spirit as a traitor and if I was like to lock him in the Tower, to be a dove among the ravens.

'The Spirit brought it hard upon me,' she said, 'that my name was Judith, the very same as that Judith who cut off the head of King Holofernes before the Lord. And that I was called to act as the new Judith upon Charles, the new Holofernes, a tyrant. And this is why my parents named me for Judith though they did not know it at that time.'

It almost caused me to blush to think that His Majestie was at this time in the closet listening to her sacrileges and calumnies. I greatly wished that he would come out and put a stop to them.

She said that it was brought unto her that these treasonous plots would fail as the Spirit was not upon them. However the undoing of these same plots would delay His Majestie and his brother the Duke upon the road and they would be put to it to sleep at a tavern on the road. She named a tavern near Rye.

She took herself to the tavern, and was employ'd there as a pot girl and chambermaid. I ask'd what others were part of her scheme. For instance might Thomas Venner and the Monarchy Men have provided her with the weapons and money to begin her scheme?

She said none knew but one seamstress who made a new dress for her. 'And she knew naught, but only that I wish'd to catch the eye of the King.' Next she says that she was prov'd right for His Majestie did spend the night there and all his suite. Here she described His Majestie in words that were enough to get her hang'd. It made me shake in my chair to think that, at my bidding, he was subject to such lies as came next – how that she had made sure she was the one to bring him his vittles and did so with coy smiles and a lecherous comportment, which he in some wise reciprocated. Later she went secretly to his chamber, he allowing her in, unsuspecting, even to locking the door so they should not be disturbed.

'Then like Judith of old, while he was naked, I cut off his head.'

'Did you have an axe to undertake such a thing?' I asked.

'None. But only a carving knife and some strength which was given me by the Lord for this especial purpose. I then made my escape and walked to London, carrying the head before me on the handle of a hoe, just as he when alive had displayed the heads of many dissenting saints.'

Here I asked her if she still had the head about her.

'It came to be too heavy. I toss'd it into a tree, like the head of Absalom. I doubt but that some body will find it by and by.'

Now there came laughter from the closet. The curtain was drawn back and His Majestie appeared. The sunlight flashed upon the buckles of his shoes as though he were winged Mercury. His brooches, sword hilt, etc., shone so that he seemed enhalo'd with grace. His laughter continued like the streams of

Olympus. He turned his kindly visage towards the woman Squibb, and holding out his hands invited her to touch them. 'In case that you should doubt like Thomas,' he said, 'do you touch my hands and side and see that there is no wound in them. Touch me. I am no ghost.'

She refused to touch him, even when His Majestie handed her a gold piece, French, saying that she had greatly diverted him on a dull day, and bidding her go home and buy bread.

He was in all ways – in grace, in kindness, in understanding, even in appearance also – so like Our Saviour that I had a good certaintie that Judith Squibb would from now be a good and grateful subject and that she would take back with her to Coleman Street good news of His Majestie.

*Private Account of a Dialogue between Judith Squibb and Josiah Early, Secretary to Lord Clarendon*

This morning at Whitehall I found His Grace, my Lord Clarendon, agitated and anxious to speak, saying, 'The woman you let have her liberty, Josiah Early, has assaulted His Majestie's person.'

'My Lord it was His Majestie himself who let her go...'

At this he became enraged for several minutes, throwing his lace handkerchief in the air and using me with some terms. 'His Majestie was ambushed – ambushed I say – while out riding in St. James – in St. James – by the woman Squibb and two others.'

At the word ambush I was much alarmed and asked if the King was murder'd.

My Lord allowed that it was an an ambush not of lead or steel but of words and breath. 'But such words! Words I never heard and the women were naked and covered in blood. Her Majestie was riding with him. She near miscarried in surprise. They called her the tatters of the whore of Babylon and worde. They called the King the flaccid organ of the Beast.' I have her imprison'd at Comptor now. Do you despatch her and that with despatch.

She was held in a cellar here in Whitehall. She was wearing nothing but a shift the which, when I came in, she removed saying that the country was plagued with counterfeiting and conspiracy. She would go naked to prove her honesty.

Josiah Early: You said you had killed the King. Was that honest? It seems he lives.

Judith Squibb: You speak carefully, Prince of Lies, when you say only 'seems'. I killed the King. Three days since.

Jos. Early: What then? Has he come back from the dead like Our Saviour?

Here she clapp'd her hands over her ears and said such things as I cannot bring myself to write. Then she began to discourse again upon the Book of Daniel.

Jos. Early: Come we need not go back so far. Nebuchadnezzar is dead these three thousand years and more. Let us go back merely to last week at Newmarket. You say you murder'd the King. Yet you saw him here in this building two days since and again this morning out riding in St. James.

Judith Squibb: Counterfeit and conspiracy. The thing you brought here, the thing out riding is an abomination confected of buckles and lace. A puppet of the Devil, it will be blown away like feathers when King Jesus comes.

Jos. Early: And when will that be?

Judith Squibb: Soon. I have made straight the way. The Fifth Monarchy will begin right soon.

I was struck then by her certaintie which it seemed no evidence could shake.

Jos. Early: Let us say that you did cut off the King's head [she smiled here] you must know that your kind have cut off a king's head before, viz. the head of His Majestie's father. Did King Jesus come then?

Judith Squibb: Ah for a time we thought so. Comrade General Harrison himself bade us wait in joyful expectation on His coming for the days of Iron and Clay were over and the day of the Flesh coming. He proposed to change the courts to Sannhedrin and to fill the Parliament with saints.

Jos. Early: You thought that Cromwell was King Jesus?

Judith Squibb: No, but only St. John come to make the way straight.

Jos. Early: But Jesus did not come and Harrison was hanged drawn and quarter'd and his haunches nailed to the city walls, for conspiracy to kill the King.

Here she looked sadly. She pulled her shift around her shoulders as if cold.

Judith Squibb: I watched all night thinking King Jesus might blow down the walls with a breath and with the same breath make those haunches walk and breathe again.

Jos. Early: But they stayed on the wall for maggots and carrion. Did you not think then that King Jesus was not coming no matter how many king's heads you cut off?

Judith Squibb: Aye. It was easy to believe when we saw the first king's head cut off. Hard to believe when the saints were routed.

I felt a great call to free her from her mistaken certainties. I put it to her that she believed King Jesus was coming and that truly you would not make so free with the cutting off of kings' heads. 'Jesus can dispose of rivals himself and has no need of your butcher's knife.'

Judith Squibb: I did not do it for his need but for his pleasure. For as it gives me joy to serve Him so it gives Him joy to behold my pleasure.

Jos. Early: If it gave Him pleasure He would surely come. And yet He does not come. Does this not give you cause to doubt yourself?

Judith Squibb: To doubt myself, aye. But to doubt Him, never. For when I did doubt myself I took up my Bible and was given these lines of John 20:29, 'How much more blessed those who have not seen and yet believe.'

Jos. Early: So the more you do not see Him, the more you believe.

Judith Squibb: As Daniel stood the cooler for every flame brought from the tyrant's fire, as he stood the safer for every growl of the tyrant's lion. When Harrison was hanged and quarter'd, we went back to Coleman Street singing songs of praise. Our faith was increased because we had looked at despair and only laughed at it. By this it was a sign that the Lord had pitched his camp in Swan Alley and we were a household of Gideons.

Jos. Early: How if I give you proofs that the Lord has not pitched camp with you but the contrary, that the King's Majestie is the Lord's annointed. His father was killed and I was thrust into a kind of grave or prison. Yet now he is now returned. Is this not a sign that man cannot frustrate his ends?

Second, that you say you killed him yet he lives. And you are his prisoner. With whom doth the Lord stand?

Judith Squibb: Why with prisoners always for he was a prisoner and not a king. Daniel was a prisoner when King Nebuchadnezzar had his dream of the great statue. And what befell that statue? It broke in pieces upon a great piece of rock. My faith is as that rock which will smash kings whether of gold or silver or clay and be not chipped itself. My certaintie is the certain rock on which your so-called certaintie will shatter. You say I did not kill the King.

Jos. Early: I do for the King lives.

Judith Squibb: If I did not kill the King, who then did I kill? For you know I killed someone.

Here indeed she gave me pause for I did see her spattered with blood and her demeanour wild.

I was also put to pause as to what to do with her. Certainly she has done enough and that before witnesses, to swing ten times over for it. But she fears not the gibbet. 'I will make of it my pulpit,' she saith, 'and prophesy in the spirit from it so all London will hear the word.'

She is indifferent too to imprisonment. 'The prison is as rich a soil for the seed of truth as any church or palace.'

She speaks the truth in both things. If she is hanged Coleman Street will void itself into London and its rats never will be returned. If she is sent to Comptor she will spread her infection through the disaffected.

We must keep her separated until I can break her of her certaintie.

*Of the Uprising of Venner and the Monarchy Men and of Judith Squibb's Witnessing thereto*

On January 1ˢᵗ 1661, Thomas Venner, carrying a halberd, led a column of men to St. Paul's and demanded the keys of the cathedral. These not being given they demanded of a passerby who he was for? When the man said King Charles, they shot him. They raided the Comptor Prison, setting prisoners free. Venner killed three men with his halberd in Threadneedle Street. All day there was talk of five thousand Monarchy Men and more, and London was alight with terror. Colonel Russell and Colonel Cox though soon had them penned up in The Blue Anchor, Coleman Street. It proved they were no more than fifty.

Hearing of this, Providence bid me take the woman Squibb from the cellar where she was held at Whitehall and bring her with me to The Blue Anchor. At this time Colonel Cox and his men were standing off. They had good intelligence that the dissenters were in The Blue Anchor. They had determined to surprise them. They cunningly muffled the steps of their ladders with cloths and thus brought several musketeers to the roof in secret. I bade them hold back and let me take the woman Squibb onto the roof with them. At my order the musketeers broke the roof tiles open with musket balls. Below I heard the voice of Thomas Venner himself call out, 'A light! A light! We have roused him up! It is the Lord who comes!' as it might be he thought King Jesus was descending to Earth through the roof of The Blue Anchor.

I bade the musketeers stand back and made Judith Squibb look down into the inn. There she saw the chief Monarchy Man, Thomas Venner, look up in hope crying and pointing, 'Behold King Jesus!' but seeing no-one there but Judith Squibb he despaired.

And she did see his despair.

I saw it too.

It was a fine thing to see the light go out in him and be extinguished.

Truth I believed had prevailed.

The woman Squibb cried out, 'Look out they are come to kill you all.'

He said, 'It matters not now.'

Nineteen times Venner was shot and did not die.

The others were shot from the roof. During this sport Squibb made her escape but I believed it to matter nowt.

When the time came for his execution it was I persuaded my Lord Clarendon that it should be done not at Tyburn but on Coleman Street itself so that every one of them could see the end of this. By reason of his many wounds Venner had to be lifted from his hurdle by the sheriff's men. On the scaffold he said that what he had done he had done in accordance with the Scripture in the best light that he had had. When the hangmen spilled Venner's guts upon the pavement, I believe that all could see that the best light he had was poor indeed. 'We have been deceived!' he cried, 'it was the Lord Himself who deceived us!'

It was a satisfaction and a reassurance to me that he died blaspheming.

About then I felt someone pluck at my sleeve. It was Judith Squibb. She spoke very quietly so that only I could hear. 'Woe to this city of gold and silver and brass and brick,' she saith, 'for lo, a great rock will fall upon it and it will be shattered. Why look you afraid?'

I said I was not afraid only surprised to see her and to see that she still clung to her certaintie when all was finished.

'My certaintie,' she said 'is the rock on which all this will be broken.'

I record this for the sake of completeness and to show that her like do not leave Coleman Street even when they have been found out. It is my contention that we should remove the whole area and make room for some great scheme for the general good.

★ ★ ★

We have been troubled but little by dissenters and radicals. I have heard nothing for years together of Judith Squibb. I was sometimes troubled by a dream of a great statue of gold, silver, brass and clay, in the likeness of His Majestie. In my dream the statue fell upon a stone and was broke in pieces. So that I would sometimes wake thinking – how if we were wrong?

But then I would see His Majestie's person and all uncertaintie would evaporate like a morning dew in the light of the Sun.

I was troubled also by a dream of Daniel standing in the fiery furnace. Only in my dream Daniel had the likeness of a naked woman. I woke from this dream to find our bedchamber hot as an oven. When we opened the casement we could smell the smoke though the fire was yet many streets distant.

It was noised abroad already that the fire was the work of malcontents protesting the Restoration of the King's Majestie. I know that there were other whispers – that fire, aye and the plague too, was raised not by the hands of dissenters but was a protest by Heaven itself against the King.

Seeing the fire was not abated I purposed to remove my household to Southwark, since the fire could not cross the Thames, first going with my family to my cabinet to consult scripture. We were given these verses of the Book of Daniel...

O King live forever. My God hath sent his angel, and hath shut the lions' mouths, that they have not hurt me:

At this my daughter did clap her hands taking it for a reassurance and saying we must now trust in the Lord with a good heart and stay here at Blackfriars. 'See,' saith she, 'the Lord will send His angels and close the mouth of the fire.'

I said but little bird, how if He not send them in time? There are but five streets between us and the fire.

But father, she said, He has spoken to us and that right kindly. O King live forever... We shall stand like Daniel untouched by flames.

I was for Southwark for all her pretty words. It was my wife held me and said, 'I find great assurance in our daughter's certaintie. It is as the psalmist sang, out of the mouths of babes and sucklings hast thou ordained strength.'

I had no text nor argument to hold against their certaintie. I could put no case for leaving. Only that thought that I had met another certaintie once, the opposite of this one. Only that I had seen that a man could be certain and yet be wrong. And how if this other certaintie was the stronger? How if Judith Squibb is even now walking in the flames of London, herself as cool as ice?

Has not the fire itself its own certaintie?

This morning I am imprison'd by my daughter's certaintie. I look from my window and it seems the houses are ashiver in the heat haze. Solid objects dissolve into air. The great pall of smoke seemed like a rock about to fall upon the city. And nothing seemed stable to me save only the certaintie of Judith Squibb.

# Afterword: The Fifth Monarchy, January, 1661

## Dr. Ariel Hessayon
Goldsmiths, University of London

FRAMED BY THE GREAT Fire of London of 2nd-5th September 1666, 'A Fiery Flag Unfurled' focusses on events from December 1660 to January 1661. Before looking at the sometimes violent yet ineffectual reactions to the restoration of the Stuart monarchy, it's worthwhile recapping the preceding twenty years. Censorship had effectively broken down, with the result that more than 33,000 printed titles were issued between 1640 and 1660. Courts which had facilitated the exercise of royal power were abolished by act of Parliament. There was bloody rebellion in Ireland and then devastating Civil Wars throughout the British Isles. An estimated 80,000 soldiers were killed or maimed out of a population of probably no more than 5.3 million. The Archbishop of Canterbury was executed, bishops deposed and the Church of England stripped of its authority. For the first and only time in English history a reigning monarch was put on trial, charged with treason and publicly executed. A Commonwealth was declared and the House of Lords abolished. Most of the Royalists who had supported Charles I were disarmed. Some were imprisoned and a few executed. Many more had to pay fines to keep hold of their homes and property. As for the Crown and the Church, much of their land was confiscated and sold off. The biggest beneficiaries were army officers on the winning Parliamentarian side who bought up large estates on the cheap. Meanwhile some regiments began to mutiny over arrears of pay. But there were also the widows and orphans of slain combatants who had to beg to survive. So too did the wounded. Bad weather did not help. There was famine as harvests failed, animals died and humans succumbed to plague. To paraphrase a couple of contemporary pamphleteers, the old world had been turned upside down and was burning up like parchment in the fire.

Yet with the King defeated the winners began arguing among themselves as to how the kingdom should be governed. Within this vacuum new political movements and religious communities emerged. Among the best known are the Levellers, who demanded social justice and the introduction of religious toleration; the Diggers, who were essentially pacifists as well as communists; the Ranters, who believed that individuals were free to do as they wished since sin had been abolished; and the Quakers, who were initially more transgressive and provocative than their modern counterparts. Many believed that the Apocalypse was imminent and that Jesus Christ would come back to reign on Earth. Using a combination of the bible and cutting edge mathematics they calculated the promised date as 1650 or 1656. Then, when those prophecies failed, they fixed on 1666; that is a millennium (1000) plus the number of the beast (666). It's here that the Fifth Monarchists of 'A Fiery Flag Unfurled' come in.

As Cottrell-Boyce notes their name was taken from Daniel. This biblical book is set in ancient Babylon at the time of Kings Nebuchadnezzar and Belshazzar, although it was actually written much later in the mid-second century before Christ. Parts of it relate various dreams and visions concerning a statue made of different materials and four great beasts. Taken together they were usually interpreted as four world empires: (1) Babylon; (2) the Medes and Persians; (3) Greece; (4) Rome. All would be destroyed, after which there would be a fifth monarchy ruled by King Jesus. Since they were not an organised religious community like the Baptists or Quakers it's difficult to date the precise beginnings of the Fifth Monarchists. But winter 1651 – shortly after Cromwell had defeated the enemies of the new republic in Ireland, Scotland and England – seems about right. Certainly by 1653 the press was full of accounts about Fifth Monarchists meeting at several London locations. Thereafter the movement spread, particularly in southern England. Outside the capital support was concentrated in Suffolk, Norfolk, Devon, Cornwall and North Wales. Yet even allowing for exaggerated reports at the height of their popularity there were probably less than 10,000 Fifth Monarchists. By comparison, there were perhaps as many as 25,000 Baptists and 60,000 Quakers in 1660.

Besides the cry 'no King but Jesus', Fifth Monarchists were also interested in Jewish law. The most extreme adopted Jewish rituals and customs – dietary regulations, circumcision and celebrating the Sabbath on Saturday. Among the mainstream there were demands for the revival of the Sanhedrin, an ancient Jewish law court which was seriously considered as the model for parliamentary government in 1653. It's this proposal that Judith Squibb recalls in her dialogue with Josiah Early, attributing it to the parliamentarian army officer and regicide Thomas Harrison. It's also worth mentioning that in 1656 Jews were tacitly readmitted to England. They had been expelled in 1290 and Cromwell had to overcome widespread opposition so as to turn a blind eye to their presence. Potential economic benefits were a factor, but more important was hastening the coming of King Jesus by creating a first-hand opportunity to convert Jews to Protestantism. 1656 it should be remembered was the predicted year when Christ would begin reigning on earth with his so-called saints. Beforehand, however, anti-Christ had to be defeated and the world destroyed by fire. To speed things along, and in a foreshadowing of the Great Fire of 1666, the followers of Theaurau John Tany, a one-time puritan claiming to be the High Priest of the Jews, deliberately burned a number of buildings in London causing thousands of pounds of damage.

Then in April 1657 there was a minor rising against Cromwell's Protectorate. It was instigated by a Fifth Monarchist faction who regarded Oliver as little better than an uncrowned dictator propped up by an unsteady alliance of local magistrates, obedient ministers and large sections of the army. Among the Fifth Monarchist plotters was Thomas Venner (c.1608–1661), a cooper with artillery training who had spent time in Massachusetts. The rebels' standard was indeed 'a fiery flag': a red lion resting on a white background bearing the motto 'Who shall rouse him up?' (Genesis 49:9). The rebellion, however, was a shambles. Thanks to a well-organised government surveillance system it was swiftly crushed with no recorded loss of life. Venner was imprisoned without trial in the Tower of London where he remained until at least 28th February 1659.

Oliver Cromwell died on 3rd September 1658, the anniversary of his two great military victories at Dunbar and Worcester. He was the man who had held it all together and within nine months the Protectorate of his son and successor Richard had unexpectedly collapsed. The restored Rump Parliament which replaced him fared little better, lasting less than a year. On 25th April 1660 a new Parliament assembled. Known as the Convention Parliament it consisted of both a House of Commons and a re-established House of Lords. A month later on 25th May Charles II returned from exile, landing at Dover. On 29th May, his thirtieth birthday, he entered London. Immediately the restored monarch set about securing power. Potentially disloyal army regiments were disbanded, the militia resettled and a royal bodyguard created. A new royal administration was formed. Although important posts were granted as rewards to staunch royalist supporters, Charles's government nonetheless featured former Cromwellians who had shrewdly swapped sides. Royalists were also put in charge of local government and key urban areas. With his enemies purged the King decided against a bloodbath. Instead he pursued a policy of reconciliation to heal his wounded kingdoms. Those implicated in his father's trial and execution, however, were shown little mercy. Ten regicides, including Harrison, were publicly hung, drawn and quartered in October. Others were imprisoned or fled abroad. On 30th January 1661, the twelfth anniversary of Charles I's death, Cromwell's body was exhumed and posthumously beheaded together with that of his son-in-law and two other hated regicides.

Despite deep divisions quite a few opponents of the Restoration regime united against a common enemy under the banner of the 'Good old Cause'. They interpreted their devastating defeat as God's harsh judgement against their failings: 'the Lord has blasted them and spit in their faces' as one contemporary put it. Even so, they regarded this terrible change in their fortunes as a temporary setback before God granted them ultimate victory. Disaffected Cromwellian army officers, alienated republicans, disgruntled nonconformist preachers and discontented printers therefore began to form clandestine alliances. The results ranged from ill-fated plots and insurrections to the secret publication of incendiary pamphlets including collections of prophecies, portents and natural disasters interpreted as signs of the Stuart monarchy's impending destruction. Although fearful of this radical underground the government infiltrated it with a highly effective network of spies and agent provocateurs. Enemies of the state were flung into prisons where many died or were debilitated because of the noxious conditions.

It's against this volatile backdrop that we can situate Judith Squibb's dream of assassinating Charles II – a potentially fatal fantasy since imagining the king's death was deemed high treason punishable by death. Having Judith working as a chambermaid in a tavern near Rye is also interesting since this alludes to the Rye House Plot of 1683; a failed attempt to kill Charles II and his brother James, Duke of York which resulted in several executions. Then there is the reference to tossing the King's head into a tree 'like the head of Absalom'. This anticipates the poet laureate John Dryden's famous satire *Absalom and Achitophel* (1681), an account of Absalom's botched rebellion against his father King David of Israel. Defeated in battle, 'brave' and 'beautiful' Absalom is trapped when his long hair becomes entangled in the boughs of a great oak tree. Contemporaries read the poem as sophisticated pro-government spin on the Popish Plot (1678) and the Exclusion Crisis (1679-81). It was also prescient: in 1685 Charles II's illegitimate son the Duke of Monmouth was executed following his failed rebellion against James II.

Turning to Judith's forename, she likens herself to 'that Judith who cut off the head' of the Assyrian general Holofernes. English Protestants regarded Judith as a heroine who resisted tyranny by seducing and then decapitating an enemy of her people. Queens had been compared to her. Continental painters and dramatists had glorified her. Yet by this period Protestants no longer considered her story part of the Bible. Although it had inspired a sixteenth-century Anabaptist imitator called Hille Feyken (she was tortured and executed), the Church of England had determined that Judith was apocryphal. Indeed, puritans were extremely hostile to the Apocrypha. To take the example of the separatist and later Fifth Monarchist John Canne (mentioned in 'A Fiery Flag Unfurled'), he railed against the 'shameful lies, horrible blasphemies' and 'ridiculous fooleries' contained in these 'false, wicked and abominable' books. As for Judith's surname, this links her to the Fifth Monarchist politician Arthur Squibb, MP for Middlesex in 1653.

While Arthur Squibb steered clear of rebellion Thomas Venner made a second attempt on Sunday, 6th January 1661. Pamphlets, newspapers, letters, diaries, memoirs, chronicles and court records enable us to partially reconstruct events. Cottrell-Boyce's story faithfully captures a number of reported details. Setting out from their meeting house in Swan Alley in Coleman Street, 'that old nest of sedition', about fifty heavily armed Fifth Monarchists marched on St. Paul's cathedral where they demanded the keys from a bookseller. There they shot a man who declared for King Charles rather than King Jesus. With the alarm raised the city guard sent musketeers against them but they were put to flight. London's mayor then led a troop of reinforcements. Outnumbered the bulk of the Fifth Monarchists retreated towards Aldersgate. After killing a constable they withdrew to Kenwood, situated between Highgate and Hampstead. On the morning of Wednesday, 9th January, weakened by hunger, they entered London again. Once in the city the Fifth Monarchists seem to have split into groups or else were reinforced by a contingent coming from London Bridge. Venner's party intended to capture the mayor in his bed but were attacked by a company of the trained bands in a fierce engagement at Cheapside. They withdrew into Wood Street, holding it for about fifteen minutes. During this skirmish Venner wielded a halberd with which he killed three men. Perhaps during a lull in the fighting Venner and some companions entered Wood Street Compter demanding the release of prisoners – presumably seeking reinforcements. They were then fired upon by troops under the command of Major (or Lieutenant-Colonel) Cox. Venner was seriously wounded and appears to have been captured at this point. The survivors fled and dispersed. Some were chased to a locked postern gate in London Wall. With escape impossible between seven and ten holed up in an upper-room at The Blue Anchor alehouse near Cripplegate. Cox's men surrounded it before climbing up an adjoining roof. They then threw off the tiles and fired inside at the same time shooting down the door and storming up the stairs. Five or six Fifth Monarchists were killed before surrendering. Others may have joined up with a different band still loose in the city since a bloody engagement was also recorded at the upper end of Bishopsgate Street. Here some Fifth Monarchists took refuge in an alehouse called 'The Helmet'. Having withstood two volleys of musket fire and two charges these rebels routed after taking casualties when hit by yet more shots.

Altogether there were about thirty survivors of Venner's rising. Twenty five, including seven wounded, were captured and imprisoned in Newgate. However, at least four escaped.

According to Samuel Pepys their battle cry had been 'The King Jesus, and the [regicides'] heads upon the gate'. At their trial at the Old Bailey, sixteen were found guilty and four acquitted. On Saturday, 19th January 1661 Venner and another ringleader were drawn upon a sledge from Newgate to Coleman Street. At the gallows erected outside their meeting house Venner proclaimed that 'what I did was according to the best light I had, and according to the best understanding that the Scripture will afford'. Refusing to confess he insisted that all the doctrines he had preached were the truth. Together with his companion, a button-seller by trade, Venner was hung, drawn and quartered. Within days eleven more Fifth Monarchists were hung and beheaded. Their heads were set on London Bridge and their dismembered bodies on four of the city's gates. King Jesus had not come.

# Trying Lydia

## Andy Hedgecock

6ᵀᴴ APRIL 1817, LEICESTER COUNTY GAOL.

WITHERS STAGGERS INTO THE darkness. Flinders the gaoler clutches a ring of keys attached to his frockcoat by a chain. With him is the new turnkey, a younger, well turned-out man who grips a truncheon and glares at Crowder and Bromwich, manacled to a wooden bench against the back wall.

'You'd best have kept your bonebox shut,' Crowder growls, the tear in his lip making speech an effort.

'Quiet,' barks Flinders, 'unless you want another basting.' He holds the iron door open and glares at the prisoners. 'Bromwich, get yer sen out here.'

'Don't be a nose,' Withers hisses, as his cellmate struggles to his feet. Hindered by the heft of the irons, Bromwich lumbers clear of the stinking wooden pail, into the doorway, and calls back to his fellow prisoners, 'don't worry I won't say –'

He gets no further. Flinders truncheons his gut – a precisely weighted swing – and, as he falls to his knees, the younger gaoler toecaps the side of his face.

'Don't rile 'em Bromwich,' mutters Withers.

Lying on his side, Bromwich strains to focus on the boots in front of his face, dry retching as the door clangs shut.

'Up. Now.' Flinders' eyes skulk beneath the peak of his

71

shapeless black cap. Bromwich fights his way to his feet, breathing hard and struggling not to vomit.

He shambles down the corridor, sandwiched between the gaolers, boots rasping against the stone floor and shoulders brushing the plaster. He glances into the cell holding Savage, Amos and Mitchell – the last with a violet crescent on one cheek. 'Eyes front.' The command is reinforced with a swipe of the truncheon to his upper arm.

At the end of the corridor Flinders barges through a door and nods towards a high-backed chair opposite a plain oak table. 'Sit.' As soon as Bromwich slumps onto the chair the gaoler kneels to unlock the leg irons. 'Off with the garters,' he grunts, 'now for the cuffs.' Having unlocked the manacles, he leaves. Bromwich shows no surprise when the younger gaoler walks to the other side of the table, slams his truncheon onto the table top and drops into the chair facing him.

'Sorry about that Bromwich. We are still calling you Bromwich, right? Need to keep things authentic, you know, to keep you breathing.'

'It's only by God's will I'm still breathing, Major Wells. Flinders could have maimed me. And as for that poor man, Mitchell, are you going to let that dullard keep battering him until he dies? He's no more than a child.'

'Getting sentimental, are we?'

'I simply need you to get me out of here before I'm milled by Mister Fisty-Cuffs out there. I need out, Wells. Sharpish.

'Not like you to lose your nerve, Bromwich. You're pining for that Nottingham barmaid of yours, I know you are.' He taps his chin: 'What's her name? Abigail? Don't worry, we only need your services on this one for a little longer. The watchman didn't die, but we can still hang these nicky ninnies, as an example to the discontented.'

# TRYING LYDIA

Six hours after tramping over the Trent at Heth Beth Bridge, Jim Towle's army of stockingers cross the Soar into Loughborough. Raw-footed, broiled and a hundred strong, they binge their way into town, discomfiting the patrons of The Marquis of Granby, The Windmill and The Old Pack Horse.

At midnight they muster in the dusk-veiled market square and make for the mill. Bromwich is at the head of the procession with Jim Towle, both of them grasping battered flintlocks. Blackburn, another of the ringleaders, waves a sabre with a crudely fashioned hilt. Mitchell is lushy and reeling, propped up by Amos who crows 'Bonny Black Hare' and cajoles his comrades to join in. Mrs. Mackie, whose prying led her into the path of the Nottingham neds on Mill Street, is marched towards Heathcot and Boden's. Between stints of sobbing she yells at her neighbours to snuff their candles and keep clear.

The Loughborough stockingers look on blankly as the mill gates are forced. Special constables summoned in anticipation weigh up the size and mood of the mob. Most retreat when Jim Towle levels his flintlock at the guard dog and fires. Mrs. Mackie screams.

They enter the mill through the casting room. Three watchmen bar their way. One is armed and fires a warning shot. This is Bromwich's chance to raise the stakes: he levels his flintlock at the watchman and fires a ball into his shoulder. The man collapses and is dragged away by his fellows.

The neds surge into the main workshop wielding axes, hammers and iron bars. The watchmen and remaining specials are forced to the floor between the workbenches.

Suddenly Jim Towle falls silent. There it squats. The Loughborough monster: Heathcot's Bobbinet. A gigantic, brooding spider with protruding rollers, warp beams, guides, bobbins, handles, comb bars and driver bars. Towle stares, as if deciphering some message wound into its ligatures. He looks up to see ranks and files of identical miscreations, the hated 'spider work' hanging from each machine – warp and weft yarns looping to produce hexagonal webs. Grabbing a sledgehammer from a comrade, Towle strikes at the Bobbinet and sends a roller spinning off. Savage and Crowder swing their axes and bobbins and handles clang to the floor.

Towle's army are unchallenged as they clout and shatter their way across the workshop. Bromwich drops his flintlock, turns away from the cacophony and tumult, and heads outside. Near the mill's main gate he spots Mitchell lying in a stupor, steps over him and heads for the address specified by Major Wells.

6ᵀᴴ APRIL 1817, LEICESTER COUNTY GAOL.

'Fifty-five frames wrecked and the finished lace burnt,' said Bromwich.

'And nothing else to report until the yeomen snatched you from your barmaid's bed,' Wells replied. 'I should have moved you on by then, but there were other activities that merited our attention.'

'We thought we'd heard the end of it when Jim Towle swung,' Bromwich replied. 'Then that weasel Blackburn sold us to the King's men.'

'*Us?*' Wells stared across the table. 'Us the stockingers, or us the comrades of Captain Ludd? Be careful, Bromwich.' The threat was undermined by the Major's smile.

Bromwich ploughed on. 'I'm not close to these men but I do know that Amos and Withers played no part in the planning, and Mitchell will go along with anything once he's sluiced. You got Jim Towle, you have the brother – no-one will miss Crowder, he's a lunatic – and you could have had Blackburn. None of the others offer the slightest threat.'

Wells' smile evaporated. 'Leave justice to the just, Bromwich, let us worry about such matters. Perhaps you should be concerned with your own health. And Abigail's.'

Bromwich winced. 'Is that a threat? If anything happens to her, or my head gets anywhere near a noose, there are stories to be told, stories within stories.'

'No need for us to fall out.' The smile returned: 'I can assure you of this, at least. The gallows aren't for you, and we'll make sure no harm comes to the lovely Abigail. Not only that, I promise you'll meet her again very soon. Trust me.'

17ᵀᴴ APRIL 1817, THE SALUTATION, DONCASTER.

I nod farewell to the stagecoach driver and walk down South Parade towards our meeting place, feeling dishevelled and grimy as I pass smart ladies in their walking dresses of embroidered muslin, and gentlemen in high-cut tailcoats. The Salutation Inn is easily spotted, with its whitewashed front wall and wrought iron balconies decked with flowers.

I draw a few stares as I walk towards the bar. 'Yes?' The Barman's greeting is less than warm.

'Major Wells is expecting me,' I announce.

'This way please.'

I follow him down a short corridor. He knocks on a dark oak door and turns a meticulously polished brass knob. 'Your visitor.'

I sweep past him. Wells is slumped in a high-backed leather armchair and gestures to its twin on the opposite side of a lacquered drinks table. 'Coffee or something stronger?'

'Porter, please.'

'Porter? A genuine predilection, or are you rehearsing your next role?' Wells asks as the barman closes the door with a discrete click.

'I'm always rehearsing,' I say in my best Nottingham accent, 'it's what you pay me for.'

'You might need a different voice for the next performance, but we'll come to that, by and by. To begin with, you might tell me how you resolved that problem of mine.'

I sigh. 'A few dashes of white arsenic and two men with spades. He's changed residence to somewhere just below the summit of Robin Hood Hill, near a village called Oxton. Do you know it?'

Wells shakes his head. 'If I note that you're cold blooded, it isn't a criticism, merely an observation.'

He reaches into his grey tailcoat and drops a hessian drawstring bag onto the table. 'Your fee, in the new sovereigns as agreed. I have another engagement for you, something short and simple. I want you to go to Derby, I've secured you a berth at an Inn called The Three Salmons. Jeremiah Brandreth, known as the Nottingham Captain, and his associates from Pentrich, will meet there soon. All arranged by William Oliver, General Byng's queer rooster – far more reliable than Bromwich, because he's in greater debt, but we fear Brandreth may have spotted the trap.'

He leans towards me. 'Keep your ears open and let me know if Brandreth and friends have any suspicions about our William.'

There is a knock on the door and the barman returns with my glass of porter.

I pick up the bag and, without checking the contents, tuck it into the pouch sewn into my lavender gown.

Wells smirks. 'Oliver has been Castle. Like you, he has a taste for changing his name, Miss Tyers, or should I call you Abigail?'

I sip at my smoked, malty drink. 'Bromwich favoured Abigail. I'm trying Lydia for my next engagement.'

# Afterword: The Luddites, 1817

## Dr. Katrina Navickas
University of Hertfordshire

'Luddite' is now a pejorative term referring to mistrust of technology, but two hundred years ago it meant textile workers defiantly defending their customary rights. The last great outbreak of Luddite machine-breaking occurred in Loughborough, Leicestershire in 1816. Lace manufacturer John Heathcot had invented and installed a new type of 'bobbinet' frame for cheapening and automating production. In reaction to the huge economic depression after the end of the Napoleonic Wars, his firm cut wages by a third. On 28 June 1816, sixteen artisan lace makers, or framework knitters, led by James Towle from Basford, forcibly entered the factory and destroyed over fifty of the new frames. Towle was arrested, tried at Leicester and executed on 20 November 1816. He had refused to reveal who his fellow machine-breakers were, but later another participant shopped some names, leading to the trial and execution of six more Luddites on 17 April 1817.

The East Midlands rebelled again the following year. In Derbyshire, on the night of 9 June 1817, about two hundred framework knitters, stonemasons and labourers from the villages of Pentrich, Wingfield and Ripley marched towards Nottingham, in the belief that the surrounding towns would also rise up against the authorities and start a mass march on London. Early the next morning, the rebels were arrested by local magistrates on the road. This time, it was less to do with their employment and was more of a political act, though the economic depression had pushed the rebels to physical force. Thirty-five men were tried at a special commission for High Treason: twenty-three were found guilty, of whom fourteen were transported to Australia and three, Jeremiah Brandreth, William Turner and Isaac Ludlam, were executed at Derby on 7 November 1817.

The Loughborough Luddite attack and the Pentrich Rising might be among the less well known events covered in this anthology, and perhaps also feel somewhat removed from our own experience and contemporary protests in today's post-industrial, post-truth Britain. But Hedgecock's portrayal of machinations in secret spaces in the East Midlands in 1816-17 highlights three major features that resonate with current issues: first, the 'precariat' and unrepresented; second, government attitudes to protest; and third, privacy and surveillance.

Formerly well paid artisanal trades such as the framework knitters of the East Midlands became the precariat of their day. With the removal of restrictions on apprentice numbers in 1813 and employers increasingly enamoured of the free market principles espoused in Adam Smith's *Wealth of Nations*, textile workers were increasingly reliant on precarious piece work, while their main trades were replaced by machinery operated by less skilled operatives in large factories. The attack on Heathcot's factory was precipitated by a rumour he was to shift production to Devon. And the attack on his machines did indeed push Heathcot to move to Tiverton, thus leaving the Loughborough framework knitters even more desperate. The actions of the Pentrich risers were political as well as economic. The rebels sought political change, though their aims were admittedly ill-defined, including an end to the ballooning National Debt. Though desperate, they were part of a long tradition of radical and revolutionary behaviour in the region. The Pentrich rising was 'one of the first attempts in history to mount a wholly proletarian insurrection without any middle-class support' according to E. P. Thompson in his classic history of political radicalism in this period, *The Making of the English Working Class*.

Who has the right to protest and in what ways? The Luddites and Pentrich rebels were active in the middle of a major period of government and local authority repression of working-class collective action. Rights we take for granted today – to vote democratically and to join a trade union – were regarded as anathema and politically dangerous by the government and social elites in the early nineteenth century. The 1799-1800 Combination Acts banned collective bargaining by trade unions. In reaction to the earlier outbreak of East Midlands Luddism in 1811, the 1812 Frame Breaking Act made the specific act of destroying stocking frames a capital offence. In 1817, the Tory government under Lord Liverpool set up a secret committee to gather evidence of a mass rebellion being planned by the working classes. The Spencean republican plot at Spa Fields in London, and the Derbyshire and West Yorkshire risings led to the passage of legislation prohibiting 'seditious' publications and any meetings campaigning for reform of Parliament or the vote for working men.

The other arm of repression involved spies and *agents provocateurs*. In the age of internet hackers, trolls, surveillance and concerns about privacy on social media, who records what we say and do? During and after the Napoleonic Wars, Britain was a murky world of spies and government informers. Before the setting up of a national police force in the Victorian period, spies were often the only way the local authorities could attempt to keep track on the activities of workers suspected of involvement in the new political and trades societies. Magistrates in the industrial regions of England paid anyone prepared to infiltrate the secret meetings of trades combinations and radical societies. At these points of political and economic crisis, no-one could trust a 'stranger'.

The Pentrich rising is thus as much the story of 'Oliver the Spy' and his fellow informers as it is about the thwarted attempt of the East Midlands textile workers to rebel, and this is reflected in Hedgecock's vignettes. Oliver got the confidence of Joseph Mitchell, a Liverpool radical, and joined him in touring former Luddite heartlands in the North and Midlands, promising the local radical groups that 70,000 men were waiting in London for the signal to rise. Oliver visited Nottingham three times, where he and another local informer encouraged former Luddites and radicals in their plans. On 25th May 1817, a meeting was held in The Three Salmons pub, as mentioned in Hedgecock's narrative, and secret agents continued to report back to government about the preparations leading up to the rising. The actions and spaces of the story illustrate the desire for privacy, darkness, aliases and disguises of a movement forced into secrecy by repression: tramping along river valleys, mustering at midnight, and meeting in back rooms of pubs.

Of course many of the dark secrets of the spies remain hidden from the historian. Oliver did not act alone; the magistrates and Home Office were inundated with information from home grown spies like Hedgecock's 'Bromwich'. The betrayals by these local informers are difficult to find in any archive, done as they were by word of mouth and personal visits. All the written spy reports in the archives were by men, so we do not know if characters like 'Lydia' existed. Could they have operated within this masculine and indeed homosocial world of the framework knitters? Women are always more difficult to find in the archive, though this does not mean they did not act as informers: there were several postmistresses in the cotton weaving towns of Lancashire who forwarded on the post of anyone deemed suspicious to the Home Office.

Five days after the arrests at Pentrich, the *Leeds Mercury* newspaper ran a sensational exposé of Oliver, real name W. J. Richards, as a government-paid *agent provocateur*. The revelations of Oliver's involvement in encouraging the rebels at Pentrich and in West Yorkshire hit all the headlines and were raised in Parliament by MPs sympathetic to the parliamentary reform movement. The magistrates' use of spies was widely criticised as wholly alien to the spirit of English law. The Tory government maintained its stance and resisted calls for an enquiry into Oliver's conduct. As E. P. Thompson noted, Oliver became a Judas figure in radical legend: he became the archetypal betrayer in the midst of men meeting to fight for democracy and workers' rights under great pressure of being repressed. Who is the modern day Oliver?

# Spun

## Laura Hird

WHO KNOWS HOW MANY there were on Glasgow Green that day, compelling us to unite with our English brothers? I confess, Pink and I were more concerned with nipping behind trees to drink, before heading down Flesher's Haugh for the other bottle he had hidden there. Alec was already fou by the time we found him, dancing on his back under a bush.

On the way, I spotted Mr. Hardie addressing a crowd and dragged them both to listen. Mother had taken me to a talk of his on the Drygate, after father's accident. As then, I soaked up every word as he spoke about the deceits of the Manchester massacre report that everyone had been talking about. My friends were less impressed.

'Ah, so he's some angel from your da's union, a politician and a war hero? My arse, Andy, the boy's not much older than me,' said Pink.

'A weaver too? Can I get a job with him? I scarce have time to piss when I'm not working, let alone fight Napoleon,' added Alec.

Their mocking continued as we made our way to the Haugh. It was only when Pink pulled two, rather than the expected one bottle from the brush by the river that I decided not to leave. Our fat friend never fails us. His uncle, employed by the exciseman, oft stricken by the white spirit himself, foolishly confides in his nephew before raids on illicit stills. Folk are most grateful for Pink's subsequent forewarnings and keen to lighten their loads. He drinks so much of the stuff, though, he half the time forgets where he's hidden it.

Made foolish from a few more swallies, it seemed a good idea to board the leaky boat by the bank. No sooner tumbled in, Alec started.

"'*I have to get up for work. Can I leave you here, Andy, lover?*'" he whined, as we pushed off into the Clyde. "'*Of course you can, my dearest, prettiest, darling.*' Aye, more sleep in her scabby bed. You must be loupin. You're better on my work's floor with me, *darling*.'

'It'll be you next week,' belched Pink.

Alec squirmed. 'I wouldnae touch anything wi' a mooth like that.'

'See when you first arrived in Glasgow in your auld pa's army jacket, waving his musket, I thought you were an idiot.' His grandfather's band were arrested for playing 'Scots Wha Hae' at a demonstration in Lanarkshire and so he sent wee dafty here to join the radicals. 'Then for some reason, I warmed to you, but I was right first time. You are an idiot.'

'Your ma warmed to the meat and fish I poach for her, more like. Hark you, Andy, so distressed I speak ill of your sweetheart.'

'No sweetheart of mine. She merely ridded me of an affliction you'll always have.' In truth, Mary wouldn't even let me kiss her. She just took pity on me one night, and let me share her bed and her warmth.

'Affliction? Are you joking? I've slept wi' loads of lassies.'

'I thought you only had one sister,' snorted Pink, causing the boat to shake from our collective laughing, coughing and spewing.

As the drink kept getting passed around, the sweet spirit burned my insides against the cold day.

'When did you last see the sun?' Pink's question roused us.

We looked up at a yellow thing, trying to shine through the dreich.

It felt good and safe, lolling in a peaty haze, surrounded by the contented faces of my friends. I laid with my head over the side, thinking about Mary's soft body, singing to myself. *'Oh the summertime is coming, and the trees are sweetly blooming, and the wild mountain thyme, grows around the blooming heather.'*

Next I recall, pelting hailstones awoke me. Kicking Alec to rouse him, I was quickly thanked by having his musket waved in my face, and a barrage of nonsense about the Cato Street affair. 'I'd have killed the whole fucking cabinet,' he slurred, rocking the boat severely, waking the others. Pink managed to wrestle the weapon from him, just before I noticed Mr. Hardie, through the torrent, with an elderly couple, hurrying along the bank, to take shelter.

Pointing them out to Alec, I tried to bring him to his senses, but instead he staggered to his feet, waving and pulling at his clothes.

'I shall cast off this yoke of slavery,' he yelled, struggling out of his grandfather's jacket and throwing it at me, '…and this shirt of tyranny.' As I pulled it from my face, he had started on his breeks, but thankfully collapsed in a heap at the bottom of the boat. With a mind to punch him, I stood up and drunkenly tumbled into the bitterly cold river.

Humiliated by my obvious inebriation, and Alec's childish behaviour, and fearful that both were witnessed, I swam to the other side. Cramp-stricken and frozen on reaching it, I looked back across the river but thankfully, Mr. Hardie was gone.

I avoided Alec for the next few days, though I did miss the fool's company. The next I saw Mr. Hardie, was at church, the following Sunday, with his lady, Margaret. Approaching him afterwards, I told him I was much moved by his speech on the Green, before apologising for my friend's behaviour.

'I have been meaning to visit your family for some time, Andy. Is your father, James, surviving?'

'If you do not find me too disrespectful, sir, I regret he is.' His eyes reassured me of his understanding. The accident was but one of several occasions on which Father required Mr. Hardie's skills of defence, as shop steward; due to his violent rages and brawls with colleagues. Now a cripple, he lives in a near imbecilic state, having also, since taken a shock. Mother tends him admirably, but still the walls reek of his rotting sores and regularly soiled undergarments.

To my delight, Mr. Hardie invited me to walk with Margaret and himself, to his mother's dwelling on the High Street. There we spent a most stimulating afternoon, discussing politics; reform; books; music. His mother even asked me to, 'sing a song by Mr. Burns,' which I did, gladly, to great appreciation. He complimented my 'keen, sharp, mind,' suggesting writings I should seek out by the likes of Thomas Paine and Richard Carlile. He also encouraged me to join one of drilling groups, around the city, combatting excessive drinking with exercise and self-restraint, adding: 'Your young friend might also find benefit in becoming involved.'

And so, with his blessing, I sought out Alec, to make amends. The following evening, at ten, we met with others next to the martyr's grave in Partick, to commence our first, since nightly, drilling session.

Though accustomed to walking long distances, understanding and honing that most natural act within a group was a very different beast, as the marching pace and distance increased. I have become stronger; my breathing easier; my thoughts and ideas finding direction through the stimulation of men of like mind. Many are former soldiers, embittered at their neglect by the government they fought for, not even classed worthy of the right to vote. They thrive on the discipline, not just for their bodies, but minds, to stave off low spirits.

Within two weeks, we are covering the same ground in half the time. Our step increases from standard to infantry, to double march pace, across varied terrain, in rain and snow. Then, the same process, weighted, then carrying towering poles.

Mr. Hardie continues lending me reading matter, including precious copies of 'The Spirit of the Union,' 'The Black Dwarf' and other papers and pamphlets. He encourages me in the importance of clear oration, which I have been practicing in the evenings after tea, reading articles to my family. Even Father quietens.

Aunt Jean is particularly enthusiastic. She and her sickly bairn recently came to stay with us after being violently evicted from their croft in Culrain. Uncle, shot in the skirmish remains in an Inverness infirmary so now my meagre wage from the book binders has to go even farther. Not long returned from battling the Arabs in Egypt, his home and belongings were burned by the same, parasites he lost his leg fighting for. The reason? Sheep are more profitable use for Laird Munro's land, allowing him more to spend on his art collection. It is shameful. In Glasgow, Aunt now scrubs floors of similar idlers and serves in a dram shop in Argyle Street to make a paltry contribution to our household.

Notwithstanding the small, monthly stipend which Mr. Hardie helped secure from the union, I am main provider for us. Though I enjoy my work, I regret it involves making lexicons of genteel, English words, in a bid, I fear, to obliterate the language of my own people completely, as happened with Gaelic. I read them, as I read everything, and feel guilt at my collusion.

My sweet sister Anne, still at school, helps Mother with her seamstress work, for which there is great demand from returning soldiers. They both also care for Grandmother, who sits in the corner of the room like a gnarled crow, in her widow's garb, repeatedly re-telling a tale about a fellow with silver buttons on his coat. In her day, she was a much demanded storyteller, invited to speak at all manner of gatherings, however, she can recall only this story, now. Occasionally she barks out something pertinent, then falls back into blethering about her damned man and his buttons.

These last few days others have crammed into our small scullery to listen to me. Aunt Jean invited the landlord from the Buck's Head Inn where she works, who brought a small keg of ale. Neighbours, alerted by the sound of him clanking it up the close, also stayed after coming to complain about the noise.

At drilling this evening, Alec would not speak to me until I demanded to know what was troubling him. 'Christ, is it not enough I have to share you with your beloved, Mr. Hardie?' Though I reassured him that he is my closest friend, he remained sullen. In truth, his infantile behaviour and dark moods are sorely trying me.

Walking home, I curse myself for allowing the fifteen year old fool to so enrage me until distracted by a sign, posted outside the haberdashers. A declaration by 'A Committee of Organisation for Provisional Government', it calls for works to immediately desist from their labour and to take up arms '*to show the world that we are not that lawless, sanguinary rabble which our oppressors would persuade the higher circles we are, but a brave and generous people determined to be free.*'

Greatly moved by the declaration, I hurry to Mr. Hardie's to share with him what I have read but minutes before. Having never heard of this committee, I pray it is genuine.

On arrival, my excitement quickly disperses. He has already seen it and seems strangely anxious.

'What ails you, sir? Surely this is what we have waited for?'

He pulls a chair next to his and bids me sit.

'It does appear that our time to seek recourse has arrived. On that, I am as happy as yourself. I am but fearful that I may have compromised my own involvement.'

'What do you mean, sir?'

'As I read it, earlier on the corner of Duke Street, a man attempted to tear it down and destroy it and on my scuffling with him, to prevent this, he stumbled onto the road. In front of a crowd, by then gathered, head bleeding, he informed me that he was a magistrate and would assure I would be punished.'

I listen, my spirits sinking.

'I had no mind to cause the man harm. I was merely trying to stop him taking it down, as he struck out at me.'

'Hopefully, the law will have other concerns now to

bother with such a trifle, sir.'

'I hope that is so, Andy. As we have,' he says, crushing my hand as he shakes it.

Alec is there, when I arrive home, the women studying copies of the notice the witless buffoon has collected. He is dancing; waving his musket aloft, until I take it from him.

Mother is concerned how long the strike may last, with no pay to support us. 'As my workplace is here, does that count?'

Aunt Jean's boss, arrives again with whisky, porter and a damp, stained copy of the declaration. 'I'd not seen it till a half an hour ago when a hussar thrust it in my face and called me a strike breaker. Their horses are saddled outside and the inn is bursting with them, clawing at my daughter and addressing my wife as an 'ugly bitch.' Let us drink this, rather than those pigs.'

The liquor is passed as I recite. Others, gathered by mother, also arrive, probably more for the drink than my skills of oration. I am near fainting from the heat of the throng and a hare, boiling next to me. Alec still finds room to prance; Anne sits at my feet; Mother, Jean and the neighbours, clap and cheer; Father whines and passes rank wind throughout. Grandmother, uncharacteristically engrossed, at one point, shouts: 'Magna Carta? Phhh. Who wrote that? The dead, mad king?' prompting Alec to snort, the residue of which hits the grate and makes it spit. Father's countenance, as he surveys us all in such intoxication, unable to partake, allows me guilty satisfaction.

I only start to sober, after the walk to Partick with Alec for drilling. Nothing further has arisen from Mr. Hardie's encounter with the magistrate, I am relieved to hear. Reading extracts from the declaration, Mr. Hardie tells us, 'I am assured that workers throughout Scotland have followed the order and will be joining on Glasgow Green to display unity tomorrow. I suggest we use our time tonight garnering support.'

We make the mistake of heading to Pink's to tell him first. He thrusts a bottle in my face. 'Come in boys. Let us celebrate.' Though I initially refuse, it takes a single swallie to sway any resolve to remain clear-headed. Here ends our preparations, besides banter and singing 'The Deil's Awa Wi' the Exciseman,' 'A Man's a Man for A' That,' 'Cock Up Your Beaver,' and the like until dawn.

Approaching the Green a few hours later but still fuddled, having left Pink still out cold, Alec, and myself are met by a most splendid spectacle. Thousands, if not ten times that, have gathered. Groups, already in formation, marching, with bold, bright banners; speakers, engaging lively crowds; musicians playing; people joining in song and dance. Everyone seems to have a story or rumour to share.

There is talk of raids on foundries and forges the length of Scotland and England. By afternoon many have set up, selling pikes; gunpowder by the pound; lead stolen overnight to make pellets; things called wasps and clegs that Alec has to explain to me. There is word of a man we drill with being arrested in Sauchie-haugh Road leading a group to plunder the vast munitions of the Carron Iron Works.

Amidst the crowd, I meet Mother and Anne distributing caps of liberty she has stitched. Many paid without her asking. She places the coins in my hand. 'Buy something to protect us, sweet brother.'

As the hours run by, others arriving bring stories of disturbances breaking out all over the country. Some have been walking since late on Saturday when first the declaration was posted.

Alec and I join one of the groups who are marching. Immediately, the steps, now so familiar, take on deeper meaning, with drummer behind us, a 'Scotland Free or a Desert' banner affront; women and children skipping at our side.

By dusk, others arrive from similar demonstrations in Dalmarnock, Pointhouse, Tollcross. We gather around one of many fires to drink and sing with a group of fiddlers deep into the night.

'There is no-one I would rather have spent this day with,' I say to Alec, foolishly sentimental as we stagger back to his work to sleep. The streets of Glasgow already look different. What may be happening on them by morning? The road is now strewn with notices. Alec bends, scooping some in his arms and throwing them several times, before stuffing a bundle in his jacket and eating one.

Sunrise again, by the time we wake, I study one of the notices that I have been using as a pillow, to assure myself. But what is this? It is not the declaration, but some offer of a £300 reward to anyone willing to reveal the identity of those involved in the 'Treasonous Proclamation.'

'Is that not good? They are taking us seriously,' Alec says, perusing another. 'This is different again. From the Provost and Magistrates, ordering immediate return to work.' He reads on as I seek it, amongst the others. 'If not, "consequences will be fatal to all who venture to oppose and resist the overwhelming Power at our disposal." Very seriously.'

We find three new notices in total. I fold a copy of each to show Mr. Hardie after the tasks he set us for today.

I make Alec promise to say nothing to Mother, should she not already know. No need cause her added worry and I cannot afford any reluctance, on her part, to my involvement. Having prepared for us oaten bannocks and a treat of tea and sugar, we share our stories from yesterday. She then wakes Aunt Jean, so we can help bathe Father.

'Whatever lies ahead, I want him to be clean.'

I respect her pride, but the task deeply offends me. As much as Father beat me, he did worse to Anne and Mother. Dutifully, though, Alec and I journey up and down the two flights of stairs. 'Jesus, Andy. You say it's hard to be *my* friend?' he retches, as we carry buckets from the rancid, local well to fill the tin bath. Aunt Jean asks to wash the baby first, but Mother insists that the man of the house has cleaner water. It repulses me, undressing him and the four of us lifting his stinking body into the water, as he greets and howls. Then the same struggle to lift him out again, so the bairn can finally be bathed, followed by Grandmother, Aunt Jean and Mother.

It is great relief to escape back to the Weavers where we sleep, to carry out Mr. Hardie's instructions. We are to borrow as many dyers' poles, not already secreted out for drilling and take them to Alan Murchy, the local blacksmith, to allow pike-heads to be attached. They can then be collected and hidden until needed. We visit Pink on the way, and find him bilious but sober having finally drunk his latest treasure dry.

At over eighteen foot, the poles can at most be carried four at a time. A wheezing Pink and myself take ends, with Alec in the middle, it thus taking three journeys to transport the twelve we find. It seems folly to attempt this in daylight, but the streets are auspiciously deserted.

Anne's coins I use to purchase pellets for Alec, from Murchy, the few his grandfather supplied now squandered killing rats, crows and the hare which still boiled on the grate this morning.

Returning home later to empty the tub, the beast has finally been liberated from the pot, its pelt drying over the grate. Pouring the filthy water, using buckets, then jugs, through the window to the close below, I decide to share the latest declarations with Mother. She is fearful, as expected, but better that than she find out from others and know I concealed it. Wishing to summon the neighbours, I refuse, unwilling to convey the provost and magistrates' bribes and threats. Still ragged from drink and weary from the day's chores, I rest on the empty mat.

Next I know, I am startled by loud banging. Afraid we were spotted, transporting the poles, I run to the window. I know not if it is morning, or night. The glass is so stoury, it is always hard to tell.

The bairn starts crying and Mother frets. 'I warned you. Oh God, we are done for.' As I try to console her, however, I realise the voice shouting my name through the door is that of Mr. Hardie, who bursts into the room upon my opening it.

'My sincere apologies for this intrusion, but the time has come. We must move quickly, Andy. I will explain on the way.' I splash the remaining bath water on my face as Mother demands further explanation. Father is squealing, his gaze focused on our visitor.

'The workers at Carron have joined the strike and are ready to dispense arms and ammunitions. It is imperative, we gather these before our English brothers stop the mail cart reaching the border – its absence being the signal of their joint revolt.'

Mother thrusts the new declarations at him and starts furiously cutting up the hare.

'Precisely, Isobel, hence the urgent need to prepare ourselves,' he explains to her. Snatching them back, she uses them to parcel the portions of meat.

'We have scared our oppressors. They must address us now. We must make haste.'

'All respect, sir, I am eternally grateful for your aid after the accident and for proving a guide to my only son, but he is barely sixteen years old, and so will not leave until I say!'

I am horrified at her impertinence. 'Then all respect to you, I must go, in hope you allow Andy to join me,' Hardie says, squeezing Father's shoulder. 'If ever God blesses me with a son, James, I pray he is as fine as yours.'

I turn to hide my emotion.

'We are assembling at the Weavers' Tavern in Germiston with mind to set off by 1am. Gather as many as you can,' he says as he leaves.

I try to follow as Mother brings a large box from the other room and opens it.

'Please, I must go.'

'This is your father's wedding jacket. I have shaped it to your size, and your initials on the lapel were embroidered by your sister. I was saving it for a happier occasion but I want my boy to be smart,' she snuffles as she forces me into it, placing the parcelled hare pieces in a pocket.

Anne plunges socks she has been repairing into another pocket and a liberty cap she has stitched upon my head.

'Keep them safe, dear sister. Tell Alec to meet us, with his pike and what other men he can muster.'

As I walk out, I spit on my palm, grab father's limp hand, and whisper in his ear: 'I am not your son and you are not my father.'

Retrieving my pike from behind the close, I am relieved to find Mr. Hardie and a gammy-legged fellow still knocking on doors. Many, possibly fearful after the latest proclamations, seem reluctant to answer, though after the mighty gathering, yesterday, it is mortally disappointing if this is so. With assurances from several that they will follow after collecting pikes from Murchy, we head off.

Mr. Hardie talks with the limping man on the way but I hear not what is said for the driving rain and my wheezing from the pace and now weighted pole. I am rather irked that he prefers to converse with a cripple like father, after arriving at my door in such a startling fashion.

Soaked through on arrival at Germiston but warmed by the sight of forty or so spilling from the inn, I discard Father's dreekit jacket by the fire. We are ushered to a table and introduced to a smartly dressed man with finely groomed blonde hair, called Kean, and his paunchy, red-faced colleague, Turner, who gammy-leg knows from the Glasgow Radical Committee. They are in discussion with a man they keep addressing as Smith, as if to irritate him. He is to lead us with Mr. Hardie, but seems reluctant.

'It is folly to leave before the Anderston group arrives. Fifty is not sufficient. If we fail to meet with others, how can further weapons be carried?'

Arguments are exchanged, and repeated but Smith is unwavering. The man Turner is furious, his face a ripe beet. 'In the name of God, I would lead them myself but must go directly, to manage the other groups on their arrival.'

Not wishing he risk the journey alone, Mr. Hardie chooses a man to escort him. Turner protests, 'I do not need my hand held, sir,' but he is insistent. I then follow Hardie to the door, where he addresses the men:

'Have we gathered here to fight amongst ourselves? We must move now to avoid detection. Who will join me?' Myself, and a few others raise their hands. 'Then I will lead, till we meet the others, as summoned to.' A cheer goes up, though some look less inspired. Patting him on the back, the still purple, Turner hands him a card. 'I heard you were a wise and decent fellow, and now see this myself. Make sure the comrade who will lead with you from Condorrat shows the other half of this, to ensure he is our representative and not an infiltrator.'

Pushing through, the man they kept calling Smith demands those wishing to proceed cross to the other side of the road and those, to wait for the Anderston group, remain. Of the sixty or so gathered, only half join us, Mr. Kean included. He has the look of an army officer. Will he and Mr. Hardie be leading us now? I notice a pallid-looking Pink and Mr. Murchy have arrived with Alec, musket protruding from his breeches.

'Oh thank God, Andy. When we could not see you, I was fearful you had already left.'

Realising I have left Father's wretched jacket inside, I ask Alec to fetch it, so I may give it him as a gesture of friendship in exchange for his own. 'It has been drying and is warmed by the fire.' I have only just struggled into his when Mr. Hardie orders us take up our pikes, in lines of four and assigns us numbers to identify each other with.

'How do you know that man, Turner?' Alec asks, as we march out. I say I met him but an hour ago. 'He appeared at work, summoning support last week, but is very disrespectful. I was told he is a master weaver but when I sought his aid regarding a loom, he spoke to me like I was a dog. Some say he is more a spinner, than a weaver.'

'Meaning what?'

'I know not. I am just relieved he is not joining us, for fear I shoot the whoreson on the way.'

Mr. Hardie appears between us, having been leading from behind. 'Save your breath, boys. We have ten miles to cover.'

The sleet and hail are biting. As we march on through bogland by Hogganfield and Frankfield Lochs, mud pours into my already leaden boots. My shoulder aches under the pole, heavier the wetter it gets. Several men have lanterns, but Alec and the other two at our sides have only the clouded moon to proceed by. Were it not for the tight formation, we would certainly be lost.

As we leave Chryston, I notice Alec's eyes are brimming with tears. He tells me we passed the path to his home, a mile back and he had been tempted to join those who left at that point, as he misses his mother terribly. It is the first time I have heard him speak of her. I had not noticed the men leaving. Thus alerted, I spot several others sleeking off as we continue.

When we pause to tidy our ranks outside Condorrat, our number is down to twenty-five. We enter the village as the night sky begins to lighten.

Kean and Mr. Hardie speak with two armed men guarding a small cottage. I push forward. 'May I join you, sir?' I am not resisted. The half card, given by Turner, is taken inside before entry is granted and door closed to the others.

We are introduced to an upper-class sounding man named Andrews and John Baird, holder of the other half, who is quite the opposite. Despite his coarseness, he has a jolly warmth about him which Mr. Hardie seems to immediately engage with, despite his contrasting temperament. As they share experiences of the military and respective unions, however, Baird's brother Robert becomes irate.

'Much as I would love to offer you a drink... unfortunately...' he says, loudly, holding up two empty bottles and gesturing to Mr. Andrews who, having looked outside, is bemoaning the inadequate number of our group.

Mr. Hardie is astounded. 'I beg your pardon, sir, but these men have walked over ten miles in driving sleet and rain. The rest await our brothers from Anderston.'

Slamming his fists on the table, Robert Baird glares at his brother. 'Just as I told you, John. Your number is not enough.

Listen to this man, not that English Glaswegian arse.'

Mr. Andrews responds, as if to a child. 'As I continue to explain, a sizeable group of armed men, many also former military, will join on the way. Refrain from trying my patience with your outbursts and be decent enough to listen when I speak.'

'Again, I beg your pardon,' says Mr. Hardie. 'The only former military I am aware of, in this room, are myself and Mr. Baird. My groups' morale is low enough, having been met by only two men, when promised upward of sixty.'

Mr. Baird stands up. 'If this man and me are to lead, then for Christ's sake, allow us at least to confer.'

'Please do, with haste. Enough time is already lost.'

Mr. Hardie bids me sit, as Mr. Baird leads Kean and him, to another room.

'Why don't you try sitting too and make some attempt to control your boorish behaviour,' Andrews sneers at the brother.

'You arrived at my home, last night, issuing orders?' he spits back. 'I should kill you for the way you disrespected my wife, after she fed you, gave you drink, changed sheets to allow you rest in our bed. Then you start on my brother. I'd sooner continue suffering than deal with birkies like you.'

Staring at the table, I know I should wait but, as the exchange of insults continues and mood becomes increasingly charged, I take leave. At the door, only the two armed men remain. 'Still a bit heated in there?' the younger one laughs. 'The inn round that corner,' points the other.

Arriving there, I am relieved to find my friends, slouched outside.

'Did no-one think to bring money?' groans Pink, his yellow skin shimmering with sweat, despite the cold.

'The landlord was rather vexed at being awoken, so not forthcoming with free ale,' Alec explains.

Those who could afford drink now empty out to ask what's happening. Numerous stories circulate about who is joining us and why others have not. Several mention Mr.

Andrews: some in praise of his gathering support these past weeks, others insulted and patronised by him. One of the Cordorrat men tells of another of the Provisional Government, called King, who has been doing the same, and oddly refers to him as the 'English Glaswegian' also.

We head back to the cottage, just as John Baird and Mr. Hardie emerge, hands raised and clasped, Hardie announcing, 'we are confident to lead those who will join us. Any man who does not wish to continue, leave now, but we must go forth.'

A now bloody-nosed Andrews wedges between them, embracing both. I'm glad I left the cottage when I did.

'You are brave men. Anderston now follows, delayed only by growth in support, which now approaches one hundred. Those from Falkirk await you at Carron. And it is confirmed, the mail truck is stopped and English brothers are assembled. Go forward and unite.'

During a muted cheer, I notice two men handing over their pikes. One is Mr. Kean apparently returning to Germiston to ensure our path just taken is blocked to all but radicals. I regret he is leaving us.

The landlord grudgingly allows us to replenish our water, we are formed into ranks and proceed. Having paused, my legs are stiff and feet raw, the mud in my boots now hardened. Such is the pain in my right shoulder, I bear my pike's weight on the left, which feels most awkward.

Two men march between Alec and myself, though I can still hear his gabbing. I see Pink, a couple of rows in ahead. Having recalled the hare in the pocket of Father's jacket, my belly rumbling, I can think of nothing else for the next few miles.

I drop back to speak with Mr. Hardie. 'Sir, with respect, we are weary and hungry. How far still to go?'

'Bear with us, Andy. Refreshments promised seem as elusive as our reinforcements. Trust me, I will secure sustenance soon.'

I march asleep to the sound of footsteps, then use the rhythm of songs in my head to spur me. At points, it is only my own, laboured breathing I have to keep going.

Finally reaching another tavern at a place called Castlecary, we're met by an innkeeper understandably alarmed at the sight of our dishevelled company filling his premises. Introducing himself, Mr. Hardie tells the man he has been informed by the Provisional Government that we can depend on him for provisions. 'The who?' he asks, bewildered.

'No less, I would appreciate if you could provide some form of nourishment for these men, who have been walking all night.'

The man calls two women who have been watching anxiously. 'Bring forth twelve bottles of porter and what remain of the loaves,' which they do. 'Apologies, stocks are low, having had no delivery since the strike. The baker remains shut also.'

I suggest to Alec we find Pink and divide the hare with him.

'Sorry, friend, we scoffed that, waiting for you in Conderrat.'

How does he always manage to incense me? 'Have this,' he insists, giving me his half of our shared bread. I take it, along with the rest of our bottle of porter.

We all remain standing as food and drink are quickly consumed, afraid our legs should seize up again. I notice Pink skulking around looking for dregs. Not a chance.

There is some disagreement with the bill, which comes to 8 shillings, as Mr. Hardie and Baird, only have 7'6 between them and will not permit any of us to contribute. 'That will suffice, sir,' reassures the landlord, but Mr. Hardie insists on signing a receipt, on behalf of the Provisional Government, with the 7'6 deducted, assuring he will be reimbursed.

Gathering our pikes outside, he addresses us again. 'As we approach Carron, we will split into two groups, one taking the main path, with myself, the other the canal, with Mr. Baird, to ensure we do not miss others headed to join us.'

'Johnny McMillan, you ken the area well, so jine the road group wi Mr. Hardie,' says Baird to a swarthy giant of a man. An old boy with a huge beard called Hart, a lad from Berwick, myself and a weasily looking thing called Henderson are also chosen to go by road.

'Can I not come with you?' Alec pleads, but is called to Mr. Baird's group, put in formation and they depart. My relief is great.

McMillan suggests boosting our numbers before leaving, as a number of weavers, passionate for the cause, bide here in Castlecary. This proves fruitless, however, only one answering his door. The elderly fellow declines joining us, but wishes us well and offers his rifle, for which another receipt is issued, with assurance of its return. I suspect his compliance has more to do with the unexpected arrival of an imposing lump like McMillan, at such an hour, than genuine support of our aims. It being three miles to the point we are to rejoin the canal group, we proceed at double pace.

Having barely left the village, an official-looking man in an ornately embroidered cloak approaches, on horseback. The animal, startled by our rapid movement, rears up. Mr. Hardie manages to grab the reins, and settle it, however, the man is ungrateful. 'I neither know, nor care, what your business is, but I will thank you to let me pass.'

'Sir, we mean you no harm, but merely enquire, where you are headed?'

The man, apparently unaccustomed to being addressed by commoners, adopts an irritating air of superiority.

'Not that it is any of your concern, but to Glasgow and suggest you get off my path.'

'I would recommend abandoning your journey, for now. The city is up in arms. For your own safety, it would be prudent to turn back.'

'I do appreciate your interest in my well-being, but will take the risk,' the man scoffs. 'So if you would, kindly, take your hands from my beast.' Mr. Hardie doing so, the man digs his stirrups in and takes off.

Still chuckling to myself about his pompous attitude a mile on, he passes us, heading back. 'I left something at home, so will postpone my trip till this atrocious weather improves. No right-minded man, would travel in this?'

So used am I to the sleet and rain, by now, I cease to even notice them, as we proceed, again at double pace. My spirits, strangely high, I shout to Mr. Hardie that, for the main trade route between Falkirk and Glasgow, it seems quiet for a Wednesday morning.

'The strike continues, Andy. The strike continues,' he bellows back.

It is another mile before we happen on anyone else: a mounted hussar, who appears from a side path. Not knowing how many may be behind him, we form in a line, ordering him to halt.

'What is your business that you will not let me pass?' We pause, to see if any follow. 'Please divide the road with me, sirs,' he asks.

'Damned if I will,' growls McMillan, striding towards him, the ground seeming to shake beneath. 'Surrender your arms!'

I fear for the man, as do Hart and the Berwick boy, who step away, but Mr. Hardie immediately reprimands McMillan, which mercifully, quietens him.

'Apologies for my friend's behaviour. I was a soldier, like yourself. We are merely seeking our rights, as honest men ought to. May I enquire, what business you are headed for?'

He is attempting to rejoin his regiment, from dispatches in Stirling. 'Much as I am sorry for your situation, gentlemen, pray let me continue. I have just kissed my wife and children farewell, after stopping, as my son was ill. I will be in trouble, should the others reach Kilsyth without me.'

We converse with the man for some time, much moved by his story. His own father took his life after returning from fighting in France with the 95th Rifle Brigade. His wife's worked in the family weaving business for sixty years, before doubled taxes forced its closure. 'I was speaking but an hour ago with a man from that same regiment who, like myself, is now a weaver. It is everyone's struggle, sir,' says Mr. Hardie. As we bid him farewell, Henderson produces a roll from his jacket, pulling off one of the original declarations.

'I have seen this, but thank you for this copy, which I can show my father-in-law and again, good luck.'

As cordial as our discourse with the man appeared to be, Mr. Hardie storms ahead, in a seeming rage, immediately upon his departure. Continuing on alone for the next mile, then waiting until we catch up, he throws down his pike and rushes towards Henderson.

'Why are you carrying these?' he demands, tearing the declarations from the man's jacket, throwing them against the rain. 'And what possessed you to hand a copy to a hussar?'

Mr. Henderson stammers: 'I'm sorry, I… they are copies I kept… for myself… since Mr. Turner had me collect them from the printer.'

'Mr. Turner had it printed?'

Henderson is struggling to understand.

'He is a key figure in the Provisional Government.'

'Then why did he, or no man, think to mention this?' he screams, before again striding on ahead. I am distraught, not understanding his upset as McMillan guides us to the moor where we have been told to reconvene. We settle on the slope of a small hill, so the others can see us, and us them, when they arrive. Woods to our right and behind offer no protection from the wind and sleet which is blowing straight at us. My exhaustion is such that my body, yearning for rest, gives way beneath me.

Unsure how much later, I hear someone crying out and open my eyes to the canal group, clambering across the slope from the left.

'Oh, Andy, I am raw from nettle stings and eaten up with midgies. That awful man, McFarlane, has been wicked to me. He stole my water.'

Several, who arrived at the same time, yell at Alec to 'shut up' as they try to rest.

'Are others coming? No-one would say,' he whispers, clawing his puffed-up face. 'Mr. Baird is a good man, like Mr. Hardie, but with a mooth on him like your Mary.' I wince as he rests his head on my still throbbing shoulder. 'Oh Andy, I'm so thirsty,' he whimpers, but I have no water left myself.

About to ask where Pink is, I see him staggering towards us, with two poles on his shoulder, which he lets clatter to the ground on spotting us. An older man from their group grabs him in an embrace. 'Bless you, comrade. I could not have carried it another inch.' I think I hear thunder and wonder how this can be, when it has been snowing, then one of the men shouts, 'Hussars! Hussars!'

My first thought is that they are joining us, but quickly sense the others' panic. Baird gestures to a stretch of wall, further down the hill between us and the approaching soldiers, ordering we take cover there. Screaming out, we slide and stumble towards it, with our unwieldy poles. At only around fifteen feet in length and collapsed in the middle it makes a paltry shield but is better than nothing. Mr. Hardie orders us kneel, two deep, at each side, the rest gathered to plug the gap. This offers no real protection, other than, at best a slight hesitation should they choose to attack.

As the rumble of horses gets louder, several men, including the weasel, Henderson, who I sensed no longer wished to proceed after his scolding, take fright, drop their weapons and run back up the hill towards the woods.

Unsure how many troops there now are, fearful of raising my head above the wall, I hear musket fire and brace myself, before realising that Alec is shooting randomly into the air, screaming. As his shots are returned, a couple of men try to grab him, McFarlane punching the side of his head. 'Are you trying to sign our death warrant, you imbecile?'

A demand is shouted, to lay down our arms but Alec fires again, returned by a barrage and in an instant we feel ourselves pushed back by a charge to break through, stones tumbling onto us from the dyke. A man I met at Condorrat, is struck by a Yeoman's sabre and bleeds heavily from the shoulder. Trying to give me his musket, I decline. Dropping it instead, he takes off but is spotted by a hussar, who gallops past our left flank, yelling, 'Cut the radical bastard down!' Those of us remaining, move forward in a fruitless attempt to secure the dilapidated wall.

Again, they make the call: 'Lay down your arms and we will do you no harm.' Conferring with Baird, Mr. Hardie orders us to comply, but retain our pikes. Some shout out that they could not hear. Standing up, making himself visible to the troops, he holds his firelock, aloft, emptying the cartridges onto the ground. 'Defend yourselves, but refrain from attacking, unless necessary.'

During the slight relaxation in our stance, one of the cavalry attempts a solitary charge at the widening gap but his horse is deflected and stabbed by McFarlane. Cursing, he shoots the old man in the face, blowing off part of his jaw.

As we reel from the horror of the attack, the hussars make an almighty push and manage to stream through, knocking half of us on our backs, allowing Yeomanry to overcome us from each side, striking out with swords.

I stand motionless, in shock and fearful for my friends. I cannot see them. As a voice pleads, 'Have mercy, we will treat with you!' one of the Yeomanry, most brutally, sabres old Hart, turning his huge beard crimson. 'Look at him now with his head like a cloven pot,' the man laughs obscenely, trying to get his horse to trample him.

With them now among us, the pikes are useless and lie scattered, making it difficult to stay on our feet, without having our ankles twisted under them. Walking through us, raising both arms in surrender, Mr. Baird discharges his musket, towards the sky, until empty, then offers it to the Lieutenant of the hussars. 'Take the fuckin' thing, but I swear, if you dinnae stand off, we will die killing you.' The soldier, glassy eyed lifts his own gun, as if to return the gesture but his weak arms slumps pointing straight at Mr. Baird as it sparks. Thanks to God, by the time it discharges, it has dropped and instead blasts the side of his horse.

'I'll get him,' cries a sergeant, raising his sabre. I run forward, to do I do not know what, but am knocked over, as Baird swings a broken pole, blindly at the man, instead piercing the already injured Lieutenant in his side. Several Yeomanry, now on foot, lunge towards him, wielding daggers and swords but the Lieutenant leans his wounded horse in their path, crying out, 'Cease, pray, cease, there is too much done already,' as the beast collapses, taking him with it.

There is an eery, bloody stillness. Aside from the muffled sound of soldiers still pursuing our deserters into the woods, like a blessed miracle, it suddenly seems to just stop. For a moment or an hour, nobody seems to draw breath.

As the Lieutenant is freed and carried off, we are gathered with no resistance. Further Yeomanry arrive with carts from local farms. Mr. Hardie is permitted to tend the wounded but I am not allowed to join him. I find Alec, banging his musket against the remains of the wall, screaming curses. Comforting him, we walk towards the first cart and watch as our bloody, muddy pikes are loaded onto it. The air reeks of rotten egg smoke and open wounds. I am so hungry, I could eat it.

Hussars return with fugitives from the woods. There is no sign of the heavily injured man who tried to give me his musket. Having heard a distant gunshot, I pray he has made it away. 'Auld Hart and McFarlane are grave,' Mr. Baird announces, 'and the shoemaker lad frae Glasgae, is buggered. He's no' gonnae make it.' Alec collapses.

Holding him on my dead shoulder, we are loaded onto the second cart. I ask a soldier if he can be given water, which is refused. The ox, McMillan is grovelling to them: 'I didnae know why we were marching. I didnae mean to get caught up in this.' The same man who, just hours ago, had us knock on every door in Castlecary, to swell our ranks. He is ordered to be silent, as we all are.

The seriously wounded are loaded onto the third cart, several squealing in pain, others too weak to. The injured Lieutenant returns on a black horse, his wounds dressed. I am relieved he has survived. Were it not for he, countless of us would certainly be dead. He asks which is our leader, Mr. Baird.

Baird pushes through to the front of the cart, 'You mean

me. Now, can we get some water for thae poor bastards?'

The Lieutenant does not seem to recognise him but immediately orders this be done.

Mr. Hardie joins him. 'May I ask how you know this man's name, or that he, like myself, were leading the men?'

'That is of no consequence.'

I immediately suspect the duplicitous hulk, McMillan.

'This is a slur on the military I was once proudly part of. Why maim men who could have easily been arrested? I must express disgust at our treatment. The Yeomanry were particular brutal, after we had laid down our arms. Have no lessons been learned from Peterloo?'

The officer studies a note. 'With due respect, sir, several of my men, myself included, have been injured, two horses have been wounded. My own steed, I have just had the rueful task of slaughtering. Five muskets, two pistols, sixteen pikes, one hayfork and a significant quantity of ball cartridges have been recovered. And, to clarify, my troops merely responded to being fired at. You were invited, three times to surrender.'

'And we did. We retained poles only, to defend ourselves against sustained attack by your men.'

'Then, respectfully, our recollections differ. Anyway, it is for the courts to decide now.'

As the carts transfer us onwards, for incarceration in Stirling Castle, we fall into another stupor of silence. My disappointment is stifling, along with a dreadful sense that we have been lead, like sheep, not by Mr. Hardie or Mr. Baird, but some hateful, ungodly force.

On arrival at Camelon, a large number of townsfolk are gathered, jeering and pelting the troops, blocking the road to prevent our progression, until the hussars are ordered to load their muskets and fire above them. One of the Yeomanry, mutters, 'Lower, get them like the Manchester vermin.'

On overhearing the comment, a number make for him, but are held back. One man, however, manages to thrust his hand through the bars of the cart, clutching to touch one of ours. 'God save you, proud brothers. I pray for your vindication.' He is hauled away, but the crowd again engages, cheering, stomping their feet, clapping, chanting – 'Onward we go,' 'Liberty or death,' 'Never surrender.' A bagpiper starts up. Drums are beaten.

Suddenly I am convulsed in tears. Everything held within, these last few weeks, bursting forth. Ashamed as I am, I cannot stop. Instead, Alec embraces me. 'Cry not, Andy. We are alive. Whatever may follow, this is the proudest day of my life, and you, dear friend, gave me that.'

His words serve only to swell my crushing sorrow. How many are dead? Oh cousin, Mary, if only to feel your warmth and softness, now.

'Come, friend, sing. You have such a beautiful voice. Let me hear it.'

A few men nod in agreement. Alec starts whistling, 'Scots Wha Hae' along with the bagpiper. Pink and McMillan tap their feet, others slap the side of the cart. The drumming of the crowd gets louder. I notice Mr. Hardie, sitting thoughtfully and watch the words on his lips.

# Afterword: The Scottish Insurrection, April, 1820

## Dr. Gordon Pentland
University of Edinburgh

RECONSTRUCTING THE INNER LIVES of ordinary men and women remains one of the most important, enticing and frustrating tasks of the historian. We have no 'ego documents' (diaries, letters or autobiographies) from Andrew White, the young sixteen-year-old boy who is the main protagonist of Laura's story. We know the bare outline of his involvement in the Radical War of 1820 and of his appearance with a group of activists who confronted troops at Bonnymuir near Falkirk. His fleeting cameos on the pages of history are rendered in other people's words: what lawyers said about him at his trial or stories told by later radicals and historians.

E. P. Thompson's rallying cry to rescue the poor stockinger and his ilk from the 'enormous condescension of posterity' runs up against this stubborn obstacle of deficient sources. With great effort historians can reconstruct the social lives, the habits, customs and political activities of men and women *like* White, but in doing so for groups – classes, communities, nations – the individual voice remains elusive. It is a proper task for writers of fiction to take the birdseye views of historians and use these to paint the wormseye view, to suggest what men like White thought, felt, feared and loved as they were caught up in a period of intense political dislocation.

The Radical War of 1820 was an abortive attempt to stage

an insurrection in the lowlands of Scotland against the government. Its background was provided by a period of withering economic hardship and dynamic political activity that had followed the end of the long wars against Revolutionary and then Napoleonic France in 1815. Faced with rising taxes on consumption, an economy painfully transitioning from a wartime footing, and a labour market strained to breaking point by returning soldiers, small wonder that young men like White became politicised.

A mass movement across Scotland and England, which explained economic distress as a result of corruption within the political classes and called for radical reform of the representative system, had emerged between 1816 and 1819. The activities of men and women who were increasingly called 'radicals' – reading and discussing contemporary politics, marching and demonstrating – embraced entire communities. While the desire to improve material conditions and the conviction that politics was broken underpinned their critique, there was a joyous and carnivalesque atmosphere to much of their politics. Accounts of radical mass meetings comment on the involvement of entire families, dressed in their Sunday best to highlight their 'respectability' and their fitness for citizenship. Women played increasingly prominent roles, making and presenting 'caps of liberty' to the male radicals. It was a 'day out', albeit one with a deadly serious purpose.

Two factors created a situation where insurrection seemed either desirable or unavoidable to many committed radicals. First, the Peterloo Massacre of August 1819 (when troops and yeomanry had charged on unarmed protesters in Manchester) created a tense political situation and an escalation in violent words and actions both by the government and by radicals. Second, legislation at the end of 1819 limited the available means of constitutional protest, including freedoms of speech and assembly. Within that increasingly restrictive political space, conspiracies and risings seemed, to many, the only available option through which to effect change.

On the evening of 1ˢᵗ April 1820 a proclamation, which purported to be the work of the 'Committee of Organisation for forming a Provisional Government', was posted in public places in Glasgow and large parts of west and central Scotland. Church doors, shop windows, toll bars and water pumps were the natural means of publicising a revolution. The proclamation called upon 'all to desist from their labour from and after this day, the First of April, and attend wholly to the recovery of their Rights'. Estimates vary, but some 60,000 workers seem to have struck work in and around Glasgow during the first week of April.

Far fewer seem to have responded to the call to arms. To do so must have involved considerable inner turmoil as individuals weighed up possible consequences. What would the effect of their own decision be on family, on friends, on workmates? Decisions on whether to participate or not and how far to go were complicated by the imperfect information available. The spring of 1820 was rife with paranoia. A plot to assassinate the cabinet had been uncovered in February (the 'Cato Street affair'), and rumours of a general rising had been omnipresent ever since. Would English radicals rise as well? Would Glasgow? Would people in the next village? The exchange of information might have been swift and efficient within face-to-face communities, but it was much more frayed and distorted between them. In such an atmosphere instinctive distrust of strangers and uncertainty about intelligence were almost obligatory. Laura captures some important truths about the kinds of partial visions and hesitancy which must have shaped and characterised participants' actions during those days.

The week of the Radical War saw a group of radicals from Glasgow, including White, defeated and captured at the Battle of Bonnymuir on 5ᵗʰ April. They had been on their way to attempt to take the Carron Iron Works in the story, the largest in Europe and a key manufacturer of artillery. Whether the radicals actively sought to engage the mounted troops of the 10th Hussars and the Kilsyth Yeomanry, or were simply attacked by the troops is unclear. In court each argued that the other had struck the first blow. The result was, however, a foregone conclusion. An English radical, Richard Carlile, hailed it as 'the first battle between British soldiers and British subjects in the present age', but added the cautionary note 'it is madness for undisciplined men, however brave, to attempt to take the open field, against trained and well disciplined soldiers, such as compose the standing army of this country.'

Further arrests were made after a contingent of men from Strathaven marched out armed, before returning home on 6th April. The most bloody encounter, which left eleven dead, occurred when a crowd rescued radical prisoners who were being escorted to Greenock Gaol on 8th April and was fired on. In the trials that followed the Radical War true bills for high treason were found against ninety-eight individuals, many of whom fled before trial. The crown secured twenty-four capital convictions and three men (Andrew Hardie, John Baird and James Wilson) were executed for their role in the events. Nineteen others, including White, were transported to Botany Bay.

The events of 1820 have retained a place in popular memory and have intermittently provided inspiration for political and industrial action by Chartists and Scottish nationalist and labour activists. They have appeared in novels, poems, plays and paintings, most notably perhaps in Ken Currie's series of history paintings for Glasgow's People's Palace and in James Kelman's play *Hardie and Baird*. Much of these efforts have focused on the three executed 'martyrs' – John Baird, Andrew Hardie and James Wilson – commemorated by monuments in Glasgow, Paisley and Strathaven.

White's story has attracted less attention, though we know slightly more about his life after Bonnymuir than before it. He was a 'lucky' transportee, in the sense that his experience in the penal colony was more positive than those of many others. On arrival in Australia he was made a house servant to a progressive master, Dr. Douglass, who was interested in the rehabilitation rather than the punishment of convicts. White secured an absolute pardon in February 1824, fully twelve years before his peers, and returned to Britain with his master immediately.

He is hard to trace in the records, but there are suggestions that his youthful radicalism was undimmed. White probably became an active Chartist in the 1830s. A very slim notice in the *Northern Star* reports that he addressed a crowd in the People's Hall in Birmingham in 1849 on his involvement in the Radical War. There was an obvious political purpose to the address. There were calls for transported Chartists such as John Frost, who had led the Newport rising of 1839, to be pardoned and so the political capital of former transportees was high. White was adding his voice and his experiences to seek justice for another victim of the laws.

White died in Glasgow Infirmary in November 1872 and a short notice in the *Glasgow Herald* recorded: 'He is to be interred today in Sighthill Cemetery, and in accordance with his dying request his body will be laid in the same grave which contains the remains of Baird and Hardie.' While there is some dispute as to whether White is, in fact, buried alongside Baird and Hardie, the report of White's request, however, rings true. How fitting that his bones should be mingled with those of the men who had directed the single most formative and traumatic event of his life. Baird and Hardie's names have, for a long time, been familiar, even if they are still not as well known as they might be. Laura has finally provided White with a voice.

# There Are Five Ways Out Of This Room

## Michelle Green

ONE: CRACK IN THE corner, where the wall meets the floor, where the sun performs a quick seven minute sweep early each morning before disappearing across the prison walls for another day and night. It's wide as a pin, that crack, maybe two pins side by side, but big enough for the small army of fork-tailed silverfish that emerge when it's quiet enough and still, surveying the floor and eating what I don't.

Boiled potato, piece of grey meat.

Two is the window, of course, and were I eight feet tall with hands like a blacksmith's vice, this would be my way out. Brush aside the bars as if iron were a lock of hair grazing a cheek. No rats from the window because it's too high, but rain sometimes, and cold. Bone deep. I lie on the plank that serves as my bed and press myself against the wall so the breeze misses me. Push my feet up against the hot water pipe. Arms down, chin down. I breathe into my hands, long slow breaths, knit my fingers together and close the gap where the tenth should be. All that blood on the weaving shed floor, and the neat white bone, the broken bobbin – now just a ragged scar and an empty space.

When we're allowed out into the yard together, Lizzie runs her fingertips across the scar, traces rings around my swollen knuckles. Finding the spots where the skin stayed thin. Between the fingers. Inside the wrist.

E39, that's her name in here, after her cell number. I'm E38. When the guards are posted to the end of the hall, we stand at the small window in each of our cell doors and meemaw across the gap. We talk about anything and everything: Asquith's latest speech; our plan for the Liberals; which of the guards might be with us. They can't see us, the guards, and even if they did they wouldn't understand. Just two hungry mill girls, mouthing nothing.

'Will you martyr yourself?' she wants to know, and my answer is quick.

'The dead can't fight. I want victory, and I want to see it,' I tell her. 'With you.' She smiles at that.

'Big Barbara Brown beats boys before bowing,' she mouths, and I stifle a laugh.

'That doesn't make sense,' I mouth back. 'Barbara's tiny.'

'Okay. Proud Pankhurst pulls pillows from pedants.' Her eyes gleam.

'Kind Kenney kills kicking kings,' I say, and she looks shocked, covers her mouth in mock-horror. She's so pretty when she laughs. We will keep this up until 8pm when the electric light goes out, and then we're mere shadows against the cell walls, alone again, until daybreak.

The third way out of this room is more inventive, metaphysic. Perhaps closed to the non-believers, this shining path grows brighter with hunger and thirst. The walls of my cell disperse like mist in the sun, my skin sings. Let the sea roar, let the fields rejoice, let the trees of the wood sing out, because it is nothing at all, this drafty hallway between us. I feel her here beside me, coy in her prison cap. Her palms on my palms. I close my eyes, and reach for her face. She is the May Queen, more precious than rubies, arms outstretched, her hair dancing, her feet bare. Around her is a wreath of daffodils, cowslip, daisies, and the ribbon above her head declares all of Merrie England for the common folk. I remember copying the picture when I was small, from the cover of *The Clarion*, and here she is now, born into flesh as my dearest love, ageless and timeless, leading the parade of the righteous. I keep my eyes closed, stay here as long as I can.

The fourth way out of this room is through the door, but there is little hope of that today. First they come to collect the tray of potato and meat, untouched but for the silverfish, and when they enter again I set my chin high, defiant. My hunger is my weapon, and I hold it with both hands, Boudicca's long sword, Joan of Arc. After the tray, we fight. Six nurses and the doctor in his hat, and when they hold me down I tense every muscle, push against it. I clench my jaw just so, and the doctor runs the clamp back and forth, its teeth on my teeth, searching for gaps. This is when I must be most fully alert, all my focus on keeping my jaw set for as long as I can. I see it in his eye, the slight glint of discomfort, of shame. He hides it well, but this place has sharpened me. It's the routine. Fifty seven, this is the fifty-seventh time. Lizzie and I keep count, and this time instead of clenching my eyes shut, crying out, I look, and I see. Look him in the eye. Fifty seven, Doctor.

He finds the gap, of course, left by my treacherous missing tooth, and the steel jaws open with each turn of the screw, forcing bare the softness of my throat. The blood is running from the tracks scored across my gums and he turns it once more, pushes my jaw wider, wider, so wide I feel my face will split, and it clicks, the crack of a tooth, then sharp bright pain, rush of blood.

My next line of defence is my throat, and so I hold it closed, as much as I can with my mouth forced wide. I tighten every muscle, but now he comes with the tube, two yards of terror. The nurses shift their grip on my limbs, and I cannot resist. Thick as a finger, India rubber, and as he forces it down my throat I taste the bile of another outlaw, the tang of infection, her mucus still clinging to the sides. He pushes it down, further down, and I feel as if my eardrums have burst, as if my chest were flayed by the butcher's knife. The pain is so much that, at one point, it blinds me. I see only shadow and shape. Hear the clang of the metal bowl, the fork, mixing. Splash of warm milk.

I know what's coming. Bread as hard as a stone, in pieces, and I press against the tube, against the nurses, until I feel it hitting my stomach and collecting there.

I hear Lizzie call out to me. When they leave, I am not I.

I was never meant to survive, that's what father said. One month early and too small, but somehow I did, even without his confidence. He sent me a letter yesterday, to tell me that the heather is in bloom, every hilltop, and when I closed my eyes and pictured it, I saw the green and purple against the cold Oldham sky, balancing pale between rain and snow and sunshine.

Janie is half time at the mill now, he said, the last of the family. The girls from the weaving shed send their best.

Keep your chin up, my girl. I read it again and again, ran my finger over the letters. It's more than he's ever said to me, directly to me. And so I did. I kept my chin up.

They gave us each a book when we came in, in addition to the Bible of course: *Fresh Air and Cleanliness.* I told Lizzie that if they wouldn't give me writing paper, I'd tear a page from it and write back to him in the margins, next to the instructions on how to scrub a stone floor.

The light is still on. I'm numb for a time, eyes on the silverfish crack, my throat burning from the tube. The scrape of metal on stone, an iron screech breaks through. Lizzie's cell door, and for the fifty-seventh time I prepare myself for her cries. Though I can't yet speak I mentally repeat the line for her: 'Dismiss whatever insults your own soul, and your very flesh shall be a great poem.' She does not reply. I vomit hard against the wall, wipe my eyes, and then vomit again. Lie down on the plank, feet on the hot water pipe, and listen. Force myself to listen. I clear my throat and speak – 'Your very flesh shall be a great poem.' My voice sounds weedy in here, high-pitched, and I still can't hear her. I clear my throat again, spit to the corner and speak: 'Your very flesh shall be a great poem', and then again, louder, enough to fill this room, then again that it might creep under the door and across the hallway, your flesh shall be a great poem, into her cell, and the next cell and the next and your flesh shall be a great poem and your flesh and the next, I can't hear her, across the prison grounds, and again, I am shouting now, out past the gates, dismiss whatever insults your own soul, onto Southall Street, your very flesh shall be down Manchester stone and into the office of our opposers, whatever insults your own soul, a tide of women, of outlaws, of voters, a great poem and you shall be you shall be and I shout as loud as I can against the cold metal door and the silence from her cell your flesh your very flesh shall be a great poem.

# Afterword: Hunger Striking for the Vote

## Elizabeth Crawford

'YOUR VERY FLESH SHALL be a great poem.' Walt Whitman's words, the refrain of Michelle's story, characterise one extraordinary element of the suffragette campaign. Women were prepared to suffer physical and mental torture in order to achieve their goal of 'Votes for Women'. Whitman's words and philosophy had been absorbed from a young age by those brought up in radical households, while others were introduced to him during the course of their active suffrage service. When given as a present, Whitman's collection signified mutual trust, respect and close comradeship. His poetry spoke to and for all people, regardless of class. Whitman's words were cherished by mill girls and middle-class suffragettes alike, from Annie Kenney to Sylvia Pankhurst, both of whom went on hunger strike when imprisoned for their Cause.

Sylvia Pankhurst suffered forcible feeding in 1913 and recounted her experience in *The Suffragette*, the newspaper published by the Women's Social and Political Union. She was in Holloway Gaol and had employed the tactic of the hunger strike as a means, she hoped, of reducing her sentence.

'I set my teeth and tightened my lips over them with all my strength. My breath was coming so quick that I felt as though I should suffocate. I felt his fingers trying to press my lips apart – getting inside – and I felt them and a steel gag running round my gums and feeling for gaps in my teeth. I think there were two of them wrenching at my mouth... I heard one say 'Here is a gap', and the other reply, 'No, here is a better one; this long gap here.' Then I felt a steel instrument pressing against my gums, cutting into the flesh, forcing its way in. Then it gradually forced my jaws apart as they turned a screw. Soon they were trying to get the India rubber tube down my throat. I was struggling madly and trying to tighten the muscles and keep my mouth closed up. They got it down, I suppose, though I was unconscious of anything but a mad revolt of struggling... Day after day came the same struggle. My mouth got more and more hurt... This went on for a month.'

What had led women to take this extreme action and expose their flesh and their minds to such appalling treatment?

With thousands of others, Sylvia Pankhurst and Annie Kenney campaigned to obtain the right of women to vote in parliamentary elections on the same terms as men. This had begun in 1866 and for nearly forty years women had played by the rules, petitioning Parliament, lobbying its members, and, day after day, week after week, holding meetings throughout the country – in drawing-rooms, public halls, cottages, and market places – to demonstrate to the government that they were in earnest. As a result of their campaign the social and political position of women had improved, with Acts passed that, for instance, allowed married women control over their own property and permitted women to take part in some areas of local government. But still they were denied the parliamentary vote. It was in this context that in 1903 Mrs. Emmeline Pankhurst, who had been involved with the campaign since the 1880s, founded a new organisation, the Women's Social and Political Union, known popularly as the WSPU. She had tired of the well-tried methods and resolved to take more direct action. This new policy was first made evident in Manchester in

October 1905 when Annie Kenney and Christabel Pankhurst, Emmeline's eldest daughter, were arrested and imprisoned after heckling Liberal politicians. They were ejected from the meeting and in the ensuing confusion Christabel was accused of spitting at a policeman and Annie was arrested on a charge of obstruction. They both refused to pay their fines, instead choosing imprisonment with all its attendant publicity. The WSPU was well and truly launched.

'Deeds Not Words' was the WSPU motto, with action favoured over lobbying, and it was the deeds of its members that increasingly brought them to the attention of law enforcers. Christabel Pankhurst later noted that, with the arrest in June 1906 of three WSPU members who had barracked the home of H. H. Asquith, then the Chancellor of the Exchequer, 'Militancy had now begun in London. The first prisoners for the vote were in Holloway Gaol.' These three were Annie Kenney and two working-class women from the East End of London. Kenney was at this point a paid organiser for the WSPU and an inspiring speaker. Despite her humble background, she was at ease in the company of much wealthier women involved in the movement. Another WSPU member later commented that it was in every way worse for working-class women to undergo imprisonment for the cause; not only did they lose their income, but they suffered the stigma of gaol at a time when the concept of suffrage martyrdom was not yet understood, least of all by their peers. A few months later, a group of middle-class WSPU members went to prison, to be followed over the next three years by many others.

Suffragettes were held in prisons throughout the country, for instance in Holloway (London), Strangeways (Manchester), Winson Green (Birmingham), Aylesbury, Maidstone, and Calton Gaol (Edinburgh), magistrates generally sentencing them to the 'second division' despite the women protesting that they were political prisoners and, as such, should be granted 'first division' status which granted some privileges. Indeed, when the militant campaign showed no sign of abating, magistrates became more resolute and imprisoned suffragettes were on occasion sentenced to hard labour in the 'third division' for merely obstructing the police.

It has been calculated that during the course of the militant campaign 1085 suffragettes served prison sentences. In the early years, particularly, the prisoners included working-class women but, later, the WSPU activists who conducted an increasingly violent campaign against property were mainly middle-class.

In the summer of 1909 Marion Wallace-Dunlop, a WSPU member imprisoned in Holloway, warned the governor that unless she were placed in the first division and treated as a political prisoner she intended to hunger strike. Four days later, after she carried out her threat, she was set free. This method of acquiring an early release, emulated by subsequent WSPU prisoners, may have been familiar to Wallace-Dunlop through her family's links with Ireland and India, countries in which fasting had a traditional ethical force. However, by the end of September 1909 the Home Office decided that this mockery of the sentencing process could not continue and suffragette prisoners in Winson Green were forcibly fed to ensure they served their full term. The policy was never consistent; some prisoners were released because they were on hunger strike, others were forcibly fed. In March 1910, Churchill, as Home Secretary, introduced a compromise measure, known as Rule 243A, which, while not giving first-division status to suffragette prisoners, did bestow some privileges. However, in May 1912, after the WSPU leaders, including Mrs. Pankhurst, were given first-division status, the many suffragettes imprisoned with them protested when they were not accorded the same treatment. The result was a mass hunger strike, during which many of the women were forcibly fed, with some released early from their sentences. The Home Office never dared to feed Mrs. Pankhurst although, as we have seen, had no qualms at so treating her daughter Sylvia.

For, in April 1913, as the militant campaign escalated with bombings and arson now daily occurrences, the government felt it could no longer be seen to allow suffrage prisoners to set their own terms of release. The result was the Prisoner's (Temporary Discharge for Ill-Health Act), popularly known as the 'Cat and Mouse' Act. By this the Home Secretary was given the power to set a hunger-striking suffrage prisoner free temporarily, without remission of her sentence, thereby avoiding the need for forcible feeding. It is known that the Home Secretary, Reginald McKenna, privately thought that the prisoner's 'licence' could run on indefinitely so long as its holder no longer took part in any suffragette militancy and, indeed, the police made no serious attempts to recapture many of the 'mice', as long as they were not known to be involved in further militant actions. Mrs. Pankhurst, while still a 'mouse', was even allowed to sail to America to raise funds for the WSPU. In April 1913 Annie Kenney was charged with inciting riot and sentenced to three years' imprisonment and from then until August 1914 was either on hunger- and thirst-strike in prison or a 'mouse' on the run. She became increasingly frail but was never forcibly fed, the Home Office wary of causing damage to such a charismatic figure. Annie was not involved with the arson campaign but other 'mice' were, as outlaws the bonds between them tightened and, with nothing to lose, any restraint on their law-breaking relaxed and the campaign against property escalated. The WSPU was adamant that no human life would be threatened by their actions, but with hindsight it can be seen that it was a matter of luck that this was so. It is difficult to escape the conclusion that attempts to coerce the government by threatening violence amounted to 'terrorism'.

Thus by December 1913, when Mrs. Pankhurst was due to return to England, the government's attitude to the WSPU had changed and she was arrested on her arrival. The Home Office was no longer prepared to release known repeat offenders under the 'Cat and Mouse Act' and rank-and-file activists deemed dangerous by the Home Office were kept in prison and forcibly fed. One prisoner, Grace Roe, attempted to shorten her sentence by arranging for an emetic to be smuggled to her, the plan being the drug would cause her to vomit when fed. Although this drug was discovered by the prison authorities others were by no means absent from the prison regime, sedatives being given to hunger-striking prisoners to make them less able to resist the feeding process. By the beginning of August 1914 ten suffragettes had endured a regime of constant forcible feeding for as long as thirteen weeks. Would they have been forced to serve their full sentences? We have no way of knowing because, on the outbreak of war, the WSPU suspended its campaign and on 10th August the remaining suffragette prisoners were released under the terms of a general amnesty. However, between July 1909 and August 1914, hundreds of women had willingly gone on hunger strike, using their only weapon, their body, to protest against the government's refusal to treat them as full citizens. No prisoner died as a direct result of the hunger strike or, indeed of the forcible feeding. However, many suffered from the after effects for the rest of their lives. Each hunger striker was rewarded with a WSPU medal. A length of ribbon, in the purple, white, and green colours of the WSPU, ends in a silver pin bar, from which hangs a silver circle with the name of the prisoner on one side and 'Hunger Striker' on the other. The pin bar is engraved 'For Valour'.

# Kick-Start

## Sandra Alland

1.

DID SHE SMELL HIM before she met him? Was his aroma so heady that it overpowered the reek of Manchester's factories, compelling her to feel her way along dark halls to find its sweet source? Truth be told, when Ada got close enough to inhale George on 15th April 1900, he did smell delicious. *But no, Manageress*, she thought. *No, you silly men of the board, impatient to pass judgement as I sit powerless before you. The answer to your dilemma does not lie in having the men in your workshops bathe less after weaving baskets, twisting rope, or dipping brushes in hot pitch.*

Ada could indeed find George in any darkness. She smiled at the thought of his scratchy face, laughter, inability to hold a tune. She could track him by voice, breath, the pace and heaviness of his walk. And yes, by smell. But no more than any lover could find their beloved in the dark. The secret to her being able to meet George properly, despite the strict separation of genders in the blind asylum's dormitories and workshops, despite curfews and matrons and the terror of snitches, should not have been a surprise to the board. The secret was her tunnel vision.

It was exhausting that sighted people never failed to be amazed and outraged upon discovering a blind person could see. Should she remind them now, or would it feed their wrath? Did they prefer to think she had invoked some sort of sightless sorcery to lure a blind man to her bed? Many of the women could see. Some detected only large objects, some a blurred version of everything. They saw out of one eye, in specific light, close to their faces, through a magnifying glass, on the peripheries. Or, like Ada, in diminishing yet useful circular tunnels she had learned to navigate to her advantage.

So she had *seen* George before smelling him. Before she heard him cuss a unique stream of words that sounded almost like poetry. Last April, tired of behaving herself, Ada had walked to the chapel alone. In honour of Easter and the start of the new century, she had vowed two things: to evade her chaperones each morning before dawn, and to never again read the Bible in Braille for the manageress. She cursed whoever had dedicated themselves to the job of pounding out twenty-one million blows by hand – just so someone like her could be redeemed via her fingertips, through forty-seven volumes. Ada had a strong visual memory; if they wanted her to accept Jesus they should have given her a printed version.

As she sat on the cold pew, lines from her favourite poem had floated into her head: *I love thee with the passion put to use / In my old griefs, and with my childhood's faith. / I love thee with a love I seemed to lose / with my lost saints.* Now *that* would have been worth hammering into Braille.

Ada wasn't supposed to be in the chapel on her own, or anywhere near men, specifically that mythical creature who lived and worked close to her but was kept obsessively far: the Blind Man. But while she sat thinking of poetry, just such a man had suddenly appeared from behind the chapel piano on the other side of the room, feeling his way to the keys. After randomly hitting flatter and flatter notes, he plunged into the top of the housing, swearing. Presumably he was making adjustments, but they seemed to have no effect on the tuning, except perhaps to make things worse.

If she tilted her head, Ada could see the piano tuner clearly as he felt around on a table for an instrument to aid his cause. Without thinking, she got to her feet − even if she had thought it through with all the consequences that would lead to that very moment with the board of Henshaw's Asylum, she probably would have done it anyway. Striding over to the piano, she grabbed his hand, placing it closer to his assortment of tools. Then she didn't let go.

They both froze. Ada could tell he was blushing. He didn't speak, just tilted his head towards her, and when she re-angled her circles, she encountered the most alluring smile she had ever half-seen. Moving closer, she whispered, 'Can none of them tell you're tone deaf?'

The piano tuner had remained silent, but reached to find her other hand.

Ada continued, 'My embroidering's equally bobbins, and I'm just passable at teaching music. But they insist we have natural skills. Or they like us to do things badly. It comforts them to feel sorry for us, it does.'

She laughed, feeling braver. 'I'd help you, but it'll be far more fun to listen to how horrible the choir sounds and see the pianist's face turn all shades of red. And to try to spot you somewhere in the room, shifting about and dead uncomfortable.'

His smile widened.

'I'm George,' he whispered. 'I make better baskets, I swear. I'm just filling in for the regular tuner who's off at a union meeting planning our much-improved future.'

'By gum, I bet your baskets are terrible, too.'

Then, at the caress of his hand on her shoulder, it was Ada that didn't speak. Neither of them did, the piano joining them in their silence. As they fell towards the floor, Ada's final thought, before *My God, at last*, was of her mother's favourite saying, 'Watch out − I make up for yous all, because I've got eyes in the back of me head!'

Only two months later, George had snuck onto a tour of the women's ward and proposed to her. She had known he was there, of course, and had been coughing the whole while to cover her laughter, so much so that one of the visitors asked if blind women were ill more often than normal women. When the wealthy patrons had finished ogling the inmates they thought couldn't see them, George had stayed behind and got down on one knee next to the bed where she was folding sheets.

'Ada,' George said, 'in this horrible room with no doors, I ask you to be my wife, to come with me to a tiny home with at least three doors, and mock me while I peel potatoes badly.'

They had married shortly after, and rented a house where they had laughed together, every night after work, for the past six months. Finally free from monitors, they hosted meetings for the National League of the Blind, the first union formed for an identity instead of a trade. Ada adored the League's anti-charity newspaper, and invited partially-sighted guests to read from it aloud. And whenever her manageress, Mrs. Blackstock, would sneak a fag out the back of the shop, Ada hid in the toilets to read the rage-filled, poetic essays of Manchester's Will Banham, Glasgow's Charles Lothian, and League president, Ben Purse. Between work and home, she devoured every back issue of *The Blind Advocate* since 1898, when a young Purse had started the paper with £60 left by his aunt.

Ada learned about eugenics, how one of the worst crimes used to be for charity's recipients to procreate, for women to dare to bring more blindness into God's world. But those ideas had lost traction. So three weeks ago, when the board called George into a hearing about their marriage breaking the rules of the institution, Ada knew it wasn't really about her womb. Henshaw's was using the rule against blind families as a smokescreen; their true concern was her husband talking too much with the League.

At the interview, George had dismissed the rule as dead letter. Reminding his interrogators of the recent marriage of his co-worker, Hartley, he surprised them with the revelation that Hartley still worked at the asylum, despite having a blind wife. But in a move of politically-motivated absurdity, Henshaw's had insisted the rule stood.

After the meeting, the board had dismissed George from Deansgate Workshop, and had not budged since, despite the League fighting George's cause. The article on his hearing was currently stuffed behind one of the toilets in the women's dormitory; Ada had learned it by heart and passed it on to the others.

With Mrs. Blackstock frowning on, the board was now staring expectantly at Ada. Gripping the arms of her chair, she swallowed back her nausea and concentrated on Mr. Helm, who had also led George's interrogation. He had a hard face, pale against his black suit, and his mouth barely moved but somehow words came out.

She wasn't sure why he kept asking her questions: How long had she and George been married? Were both their mothers blind? Had Ben Purse visited their house? Henshaw's already knew everything from interviewing George, and from sending spies to talk to their neighbours. This meeting was pure formality; she would be let go, too.

Ada swallowed. Without her income, she and George could soon be in the workhouse, or worse, the streets. There was nothing left to lose.

Shaking with anger, she conjured the words she had memorised from the *Advocate*, and addressed them to Mr. Helm. 'Mr. George Edge', she quoted, 'has been brutally and deliberately VICTIMISED by the officials of Henshaw's Charity for the Blind.' Although Ada thought the League overused exclamation marks, she did share their passion for capital letters.

The board members were looking at her as if she were mad. Clearly they didn't read much, or none of this would be a surprise. Ada closed one eye and studied each of them; not a one flinched.

'Excuse me, Mrs. Edge?' Mrs. Blackstock cleared her throat.

Shutting them out, Ada continued, 'Nominally, for the crime of marrying without asking the permission of the pseudo philanthropists who run this establishment...'

She let 'pseudo' sink in, almost re-opened her left eye to see their reaction. '...but practically for being actively identified with the National League of the Blind, and possessing the courage to voice the demands of his fellow-sufferers for justice in the place of degrading charity – administered by overpaid and tyrannical officials!'

A sharp intake of breath, six throats sucking at air.

Inside Ada's womb, a tiny leg began to kick. The kicking grew with the pictures in Ada's head, of thousands of blind families begging in the streets, of people with no sick pay, funerals, lawyers, pensions. Ada moved in her chair, but the pain and nausea increased. The baby put its small feet up against all her fears, and shoved – life without George, kick, the poorhouse, kick kick, losing her children, kick, kick, kick. The feet began to chip away at even the worst things, like the times uninvited men had visited the women's wards at night. She would never again have to hear about God's punishment for her sins.

The kicking stopped, and Ada's head was clear. Placing her hand on her stomach, she stood up.

'I can find my own way out,' she said.


2.


Alexandra Park was buzzing in the way it did if the sun was likely to make an appearance. Glaswegians knew how to make the most of a mostly good day, especially in January. In the blind section of the park, Charles Lothian was kicking a ball around half-heartedly. Behind him, men were playing dominoes up on the wooden pavilion, or stretching on bits of pitch not turned to frosty mud.

In the distance someone shouted, 'Happy 1919!'

If his fellow players had been able to see his expression, they would have known something was amiss. Instead, they only heard the jingle of the bell inside the football, which informed them Charles was warming up as usual: bouncing the ball on one knee and then the other, sending it flying high then catching it with a reverse kick behind him, the bell announcing its direction.

Sitting at a picnic bench lacing up, a few of the lads sang one of the League songs Charles had written for last year's strike. Some were still drunk from the previous night's joint celebration of New Year's and the strike victory.

'Awake, awake, ye toilers of the land,
Arise, arise, and list to our demand,
We only ask for justice, we ask for nothing more,
We only ask for justice for our sightless poor.'

Charles smiled for the benefit of the players who were partially sighted, but he couldn't bring himself to join in. The song felt like a taunt, proof of his foolishness, and lack of poetic talent and women friends.

Charles was anxious. The click of dominoes on nearby tables reminded him of the manager's fingers tapping on the desk each night while he finished tarring brushes before retiring to the dorm. In October of the previous year, after months of ignored requests for meetings about grievances, Charles was one of twelve men who had marched into the managers' office to demand improvements. The men still didn't earn a living wage, worked long hours in dangerous conditions without breaks, and had no sick leave.

After the meeting, Glasgow Asylum had dismissed all twelve men from their jobs. When others refused to take up their work, they were suspended too. In retaliation, the League's Glasgow branch called out all the workers for their largest strike ever. Glasgow Trades Council, Clyde Workers' Committee, and the public were onside. As the strikers picketed through November and then December, supporters cheered, joined in songs, even donated change. Some days the workers froze in horizontal rain, but people brought hot drinks and news of union support from places like London and Leeds. They were in every paper, and Charles had been on top of the world.

On New Year's Eve, buckling to pressure, Glasgow Asylum had reinstated the dismissed workers, giving the men an advance of six shillings a week. Charles' co-workers recited his poetry on the tram to the League's Hogmanay dance, which hadn't pleased the driver.

'Why should this beauteous world of ours
In such confusion ever be?
The wealthy waste their precious hours
While others pine on charity.'

Bouncing the ball on his knee, Charles turned his head to face where he thought west was. The ballroom was less than an hour's walk from the park, but it might as well be in the Atlantic. He tried to imagine the rows of tenements and fields lining the hill that led to the city centre. If he shut out the dominoes, birds and football bells, he could faintly hear the trams on Cumbernauld Road. Only the night before, Charles had found himself on a large wooden floor, amazed by the sound of so many shoes thumping in time to the band – and dancing 1918 away with someone he'd just met. As he had tried desperately to keep up with Siobhan's more agile feet, she'd shouted stories into his ear.

'I stay wi' mah mother, so huv more freedom than the lassies in the asylum, but Glasgow Mission tae the Outdoor Blind still hound me tae read me the Bible or bring me tae church. Sometimes I join writin' competitions or knittin' circles, or take their trip doon the water on the paddle steamer. I dae enjoy meetin' isolated blind women wi' nae friends or education apart fae God's word.'

'Why's that?' Charles asked.

'I view it as mah purpose on Earth tae corrupt 'em!'

She spun him round, nearly knocking him over. He thought of the sound of birds when a flock took off all at once.

'But mostly I've ditched the charities and the mission,' she said, blowing smoke past him. Without missing a beat, she had somehow lit a cigarette. 'Mah Mum loves Labour, so she helped me intae the Women's Social and Political Union.'

'Suffragettes! Och, my.'

'I was in the rent strikes, back in 1915. I've broken windaes, poured acid in postal boxes wi' oor Jessie Stephen, even wrestled polis in St. Andrew's Hall.'

Glaswegian women were known for their determination, and the war hadn't slowed the suffragettes' momentum. Charles' feet, however, were slowed by all the stout he'd had since four o'clock. He tried to concentrate on Siobhan's breath in his ear, and something smart to say.

'But they cannae catch me, the closest I got tae Duke Street Prison was takin' flowers tae the poor jailed lassies on their release. At least they didnae force-feed 'em there.' She paused to exhale a large cloud of smoke. 'So what dae ye dae, Charles?'

'Oh, och, I'm jist at the asylum,' he muttered.

'What?' she shouted.

'The asylum!' he shouted back. 'We jist won the strike?'

'And what dae ye think of your victory?'

'Justice is blind indeed!' Charles exclaimed, accidentally kicking her left shin.

'I'm rollin' mah eyes,' she told him. But he thought maybe she liked him.

'But, Charles,' Siobhan said, grabbing his hand tighter. 'Why huv the men got six shillings and the women three – they work aw day jist as hard, they supported the strike. But they dinnae get paid the same or even huv the vote unless they're over thirty and huv property. That leaves oot the poor, Charles, and maist women fae other countries.'

'Well… we cannae win all the battles at once, can we hen? We've got eight women secretaries this year, and they're considerin' Mrs. Fairhurst as regional secretary in London.'

'And sixty-five men secretaries,' she scoffed.

'The League takes its women seriously. It isnae oor fault

what the prime minister decides, is it?'

Charles put his arm around her waist, pulled her to him. But Siobhan stopped dancing and let his words hang in the air until he wished he hadn't said them. As Charles reached for her hand and did not find it extended, the day's victory dimmed.

'Charles', Siobhan said soberly. 'I'm no lookin' for a fiancé, I'm lookin' for comrades.' She lowered her voice, 'I prefer dancin' wi' women, if ye get mah meanin'.' But some lassies might want husbands, ones who respect 'em. You're pure lovely, Charles, but even us blind folk need tae think a' the bigger picture.'

When she left him standing there with a quick 'nice tae meet ye', he realised that business would continue as usual, with Glasgow Asylum exploiting him and his co-workers for even less money and security, and more hours, than sighted workers were unhappy with. Siobhan was right, the League was letting the women down. And for nothing but empty promises.

Charles had gone home in a fog, walking instead of using his tram token stamped 'BLIND'. He wasn't in the mood to count stops or deal with anyone who could see, even if it meant getting lost. As he finally passed beneath the stone gates of the asylum, just before curfew, the nine-foot wall closed him in, its shadow a cold weight on his head. It seemed the hands of the sculpture above the entrance were pressing down on his shoulders, too: Jesus healing a blind child, a statue he had heard explained a thousand times to wealthy patrons looking for a charity that elicited enough pity to get them into heaven.

Even now, on a field in the slanted sunlight of a new year, free as a man could be, he could not shake the heaviness of the asylum. Charles rubbed his hands together, suddenly furious at the calluses and cuts he had from binding brush bristles and dipping them in tar for ten hours a day, six days a week. After months of not working, his hands were still swollen and stained, with the scars of pitch burns reaching his elbows. He needed his fingers to read Braille, feel his way around, know the difference between a fine dress and a cheap one if he ever managed to not make an arse of himself with someone like Siobhan. Well, someone almost like Siobhan. Something much bigger would have to happen to change the way things worked.

Charles kicked the football towards the goal and listened for the clap of a goalie to tell him he'd scored. Instead he heard only the bell, ringing repeatedly as the ball bounced out of bounds.

'I'm rollin' mah eyes,' it seemed to say. And the sky opened up as if on cue.

3.

On 12th April 1920, 250 blind marchers convened in Leicester Town Square. Thanks in part to appearing half-drowned, the men had raised massive popular support. They had walked for a week already, in groups from every corner of the country, through heavy rains and with no change of clothing. Hoping to get Ben Tillett's Blind Bill passed in Parliament, they followed the League's David Lawley and his 200-mile plan to win blind workers economic emancipation.

Banners with slogans like 'Justice Not Charity' draped the square, whipping noisily in the wind. A reception awaited, as it had at every stop, with local labour organisations, the mayor, friends, musicians, soup. Soon they would carry on together to London for the largest mass protest march in history – with demands for state aid and a meeting with Prime Minister Lloyd George.

Ada and George Edge had arrived among the marchers from Birmingham, where workers had met from places like Manchester, Oldham, Liverpool, Dublin, Newport and Swansea. Henshaw's men didn't march, maybe because of threats from management. But Ada and George weren't with Henshaw's, they never got their jobs back. They did, however, have three sighted children, supported largely by music lessons Ada gave from their home. Since Manchester, Ada and their daughter

Lucy had helped guide the march, just as they had guided George to the celebratory pint of stout he now held high as the final group from the Northeast marched down the muddy road into town, soaked but happy.

Sitting next to George and Lucy as they awaited the ceremony in the square, Ada described what she could see through her remaining narrow circle.

'They're arm in arm in fours,' she said. 'The paper said this group didn't even use a rope to guide themselves. There's seventy-four men in total, from Edinburgh, Glasgow, Paisley, Sunderland, Southshields, Newcastle, Leeds, Bradford and York. The paper said they looked bedraggled. Do they, Lucy?'

At a whistle from the leader, everyone stopped in unison. The Edge family cheered.

'I favour that reporter from *The Herald*,' Ada continued. 'The one who's marched along with everyone. I like his words: cheerful, justice, organised, no complaints, kindnesses, gratitude, invincible patience. He writes about begging and unfair wages, but never says "pitiable".'

George replied, 'A good man indeed. Does anyone see Charles Lothian? We must meet him!'

As Ada squinted and shook her head, Lucy replied, 'Yeah, Dad, aye. There he is, right at the front of the marchers. Can you hear him singing?'

George laughed, and joined in for the chorus of 'Pack All Your Troubles in Your Old Kit Bag' as the men started to break away from their organised lines.

'George, can I tell you what Mrs. Fairhurst, our woman in London, said to the papers?'

George grabbed Ada's hand. 'You can tell me anything right now, especially if it makes you happy.'

'"I am disappointed that our organisers will not permit us women to march with the men." That's what she said, George. Just like that. And after all the suffragettes did, and all we working women still have to gain, it did need to be said.'

George smiled. 'And what did the reporter say?'

'He said: 'Surely, as a woman, you do not agree with the undue hardships suffered by the men who are marching to London.''

The men in question were now being offered stout and led to chairs around Ada, George and Lucy, in preparation for the speeches. The rain was starting first, though. George reached for an umbrella.

'And what was our Mrs. Fairhurst's reply?' he asked, opening it above them.

'She said – listen to this, she said: 'On the contrary, our blindness is not of a temporary character caused by excessive drinking, therefore our legs are not usually affected.''

'She ain't met you, me love.'

Ada smacked him softly. 'Then she said the bill only represents the minimum we need, and that the financial clauses must not be whittled down, or many blind people will remain in beggary. She spoke so well, George. They should've let the women workers march.'

'You're right, love, of course you're right. But most men still don't take kindly to women leading, especially the prime minister. We need to sway him, but he's an enemy to suffragettes, he is. He won't forget they tried to blow up his house.'

'If people had told any of you men from the League that your blindness was getting in the way of the general working man's cause, you wouldn't have stood for it. By gum, we can do both, George. Nowt will change unless we do.'

The ceremony was starting. After the mayor's greeting, a brass band played a soggy yet delightful welcome.

'Who's up first, love?' George asked.

'It's hard to tell, but I think it might be David Lawley himself. His hair looks fair enough. He's done so well organising all this. We're lucky to have him.'

'Aye, it's him,' Lucy nodded. 'I can't wait till he and Ben Purse get the prime minister in a room.'

As David Lawley stepped onto the small wooden stage, the crowd clapped and hollered, then quieted down.

'I spent twenty years working in a quarry before I was blinded,' he began. 'I haven't had to suffer the charities, the church and the workshop like many of you…'

Ada whispered, 'Oh yes, that's him indeed. I love hearing him even more than reading him.'

'Voluntary charities are a great ring of vested interest by which the blind are exploited,' Lawley continued. 'They are prepared to do everything for the blind but get off their backs. It is a case of salaries for the officials and doles for the blind. And to these organisations Lloyd George granted £170,000 last year, not to the blind!'

When the speeches ended, the crowd sang the socialist anthem, 'England Arise', but with Lawley's lyrics, 'The March of the Blind'. Having given up on politics since their failed suit against Henshaw's for wrongful dismissal, Ada and George had found their love of protesting rekindled by joining the march. Despite blisters and aching calves, their steps felt lighter as they found their way to the pub.

Inside, more food and drink awaited, next to a much-needed fire. A local family had prepared gifts of wool socks for the marchers. Throwing them into the middle of the room and shouting 'Catch!' was the latest game of the Northeast contingent, and men jostled about with hopeful hands in the air. The rooms were a sea of white shirts, black ties and white canes, with space for standing only, but Lucy found the Edges a round table in a corner.

As everyone settled in, Lucy disappeared to get drinks, then returned with an overflowing tray and Charles Lothian. Cigarette in hand, Charles exclaimed, 'The family that stood up tae Henshaw's!'

'The fella who made the consequences bearable!' Ada replied. She quickly fell to gushing about Charles' work with the *Advocate*, and in return learned of his shared love of Mrs. Fairhurst's newspaper quotes. Charles called over one of his younger comrades from Glasgow.

'I present Sean, another admirer of oor women secretaries,'

Charles said, without removing the cigarette from his mouth. Sean was smoking, too.

'Any friend of Charles Lothian is a friend of ours,' Ada said, waving the smoke away and shaking Sean's hand, which seemed soft for a basket weaver. 'Either you're a writer or you tune pianos!' she said as he sat down on the stool next to her.

Ada tilted her head and thought she could see Sean smile. 'I cannae even sing, ma'am. A pure embarrassment tae the cause, I am, huv tae march in silence. But aye, I hope tae one day be a famous newspaper man like Charles here, or a union secretary the likes a' Mrs. Fairhurst.'

'Wantin' tae be like a woman, are ye?' Charles asked. 'That's a fair aim.' Ada saw Sean reach to find Charles' leg under the table across from him, then deliver a kick to his shin.

'A noble aim,' George added seriously. 'The best aim. The only aim. Someone tell me – is my wife smiling at me yet?'

'Your wife?' Sean said, turning towards Ada. 'She reminds me of mah own. I'd wager Mrs. Edge is rollin' her eyes, she is. Everyone knows one suffragette is harder than aw the men together.'

'And less likely tae wind up in a pub on the road fae Huddersfield!' Charles added, filling everyone in on the marchers who had temporarily stumbled off their path, finding a place to sleep with local police.

Ada moved closer to Sean, placing her hand on his shoulder. 'I admire your writing,' she said into his ear. 'What was that one from ages ago? "An impression of the suffragette's raid. By one who was present." It's so grand that Glasgow's *Forward* has kept printing your articles.'

At Sean's silence, Ada asked, 'Are you still here?'

Lowering his voice, he replied, 'I'm speechless, Mrs. Edge. Women dae read a lot these days, even the blind yins. There's nae foolin' yous.'

Ada laughed. 'My favourite will always be *The Blind Advocate*, it will. But I also enjoy *Votes for Women* and *Suffragette*. Like you, Sean – and I imagine your wife, too – I'm no supporter of charity *or* patriarchy.'

Ada stood up. 'A toast! To no gender being pushed about by another, to people choosing their own destinies. To blind people of every kind, to victory over all that keeps us down!'

'But are you smiling at me yet?' George asked.

'Always, my love.'

Everyone was smiling. After resting, they would begin the ten-day march to the capital, where 10,000 supporters would greet them as they challenged a post-war government that had made its bed with Conservatives. But for now, they were in a dark pub among friends, happy to see even less of the world than usual.

# Afterword: The Blind Men's March, 1920

## Francis Salt

ON THE 5ᵀᴴ APRIL 1920, 250 blind men set out from three starting points – Manchester, Leeds and Newport – to march to London. On the 30ᵗʰ of that month, after 20 days of marching, and a further five days of waiting, they finally met with Prime Minister Lloyd George in Number 10 Downing Street; a meeting which resulted in the first law specifically targeted at a particular group of disabled people, the Blind Persons Act of 1920.

This march and its effect on blind people, who at the time relied on the poor law and charitable donations for relief from poverty, appears to have been largely neglected by historians.

As my own research has demonstrated,[1] blind people began to organise in Britain in the late nineteenth century to change how the rest of society perceived their impairment and their ability to work. Until the turn of the century, a blind person's best prospect was to be housed, educated and employed in a charitable asylum – like the Manchester-based Henshaw's Institute for the Blind, referenced in this story. The asylums owned workshops nearby that occupied the blind members in a number of predetermined tasks, including brush making, basket weaving, mat making and shoe repair, as well as some more skilled occupations such as music teaching, and piano and organ tuning and playing. Working conditions were often poor, safety lax, and pay far below what sighted artisans and craftsmen could expect for the same work. To many, this cheap labour felt like a condition of the charity provisions they were receiving, not fair and dignified employment.

Many of the asylums also came with strict rules; men and women were kept apart, in the same asylum, with different workshops and segregated dormitories for those not living locally. Fraternisation between them was strictly forbidden. The implicit reason for this being that blind couples were deemed more likely to produce blind children, and thus further burden the state.

The National League of the Blind was established in 1893 and became a trade union in 1899. Its mission was not just to change the rules and conditions imposed on blind people by the charities they were at the mercy of, but to change the charity-based approach itself, and to call for statutory rights and 'state aid' for all blind people in education, employment and maintenance.[2]

The launch of its monthly journal, *The Blind Advocate* – founded and initially edited by Benjamin Purse, himself educated at Henshaw's – allowed accurate information to be communicated to members. The influence of *The Advocate* cannot be underestimated. Although it was a printed journal, not Braille, it was read, out loud if necessary, by and to members of the NLB up and down the country. In its pages we can trace many of the real-life characters in Sandra's story. Articles by activists such as Charles Lothian, the Scottish regional organiser, appeared regularly alongside appeals for funds for campaigns such as the Glasgow Workshop strikers in 1918. Another frequent contributor was David B. Lawley. Blinded in a quarry accident in his twenties, Lawley was the Northwest regional organiser, and Blackburn branch secretary, who stood for election to the local council, and in 1918 stood in the General Election for Labour in Warrington.

Other characters in Sandra's story are equally real. George Edge – educated and trained at Henshaw's Asylum in Old Trafford, and employed as a basket maker at their Deansgate workshop – was indeed dismissed by Henshaw's in 1901 for marrying a blind woman, Ada, a music teacher also educated and employed by the Asylum. The NLB demanded his reinstatement arguing that it was really George's activities with the League that had brought about his dismissal, as by this stage other cases of rule-breaking were being overlooked. Various 'agitations' by League members then followed. Cognisant of Henshaw's rules, as a charity, in 1902 Ben Purse, the League's president, and George Edge made a donation to the charity which allowed them to attend its annual general meetings and to speak to the board, which they did several times. Despite these 'agitations' and local press coverage challenging Henshaw's ruling, however, George was never reinstated.

Agitations such as these, as well as the League's affiliation with the Trades Union Congress and the newly formed Labour Party, all helped to strengthen its membership. The union's influence grew and grew with successive governments. In 1901 Keir Hardie, the sole Labour MP, presented an NLB petition to Parliament; as early as 1914, the NLB had a representative on the government's new advisory committee on the conditions of the blind. And by 1917, despite the war, pressure brought by the NLB forced the government to publish the committee's report on the blind and take measures to begin to implement its recommendations.[3] During this period, the League also showed a great understanding of the value of public demonstrations and media coverage (including on two occasions coverage by Pathé News, which was shown in early cinemas). Demonstrations were staged on a national scale – with large gatherings in Trafalgar Square in 1909 and again in 1918 – as well as locally, including the regular appearance of floats in town and village carnivals, to present the case for 'state aid', as opposed to private charity.

In 1919 members of the NLB disrupted a sitting of the House of Commons and later members attended a mass demonstration in Hyde Park. 1919 was a critical year: the NLB's third attempt at legislation was being put to Parliament by Ben Tillett, the new Labour MP for Salford. But realising that the bill would again fail, the League began to plan its march for the following April.[4]

Although the march set off from three cities, it featured NLB members from across the UK. Those from the Northwest and Ireland met at Manchester (and marched via Stafford, Wolverhampton, and Birmingham). Those from the Southwest and Wales started at Newport, and marched via Abergavenny and Worcester, joining the former march at Birmingham. And those from Scotland and the Northeast marched from Leeds, via Sheffield and Nottingham, to join the others at Leicester. From there, they proceeded towards London, meeting London-based marchers at Watford, and eventually arriving at Trafalgar Square on Sunday, 25th April.[5]

At the front, men carried a banner bearing the words 'JUSTICE NOT CHARITY'.[6] The general consensus of the time may have been that blind people were 'well cared for' by voluntary provisions, with the charitable institutions using donated funds 'for the good of the blind'. The League, however, contended that more of the donated funds went to sighted employees of the charities than to the people for whom they were intended.

In what may have been an attempt to encourage the public to question the view of the conditions of the blind, the men set off carrying only white canes. They took no provisions, 'not even a change of underclothes',[7] relying for the three weeks on the support of cooperative societies and trades councils for food and lodging. The League's officials, who marched with each of the three groups, were well aware of the power of publicity, and engaged themselves effectively in what today would be called 'spin'. The speakers delivered anti-charity and anti-government oratory and leaflets[8] to their audiences, who responded with collections of cash to support the 'blind crusaders'.[9] In the towns and cities through which they passed, large meetings were arranged; civic receptions with local dignitaries and workers' brass bands were not uncommon.

In one speech, David B. Lawley accused the 'charity mongers' of living off the backs of the blind and taking food out of the mouths of blind children.[10] And when the Deputy Prime Minister, Bonar Law, offered to meet the delegation instead of

Lloyd George, Patrick Neary, the Dublin branch secretary, told a large gathering in Birmingham, 'We want Bonar Law no more than we want the Poor Law.'[11]

The 250 blind men marched by either holding onto a rope that passed through the centre of the column of two, or by linked arms four abreast, with whistled commands to walk or stop given from sighted helpers marching with them.[12]

The decision of the organisers to present such a spectacle of vulnerability (and poverty, considering the lack of provisions) in order to challenge the view that blind people were 'well cared for' by charity seems to have had the desired effect. Contemporary reports in the *Daily Herald*, the *Manchester Guardian* and other local newspapers speak of 'a pitiable group', so dishevelled were they marching through so many days of rain, and of women in tears rushing to kiss them as they entered London. One reporter even suggested their banner could have easily read 'JUSTICE NOT PITY', so forlorn was their appearance.[13] But anyone who knew the League would have known this to be an insensitive joke; blind men and women would have reacted angrily to any form of pity, no matter how well intended.

And so, on 25th April, the marchers finally arrived in Trafalgar Square where they were joined by 10,000 fellow trade unionists. Again, there is evidence of intelligent 'media management'. The marchers were arranged in rows upon the steps of the National Gallery forming a 'sightless' background behind the speakers' plinths.[14] The gathering was addressed by various union leaders as well as Herbert Morrison, the chairman of the London Labour Party, each demanding government action on improving conditions for the blind.[15] But the marchers had to wait five days before Lloyd George eventually relented and met with a delegation including Ben Purse, David B. Lawley, Charles Lothian and Pat Neary.

The way in which the NLB's March of 1920 changed the law was unique. The Blind Persons Act 1920 was amended several times and became the basis for other acts which legislated for disabled people. It could be argued that the more recent Disability

Discrimination Acts of 1995 and 2004, and the Equality Act of 2010, finally legislated for many of the changes the National League of the Blind were calling for as early as 1899.

But the march itself is rarely talked about in the history of social reform. Much better known, for instance, is the column of unemployed people who marched from a small town in the Northeast to London sixteen years later. That Jarrow 'crusade' took much of its inspiration from the NLB march, and despite failing to change government policy[16] is still better known than this, its antecedent. That in itself speaks volumes.

## Notes

1. Salt, Francis Wilford, 'The Forging of a Blind Radical: Ben Purse and the National League of the Blind 1874–1925: Recovering a Lost History' (MA Thesis, MMU, September 2007).
2. Smith, T. H. (ed), *Golden Jubilee Souvenir Brochure: The National League of the Blind of Great Britain and Ireland 1899-1949* (NLB, London, 1949).
3. *Seventeenth Annual Report* (NLB, December 1917).
4. Smith, 1949 op cit.
5. 'The March of The Blind,' *Leicester Daily Mercury,* 13 April 1920.
6. Coverage of the Blind Men's March to London, *Daily Herald,* 7, 12, 20, 21, 23, 24, 26 April, and 1 May 1920.
7. 'Blind Men's March,' *The Times,* 6 April 1920.
8. *Facts for the British Public* (pamphlet); *Justice or Charity. Which?* (pamphlet); and *What The Government Have Done* (all NLB, 1920).
9. *Daily Herald*, 1920 op cit.
10. *Ibid*.
11. 'Blind March in Birmingham,' *Birmingham Gazette*, 12 April 1920.
12. *Daily Herald*, 1920 op cit.
13. 'March of the Blind Ended, Cheery Welcome from London Crowd,' *Manchester Guardian,* 26 April 1920.
14. *Daily Herald*, 1920 op cit.
15. *The Times*, 1920 op cit.
16. Fraser, W. Hamish, *A History of British Trade Unionism 1700-1998* (Basingstoke, Macmillan, 1999).

# The Blind Light

## Stuart Evers

THE CHAIR-WHEEL TOOK his standing leg, interrupting their saying nothing. Though he buckled from the shunt, almost fell, no-one, not even her, turned towards him. Like those around him, her eyes drifted on, surfing high-held banners, following shivering placards on wooden stakes, browsing the heads and hats of the assembled. She walked on and he watched her: the way she did not turn; the way she did not notice. He wanted to call her, but could not be sure if he had already done so. Had he shouted, though, she would have turned. She would, he was sure, have paused, and looked back. Of this he was certain. So, yes, he could call out to her and when he did, she would turn. Or he could say nothing. He could say nothing, stay at the site of the collision and wait. She'd soon notice his disappearance. She'd turn back. She'd turn and jink her way back through the crowd toward him. Yes, better that. Better to say nothing and wait. So he said nothing. He watched her walk and said nothing. On she moved and did not turn.

Marchers slipped around him: a branch in the brook, a rock in the stream. They smiled, they talked, they sang. He watched her walk. Men came between them, a scrag of shout and song. Women and men. Children too. How many, and how quickly. All happy, all singing. Pouring, he thought, streaming past. He heard their voices: pockets of conversation neatly stitched, hemmed with confederate laughter. A troop of musicians flowed ahead, their drum and flute, their guitar and arrogant trumpet. The swell of them. Of the hated jazz. The heavy steps, the arrhythmic handclaps, the tone-deaf voices, their teeth beneath their smiles. They flooded on and past, but he could still see her, visible through legs, past heads, over shoulders. Her gas-blue jacket and green scarf. Her half-turned face, her hair in the curt breeze, her closed and gravid lips.

Before him, a passage opened, a ricked alley past the band – boop, bop, a clarinet joining – and straight to Mathilde. I am going to join her. This he thought in a full, declarative sentence. As though for a tape, for the record. He was going to join her, but the corridor was quickly occupied by the woman and the wheelchair that had charged him. She was parallel to the musicians – a fiddle now, a saxophone – her progress impeded by their righteous chorus. He watched them both. She and the man she pushed. They were made of button badges; their coats and hats and scarves bathed in discs. Some the size of pucks, others small as pennies. Short slogans, lines inside circles: universal symbols. He could make them out, even at that distance, the glister of them in the morning shine. In front of them, Mathilde walked and did not turn. He waited for the inevitable collision, but it did not come.

The woman pushed past Mathilde. He saw her face. Old enough to have seen two wars; lined enough to have seen several more. Witch eyes and jutting chin. Hairs there, most likely. So many old women in the crowd, so many old men. Her companion looked younger: perhaps her husband, perhaps her son. Where his legs once were, flat black slacks were rolled at the cuffs. She pushed and sang, rounding Mathilde at speed. Free at last, she clattered others as she pushed on, scuffing shoes and nicking shins. They looked, under their buttons, gloriously, furiously happy.

Drummond wanted to protest. To shout at them across the crowd. You are to blame for this. You and your reckless progress. But they were old, and one a cripple, and both fully committed to the cause. Those around him, the beatnik youths in their denims, the stooped vicar, three old women and their older husbands, would turn on anyone who shouted in the face of such devotion. They would carry no pitchforks or flaming clubs, but wield a collective withering, a common glare: shame, the pacifist beating. He shouted nothing.

He raged instead a silent war. A campaign against the man and woman, their pin-mail garb, their shaking fists and singing voices. He had them against a wall and held the man's legless body and beat him. How long it lasted. With every blow, he moved backwards into the crowd, retreated slowly into its belly. The kindly faces, the competing bands – a timpani now, a banjo – the women in their pearls and flat shoes, Tory wives, children on the shoulders of men, all in laughter. Laughing in spite of it all. He looked for Mathilde. He could see her, just; the curve of her shoulder, the green scarf around her throat. Parts of her, but her nonetheless, and all of her still unturned. As he caved in the cripple's skull he lost her; lost her, finally, amongst the trotting crowd as they crested the coming hill.

★

When the blister burst, on his right foot, during the early afternoon of the first day of marching, Drummond blamed Mathilde. He said it for the tape: I blame Mathilde. He blamed her with every stride, even when she squeezed his hand, even when she whispered something conspiratorial about a fellow marcher. He blamed her as they walked the endless miles to the designated rest spot. I blame Mathilde, he said for the tape. This is her fault.

He sat at the roadside, half-shoeless, a handkerchief pressed to his heel as she stood talking to a young man called Alan. Drummond looked away, back to his foot. He saw Mathilde at their kitchen sink, suds on her yellow-gloved hands, rinsing a plate, setting it on the drainer, him studying it for food she might have missed.

'We should go,' she said. 'We always say we're going to, but this time we should.'

He picked up a plate.

'Yes,' he said. 'We should.'

His emphasis was clear: he said it the same way he would have said, yes, we *should* stop smoking; yes, we *should* visit your father again; yes, we *should* do this more often. This she had ignored. Or had not understood. She should have understood. The tape wound loudly. Yes, he said for its benefit, I know I mentioned it first. But years ago. Before Cuba. Before Anneke, even.

After their courting months and into their engagement he had suggested it, this during the winter of 1959. One of so many things he had suggested. She had laughed; he'd said he was serious. She just smiled. She tapped his hand.

'They'll be time enough for all of that,' she said. 'I know what goes on once the marching stops.'

Once married, once settled, once sexed, he did not mention it again. They did not have four days to campaign for nuclear disarmament: they *should*, but they had names to discuss, a crib to construct, privations to endure. They worked and they did not consider the coming Armageddon, though Mathilde, drunk on the stout her doctor had recommended for iron consumption, did once suggest it as a name for a boy. He watched his wife grow taut in the belly. He did not think of anything but the child and her mother. For the tape he called his daughter Anneke and, for the tape, he promised she would go to the grammar school, go to university, be a woman as singular as her mother. Only for the tape was she Anneke. When they took her away, unscreaming and blue, the nurses did not ask for a name. Had they asked he would have said, but they didn't.

So when Mathilde had said they should go, there was no excuse. And he had said *yes, we should go* and whatever the emphasis, whatever he had really meant, he knew there was no reason not to march. She booked her time off from the factory, and Drummond did the same. The tape wound, waiting, but he failed to add anything to the record.

At the roadside he blamed Bill. Bill who had been on every march and had abandoned them early, meeting with old hands and disappearing into the swell. He blamed Bill and retracted his sworn and taped statement regarding Mathilde. Bill, a friend from the Ford plant, had talked of the brilliant minds and the variety of folk, the grand breadth of those who walked. But Bill had not mentioned the song and levity, the youths, the sense of cumulative power. Drummond would not have consented, had he known. Had he known about the way young and old danced along as the world teetered, he would never have agreed. Without Bill they would not have met Alan. Alan was not Mathilde's fault. Alan was all on Bill.

Alan had been a constant since the morning off, somehow latching on to them, keeping his reefer-jacketed arm beside Drummond, beside Mathilde. He talked in unpausing, fully formed sentences, effortlessly describing his credentials, his zeal for nuclear disarmament, his disagreements with his father. His cigarettes were French and he talked of Bob Dylan in the way one might a personal friend or kissing cousin. There could be no more than a few years between them, but Drummond felt beat and faded in his wake. There were no blisters on Alan's feet.

Alan knew why he was there. He had not been duped by others. Alan was there under his own duress: to feel part of something, to make a difference, to be adored. Over the morning and afternoon, Drummond had had him against the wall several times. He blamed Bill, but it was not his fault. Drummond could not really blame Bill for the gang of similar men around Alan, their accents, their surety. He could not blame him for their lack of seriousness. For so many reasons, he could not blame him. He struck it from the tape. Erased again his statement.

Mathilde stood over him, blocking the thin sunlight.

'How's the foot?' she said. She looked down and he revealed the gore below the handkerchief. She did not wince.

She sat down beside him, took the handkerchief and pressed it to the wound. Alan had wandered off to talk to a long-haired girl of his own age.

'Is this why you've been so quiet since lunch?' she said.

'It's been murder, the last few miles.'

'You should have said something.'

'Yes,' he said. 'But you told me not to wear these shoes, and did I listen?'

Still holding the handkerchief down, with her other hand she fished in the small rucksack. She took out an envelope and removed three sticking plasters.

'I came prepared,' she said. 'Always prepared, me.'

She smiled. Her black fringe was severe, but her face soft, a mouth wide, behind it buckled teeth, coffee-and-cigarette stained. The hair was a new thing. He liked it, though he missed the way strands had once unleashed from her hairband and gently tangled over her cheekbones. For the tape, he apologised. I feel ashamed, he admitted. The tape pocked and spooled.

'I feel young,' she said. 'For the first time in, well. But I do. Feel young.'

'You are young.'

'At home I feel old. Like a crone.' She laughed. He said nothing. He affixed the sticking plaster to his ankle, the fabric staining dark around the blister.

'You're not having such a terrible time, are you?' she said.

'It's just not what I was expecting,' he said. 'That's all. The way Bill talked about it, it felt more serious. More... I don't know, more exacting.'

'You didn't expect it to be fun?'

'You call this fun?' he said.

'Yes,' she said.

She sat down next to him, tucked her legs underneath her, the same way she had when they had picnicked in the fields, shared sandwiches and kisses. With grace, he said, proudly, for the tape. She looked over at Alan and the girl. He followed her eyes.

'You see,' he said. 'Look at him. Only one reason he's here.'

'You once asked me along for the same reasons, as I recall,' she said, laughing.

He attempted a look of affront.

'I never did. I would never have—'

'Oh, behave,' she said. 'You didn't want me for my encyclopaedic knowledge of blast radiuses.'

She held his hand, soothing.

'I love you,' she said. 'And remember, it's just three more days. Best make the most of them.'

'Might be our last,' they said together.

She helped him up and they moved on, re-immersed themselves in the crowd. She kept hold of his hand as they marched; Drummond more alive to those around him. There was no sight of Alan. They walked beside a family with a pram, their girl eating a toffee apple.

'It looked like rain before,' he ventured to the father. 'But the clouds don't look so ominous now.'

'Supposed to be dry today,' the man said. He had a Midlands accent, dense and foggy. 'Tomorrow, I'm not so sure.' It was the end of the conversation and he tried no more. What is the point, he said for the tape, what is the point?

Marchers left and marchers joined. This was something Drummond had not expected, the way women and men would walk a few miles then head off, perhaps for bus stops or to hitchhike home. He eyed them jealously. There were times he felt Anneke's weight on his shoulders, her fingers pinch the helix of his ears. It was something he wanted to share with Mathilde, but it was not the time. I am thinking of the future, he said for the tape. The future and not the past.

As the sun began to down, men in dark jackets waved the marchers off the main road towards the town that would put them up for the night. It felt military, he thought, like they were being marshalled.

'Watch out,' he said to Mathilde. 'We're being sent to the showers.'

She looked up from beneath her fringe.

'Did you really just say that?'

She glowered, then reined the look in. She squeezed his hand.

'You need to eat. You forget what you're saying when you're hungry.'

He nodded. An excuse of convenience; invented by her or him, he could not recall. It was, he said for the tape, an error of judgement. The tape waited for more, but nothing came.

As they trudged into the town, they were greeted by a woman with a clipboard. She was standing beside a van from which men were throwing sleeping bags. The bedrolls were used and lumpen, some darned, some patched; most grey, some a dark green. As they got closer, Drummond could smell their must, the timberishness of the cloth. In the hand they were light, like summer coats.

'St Peter's Hall,' the clipboard woman said after they'd taken possession of their sleeping bags. 'You turn right, right again and there's the hall. You'll find something warm to eat there, too.'

Mathilde said thank you; Drummond did not. They walked as they had for hours, in the wake of others, and arrived at the lead roof and dank brick of the church hall. There were people sitting outside, eating from tin trays of bully beef and bread, drinking from beer bottles, a few smoking pot. The braying trumpet again, the strumming chords, the laughter. Here to spend the night in a draughty hall, municipally sleeping as though they were lucky survivors and the bombs had already come. He held his sleeping bag tight in his arms, determined not to sleep in it. Lice, he said for the tape. It looks like there are lice inside.

Inside the hall, rows of sleeping bags were laid out: empty stretchers, flattened corpses. Lines and lines of them. Hundreds it looked like. The remaining spaces were close to the heavy door through which they had entered. The room was chill, the walls covered in murals, artless depictions of Christ's miracles and sufferings. They nodded to each other, accepting their pitch on an untaken stretch of parquet. In the silence, he heard the snores, the pant of breath, the stifled erections, the hands inside other people's underwear.

Mathilde looked at Drummond, slowly, as though she had only at that moment caught the last of something he'd said.

'I hadn't thought about this bit,' she said. 'The sleeping.'

She set down her sleeping bag and he did the same. 'I miss our bed already.'

He nodded. For the tape he thanked Bill. For the tape he said: I knew I was right. He had money in his pocket, more than he'd said he was withdrawing. Taking it from the bank had been charged, the wait in line an adultery, the folding of the notes an erotic thrill. Rainy day money, clean and crisp. A telephone call to The Fox, the booking of the room. The delightful expense of it. He'd thought of little else but the sleeping those last hours, nothing but closing the door on their cottage room, pillows plumped on a horsehair mattress, a soft bedside light as he removed her brassiere, kissed her stomach, the patchy hairs leading downwards.

I was only thinking of her – he said for the tape – only her. Her back still plays her up. And have we had a holiday since Anneke? Not even a daytrip to the coast, not even that. And I knew she'd miss our bed. I knew it, which is why I made alternative arrangements. It's what good husbands do: anticipate.

'There's a pub,' he said. 'The Fox and Hounds or something. Other side of the town. We could slip off for a bit. A drink before we have to bunk down.'

'And how'd you know that?' She had her hand on her hip, something quick in her voice; spoken lightly but not joking.

'Bill told me,' he said. Which he had. Which was not a lie. Bill had said he would never go there again. Drummond wondered how his face looked, how he was presenting. He hoped for neutrality, pragmatism, perhaps a casual air. He worried he looked like a man holding his breath before plunging into a darkening lake.

'No more walking,' she said. 'I couldn't walk another pace.'

He held her closely, kissed her forehead through the straight black fringe.

'You want to stay here, then? Wait for Alan to come back?' She laughed.

'Well, let's go then,' he said.

'We should stay,' she said, quickly. 'We should stay and have something to eat.'

He nodded. 'Yes,' he said. 'We should.'

Silent minutes later they moved as stowaways, dodging the milling crowds, and cut down by the side of the church, past gravestones and lichened crosses. They dared not smoke or speak and held hands as they pushed through squealing iron gates. The voices and laughter fell, ghouled on the soft breeze. Past workers cottages and trees, hedgerows and scrubland, they walked until they saw the light of the inn, its gentle swaying sign, a flyblown fox at prowl.

They ducked under the doorway into the small saloon. It was, he thought, the kind of place in which children were conceived: accidentally, joyfully. Upstairs in the rooms, or out back in summer, the first spark kindling in the bar. He pointed to a table by the dying fire and Mathilde sat down.

The pub was half busy and the patrons were the right kind of men. Workers, fathers, husbands, farm-hands. They did not look up from their drinks. Or they did not look up for too long. The barman was cleaning glasses; behind him bread rolls wrapped in greaseproof paper. He looked up and Drummond ordered a 'gin and it' and a pint of best. His feet did not hurt, his eyes he rubbed like those who came in after a shift. A drink for the wife, a drink for the worker. There were no marchers. Not a one.

'I've booked a room,' Drummond said, 'in the name of Price.'

The barman looked surprised pulling his pint. He was sloped at the shoulder, pomaded, his shirt white and starched, a vest visible beneath.

'Let me get the book.'

He put the pint down on a Watney's bar towel, then went to the other side of the bar. The barman returned with the book, set it to one side. He leant in, sausages on his breath.

'Mr. and Mrs. Price,' he said. 'Yes. I got that. One night?'

Drummond nodded. He turned and saw Mathilde light a cigarette; Drummond liked to watch her do that, the way she pouted. The barman looked at Mathilde, her cut hair, her rucksack.

'Look, I don't care,' the barman said. 'But the wife? She cares. You understand me? So you stay down here until I fetch you, all right?'

'I'm sorry?' Drummond said.

'Don't come it, lad, or you can go back to the bloody church hall with the rest of 'em.'

The barman turned and poured gin, poured vermouth, mixed the drink and put it next to the pint of best.

'Like I said, I don't care. But just keep away from the wife. You stay put until I say so.'

'I don't quite know what you mean,' Drummond said. He pointed to Mathilde, checking her makeup in a pocket mirror.

'That's my wife and she's pregnant. It's only the second month, but she's already getting tired. It's our first, you know? We're on the way to break the good news to her father. Lives in Reading. Hell of a drive.'

The barman, he thought, was the kind to have a brood or none at all; vinegar in his balls or pure spunk. The barman looked again at Mathilde. I don't know why I said it, Drummond said for the tape. But I stand by it. I did what I needed to do. And I would do it again, no questions asked.

'The first one's always the worst,' the barman said. 'But it gets easier. You'll pay now for the room?'

He lopsided smiled. Drummond nodded and handed over a note.

'Best of luck,' he said. 'And sorry, but it's every bloody year here now. Don't know who's on the level and who's not.'

Drummond set down the drinks on the small table as Mathilde placed her cigarette in the ashtray. He drank swiftly and raked his fingers across his mouth, the beer cool and malty. He picked up her cigarette, took a drag and passed it to her.

'I have a plan,' he said as she sipped her drink. Did the hair make her look younger? More fashionable? More like one of Alan's lot? Even with the haircut, he saw her and nothing else, the same her as he always saw, like she was cast in blind light.

'Let's hear it then,' she said. 'But we're were not leaving the march. At least I'm not.'

She took the cigarette in her mouth. He wondered if she was imagining her face, whether she was concerned as he about presenting. She looked defensive and sharp. Was the inhalation of the cigarette meant to soften this, or calcify her position? He'd once said the first thing that attracted him to her was her strength and clarity, but this was something he had learned to say over time, a gloss over the fact that she had good skin and a dirty laugh and seemed to find him, bafflingly, good company. The reasons for a love affair come only after the affair itself is a steadied ship, eased by familiarity. He did not say this for the tape. The tape had recorded it before.

'The plan is we stay here. Tonight. Finish our drinks and sleep in a proper bed.'

The words were wrong. Better, he should have said he suspected lice in the sleeping bags. Better, he should have included her, made it a joint decision. But he was stuck now with the words, unbalanced by humour or a sly wink. He looked down on his pint, its thinning head. He could not look at her, newly young, newly fashionable. He waited for her to speak: so rare, those moments of suspense. He saw possible outcomes dart, her voice soft, her voice fizzed with rage; her eyes low, her eyes on his face. He was, despite the planning, woefully unprepared.

Mathilde looked around, swept the carpet, horse-brasses, etchings of local churches, the pewter tankards hanging above the bar. She sipped her drink and put out the cigarette.

'They have rooms?' she asked.

'They have rooms.'

She laughed. And for that he would have done anything. The first time she had laughed after Anneke, he thought he would remember it until the bombs dropped. The tape had recorded it, though he no longer remembered.

'It sounds like a bunk up,' she said. 'Like you're trying it on like you used to. Are you propositioning me, my love?'

At that moment she looked younger than when they had met. She reached for the cigarettes and lit another, though she rarely smoked much, struck a match though she looked only at Drummond. She shook the match and dropped it lightly in the ashtray.

'It was just an idea,' he said. He thought of the church hall, the cold floor on his back. He thought of the money. Of the barman coming to his table, giving him the nod. He thought of the money, the rainy day money: once crisp, now lost. The tape spooled without comment.

She waved away the smoke.

'I like the idea,' she said, eventually. 'I like it very much.'

★

No marcher stopped, though some slowed as they passed, the same way he would if faced with a man paused like a struck clock. For a time, he remained standing, then took to the roadside, a vacant spectator of blurred legs. He removed his socks and shoes and examined his blisters, a new one on his left ankle, and watched the striding legs. Here there was less drum or trumpet, these were the people he had expected: their quiet determination, their stoic faces. Had they just marched with these men and women! No Alans. No chair-bound collisions. No unturned footsteps. He thought of Alan, head on one side, saying: *a march is a plurality of opinion, not a single voice.* The way he'd almost punched the young man in his self-satisfied face. He saw him – how far ahead in the crowd? – ask Mathilde what had happened, a reefer-jacketed arm around her shoulder, the hem of his coat resting on her green scarf. Her saying he's just disappeared, and Alan stroking his chin, offering help and assistance. Drummond tried to calculate the distance: yards not yet miles, surely. He pushed himself up to standing. He started quickly on the left wing of the march. For the tape, he acknowledged his childlike truculence, admitted that he must shoulder responsibility for the misunderstanding. He offered this for the tape and the tape continued to record.

Through the march he walked, the going easy at first, shuffling past families, excusing himself as he brushed against someone, then not: in his increasing urgency, progress more important than politeness. Mathilde would now be worried, of this he was sure, checking back, possibly even walking against the tide, making her way back towards him. He would see her first, though; the gas-blue jacket and green scarf lit up as in neon. He'd see her and she'd see him, at last, and together they would walk on, hand in hand, in silent forgiveness.

The hill he reached quickly. The placards and signs just visible again, some of the marchers looking familiar, men and women he'd seen before. He stood on the balls of his feet when impeded, and when not, moved off with sharpened elbows. The further he went and the more he overtook, the more he sensed something change. There was a slight unrest, a skitter to the surrounding conversations, even to the fluid motion of the march. The music was still there, but the key had changed, or the tone, or the way it was played. It was off, and unaccompanied by voices. The road leaned rightwards, and in the distance there was an impasse of some kind, a group moving away from the main body of the marchers. Those around him seemed to have no better idea of what was going on than he did.

At the crest of the hill he saw identical pieces of paper on the asphalt; notices of some kind, dropped to the ground, spoiled by boot prints and pram wheels. He ducked past a family, and into a standing man. He had long curls, a rag beard, and was dealing out flyers.

'Direct action,' he said as he passed out the papers. 'Direct action. Direct action.'

Drummond tried to walk and read, walk and read and search for Mathilde. He looked at the photostatted paper. A picture of a non-descript building, one like many they had blindly walked past. The headline said, 'DIRECT ACTION AGAINST RSGS'. 'A Regional Seat of Government,' the sheet read, 'is an affront to us all. A secret safe haven for the ruling classes when the bombs drop. They tell us lies about survival, because they know they are safe. The time has come for direct action. We must overcome. We must show them we know their secrets and will expose them to the world.'

He walked on, holding the flyer, walked on into the impasse. The crowd slowed and rubbernecked at the few taking the other path, but the majority stayed left. It was a binary option, left or right. Drummond erred. Left or right. He could not see too far ahead, could not see Mathilde, her scarf or any part of her. A binary option: left or right. He heard the tape spool. He let it run. He did not have the words for it.

★

The men at the next table were talking of an acquaintance, a dead man, recently deceased; Mathilde was telling Drummond a story Alan had told her. It didn't matter, he said for the tape, not at all. To see her like that, to see her again think, ruminate, consider an argument and find it lacking was compensation enough. He listened to her while filtering out, when he could, the dead man's elegy. She was close and her voice soft, for which he was grateful. He could imagine living there, he thought. Amongst the fields and pastures, the world at one remove. She could talk, and he could talk, but it would feel hypothetical, without real-world basis. He watched her shake her head, but at what he was unsure. She sipped her drink. She looked at the cooling grate.

'I know things have been rough,' he said eventually. 'But things will be better now, I promise.'

'What?' she said.

'I know I can be—'

'Drum, stop. We don't need to talk about this now. Let's just not.'

She finished her drink. Drank it down so quickly he thought she would cough and splutter, but instead came up smiling.

'Doesn't this feel like that place in Petersfield? You remember, that place?'

He nodded. For the tape, yes, but he had no idea when they had gone to Petersfield. He didn't even know where Petersfield actually was.

'That was a good place,' she said. 'I liked it there. You got me drunk. You had your way with me.'

She laughed and he remembered. The patchy hairs, the way she had inched up and down the bed. He watched her eyes beneath the fringe. The way they flit from left to right. She put her hands to her forehead. She shifted her fringe but it fell below her eyes again, blunt and thick.

'We should do that tonight,' she said. The way she said *should*. The articulation within it. He could not recall it. For the tape: I have never heard that from her. Since Anneke, at least. Possibly not even before.

'I'll see if I can get the keys,' he said. 'They were cleaning the room the last I asked.'

She pulled on her cigarette and set it in the ashtray, thin tobacco lines piping from its end.

'Do that,' she said. 'And tell them to be quick. I don't mind a little dirt.'

He finished his drink and put his hand on her thigh. When he stood he felt shake-headed, disbelieving. The barman was serving two men, all three big smiles, so he went first to the lavatory. Relieving himself, he was bigger than he usually looked at a urinal. He took some time standing there, longer than usual. His urine smelled of chicken broth and he wondered if that was a sign of something.

Above a small sink there was a smaller mirror, cracked at its bottom right edge. In the glass he thought he looked younger, less spent. From his jacket pocket he took his comb, parted his hair and styled it, taking care with it. The dandruff had gone, his scalp white and clear. For the tape, he said I am calm for the first time in years, and for the tape he thanked Bill, and for the tape he said, I knew I was right. Under the warm water tap he washed his hands and washed his face. He wished he could wash himself all over.

A man entered the lavatory, Drummond putting away the comb as though caught untoward. The man looked at him as he undid his flies, looked at him as he began to piss horsily into the trough. He looked at Drummond through bagged and bloated eyes.

'Why don't you all just fuck off back to Russia?' he said.

The man's piss was now on the grey slate floor, the man was aiming piss at Drummond. The piss came seeping but Drummond did not want to open the door. He didn't want to move at all. The piss crept towards his crippling shoes. The man finished, shook his cock and put it away.

'Bastard,' he said as he pushed past Drummond and opened the lavatory door. It swung open and he saw four men sitting around Mathilde, then it shut. Drummond stood looking at the door. He inched it open, but the men were still there, sitting with Mathilde by the ashy fire; three men and Alan in their middle. Mathilde was laughing. The men who had been talking of their dead comrade had left. He had blisters on his ankles and piss in his shoes and his hair shone, pointlessly. And Alan had seen him, and Alan waved.

'What d'you want, Drum?' said Alan. 'Pint is it?'

Drummond held open the door, and paused. A struck clock. He nodded and sat at the table, not quite on the seat he had vacated. There was already a drink in front of Mathilde, and she was already taking a sip. He took a cigarette from the pack and lit it. The other men were talking in the same brash way they had on the road. They introduced themselves with handshakes, as though Drummond should already know who they were. Mathilde looked through her fringe and he could not fathom the look: deliver me, or do not constrain me. He thought of how he was presenting. He tried a smile and shifted around the table to accommodate the returning Alan.

'To a future for us all,' Alan toasted.

He thought of the cold church floor and the untouched mattress of the above-stairs room. He thought of what it had meant, what he had planned. He raised his glass and so did Mathilde.

'To a future for us all,' they said.

★

The bodies seemed closer packed. He felt hands on his shoulder, on his arms. He turned around and the crowd was monochrome, no gas blue, no green scarf. He was pushed, shoved from another angle. Perhaps, he thought, he would be swept under, trampled beneath walking boots and rubber-soled shoes, left as flat as the wheelchair man's trousers. He was charged again and he turned ready to fight, clenched fist and set jaw and by the time he was facing the right direction he was merely scared. The man who had charged him was already gone, the only thing remaining a decision. Left or right. A binary option. He could not decide. For the tape, he said, I don't know. I don't know which way she would turn.

★

'I don't agree,' Mathilde said to Drummond. 'I think Alan has a point.'

Alan held his drink in hand, weaponised and cocked. Alan was smiling behind his small, wide cigarette.

'Alan doesn't know what he's talking about,' Drummond said. 'Alan, here, Alan – he knows nothing of the world. All that education and he knows nothing about any of this.'

Alan smiled, sly and thin.

'What I'm trying to say, Drummond, is that a march is a plurality of opinion, not a single voice. It is inherently democratic, it has a space for all concerns. A protest and a march is there to show a well-spring of disagreement, not a dogmatic adherence to a particular ideal.'

'Fancy words, mate. Fancy words, but you have no idea what you're talking about.'

'I'm talking about direct action. I'm talking about standing up and being counted. Being seen. You think these people' – he milled his arms around – 'care about people walking? The quakers, the vicars, the pacisficts? About the movement? They'd care if we showed them the truth. They'd care then.'

Alan picked up his drink, downed the last of it and set it down on the table with a thud that jumped the glasses, spilled some of the fuller pints.

'Don't talk for these people,' Drummond said. 'You know nothing about them.'

'And you know it all, do you, Mr. Mechanic? Found the secrets inside a carburettor?'

The three men laughed, the wisemonkey cackle, and Drummond had nothing to say, nothing to say that would rescue the situation. He looked at Mathilde and she looked away. He gripped the handle of his pint glass. He wanted to swing it. How he wanted to swing it into the boy man's face. He should have been in bed, Mathilde in the crook of his neck, new life sparking somewhere, fixing itself to something, making future. He looked down at his drink. Four of them and one of him. One of Mathilde, just the one, withering as he swung the glass. Nothing to be done. Nothing that he could see.

The barman came over to the table. You see salvation in such moments, and watch as they slash and burn.

'Right, bar's closed,' he said. 'And I want you out. All of you.'

Alan began to protest, but Mathilde cut him off. She picked up her gas-blue jacket and her small bag. She got up and she was hot in the cheek, burning. Alan shouted something as they left, Mathilde kicked a stool and a glass shattered on the floor. Drummond followed them, his striding wife and the four whooping men.

Eventually, Drummond caught up with her. He placed a hand on her jacket and she removed it.

'You couldn't just leave it, could you?' she said. 'You had to have him, didn't you? You had to put him in his place. We could be in bed now, but you had to be right, didn't you?'

She laughed and kicked at a stone.

'I'm sorry,' Drummond said as they walked alongside the church, behind the four loud men.

She stopped on the track. She stopped and put her hands on her bowed hips. She ran her fingers through her fringe and the hair fell just as bluntly.

'You're always sorry,' she said. 'But things don't change, do they? Things never bloody change.'

For the tape, he said: I am sorry. I am so sorry. It was a blind light. It descends and then…

'You could have stopped me. You could have said that we had to go. You could have done that. It is your fault. Yours as much as mine.'

The tape spooled. Mathilde walked on. She walked to the church and said nothing.

★

He took another charge and a man called him something, an insult mindful of ladies present. It forced him slightly right, slightly over toward the small theatre of direct action. Beyond him he saw the wheelchair man and his wife-mother, and was buffeted towards them. He gave into it, followed the ruck. The crowd listed right and left, increased their pace, flurried onwards towards the gates of the RSG. A man put his arm around Drummond, encouraging him to shout, pushing him onwards until there was nowhere else to go, no more march to be had. Men and women were squeezed around him, tight packed, incited by the proximity.

He saw Alan first, then one of the men from the night before. The one who he'd properly insulted. To their right was Mathilde, her arm in the air, her gas-blue jacket over her non-protesting arm. He tried to move towards her, but was immobilised by the crowd. He watched his wife shout aloud alone, tendons in her neck stretched, her cheeks flushed. He watched her. There was nothing else to do but watch.

The sirens came, louder even than the crowd. Most turned, feet scrabbling to get away from the disturbance. Mathilde did not turn. Mathilde kept on her protest. Alan tapped her on the shoulder, but she did not turn; just kept her arm aloft and her mouth moving. Alan tried again, just the same way Drummond would have done, but Mathilde remained. Alan walked off, moved away with his boys, the sanctimonious lads, and a ricked alley opened up straight to Mathilde.

Drummond pushed past the retreating bodies, those heading back to the junction. He kept his eyes on Mathilde, on her unturning gaze. He reached her and she did not notice. He stood beside her and mimicked her pose, chanted the same things she did. And she did not notice. He shouted and she turned then. She turned and with her unprotesting hand took his. They shouted and they shouted. They stood their ground and shouted even when the police moved in. They protested until the very last. And to those around them, the two of them looked happy. They looked gloriously, furiously happy.

# Afterword: Easter Weekend, 1958–1963

## Michael Randle

THE BEGINNINGS WERE modest. In 1949, the pacifist organisation, Peace Pledge Union, set up a Non-Violence Commission to study the applicability of Gandhi's methods in the context of the British peace movement. By 1951 some of its members decided it was time to move from discussion to action and formed a group calling itself Operation Gandhi committed to using nonviolent action, including civil disobedience, with the goal of securing the withdrawal of US troops from Britain, ending the British manufacture of nuclear weapons, withdrawal from NATO and relying on nonviolent methods for the defence of the country. It was headed by Hugh Brock, then assistant editor – later editor – of the pacifist weekly newspaper, *Peace News,* who was to play a critical role in the development of an anti-war and nonviolent movement in Britain.

Operation Gandhi's first action was a sit-down by fourteen people, seven men and seven women, outside the War Office in Whitehall in January 1952. The participants were arrested, convicted of obstruction at Bow Street Magistrates Court, and fined. Though the numbers involved were small, the protest attracted some publicity in both the local and national press. In a sympathetic report, the *Railway Review* commented: 'It would be interesting to see the effects of such demonstrations if they were carried out simultaneously in every town and village in the country.' I read the report of the demonstration in *Peace News* when I was facing a tribunal hearing as an 18-year-old conscientious objector, and wrote to Hugh Brock to say I wished to join the group.

Over the next two years, the group – which changed its name a few months after its formation to the Non-violent Resistance Group – went on to organise demonstrations at various military bases and research establishments including: the USAF base at Mildenhall in Suffolk (July 1952), where two young women, Connie Jones and Dorothy Morton, lay down in front of the main gates to obstruct traffic; the Microbiological Warfare Establishment at Porton Down (March 1953); the Atomic Energy Research Establishment at Harwell (April 1953); and, twice, in April 1952 and September 1953, at what was at first misleadingly called the Atomic *Energy* Research Establishment at Aldermaston – subsequently acknowledging its true purpose with the change of name to the Atomic *Weapons* Research Establishment. The suggestion for a demonstration there came from a group member, Laurence Brown, who lived in the area. Our protests in this period took the form of participants taking a coach from London to the chosen destination, walking round it with banners, distributing leaflets, and holding open-air meetings. At Aldermaston, still under construction on that first occasion, we handed out leaflets to workers coming out of the base at noon, but otherwise our principal audience was a herd of cows in an adjacent field who took fright at the unusual spectacle and stampeded round the field in a panic.

However, another function of the group was to arrange meetings with people engaged in similar campaigning in other countries when they were passing through London. The meetings were organised by Hugh Brock and took place in the homes of members in the London area. Among them were Asha Devi Arayanayakam, a close associate of Gandhi, the African-American civil rights and peace campaigner, Bayard Rustin, and another Afro-American activist, Bill Sutherland. These and other contacts were to prove important in the development of the movement.

Fast forward five years. October-November 1956 saw on the one hand the Israeli, British and French attack on Egypt to seize back control of the Suez canal – nationalised earlier that year by Egyptian President Nasser, and, on the other, the Soviet military intervention in Hungary to crush a movement for democratic reform under the leadership of its Prime Minister, Imre Nagy. It was a watershed moment in post-war history. In Britain, the Suez crisis sparked the largest and angriest anti-war demonstration post-Second World War, and was an important factor in the emergence of the New Left. Other factors contributing to its emergence were the Soviet military intervention in Hungary, and Khruschev's denunciation of Stalin's crimes at the 20th Congress of the Soviet Communist Party. These events caused many on the left, including in the Communist Party of Great Britain, to revise their thinking about the Soviet version of communism and explore other approaches to the creation of a socialist society. (*The Universities and Left Review* was first published in the Spring of 1957 and opened the Partisan coffee house, a lively debating venue in Central London; *The New Reasoner* first appeared in the autumn of the same year. In 1960 the journals merged to become *The New Left Review.*)

This period of the mid to late 50s also witnessed growing public unease about the fall-out from nuclear weapons' tests and the threat of an East-West nuclear war. The Moscow-backed Stockholm Peace Appeal of 1950, which called for an absolute ban on nuclear weapons, probably helped raise public awareness of the issue, despite its pro-Soviet bias. In July 1955, Albert Einstein and Bertrand Russell issued a manifesto warning of the danger of a nuclear holocaust which was signed by a total of 11 pre-eminent scientists, all but one of them Nobel Prize winners. In 1957, the National Council for the Abolition of Nuclear Weapons Tests was set up in Britain and one of its early demonstrations was a march by 2,000 women wearing black sashes from Hyde Park to Trafalgar Square. NCANWT was a precursor of the Campaign for Nuclear Disarmament (CND), which was publicly launched in February 1958 with a mass meeting of 5,000 people in the Methodist Central Hall in London with four overflow venues.

These developments prepared the ground for the Aldermaston March. The proposal for the march arose out of an attempt in 1957 by a Quaker/Unitarian, Harold Steele, to hire a boat in Japan to sail to the proposed first British H-Bomb test at Christmas Island in the Pacific. A number of people volunteered to accompany Steele and an Emergency Committee for Direct Action was formed in May in support of the venture, operating from the *Peace News* offices in Finsbury Park, London. It drew much of its support from the same circle of people who were involved in Operation Gandhi and the Non-Violent Resistance Group, including notably Hugh Brock who was its main organiser. A letter published in *The Guardian* newspaper on 12th April publicising the project and appealing for support was signed by a number of well-known people including notably the philosopher Bertrand Russell.

Harold Steele was unable to complete the mission before the H-bomb test went ahead, but on his return, Hugh Brock called a meeting of volunteers and supporters to discuss how the project could be followed up. At Laurence Brown's suggestion, supported by Hugh Brock, it was agreed to organise another demonstration focused on the AWRE at Aldermaston, this time taking the form of a fifty-mile walk over the four days of the Easter weekend in 1958. An ad-hoc Aldermaston March Committee was set up comprising Hugh Brock, two members of the Labour Party pressure group, the Hydrogen Bomb Campaign Committee – its secretary, Walter Wolfgang, and Frank Allaun MP, Pat Arrowsmith, (Organising Secretary), and myself. I did not attend the meeting but was co-opted onto the March Committee.

We had anticipated a demonstration somewhat larger than the earlier actions but of a similar order of magnitude, with perhaps a few hundred participants. Within a week or two it was clear that we had not taken into account how much the political climate had changed in the intervening years. Offers of help came from all directions. Quaker meeting houses and church halls offered free accommodation, the *Universities and Left Review Club* publicised the march from the Partisan coffee house, the London Co-operative Society agreed to take charge of catering, Kenny Ball, Ken Colyer and other jazz musicians volunteered to provide entertainment during the march, the London Youth Choir and two or three left-wing folk music groups volunteered to go ahead of the march to towns on the route. A group of film-makers begged and borrowed 35mm film stock to make a film of the march, which was ultimately directed by one of Britain's most talented film directors, Lindsay Anderson. (The film's commentary was written by the poet Christopher Logue and spoken by Richard Burton.) The committee operated from a small office in the *Peace News* building, and soon phone lines were jammed with calls and a new line had to be installed. Hugh, Frank, Walter and I held weekly planning meetings in rooms in the House of Commons booked by Frank.

The public launch of CND gave a new fillip to the preparations. Canon Collins, its chairman, drew attention to the march and we arranged to have leaflets placed in advance on the seats in the Methodist Central Hall. Our first leaflets, which had been cyclostyled rather than printed, gave details of the route and speakers at various stopping places, but contained no icon or symbol. Then sometime in February 1958 – I don't remember whether it was before or after the CND launch – an artist, Gerald Holtom, arranged to come to the DAC office to show us a symbol he had designed, and some sketches of how he envisaged the march would look. The symbol comprised the semaphore positions for N (Nuclear) and D (Disarmament) enclosed in a circle. We agreed to adopt it, and the famous Nuclear Disarmament or 'Peace Symbol' was born.

Not everyone was impressed at the start. When our first leaflets appeared bearing the symbol, Harry Mister, one of the original members of Operation Gandhi, said to me: 'What on earth were you, Pat and Hugh thinking about when you adopted that symbol? It doesn't mean a thing, and it will never catch on!'

If the march had flopped he might have been right. As it was, it has gone round the world, and Harry Mister himself was never afterwards to be seen without it on his lapel. After Hugh's death in 1985, his widow Eileen bequeathed the original sketches to the Commonweal Collection, a library devoted to books and other publications on nonviolence and radical politics, housed in the main library at Bradford University. They are now stored in the library's Special Collection archive but were loaned to the Imperial War Museum for its exhibition *People Power: Fighting for Peace* which ran from 23rd March to 28th August 2017.

The march succeeded beyond anything we had imagined. Somewhere in the region of 4,000 people attended the initial rally in Trafalgar Square at which Bayard Rustin was one of the speakers. Canon Collins also spoke, emphasising the moral dimension of the choice the world was facing. Collins had initially turned down the invitation to speak. Like several others on the CND Executive Committee, he had reservations about it, but was persuaded by Hugh Brock to change his mind. Another member of the Executive Committee, J. B. Priestley, even went so far as to issue a press statement after the march emphasising that it had *not* been organised by CND. Michael Foot, however, gave a rousing speech at the rally, at one point startling the pigeons in the square who flew up in a swarm round Nelson's Column with a great clatter of wings, like a burst of aerial applause.

My own role during the march was one I found particularly difficult: it was to accompany one or other of the advance groups of singers and folk musicians to make sure they stuck to an agreed list of songs. Some in their original proposed list we judged to have an anti-American flavour, and in a period in which peace campaigns and demonstrations were almost invariably suspected of being communist-inspired, we wanted to make sure people understood that we were against all nuclear weapons, whichever country possessed them. Some of the leading members of the groups had avowedly communist sympathies or were members of the Communist Party. That was, of course, their right, but it was important that the non-aligned nature of the march itself was beyond question. The groups, let it be said, produced some excellent songs for the march which have lasted down the years such as Karl Dallas's 'The Family of Man', and John Brunner's 'The H-Bomb's Thunder'.

The second day of the march was marked by wind, rain and finally snow in the coldest Easter weather for 41 years and the wettest since 1900. Numbers did dwindle to some degree the next day, but at least five hundred persevered and walked the whole way, including many young mothers wheeling push-chairs. Even some of the right wing press were impressed. On the fourth day, numbers swelled again and an estimated 8,000 people walked the final leg of the march from Reading and attended the final rally at Falcons Inn Fields opposite the base. Speakers at the rally included Rev. Martin Niemöller who had been imprisoned by the Nazis for criticizing their ideology and opposing their plans to control the churches. But for me the most moving event was the march past the base by so many people in total silence.

As the march approached Falcons Inn Field, the twin brothers, Norris and Ross McWhirter, two right-wing journalists and co-founders of the *Guinness Book of Records*, drove Norris's black Mercedes car with a loudspeaker attached to the roof and began heckling the approaching marchers. A scuffle ensued in which the car was rocked from side to side and the wire pulled out from the loudspeaker. It was a brief incident that the majority of marchers know nothing about, and Norris McWhirter himself stated in a *Woman's Hour* programme a day or two later that none of the marchers were involved in it. Nevertheless, some press reports claimed that the march had ended in violence.

However, the success of the march set CND firmly on the path to becoming a mass movement rather than the pressure group some of its founding members had envisaged. In 1959 it took over the organising of the Aldermaston March and reversed its direction, arguing it was more logical to march from the base to the centre of power in London where political decisions were made, and from then until the mid-1960s it became an annual event. The 1959 march brought an estimated 20,000 protesters to the final rally in Trafalgar Square. By 1960, numbers had grown to around 100,000, and in the same year the Labour Party passed a unilateralist resolution at its annual conference – unhappily reversed the following year. In 1962 the venue for the final rally was moved to Hyde Park to contain the estimated 150,000 who took part in a two pronged march, one from Aldermaston, the other from the USAF base at Wethersfield in Essex. 'Easter Marches' against the Bomb also took root in a number of European countries using Holtom's now well-established symbol.

The Aldermaston march in the fictionalised account by Stuart Evers in this book is that of 1963, when the 'Spies for Peace', a clandestine offshoot of the direct action wing of the movement, revealed the existence and whereabouts of a number of underground Regional Seats of Government from which it was planned to govern the country in the event of nuclear war. One of them, at Warren Row near Reading, was close to the route of the march, and, as Stuart Evers' story relates, a number of people – estimated to be in the region of 600 – broke away from the main march to demonstrate there.

By then, however, divisions had opened up within the movement, and from the mid 1960s onwards support for the marches declined – in part also because the war in Vietnam became the focus of radical protest. It was not until the late 1970s and early 1980s, following the deployment of cruise and Pershing missiles in Western Europe, and Soviet SS 20s in Eastern Europe, that the movement regained its strength and resilience. It did so, however, on a scale that dwarfed what had gone before, with massive protest rallies not only in Britain but across Western Europe, North America, Australia, and even, to the extent possible, in the Soviet Union and Eastern Europe. Nonviolent direct action was also a much more central part of the campaign, notably with the sustained blockade by women of the US cruise missile base at Greenham Common which began in 1983 and only ended when the base was finally closed down in 2000.

The DAC, after the first Aldermaston march, focused on nonviolent direct action at missile bases and campaigning among trade unions in areas where nuclear-related arms manufacturing was taking place. It also initiated a transnational action to prevent France testing its nuclear weapons in the Algerian Sahara which took the form of a team of volunteers from Britain, the US, France, Ghana, Nigeria and Basutoland (now Lesotho) attempting to drive from Ghana across the Sahara to the test zone. Though halted by French–controlled police and military, the demonstration helped to galvanise African opinion against the bomb and was followed by a pan-African conference in Accra in April 1960 of independent African states and Liberation movements, against colonialism and 'nuclear imperialism'. One of the participants in the Sahara Protest Expedition was Bayard Rustin, by then a close associate of Martin Luther King. It was Bayard and the black trade union leader, A. Philip Randolph, who proposed the 1963 March on Washington, and Bayard who co-ordinated it. He told several of us in DAC that Aldermaston had been one of the inspirations for it.

In 1960 a new committee, the Committee of 100, was formed to organise a campaign of mass civil disobedience against nuclear weapons. The group of people responsible for this initiative included an American student in London, Ralph Schoenman and the artist Guztav Metzger, and individuals associated with the Youth Campaign for Nuclear Disarmament, the DAC and the New Left. It was launched with a public appeal by the philosopher Bertrand Russell and the anti-apartheid campaigner, Rev. Michael Scott. The Committee carried out a series of major civil disobedience demonstrations in city centres and bases, principally in 1961 and 1962, attracting huge publicity both at home and abroad, especially when the 89-year-old Russell, his wife Edith, and some well-known personalities in the fields of literature and the arts were arrested and sentenced to terms of imprisonment, albeit of relatively short duration.

It would take more space than I have available to assess properly the legacy of the Aldermaston marches and the broader anti-nuclear movement of the period. Clearly they did not achieve the central goal of British, much less global, nuclear disarmament. However, they were an important force pushing the nuclear powers to agree some measures of arms control and disarmament, such as the 1963 Partial Test Ban Treaty, and they probably acted as a constraint upon the leaderships on both sides in the Cold War. Most clearly, however, the Aldermaston marches, and anti-nuclear movement as a whole, contributed an important new element to the long tradition of dissent and resistance in this country as recorded in this volume by combining radical direct action with a commitment to maintaining a non-violent spirit and discipline. In the age of Trump, Putin and Brexit, and with the resurgence of right wing populism across Europe, that commitment and technique may again be urgently required.

# Exterior Paint

## Kit de Waal

THE ESTATE AGENT IS optimistic. That's what he said on the phone and now, at the front door, he offers his hand and smiles: 'Baxter. Mike Baxter. Baxter Byrne.'

Alfonse Maynard had been watching from the front room window for fifteen minutes. He saw Baxter pull up in his white car, get out and walk along Marshall Street looking up and down the road, in front gardens and back alleys, peering at the uncut hedge at number eighty-five, the shoddy porch at forty-nine and the permanent satellite dishes on every house but his own. Baxter made notes on his clipboard and tapped the side of his head with his Biro, then he rang the bell.

Alfonse leads him through the house from front to back, through the narrow hall and the two sitting rooms where no-one sits, rooms that smell of air freshener, beeswax and unopened windows. In the back room at least, thyme and pepper have settled in the nap of his dralon armchair, sticky spots of coffee and rum decorate a little mahogany trolley. There's a Formica dining table and chairs for his dinner, a display cabinet for his wife, his children and grandchildren, a footstool for his bad foot, a Freeview television for the news and a black CD player for Nat King Cole.

The estate agent moves the net curtains aside to look out on the garden. 'A proper garden,' he says, 'some on the other side of the road have little more than a postage stamp. And you've got a shed.' He scribbles something on his pad and taps the window frame with the tip of his pen.

'Double glazing,' he adds. 'Been here for a while have you?'

Alfonse moves aside so the estate agent can be first in the kitchen, the one Lillian had installed eight months ago, the one she used exactly five times. 'Since sixty-four,' he says. 'I used to rent it, then I bought it. My wife's idea.'

'Good, good. You'll see a handsome return on your investment then, Mr. Maynard,' says Baxter running his hand along the work surface like it's a woman's skin.

'Solid timber,' says Alfonse, knocking on the cupboard doors. 'It was my wife that wanted it. Then she died.'

Baxter doesn't turn his head, takes his time then makes his announcement in full.

'On behalf of Baxter Byrne, I would like to offer my condolences to you, Mr. Maynard. Sorry for your loss,' and Alfonse realises that for Baxter, death is a professional boon.

'You have a...' Baxter moves through the kitchen to the little toilet off the lobby. '... ah yes, downstairs cloakroom, wash hand basin, fully tiled, modern white suite.' Then back through the kitchen, noting the name of the boiler as he passes, 'Domestic hot water and central heating,' he says to himself. He motions to the staircase. 'Lead the way, Mr. Maynard.'

Alfonse shows him the little bedroom at the back with its single bed and blue eiderdown. It still has Lillian's sewing machine set up and the little vanity chair she used to scuff across the carpet to sit at it. Whatever she was sewing when the stroke knocked her backwards has been tidied away. The room is dark and lifeless and Alfonse closes the door quickly. The second bedroom lost its bed twenty years ago when Lillian declared it a dressing room. She had wardrobes built on every wall and mirrors on every door. It reminds Alfonse of a circus or somewhere you might take your child for a day out; a child that might slip your hand and run away or get lost, and the very thought of this room lately has begun to give Alfonse nightmares.

So he only stands at the door and lets Baxter go in alone.

'Useful second bedroom,' he mutters, 'large double.'

The biggest bedroom overlooks the street. Why Alfonse is embarrassed to be standing in there with another man he does not know. He has tucked in the sheets and blankets as he does every morning, his shoes are out of sight, there is no dirty washing in the pink plastic laundry basket and no dirty magazines shoved under his mattress. But the room smells of man and not woman and that's enough.

'Master bedroom,' says Baxter, 'fitted wall lights, central heating radiator, telephone socket.'

Baxter measures up and is done in fifteen minutes.

'Presentation is everything, Mr. Maynard,' he says as he shakes hands again with Alfonse on the doorstep and flicks his eye towards the peeling green paint on the front door. 'Red sells.'

In his chair that evening, Alfonse cries.


The next day, the lady at B&Q helps him choose a bloody red for the front door. Lillian would have been in charge of colour but the woman that helps him is blonde like Lillian with the same good shape and easy smile.

'There you go, bab,' she says, 'September's a good month for painting. Not too cold, not too hot.'

Alfonse buys paint brushes and sandpaper and undercoat and white spirit and a new flap for the letterbox in brass with rope edging. He puts some chicken to stew in his still-new oven and reads the instructions on the tin of paint. He pours himself a little rum in an amber glass and sits back in his chair. This will be a two-day job.

The next day, Alfonse is outside early enough to watch the children go to school. All the children are brown of one shade or another, in headscarves or cornrows, and Alfonse realises that there must have been a time, just before he came from St. Kitts, when all the children on Marshall Street would have been white, when maybe there was a white man, standing at this very gate with sandpaper in his hand and his shirt sleeves rolled up, a man with a tin of green paint, watching white mothers wheel their prams round the corner to the shops. Alfonse has brought out a kitchen chair. He will work from the bottom up, first with sandpaper and then he'll paint on the undercoat.

Mr. Kang stands in his porch next door. 'You've been a stranger,' he says to Alfonse.

'Oh, I've been busy, you know. Tidying up and throwing things out. I got a valuation yesterday.'

'Good?'

'Good.'

Mr. Kang folds his arms across his chest. 'What colour?'

'Red,' says Alfonse.

'Red is for celebrations, my friend,' says Mr. Kang. 'And when you leave, it will not be a happy day.'

Alfonse nods. 'My daughter lives in Sutton Coldfield.'

Mrs. Kang and the big-eyed Kang girls cluster at his gate. They hold hands with their mother as they cross the road. Alfonse watches them go. Watches Mrs. Kang button her coat tight around the curve of her hip, into the slip of her waist and he remembers Lillian and the tip-tip of her high heels on the pavement after dark, after her shift at The Blue Gate, after everyone had gone to bed. Alfonse would be sitting at the open window with his cigarette waiting. The sound of her shoes and her voice, that's what he first loved.

Mr. Kang brings them both a cup of tea, sweet and spicy, boiled with cardamom and spice, thick with condensed milk. 'You can't have tea without biscuits, my friend,' he says and whips the lid off an enamel tin eight inches wide. Alfonse looks inside at the Jammy Dodgers, custard creams and pink iced rings. 'If they make them, we buy them,' says Mr. Kang.

Alfonse takes two chocolate bourbons. Mr. Kang takes six. He won't ask so Alfonse has to tell him.

'The man was called Baxter,' says Alfonse. 'He said to put it on for ninety-nine thousand, but I must only expect ninety-six.'

Mr. Kang whistles. 'Not bad. When did you buy it? Things must have been cheap in your time.'

Cheap. The word makes Alfonse wince. He scours at the panelled door until the scratching noise is so loud he can't hear if Mr. Kang is still talking, until he is sure that Mr. Kang has gone back inside so that when he turns around Marshall Street will be quiet again and he can remember in peace.

There are two barmaids at The Blue Gate, Lillian and Lillian's sister. They both have the same job and the same words to say to the black men that come looking for a drink after work or on Sunday afternoons when the loneliness of the long day and the pressure of four walls bears down heavy.

'Blacks round the side,' or 'Smoke Room Only.' The difference is Lillian only says it with her mouth, not with her eyes.

You only get told once, the second time you remember but this is 1965 and there are new black men every week, new reminders from the barmaids or the landlord. The first time Alfonse goes in, he opens the door to The Lounge. Everyone stops talking, stops drinking. Alfonse looks from face to face and sees Lillian's. She gives the slightest shake of her head and he steps backwards, outside, round the corner and in again through The Smoke Room door. She walks through the bar and is there again waiting.

'Sorry,' she whispers and then louder, 'Coloureds can only drink in The Smoke Room, sir. What'll you have?'

Alfonse takes his half a stout to the corner where the West Indians sit. They're men like himself, young in the world, young to the country and homesick. Alfonse hardly joins in the conversation, his drink is untouched. He watches Lillian pulling drinks and wiping the counter.

One of his new friends tugs on his coat sleeve. 'Listen, man, over here you don't even look, never mind touch. You want a woman, you must send for the one you leave at home. Come, man, play a hand of cards.'

Alfonse holds the Jack of diamonds and the eight of clubs. He doesn't concentrate on the game and loses nearly two shillings by the end of the night. He walks home slowly with his last cigarette, the collar high on his coat. Alfonse has only come for a few years and the truth is he's not sure if he wants his woman to come, not sure he misses her. Isn't it better that she waits in St. Kitts 'til he comes back? The last time he saw her, she shouted after him, 'Write me!' That was nine months ago. Alfonse hears the tip-tip of a woman's shoes behind him and when he turns, it's the barmaid. He waits at the corner under the lamplight and she catches up.

'You left this,' she says and holds his hat in her hand.

'Oh,' he touches his hair and then shakes his head. 'I'm not myself this evening.'

'Who are you normally then? Should I call for a policeman?' If she hadn't smiled, he would have backed away. Only last week he heard that someone, an Indian man, smacked a barmaid across the face and was being hunted by the police for assault. Alfonse wasn't there and doesn't know if it's true but isn't this how trouble starts, with the pretty face of innocence and the sound of laughter?

He puts his hand out for his hat but she perches it on her blonde beehive and laughs again. 'Does it suit me?'

'Yes,' he says. And instead of taking it off her, he taps it down at an angle so she looks like one of the girls that dance with Gene Kelly or Fred Astaire. She spins around as though she can read his mind and when she stops he reaches out to steady her.

'Whoops!' she says and grabs his arm. There is a moment then in Alfonse Maynard's life when his world tilts and he understands that something has changed.

'You better walk me home,' she says and keeps her hand on his arm directing him all the way to Marshall Street.

'But I live on this street!' he says and she winks at him.

'Yes, I know.'

She tells him she lives with her mother and her sister on the posh bit of the road that bends around the corner, number seventy-five, and that when Alfonse and his friends moved in she went to have a look. Everyone was talking about it, a house full of single men, single black men, four at least, getting up to who-knows-what. While Lillian watched the house she saw Alfonse open the front door and button his coat. And just like Alfonse's world tilted when she took his arm, Lillian told him later that her world tilted in direct proportion to the angle of his trilby as he put it on and nudged it to the side.

That night, they stop at the corner and Alfonse kisses Lillian on the cheek. They both look around in case they are seen and then Lillian kisses him back.

'We'll have to keep quiet about this and be careful,' she says, 'My Mum's a bit prejudiced.'

Alfonse agrees.

The being careful bit is harder than they expect. Sometimes, on a dark night, they twist suddenly into an entry between the terraced houses and kiss for so long that it's all Alfonse can do not to ravage Lillian there and then. He feels her slender body beneath her coat, the soft pressure of her bosom, her heart against his and he wants her like food. After six weeks, Lillian has an idea.

'You go home, Alfonse and I'll finish at The Blue Gate. I'll go to my house, pretend to go to bed and slip out when no-one's looking.'

Alfonse says nothing. It was Lillian's sister that got the slap in the face from the Indian man she refused to serve. The man is still wanted by the police. There are slogans daubed on brick walls telling black people to go home. There are demonstrations by the Indian Workers' Association about the colour-bar at The Blue Gate and to top it all, Marshall Street itself is in the papers for being too full of black people. 'YOU DON'T WANT A NIGGER FOR A NEIGHBOUR' is the headline and Lillian's mother is involved somehow, part of a local crowd pushing the council for all-white streets. Alfonse knows what happens in America, black men are beaten with clubs, burned alive, hung from trees and for a lot less than sex with a white woman. This wasn't the time to let the tilt for Lillian topple him headlong into his coffin. But then again, when she kisses him, touches him and says his name....

'Alright,' he says. 'I'll wait at the window. Don't knock. I'll watch for you and come down.'

On Friday it works like a dream. On Saturday, the same. On Sunday night when Lillian finishes early, she lies down on her bed and falls asleep. Alfonse waits at the window until half past one and then oversleeps for work. On Monday night, not a day they planned to see one another, he hears shrapnel against his window just before midnight. She's grinning up at him and he takes the stairs two at a time.

'I missed you,' he says and he pulls her up the staircase.

They make love under his pink candlewick bedspread and lie in the dark with their cigarettes, her in his arms, pale and soft.

'I'm going to tell her,' says Lillian. 'We're not doing anything wrong.'

'No, no,' he says. 'Not yet.'

Christmas comes. Lillian tells him that her mother has the house full of visitors and there's not a moment Lillian can call her own. If she's not working at The Blue Gate, she's washing up and making meals. She has one cousin walking her home, another sleeping in the same bed, someone by her side day and night. Alfonse doesn't see Lillian for three whole days and he begins to wonder if she will forget about him like he has forgotten his woman in St. Kitts. He can barely recall the promises he made to her back there or the sound of her voice or whether she wore perfume. He doesn't know if she has dimples and downy hair on the back of her neck or whether the moonlight makes patterns in her eyes. Does she taste of sugar, taste of salt? Does she fit against his body like wet sand under his feet? He can't remember.

Alfonse spends Christmas Day and Boxing Day with the other boarders, sitting around their kitchen table trying to recreate the festivities of home without good rum, without fruit cake, without pepper and garlic for the small, small ham on a dry pallid bone, without stew-peas and rice and, for the first time in Alfonse's life, without the white heat of the sun.

But Lillian hasn't forgotten him. Stones scuff the window at midnight on Boxing Day and he crushes his lips on hers.

Lillian is dressing one February evening when she sits down suddenly on the bed and covers her face with her hands.

'My Mum knows,' she says.

Alfonse sits up. He doesn't reach for her or tell her not to worry. He doesn't bundle her up and kiss her face. In that moment, Alfonse thinks of himself and of the viciousness of the mother he has heard about for three long months, of her scheming with others on the street to get the blacks out and put the niggers back where they belong, on the boat home. He reads the papers each day now and listens closely to the news on the radio because everyone in the foundry, Indians, Pakistanis, West Indians talk about how bad it is and whether it can get any worse, whether it could get like America with the Klu Klux Klan, lynchings, segregation, assassinations.

Lillian raises her head and looks at him. 'She knows, Alfonse! She's furious with me. She was screaming some terrible things.'

Alfonse lights a cigarette and lays his arm on Lillian's shoulder. 'Don't worry, Lily.'

'She said I was a slut, Alfonse. She said I was cheap.' Lillian wipes her eyes and grabs his hand.

'What shall we do?'

'We have to be more careful, that's all.'

'Careful?'

'Yes, Lily. Watch our step. I don't want no trouble.'

Lillian stands up straight. 'I see.' She pulls the belt tight on her Macintosh and feeds her slender feet into her stiletto heels. She ties her headscarf and places her handbag neatly in the crook of her arm. 'When you're ready to be a man, Alfonse Maynard, you know where to find me,' she says.

Alfonse goes to speak but the door slams so hard he's

worried that it will wake the house and give the game away if there is any game left.

Alfonse sleeps not one single minute of that night. He squeezes his eyelids together and lies as still as his mourning body will allow but peace can't find him. Lily has gone. Morning comes and Alfonse doesn't move. His alarm alarms and he throws the blasted thing to the ground. Lily has left him. He smokes cigarette after cigarette until his mouth begs for water. It's Friday. Payday. Alfonse has missed his first ever day of work.

He sits up in bed and peels back the curtains. The road is quiet. He looks at the corner where he first kissed Lillian and wonders if he will ever get to kiss her again. He has to get her back.

Then Alfonse notices at the top of the road, a big group of men have gathered, some with notebooks out, some with cameras and standing in the middle of the group is a tall black man in a hat and glasses. Alfonse pushes his head out of the window as far as he can without tumbling to the ground.

'Can't be,' he whispers. 'Just can't be.'

There are two Indian men at the corner and a black woman too.

'Can't be.'

Alfonse is dressed in his trousers, shirt and socks in seventy-five seconds. He has his arms in the sleeves of his coat as he opens the front door. He stands at the gate and looks to the top of the road and the apparition.

'Can't be.'

Then suddenly the black man walks away from the crowd, just him alone. He comes down Marshall Street looking left and right at the houses, at the 'For Sale' signs in the windows and the group at the top stand and watch. Someone is filming and 'if they are filming this thing,' says Alfonse out loud, 'it's because it is true.'

The man gets closer and closer and as he walks past Alfonse, their eyes meet, black man to black man and again, Alfonse feels a shift in his world. The black man walks to the corner of the road and Alfonse has to follow.

'Malcolm X,' his heart says over and over, 'Malcolm X.'

A group of women are waiting for him at number seventy-seven. A group of white women and with them Lillian's mother. They stand in the front garden and shout, waving their arms and pointing.

'Go back home!'

'We don't want blackies here.'

'Get out of our country.'

Malcolm X doesn't turn his head, he doesn't answer, doesn't break his stride nor cower. It's as if he can't hear them, like he's thinking his own thoughts, just a man out for a stroll on a winter's afternoon. There is no jeering, no name calling. Nothing.

When Malcolm X goes back to the group at the top of the road, he faces a camera and speaks. Alfonse can't hear what he says but he knows it will be in the paper, it will be in the news, it will be all over the world that Malcolm X came to Marshall Street and walked strong with his back straight and his head high. The men slowly pack up their things, put their notebooks away and then they are all gone.

Alfonse goes back inside and straight to the kitchen. 'Malcolm X,' he says. He puts the kettle to boil and plugs in the iron. He came to England in a good suit and tie. He brings it out of the wardrobe and holds it up to the light. Yes. He cleans the nicotine from his teeth and shaves carefully, closely until his skin complains. He takes a clothes brush to his overcoat and buffs a shine on his shoes.

'Malcolm X,' he says and puts his trilby on. He nudges it down at an angle over his eye and he will never know if he really heard the next words but in his heart they are clear and true.

'Do it, Alfonse,' said Malcolm X. 'Go and do it.'

Lillian is behind the Lounge Bar at The Blue Gate. Alfonse stands in the open doorway. The talking stops. The drinking stops.

'Come, Lily!' he shouts.

Men look from him to her and back to him. Alfonse

doesn't turn his head. He can't see them.

'Come!' he shouts and she darts into the back, grabs her coat and skips across the carpet.

He pulls her by the hand past Dibble Road and Topsham Road, over Holly Lane and all the way to number seventy-five. He says nothing. By the time he rings the bell, they are both panting.

'I've got a key,' Lillian whispers but before she can get it out, the door opens. Lillian's mother. She folds her arms, opens her mouth but Alfonse is quick.

'Your daughter has come for her things,' says Alfonse, calm like Malcolm X. 'Go on Lily, and then give your mother your key. You won't need it again.'

Lily slips past and the woman gasps.

'Lillian and me will be married next week,' says Alfonse. 'We would like you to come.'

Curtains move in the front windows of all the houses along Marshall Street. Women up and down the road and in the shops and in the pubs and clubs and launderettes would talk for many years about the time a black man fronted Lillian's mother and got the better of her. Alfonse would always remind people that Lillian's mother did try and speak but he held up his hand, palm to her face and said simply. 'No.'

Alfonse carried Lillian's little suitcase and a lightness in his heart that never left until Lily died.

Alfonse wipes the sanded door with white spirit. He has gone down to the wood in some places. If he was staying maybe he would strip it right back and peel off all the layers of exterior paint that have built up over the years. But he only needs to smarten it up for the sale. Presentation is everything. He will go inside now. His chicken will be stewed and ready to eat and he will pour himself a good inch of rum tonight, two good inches. Three.

He will paint the door tomorrow and afterwards he will invite Mr. Kang and his wife and the Kang girls into his home like Lily used to, when she would lay the table with all sorts of treats and sweets and sandwiches. He will buy a nice tin of biscuits from the supermarket and orange squash for the children. Alfonse will show them Lily's new kitchen and they can all sit in the front room, sit and sit until it smells of people and not furniture polish.

It's a good thing to think about the past, to think about Lily. Nine days after he walked on Marshall Street, Malcolm X is killed. Alfonse reads it in the Sunday paper and has to sit down. He tells Lily all about it, how he and Malcolm spoke heart to heart and Alfonse found the strength to stand up and be a man. Lily kisses him and says he should send a card of condolence to the widow and children. So Alfonse does. There are photographs of the funeral a few weeks later and Alfonse imagines the grief of the crying wife and wonders if she will ever recover.

Alfonse sips his white rum and knits his hands together. There is red paint under his nails. When the 'For Sale' sign goes up people will come and walk through his rooms and touch his things. They will open Lily's cupboards and look at her clothes but they will never know her and the gentle touch of her hand and the way she made him feel. 'I love you, Alfonse,' she said just before she died.

People will come and look at Lily's sewing room and the little bathroom and they will think about changing the shower curtain or replacing the roof. They will knock the two downstairs rooms into one like Mr. Kang did and they will think how much better it would be without the dralon chair and photographs of a dead woman, without the old man that lives in one room.

Alfonse holds his glass up towards heaven. 'Lily,' he says. He goes to drain his glass and then remembers and smiles. 'And Malcolm.'

# Afterword: Smethwick, Pub Crawl Protests, and Malcolm X

## Avtar Singh Jouhl

I WAS ONE OF the men accompanying Malcolm X that day, on Marshall Street, in February 1965. But my story, or the story of my involvement in the Smethwick campaign, started much earlier.

It was November 1956 and I was in my final year at Khalsa College (an affiliate of Punjab University), and still living with my family in a village called Jandiala Manjkki, in Jalandhar District, Northern Punjab. The long-awaited return of my uncle, Bachint Singh, from England, began to draw me into a series of conversations about what I should do after graduating. Bachint had been living in the Midlands, in a town called Smethwick in the suburbs of Birmingham, where he co-owned a small terraced house with my brother, Gurbux. He had been working as a general labourer at Dartmouth Auto Castings No. 2, a large iron foundry and part of Birmid Industries.

Eventually, and reluctantly, I was persuaded by my uncle to try England myself, and to join my brother. In April 1957, I completed my BA, graduating with a degree in Politics, Economics and English, and come February of the following year, I found myself at Heathrow Airport. It was a very cold wintry afternoon when I arrived at No. 54, Oxford Road, Smethwick (just a stone's throw from the West Bromwich Albion football ground, as it turned out). And to my surprise, I

192

was greeted by ten Punjabi men, all of whom were already living in my brother's three-bedroom house.

The day after arriving, my brother initiated me into a key ritual of British culture: along with three other friends of his, he took me for a pint at a local public house. In this case, one called 'The Wagon and Horses'. Not long after entering this quintessentially British space, I needed to use the toilet, and on my return I wasn't quite sure which room my brother and his friends had entered. I tried a room that had a sign saying 'Assembly Lounge' on the door, but the second I stepped through it, a roomful of entirely white faces turned and stared at me. You could've heard a pin drop. A man from behind the bar was suddenly coming towards me at speed, shouting and gesturing: 'You coloured people in the Smoke Room!' Barging me back through the Assembly Room door, he pointed: 'The Smoke Room!'

I was shocked at this. I had been to college; I had been brought up in gentle, loving family, and I had always regarded Britain as a reasonable place. I had never been told where to sit, or where to stand, in a public place.

I rejoined my brother and his friends in our specially allocated room, and noticed that every last person in there was coloured. I asked my brother to explain this segregation to me. I was dumbfounded. He informed me, simply, that the 'gaffer' only served Indians and West Indians in the Smoke Room, never in the Assembly Lounge. But he didn't give me a reason for it; this was simply how it was. Almost all pubs were like this. Welcome to Britain.

A few days later, I went out on my own to get a haircut. There was a barber shop on Brasshouse Lane, near the park, called the 'Beacon Hair Salon'. But as soon as I opened the door, the barber called out a soon to become familiar phrase: 'Coloureds are not served here!' I asked why. The reply came: 'My customers object.' I went back home. When my brother returned from work that evening, I asked him *again* to explain this colour bar.

His explanation was again unsatisfactory.

Two weeks later I started work at Shotton Brothers, an iron foundry at Oldbury. By chance, I happened to meet an old friend of mine, working there, Jasbir Singh. Jasbir was from a village called Shankar – just four miles from my own – and had also studied with me in Jalandhar. I joined him as a general labourer working under two white 'moulders'. Here too, I discovered there was segregation. Job segregation. All the 'labourers' were Asian or West Indian, whilst all the skilled positions – moulders, core makers, grinders, fettlers, maintenance workers, etc. – were filled by white men. My weekly wage for a 48-hour week was £7 and ten shillings. The white moulder, who I served under, took home £17 a week, for 44 hours' work.

My friend Jasbir was living with his uncle, Karam Singh, on Tadbank Road in Oldbury. One weekend I went to visit them both, and Karam explained that he was a member of the Indian Workers' Association (IWA) – an association that had been set up because the bigger unions weren't serving the needs of Indian workers specifically. Jasbir and I shared our experiences at the pub, at the barber shop, and so forth. Karam explained that racial discrimination is not against the law in England and that the IWA was campaigning to have discrimination – based on colour, race, creed, and gender – made illegal. Karam gave us a contact for someone at the IWA, a man called Jagmohan Joshi, and within days, Jasbir and I had joined the union. Over the following weeks and months, the two of us began the not insignificant task of organising fellow Indian, Pakistani, and West Indian workers into specific unions for each of their respective trades.

Every two years the IWA held a General Meeting to review committee reports and elect new branch committee officers. So it was that on an October evening tin 1956, in the main hall of James Watt Technical College, I found myself elected to the position of Birmingham Branch Secretary.[1]

In the late fifties and early sixties, Smethwick became something of a microcosm for the wider national debate about race. In the late fifties, a group of Conservative councillors led by Councillor Don Finney, had set up what they called an 'Immigration Control Committee Smethwick'. Come the early sixties, the Conservatives won overall control of Smethwick Borough Council, and implemented a new policy on housing which declared that only people who had lived in Smethwick for ten years were eligible to go on the Council Housing Register (for council accommodation). This policy was deliberately targeting 'coloured' people in Smethwick because practically no 'coloured' people had been living in the town for ten years. What's more, very few of the (almost exclusively white) landlords in the town were prepared to take in non-white tenants (the reason my brother's three-bedroom terraced house was occupied by 12 of us).

To overcome this deliberately racist housing policy, 'coloured' people started to buy terraced houses jointly, pooling their financial resources and borrowing from friends. Seeing this, many white residents – most famously on Marshall Street led by a Mrs. Grove – started objecting. First they leant on estate agents to sell to whites only. Later, they even asked the council to buy up all the remaining houses on Marshall Street and promise not to sell or rent them to 'coloured' people.

Colour bars were being introduced across all aspects of life in Smethwick.

In response, the IWA, together with other black organisations, stepped up its campaign against racism in all its forms: writing letters to local papers; opposing racist publicans' licence renewals; lobbying Parliament against proposed and existing immigration controls; calling for a new act of Parliament to outlaw racial discrimination; and supporting 'coloured' residents on Marshall Street through local and later national demonstrations. In the 1964 general election, prospective Conservative MP, Peter Griffiths, played into the area's mounting racial tension with the infamous campaign slogan 'If you want a nigger for a neighbour, vote Labour'.[2] The Labour Party, led by Harold Wilson, won the election, but Smethwick went the other way. Griffiths' openly racist campaign went down a storm and he won the seat, ousting the former Shadow Foreign Secretary Gordon Walker.

Prime Minister Wilson denounced Griffiths, calling him a 'parliamentary leper' in the House of Commons. But despite this, the racists were emboldened by the 1964 election results, not just in Smethwick but nationally. A British wing of the Ku Klux Klan was formed in the area, and many coloured residents of Smethwick received burning crosses shoved through their letterboxes. In my house on Grantham Road, I had pellets shot through the window. In January 1965, Gordon Walker stood again in the Leytonstone by-election (a seat almost created for him by the elevation of the existing MP to life peer). But, being weak on the issue of race (and afraid to confront it head on), Walker was beaten again, by the Conservatives, in what had been a safe Labour seat.

However, lobbying by anti-racist organisations was beginning to take effect. Wilson seemed sympathetic and our campaign scored its first major victory with the passing of the 1965 Race Relations Act (and the formation of the Race Relations Board to adjudicate it). This Act made racial discrimination in 'places of public resort' (such as bars and restaurants) illegal, but crucially did not apply to shops or private boarding houses, and made no comment on racial discrimination in the workplace or in housing policy. It was generally regarded as a weak piece of legislation, weak in its scope and weak in its enforcement capabilities – being limited to conciliation and an assurance not to return to the discriminatory behaviour. Basically, a slap on the wrist. It was a start, however. Something to build on.

The IWA in Birmingham organised a series of 'pub crawls' to test this new law, working in collaboration with the National Union of Students, and specifically students from Birmingham and Aston Universities. Wherever a publican was found to be discriminating, the IWA filed a complaint to the Race Relations Board. After the Act was passed we needed to prove that a colour bar was being covertly maintained. For instance, 'coloured' people were often turned away at the door under the excuse that the pub was hosting a 'private party' that night. We exposed this practice through the pub crawl – dividing the crawl into two parties: white students and 'coloured' IWA members. The students would enter first, and be let in, of course, then when we arrived we got the 'private party' excuse. We did this at pubs like The Robinson Crusoe, on Suffrage Street, which after a complaint to the RRB, was forced to drop these practices. We also organised pickets outside pubs. One particularly offensive pub was The Blue Gate Hotel, a very large and popular drinking den on the High Street. Its licensee kept dodging the new rules to preserve his precious whites-only 'Lounge' room.

Inevitably this led to frustration among some IWA members, and one Indian campaigner, after many attempts to be served there, lost his cool and was reported to have slapped a barmaid. Fortunately for him, he had disappeared long before the police arrived.

Malcolm X became involved in the movement thanks to a key campaigner in London, a woman called Claudia Jones, or Comrade Claudia. In the late fifties, Claudia was living in London having been deported from the US in 1955 following the McCarthy trials for being a Communist. Claudia was a US Citizen but exiled from her own country. In London, she founded the *West Indian Gazette* (*WIG*), a revolutionary journal, and also in 1959, organised the first ever Notting Hill Carnival in response to the riots the previous year. The IWA and *WIG* coordinated their campaigns against racism and in particular the Commonwealth Immigration Bill, which had come into law in July 1961. Comrade Claudia was in contact with Malcolm X and other Civil Rights leaders in the US, and before her sudden death in December 1964, had made arrangements for Malcolm to visit the UK. After her death, the managing editor of the *WIG*, Manu Manchanda, together with Jagmohan Joshi (by then National Secretary of the IWA), pushed forward Claudia's plan for Malcolm X to visit the UK.

Thus, on 12th February 1965, the terraced houses of Marshall Street witnessed the unlikely sight of one of the world's most famous Civil Rights campaigners walking along it. Malcolm had arrived with bodyguards, of course, as well as a small crowd of reporters, TV crews, and journalists.[3] This crowd was asked to wait, though, on the corner of St. Paul's Road and Marshall Street. Malcolm informed me that he wanted to walk down the street alone. I warned him that he should expect jeering, from Mrs. Grove and friends. At this, he smiled, and said: 'Don't worry, I can handle it.' As agreed, he walked alone, slowly, up and down the street, stopping in front of one window with a 'FOR SALE: WHITES ONLY' poster. The atmosphere was highly charged. Residents came out, stared, and several shouted things like: 'We don't want black people here!'

Malcolm was very calm, dignified and composed. He didn't even look to see where the shouting was coming from, and eventually rejoined us.

We then invited him to accompany Joshi and myself for a drink. Our visit to The Blue Gate was organised discreetly. About 15 IWA members and West Indian colleagues were already there, waiting in the allocated 'Bar Room'. As we entered the main 'Lounge Room' the staff stared at us. Nervously, they refused to serve us, quoting house policy, so eventually we moved to the 'Bar Room'. Malcolm X shook hands with everyone in the room: the Asians and West Indians as well as our white comrades. It was one of the most quiet, sombre half-pints I've ever drunk. From where we were, the 'Lounge Room' could be seen clearly through a serving hatch – a room full of white faces. By the time we eventually left, Malcolm was feeling appalled.

Despite being fully briefed on the racial tensions in Smethwick, Malcolm still found the experience shocking.

What's important is that he came, though, and his solidarity with us was there for all to see. After The Blue Gate, he was whisked away to Birmingham, to speak at the University, and tragically, only ten days later, he was assassinated at a rally in New York. Despite all this, Malcolm's visit to Marshall Street acted as a great boost for the anti-racist struggle in Britain. Black and Asian people suddenly felt emboldened and confident. Malcolm's visit to Smethwick had linked our campaigns with other movements all across the planet. Our activists – just like Alfonse and Lily in Kit's story – found a new strength, to stand up and be counted as different but equal.

The following year, the actor-turned-politician, Andrew Faulds, stood as Labour's parliamentary candidate for Smethwick, and challenged Peter Griffith openly on his racist agenda. The IWA put its full force behind Faulds' campaign, and come Election Day on 31ˢᵗ March 1966, Griffiths was defeated for good. Black and Asian people went on to buy houses on Marshall Street, and indeed elsewhere in the country, without hindrance.

Writing this in 2016, in the aftermath of the Brexit vote, however, I can't help but feel a shudder of familiarity, recollecting the atmosphere in 1964 and 1965. The language and rhetoric of UKIP and the 'Vote Leave' campaign during the summer of 2016 has been frighteningly similar in tone, if not in its choice of specific words, to Griffiths' 1964 campaign. The inability of supposedly open-minded politicians to address racism and nationalism is also reminiscent of Gordon Walker's inability to face up to it in 1964. A Labour politician was murdered in the street by a 'Britain First' supporter. Hate crimes have risen by 57% nationwide since the referendum, and have increased threefold in some of the most Eurosceptic areas.[4]

In the sixties, Enoch Powell spoke of 'Rivers of Blood'. At the end of seventies, Thatcher swept into government defending people's fear of 'being swamped by an alien culture.'

Now we have Theresa May, whose rise to power has been ushered in by the jovial, 'friendly' faces of xenophobia – the ideology of the forever beer-swilling Brexiteers.

The forces of xenophobia, and the influences of countries-old imperialism, persist just as strongly today as ever. Their focus may have shifted (to East European migrants and refuges from Syria and Libya), but they remain closer to home than you think.

## Notes

1. In a separate capacity, through the Amalgamated Union of Foundry Workers, Jouhl also worked to secure £1,700 compensation for a colleague, Lachman Singh, who was blinded in one eye, in a workplace accident due to inadequate safety gear. Later, when working at Midland Motor Cylinders on Dartmouth Road, Smethwick, Jouhl campaigned successfully for the scrapping of a system of separate toilets for Europeans and Asians.
2. A recent BBC documentary ('Making the Midlands: Racism and Ignorance in 1966, 1 June 2016') decided to censor this slogan putting the word 'coloured' over the offending word on the infamous election poster.
3. Reporters from the BBC, ITV, *Birmingham Post* and *Evening Mail*, *Express and Star*, *Smethwick Telephone,* and the Associated Press.
4. 'Brexit: Surge in anti-immigrant hate crime in areas that voted to leave EU,' *The Independent*, 31 July 2016.

# Banner Bright

## Alexei Sayle

From a corner facing into the marble lined hallway, a 16mm print of *The Sound of Music* played backwards through a projector. Jagged, brightly coloured images flickered over Jack's body as he hammered wildly on a pair of bongos while a girl danced sinuously in front of him. Just like Jack none of the twenty members of the impromptu jazz band had ever played their instruments before and the noise they created, a cacophonous unrhythmic din, combined with Julie Andrews yowling in reverse, bounced erratically off the hard surfaces and high ceilings of the room. With sweat pouring down his face Jack realised less than thirty minutes had passed since he'd come into the building to enquire about night school classes.

He had passed the college many times on his walk to and from the railway station but couldn't say that he'd really noticed it, fully taken it in, until a week ago, on the day of his fortieth birthday, an event that had prompted Jack to try and make some small changes in his life. He worked as a pipefitter and welder on large building projects all around the North West and, though he was a meticulous and conscientious employee on the construction sites, he always kept himself a little apart. Jack never took part in the rowdy behaviour of his fellow workmen and so, though he was respected due to his precise workmanship and quiet reliable manner, he had no friends in the building trade.

Jack would sometimes attend folk clubs or visit the few pubs that served 'real' ale in the Lancashire town where he lived, but he never quite fitted in in any of those places either. A thought that had been bothering him of late was that if he hadn't been forced to leave school by his parents at the age of fourteen he might have become an artist of some kind. He regularly visited the town's Victorian art gallery and would spend hours in front of the gaudy second rank pre-Raphaelites, the single minor unfinished Augustus John and the painting Lucien Freud had done just after he'd left college, waiting for inspiration to strike. Now he was forty Jack thought it was time to see if he could make art instead of staring at it, not quite knowing what he was looking at. So one autumn evening he decided to stop off at the local art college, a two-storey 1930s brick structure separated from the road by a low wall and a small patch of grass, typical in style of the civic buildings constructed between the wars. Inscribed on the stone lintel above the glass double doors were the words 'Art School' and, as he entered, he didn't really notice that this inscription was now largely obscured by a homemade banner stretched over the entrance on which was written in neat black letters – by someone who knew what they were doing – 'Student Occupation'.

Once inside however there could be no mistaking that something out of the ordinary was going on. The entranceway was scattered with sleeping bags and here and there clumps of young people sat about talking together in intense little groups. A slightly older-looking man stood just beyond the doors surveying the whole scene with a benevolent smile on his face. He had medium length black hair with a thick beard and was dressed in a pink long sleeved T-shirt of the type known as a 'Frog' with flared sleeves, a scooped neck and a tail like a conventional shirt plus tight purple flares and cowboy boots. Since he seemed to be a bit in charge Jack addressed his enquiries to this man, 'What's going on?'

The man turned to him, the smile broadening into a welcoming grin, 'This, my man, is the world coming to itself, in the most literal meaning of the phrase coming to its senses for the first time. Are you here to be a part of that?'

'Not really, I was thinking of taking a night school class in pottery.'

'Ha! You don't need no night classes, my man. Do you think this new world can be taught in classes? Teaching is dead! The truth already exists inside you, you just need to find a way to let it out.'

'I see. So you're one of the students here then?'

'No I'm one of the staff,' the man said. Then he handed Jack the bongos adding, 'Hi! I'm Nick'.

Now most nights after work and all day at the weekends, Jack would hurry down to the college. It turned out that Nick was not their leader. In as much as there was a leader of the occupation it was a committee of the more earnest students. Nick did not even sit on this committee but nevertheless he seemed to be everywhere, talking animatedly in the discussion groups, proposing wild ideas, popping up here and there like an imp in flared trousers. Nick had not taught painting or sculpture or graphics at the college but had been the sole lecturer in charge of something called 'General Studies' which seemed to Jack to be basically anything that jumped into his head, which made him very suited to this sort of role. There was a song in the charts that kept going round Jack's head '…you're everywhere and nowhere baby'.

The local newspaper had at first tried to portray the occupation as a 'love-in', but in fact the atmosphere was surprisingly chaste, occasionally late at night there would be muffled grunting from some of the sleeping bags, but by and large the students reminded Jack of a more arty version of some Yugoslav pioneers he had heard speak at a Labour Party meeting in Manchester just after the war. They had declared that though men and women fought alongside each other there had been no, what they called, 'fraternisation'. Mind you he did remember reading somewhere else that any who did 'fraternise' had been shot so you could see why they wouldn't.

The students operated the college's telephone exchange with great efficiency, answering enquiries from curious members of the general public and relaying calls from the newspapers or radio to their appointed spokespeople. And the college canteen which before the occupation had reminded the building's caretaker of, as he told Jack, the food the Japanese had provided while he had been a slave labourer on the Burma Railroad, was now open fifteen hours a day and served nourishing and inventive vegetarian meals both to the occupiers and any of the local community who wished to drop in.

After about a week a little group of four others had coalesced around Nick. One was Jack, another was a pretty blond girl called Claire who wore her hair parted in the middle and then combed it severely so it fell straight down the sides of her head, as if it had been ironed, so her ears poked through giving Claire the vague appearance of a monkey – but then Jack had always really liked monkeys. The other two were a couple, Shirley and Adrian; Shirley was the more serious of the pair, listening intently and taking notes as they sat through passionate discussions on how they could make art eduction more relevant to the anti-colonial liberation struggle, while Adrian reminded Jack of some of the women he'd met at folk clubs who'd been dragged along by their boyfriends, and who kept up an air of wide-eyed astonishment which masked a much deeper boredom.

While the five of them attended as many talks and free-form jazz sessions as anybody else, the best of times, they all agreed, were when they were making their banner. It had been Nick's idea, of course. He said one day, 'There's a second Vietnam demo coming in a couple of weeks and hundreds of thousands of people will be on it. We should take all that we have learned here and put it into a banner. It would be a bit similar to all the other banners you see on demos but it would also be like... this art object. You get all these banners and flags and stuff on demos – I've always thought they're all really dull. Just clenched fists and 'Chelmsford Maoist League' or something.

But we could create an artefact that is really special. We could take elements of the folk art of those old-fashioned trade union banners but we could add in, say, the constructivism of Malevich or the pop art tropes of Lichtenstein, it would be...' and this was the first time that anybody had used the word in this particular way, '... it would be... awesome!'

Jack provided two lengths of thin but strong aluminium piping for the poles at either end, and a third longer piece to run along the top, supporting the eight foot long and four foot deep piece of canvas they acquired from the art school stores and dyed red. He also welded sockets for each end of the pole to fit into. Then they set to work on the design. Claire turned out to be good at embroidery, learned from her grandmother, and so she was responsible for parts of the banner that imitated the style but not the content of the Bayeux Tapestry. Adrian designed a brand new typeface like nothing that had ever been seen before, and Shirley painted a border of flowers interwoven with military weapons and objects of torture. Jack for his part entwined tiny pieces of metal, glass and wire into the canvas so that in the light it sparkled and glowed, while Nick directed the whole thing, took the overview, showed them where they were going right and where they were going wrong. Occasionally people would stop and stare at the banner for a long time, finding it, as Nick had predicted, 'awesome'. Some asked if they could come on the Vietnam demo too, perhaps to walk behind the banner or maybe carry it for just a short while, but the group told them no. It was their thing.

For their trip to London, Jack purchased a motor vehicle – a green mini van – he thought of it as not just his but rather that it belonged to the five of them. He had learned to drive in the army during National Service. If you bought a van version of a small car then you didn't have to pay purchase tax on it and the van version of the mini was hardly less uncomfortable than the cramped little car; it had the same door handles that were basically a piece of string and sharp metal edges everywhere, it just didn't have any seats or windows in the back. The cost of a radio, like the cost of a heater, was extra so he hadn't been able to afford either of those – though he had paid a few additional pounds for a passenger seat. Early on the Saturday morning Jack arrived first at the college. He just sat in a happy silence and waited. Claire and Nick turned up together, which surprised him, and she seemed to be wearing Nick's 'frog', the top the lecturer had worn the first time they'd met. Without discussion Nick took the passenger seat while Claire climbed into the back where Jack had put some cushions for people to sit on. Claire folded herself – knees drawn up, her arms wrapped around her legs – and did not respond to Jack's greeting. Nick by contrast was all bright chatter about how the day was going to go and what an effect seeing their banner was going to have on people. Shirley and Adrian too arrived together and climbed into the back. Getting settled took a while as they had to arrange themselves around the banner which ran the whole length of the vehicle from the double back doors to the front windscreen. Then they set off.

Pretty soon they got to the M6. Some parts of the motorway hadn't been open that long; here the tarmac ran smooth and unmarked and there was very little other traffic. Still, Jack didn't feel safe pushing the buzzing green box above 65 miles an hour. Occasionally a coach would pass them with either North Vietnamese or Viet Cong flags or both, fluttering from its open windows or strung across the expanse of glass at the back. Somewhere near Birmingham the motorway ran out and they had to take lesser A roads to get to the M1 near Rugby. The little van was passing through a small Midlands town which resembled any other place except for the fact that every single person on the streets seemed to be from India when Claire suddenly shouted, 'Let me out!'

'What?' Jack asked, alarmed.

'Stop here. Let me out!' she yelled once more.

Jack pulled up beside a row of semi-detached houses outside of which a number of Sikhs were washing their brightly coloured cars. The back door of the mini van could not be opened from the inside though Claire hammered on the door, Jack clambered from his seat and opened it from the outside. The girl was breathing heavily and there were tears in her eyes as she unfolded herself. 'What's the matter?' he asked.

'Why don't you ask him?' Claire said, indicating Nick who sat in the passenger seat staring straight ahead as if nothing was happening behind him.

'I'm going home,' the girl said and turned and walked off back towards the town centre.

'How will you get home?' Jack shouted to her retreating form.

'I'll hitch.'

'Well what was that all about?' Jack asked as he climbed back into the driver's seat.

'I've no idea, my man,' Nick replied.

Once they got onto the M1 Jack pulled into Watford Gap Services for a break and to fill up on petrol. In the foyer outside the Top Tray self-service restaurant a sudden argument broke out between Shirley and Adrian over the role of non-violent versus violent action in the revolutionary struggle. Shirley could not believe that she was hearing for the first time that Adrian harboured pacifist sympathies and wasn't really that keen on the Viet Cong. He also told her that he was thinking of training as a Church of England vicar.

Shirley was not willing to share the van with such a counter-revolutionary and the last Jack and Nick saw of her, she was getting on a crowded coach bearing the banner of the Nottingham Branch of the Vietnam Solidarity Campaign. But then Adrian decided he couldn't face going on the demo either, so the last they saw of him he had climbed over a fence at the back of the services and was walking across a field full of curious cows.

In silence Jack ate steak pie, chips, a buttered roll and a cup of tea which cost four shillings and threepence which he thought was expensive. Nick said he couldn't see anything he fancied so only had a cup of coffee which he announced was terrible. They got back in the car and headed south.

Nick talked more or less the whole way about a thousand and one things. Jack stayed quiet. He thought that after all he didn't like Nick that much and he wished he'd paid for a radio.

The M1 stopped north of the London suburb of Hendon. The group's plan had been to park somewhere near the underground station then take the tube to Hyde Park where the demonstration was scheduled to begin in about an hour's time. The two men who remained might have got through the day if Nick hadn't said as they pulled up in a North London side street, 'That Claire eh, my man? Crazy bitch or what?'

After a few seconds Jack said, 'Fuck off, Nick.'

'What?'

'You heard. Fuck off, go away, leave, beat it, get away from me.' Making sure Nick could see, Jack reached down to a large metal wrench he used for work and tightened his fingers around it.

'You're crazy, my man!' Nick shouted, scrambling out of the passenger side door and hurrying down the street, checking every few seconds that the other man wasn't following him.

For a while Jack sat staring straight ahead, his fingers clenching and unclenching around the steering wheel, then finally he climbed from his seat, walked around to the back and pulled open the rear doors. He dragged the banner from the back of the van and laid it on the ground. Rolled up it was dull and lifeless but Jack knew when the banner was unfurled it could shine with a light so powerful it would change the lives of all those who saw it. But there was nobody to hold the other end.

THE ANTI-VIETNAM WAR DEMO

# Afterword: Grosvenor Square, 1968

## Russ Hickman

On Monday 18<sup>th</sup> March, 1968, the *Daily Telegraph* ran a front page that could have summed up the late sixties (at least, as they came to be viewed by history). Surrounded by predictably reactionary coverage of the previous day's anti-Vietnam demonstration, they ran a photo: a horde of young people sitting in the middle of the road, CND banners proclaiming support for the Vietnamese people; skinny ties, David Hockney spectacles, Frank Zappa moustaches, women with long flowing hair. One guy is singing or shouting something, his hands clapping manically. In appearance at least, they seem to epitomize the art school protesters of Sayle's story.

I didn't see this front page until the day after it came out. On the day of its publication I'd been in court, as a witness for my brother-in-law, who'd been arrested for 'assaulting a police officer'. Arriving back at work I was immediately sent to the Personnel Director's office to explain my absence. Normally, a quick word with my manager and an entry in the sickness book sufficed so I guessed something was up. But I was totally unprepared for what followed.

Personnel Director: 'You were off sick yesterday.'
Me: 'Yes, I had a sore throat.'
Personnel Director (theatrically throwing the *Telegraph* on the table): 'Is this you?'

Me (leaning in to carefully study a picture of me, my sister and my brother-in-law sitting at the front of a group of anti-Vietnam war demonstrators in Regent Street): 'Maybe.'

Personnel Director (without any sense of irony): 'If this happens again you will be sacked, we won't have anyone working for us damaging our reputation like this.'

Most of the demonstrations in the 1960s were indeed organised and populated by the kind of students depicted in Alexei's story; the number of people entering higher education had grown exponentially, and with this new army of students came a new political force. But many of those who took part on the day, like me, were not students, and had ordinary jobs, working for companies that were steeped in conservative cultures, both in the boardroom and the workplace. It wasn't just the Personnel Director who took my participation in this demo personally; my co-workers were also angry with this 'unpatriotic', 'communist-sympathising' behaviour. As news of my reprimand got round, I soon learned how hard it was to convince people who trusted their government and their country's media that not everything is at it seems.

Previous marches I'd been on had been fairly sedate affairs; cheerful walks with CND banners, lots of singing and chanting, my younger brother in a push chair shouting his first sentence 'Ban the Bomb', the Rev. Donald Soper on his soap box at Hyde Park corner. The only note of discord I recall was Randolph Churchill, agitated and red-faced, heckling us through a megaphone from his Rolls Royce. But the demonstration of March 1968 felt very different, more visceral; we knew people were dying in Vietnam whilst we were protesting. The US and UK were finding it hard to suppress the stories and photos of the atrocities being committed. Like many others I had just read Thich Nhat Hanh's *Vietnam: The Lotus in a Sea of Fire*, with its shocking cover photo of a Buddhist monk making the ultimate protest by immolating himself. The intensity of the war had risen steeply since the Tet Offensive by the North Vietnamese army a few months before and the US military appeared to be out of control in its rage to gain the upper hand. This, and the possibility that our own government was about to increase its involvement added an extra urgency to the day.

If there is such a thing as a natural demonstrator, then my brother-in-law, Eric, was your man. A confident and humorous orator, persuasive, brave and happy to challenge authority. As we marched down Regent Street and came to yet another standstill, the kind that happens on most protest marches, Eric seized the moment and called for us all to sit down. This seemed a good idea; the solidarity and good humour experienced at demos also comes at the cost of sore feet, sore throats and, when the crowd bunches up, the feeling that the air is being sucked from your lungs. Sitting down in a street normally bustling with traffic felt odd but I remember feeling grateful for the rest, the cooler air and the brief moment of peace. As is often the case in crowd situations, once two or three people heed the call others will follow. So after my sister and I sat down with Eric we soon had a 'sit-down demonstration'. 'Hey! Hey! LBJ! How many kids did you kill today?' went the chant. But someone who didn't join in, it turned out, was the *Telegraph* photographer.

Eventually we got up and resumed our march towards Trafalgar Square where Tariq Ali and Vanessa Redgrave were due to make speeches, but again the crowd bunched up and again we couldn't move forward. The police started to push people, including my sister who was 6 months pregnant, her presence on the demo an indication of the sort of day we had anticipated. Eric called out to the policeman to stop pushing as his wife was 'delicate', but the response he got was not what he expected. 'OK, arrest him', came a shouted command and the policeman dragged him off to the station. As Eric later explained, after being taken to the station the policeman who arrested him was sent back to the demo. When he reached the front of the queue of protesters waiting to be charged, the desk sergeant called out to an officer Eric hadn't seen before and said, 'This man hit you in the face, isn't that right officer?' 'Yes, sir,' came the reply.

My memory of the later stages of the demo consists of vivid events but vagueness on how one thing led to another. I remember the buzz going round about GIs positioned inside the American Embassy with loaded rifles. What I have no memory of is what possessed me to join the splinter group breaking through police lines into Grosvenor Square itself. The guilt I felt damaging a bush as I squeezed through the hedge into the square soon left me as I picked up stones and handfuls of dirt to throw at the US Embassy. I have no idea whether the stone broke the window, the light was fading and the noise of the crowd too loud to hear glass shattering. Not that it stopped me from boasting about it when it suited, and now, of course, I can claim that my my actions probably didn't hurt anyone.

But the most lasting memory of that day is of the mounted police charging towards us in Grosvenor Square. It wasn't so much the fear of getting hit or the clattering hooves of the horses; it was the whooping and screaming of the riders: police acting like warriors, rousing themselves before cutting down their enemy with their truncheons. As I looked around for a safe way out I noticed there weren't that many of us for them to charge at. I learned later that photographers and reporters had been cleared from the square and the police had already dragged many of the protesters away. But now there was no escape route; police enclosed us on all sides. This was clearly not an attempt to move us on, this was about teaching us a lesson.

I tried dodging the truncheons but man against horse is a one-sided sport and it wasn't long before I received a thwack to the back of the head. I can't remember how I got out of the square, just the glare of the camera lights and how the mood had darkened. Archive film shows big crowds in the square and evenly matched collisions between police and demonstrators. The absence of film-footage or photos from within the grassed area of the square, once dusk had fallen, will probably go unnoticed by all but those who were there.

As I finally emerged into the flashing bulbs and curious onlookers I just wanted to get as far away as I could. I had glimpsed behind the curtain of respectability that screens us from the workings of the state when it is under threat. A sight not easily forgotten.

# Rivers of Blood
## Stories in Two Voices

## David Constantine

ALICE MAPENDA: I REMEMBER THE SILENCE. Thinking about it, that's what first came back to me. If I remembered nothing else, that would be something, wouldn't it, the feeling of silence? But tell me – since I am very interested in the truth – did we really walk in silence?

HARRY CLAYTON: We did. And the people on the pavements, they stood in silence. Actually, to be precise, two voices were raised against us, separate voices, an elderly man, and ten minutes later another elderly man, they shouted out against us.

AM: You remember that?

HC: No, I read it. To be honest, I'm not sure I even remember the silence, not myself. But I've been reading up about it. The papers said we walked in silence, 'the coloured people' along the way stood in silence, and there were two hecklers, two elderly men. And apart from that: it was May Day, early evening, and it was raining.

AM: And we gathered at Rose Lane. You were already there.

HC: Yes, I was watching for you. To be honest, I was hoping you would come on your own, but you arrived hand in hand with Jack. I looked at you, the pair of you, for half a minute before you saw me. Funny how these things never die. It goes through me again and still, even now.

AM: It wasn't silent while we were gathering.

HC: No, there was the noise of an increasing crowd, that murmur, like starlings before they swarm, louder and louder, only the nearest voices speaking in words you could understand, the rest, the mass, all a murmur, the murmur of a gathering solidarity, like nothing else on earth.

AM: Unfolding the banners, handing out placards, the stewards going round. And before we set off everybody hushed.

HC: You remember that? So it must have been before we moved off that Jack said the lines. Jealousy is a horrible thing. He was still holding your hand. I can see his face, quite the most beautiful I ever saw on a man, and even then I knew in my heart that he wasn't showing off, he spoke very softly, not to you nor to me, more to himself, in a musing sort of way. Of course, I didn't understand what it meant, but even that wouldn't have mattered, only for the jealousy.

AM: 'O tandem magnis pelagi defuncte periclis!
sed terrae graviora manent. In regna Lavini
Dardanidae venient; mitte hanc de pectore curam;
sed non et venisse volent. Bella, horrida bella,
et Thybrim multo spumantem sanguine cerno.
non Simois tibi, nec Xanthus, nec Dorica castra
defuerint; alius Latio iam partus Achilles,
natus et ipse dea; nec Teucris addita Iuno
usquam aberit; cum tu supplex in rebus egenis
quas gentis Italum aut quas non oraveris urbes!

216

Causa mali tanti coniunx iterum hospita Teucris
externique iterum thalami.

HC: So you know it too?

AM: I learned it later, many years later.

HC: And he wasn't even reading Classics! Did he not do
Engineering?

AM: Yes, he did. He thought it would be more useful. And I
suppose he was right. Engineering would have been more
useful.

HC: Rose Lane. Then over Magdalen Bridge and round the
Plain. And on very slowly down the Cowley Road. Do you
know I'd never been down the Cowley Road before that
evening? If I ever crossed the bridge it was to go left to the
Moulin Rouge or right to the river. Never once till that 1ˢᵗ May
did I walk down the Cowley Road.

AM: Who did?

HC: I'll bet you and Jack did. I'll bet you leafleted at the
Cowley Works.

AM: So what if we did? The past isn't everything. You can't live
off the past.

HC: You're not like me. I have to keep persuading myself there
was once a time of hope and I lived then and acted hopefully
and thousands around me were doing the same.

AM: You mean to say you can't live hopefully now without
believing there was a hopeful time back then, half a century ago?

HC: No, I can't. Can anyone live without believing in such a past?

AM: Millions have no such past. And most of those who do, live without ever giving it a thought.

HC: Still I do live like that. Seeing you again makes me know it. It's a way of the imagination. Convince yourself there was once a time of hope, really, here on earth. Believe it. Better still: remember it. Remember you were there.

AM: By 'remember' you mean read up about it?

HC: I remember the feeling of the occasion, I read up the real details if they're anywhere still to be found.

AM: Tell me some. Perhaps we're not so very different, you and I. Tell me a few of the details you have unearthed.

HC: Heath sacked him from the Shadow Cabinet. London dockers and meat-porters went on strike and marched to the Houses of Parliament. They wanted him reinstated, they wanted him for the next prime minister. Our little march − not that little, the biggest since Cuba, two thousand or so − our little march was eleven days after his speech, on May Day, International Labour Day, Red Flag Day. Ruskin called for it. Listen to this: 'There must be many people in Oxford who would like to express their dismay at the recent upsurge of racialist innuendo. A whole complex of insecurities has emerged, which put in question this country's entire moral and social state. The fate of the immigrants has been discussed as though they were so much scrap, to be shunted hither and thither as the vagaries of opinion − and the movements of the economy − heartlessly dictate.' *Cherwell* carried a photo of an Oxford student, an Anarchist by the name of Piers Greenwood − did you know him?

AM: Maybe. But I wasn't with the Anarchists then.

HC: In the photo he was shown on the ground being kicked by pro-Powell dockers. It was in London at a printmakers demonstration. Apart from that, the Race Relations Bill was being debated in Parliament. The Nigerian government were slaughtering Igbos with British arms and employing famine as a weapon of war. *Rebel without a Cause* was on again at the Scala.

AM: Yes, I went to see it with Jack. He didn't much like it. He said there were any number of causes. Open your eyes. Look around.

HC: To be honest, I'm not sure I'd have gone on that march but for you. And when you turned up with Jack I felt there was no point me being there and if I'd had the nerve I'd have left you to it.

AM: Then you'd have missed something good. It was an occasion, like Grosvenor Square or the big Iraq War demonstration. Surely you were glad to have been there?

HC: Yes, I was glad. Trouble with me is, I'm often gladder afterwards. Sometimes *long* afterwards. That may be because it takes me a long time to take things in. So perhaps when a thing is happening and when I'm there I'm not quite sure whether to be glad or not. That march from Rose Lane, down the Cowley Road, right at James Street, back down the Iffley Road, down the High and Cornmarket to St. Giles, I thought about it on and off for several years, along with much else in that particular year, and, yes, I was glad I had been there. But only these last few weeks, knowing I'd see you again after half a century, did I set myself to remembering all I could and to reading up on what I couldn't, and then, like two or three other events in that same year, the silent march through the immigrant area became very clear and luminous to me, and I am deeply glad of it. I looked for us, the three of us, in all the photos I could uncover but was never sure of a sighting, though the *type* – you and me, at least – was everywhere visible. I didn't see Jack. He was a rarer kind and it's a pity I saw no photograph of him. There were several of the people along the route. They were watching with great attention. My impression now – I don't know how I felt then – is that they didn't quite know what to make of us, or of it, the occasion, but at least they knew our incursion into their territory was friendly.

AM: There was a banner – Somerville International Socialists, if I remember rightly – it said: 'WOULD YOU LET YOUR DAUGHTER MARRY ENOCH POWELL?' Do you remember it?

HC: Can't honestly say I do – not the thing itself, so to speak. But I came across it in my reading up. If it wasn't Somerville, it was St. Anne's. What did your mother and father say to you marrying Jack?

AM: We didn't tell them. I only took him home after we'd done it. I wasn't very considerate in those days. They didn't exactly shut the door in our faces but nor did they ask us to stay. So after a couple of hours and nobody saying very much we walked back to the railway station.

HC: Why did you marry him?

AM: Because I loved him.

HC: Quite a few of your sort – of our sort – had given up on marriage by then.

AM: He got citizenship, but that's not why we did it. But just as well we did, as things turned out. I was pregnant when he left, though he didn't know that. He was dead when Elsa was born, though I didn't know that. I went home and they took me in. They took me back into their hearts when the baby was born, and when I learned her father was dead they kept me safe in the land of the living when all I wanted was to go down among the dead.

HC: I wrote you a letter when I heard about Jack. Perhaps you never got it? I wrote to College, I thought they would forward it.

AM: They did.

HC: You never wrote back.

AM: But I read your letter and I was grateful to you.

HC: I supposed you thought it would encourage me if you wrote back.

AM: What have you done with your life, Harry? Forgive me for asking, I always wonder and if they're still alive and I meet them I always ask people who knew Jack what they have done since he got killed.

HC: I don't mind you asking. I do the same. I often ask myself what I've been doing since Jack died, and not only Jack, three or four others besides him, I ask myself what I've been doing, what am I doing now, in the time that has been allowed me beyond theirs. Well, I've done various things, none of them heroic, nothing you'd put up in the firmament and that people would look out for at nights and be thankful for and be steadied and orientated by, nothing like that, nothing fit to be up there among the deeds of my own pantheon of saints and heroes.

AM: What, then?

HC: This and that, different forms of the same idea, I'd say. For nearly twenty years I had a partner called Masouda. She was much younger than me but we couldn't have children. She died not long ago. Anyway, we opened a library together, we called it the People's Library. It's still going, still called that, up five rickety flights of stairs in a part of town they keep saying they'll develop one day but they never have and now there's no money so with any luck they never will. Quite a big room when you get there and all the books properly in order around the walls. People donate books, and pamphlets, newspapers, posters, all sorts of ephemera. Only last week an old lady left us a suitcase of stuff from the Munich Soviet, priceless. Once a month there's a talk and a discussion. We've had speakers from all over the world, we're on the network, it's almost the old International, the idea of it at least, the survival, the new beginnings, who knows? When nobody else offers, Masouda or I would do something. Her last talk was about women in the Commune. Everybody's heard of Louise Michel, but there were others, many others, needless to say, making a start at least in that brief interlude of a possibility of justice. I'm giving a talk on Kropotkin next Thursday. It's hard without Masouda, quite a struggle, to be honest, but it's like with Jack, I'm alive and he isn't, I'm alive and Masouda isn't, they need me, if you take my meaning, in a way none of the living do. Did you ever blame Jack for going to Mozambique?

AM: Yes, I did. Not when he left. When I was twenty-three I didn't believe in death. A year later I did, and I felt I would never forgive him for going away and dying when I needed him so much. When Elsa was old enough, I told her the whole story. She was furious. Typical man, she said. Typical stupid man.

HC: Does she still feel that?

AM: Yes, I think she does. She forgives him, but she still thinks he owed allegiance to me first, not to an idea. When FRELIMO notified me of his death – on a cyclostyled form with a gap for the name – they sent me also, wrapped up in silver paper from a cigarette packet, the silver ring I had bought him in a junk shop on Folly Bridge. It was in the form of two entwining snakes, good magic, we said, against all evil. I wrote to the office in Dar Es Salaam, asking could they tell me where and in what circumstances he had been killed, but I got no answer. I wrote three more times and never got any answer. Then when the War of Liberation was won, I made a plan to go to Maputo, leaving Elsa with my parents, to discover what I could about Jack myself. But almost at once the Civil War began, and lasted another fifteen years, and I felt very bitterly that he had laid down his life for just the usual human mess. Why do you like Kropotkin? I know I used to, half a century ago.

HC: Because he was born into privilege and moved from that into revolt. Once a *page de chambre* of Czar Nicholas I, in 1882 he came to the Durham coalfields, he went into the pit villages, he talked to the miners and their families in the hovels they rented from the Company. He wore a working man's cap, which he took off on entering. That bald head, that big grizzled beard, that look of wondering innocence, he must have appeared to them like a visitation from another world, one in which the brotherhood of man was already achieved and he had come to spread the word of it to those who needed it first and most, the poor, the labouring classes, to foster solidarity for their struggle. He addressed their Big Meeting! I often think of that. His life had a purpose and a shape, it is fit to be looked at. And here's a thing – one of those emblematic moments: Escaping from prison in 1876, he crossed Russia and Sweden as fast as possible and spent a few days at Christiania, hoping for a passage to England. Seeing a likely steamer – let me read you this bit: 'I asked myself with anxiety, "Under which flag does she sail, – Norwegian, German, English?" Then I saw floating above the stern the Union Jack, – the flag under which so many refugees, Russian, Italian, French, Hungarian, and of all nations, have found an asylum. I greeted that flag from the depths of my heart.'

AM: I learned the other day that Powell wrote poetry. Every year he gave his wife a poem on her birthday.

HC: Yes, that's right. I read up about him in the *DNB*. He married Margaret but really, in his early years at least, like A. E. Housman, he preferred young men. And he wrote like Housman: 'The years that took my youth away,/ They brought to me instead/ The hunger that from day to day/ On other youth is fed…' And, also like A. E. H., he applied himself to the editing and explication of obscure ancient texts. Few know anything about the Rendel Harris Papyri, for example, but he knew all there was to know. That seems to have been part of the discipline: a sort of chosen pointlessness, meaningful as an act against the pointlessness of human existence because you yourself chose it. A scholar, a poet, master of many languages (including Urdu), 'a fine mind', fiercely independent, nobody's lobby-fodder, in that year after the Sexual Offences Act, had he gone back to young men and classical scholarship, he might well have caused no trouble to anyone. But instead it was Smethwick again: 'If you want a nigger for a neighbour, vote Labour!' And ancestral voices, his at least, prophesying rivers of blood.

AM: 'At length having passed through the sea's great perils
Worse awaits you on land: oh rest assured, Trojans
You *will* come to Lavinium, and coming there
Will wish you had not. Wars, horrific wars
I see and the Tiber foaming with much blood.
Simois again and Xanthus and the encamped Greeks
Again, in other shapes, and in Latium another Achilles
Born, like him, of a goddess and nowhere will Juno
Let you rest but you in your dire need to every tribe and city
Of Italy will go begging, and the cause of so many ills
Again will be a bride who is a stranger among the Trojans
Again will be marriage to a foreigner.'

HC: If it was only the Tiber. After the Siege of Magdeburg in 1631 the Elbe couldn't move for corpses – she was quite choked, couldn't take any more, halted, clogged up. And that was back then, by our standards quite a trivial slaughter. I often think of the *effort* of the old massacres, Constantinople, say, or Chios, the terrible labour of it. Born when we were, Alice, our generation, I've often said we're the living emblem of the beginnings of the makings of a fair society – the Education Act, the Labour government, the NHS, the welfare state, the chance for all our citizens to realise themselves – then, after 1979, the counter-revolution, the systematic rolling of it back, to the state we are in now. That's one way of looking at our social selves. Another is blood – rivers, lakes, seas, oceans of blood – the inescapable, all-pervasive knowledge of the shedding of so much blood: the opening of the camps, Belsen and Auschwitz, Hiroshima and Nagasaki, the Nakba, Korea, Vietnam, Biafra, Cambodia, Ruanda, the Balkans, on and on and on, the mass graves, the trials, the films, the memoirs, the exhibitions of photographs, the forever increasing archives, the *consciousness*, the unexpungeable knowledge of what we have done, of what we have let happen. Look at us that way, we are steeped, steeped, steeped in blood and our waking and dreaming lives are brimful with the knowledge of it. A man helps in our People's Library, he shelves the books when our borrowers have returned them. He speaks rarely and with great difficulty. He has come out of Syria with his wife and three children. He tells me that when his children first went to school here he stood at the gates all morning, fearful of what might happen to them inside. Advised he must spend a night in hospital here, in England now, to mend at least one of his physical injuries, he did not dare to, he refused, he fled. Hospitals and schools, for him, are places that get bombed.

AM: Where was Masouda from?

HC: Her family were driven off their land in Palestine and finished up in the camps. She was born in Shatila. When we fell in love and admitted it to one another she asked could she come and live with me in my house but have a room of her own and not sleep together for twelve months. I agreed, though I didn't want to wait even twelve minutes. I gave her my big bed upstairs and slept on a couch in my study-cum-lumber room downstairs. That was the arrangement and I didn't ask her why it had to be. I viewed it as an ordeal such as a lover might have agreed to in a legend. I supposed that in her tradition there might still be a *pudeur* long gone in mine. So the year passed and in that chasitity I loved her more and more. On the first evening of our new life we ate together as always, then she moved my things upstairs and we went to bed. In the dark, after we had made love, she told me the waiting year had nothing to do with modesty but she had wanted to try in that time, sleeping apart from me in my house, whether she could get rid of or at least reduce the violence of her nightmares. In the massacre of 1982, when she was four, all her family – mother, father, two brothers, two sisters – were butchered. Her mother hid her under a pile of bedding. Hours later, when she crawled out, she saw what had been done.

AM: And the nightmares?

HC: No, wherever these things live in a person, there they still lived. But they tortured her less often and when they did I was with her, she was in my arms, I helped. She was ashamed and it made her miserable. She said she had not wanted to infect me with all that, she loved me, it was horrible to bring me that, as she put it, for her dowry. But over the years her sleep got quieter and deeper, for weeks at a time not once did she wake screaming. Then would come another bad phase, but it passed, it always passed. I woke more often than she did, I woke and lay listening to her quiet breath, and I was gladder of that than of anything else ever in my life.

AM: I live just round the corner from Elsa and her family. She and her husband are both teachers. They have three children.

Coming here today, I was early for our meeting, so I walked the first part of the march to see what I might remember. I walked from Rose Lane to James Street and down as far as the Iffley Road. Then it was nearly time to meet you, Harry, and I turned back to the Cowley Road. The traffic had halted at the zebra crossing outside Sainsbury's and two classes from the primary school were being shepherded across by their teachers and the teaching assistants. They were Foundation Year, I should say, they were hand in hand, boys and girls mixed, and many looks and colours and kinds of dress, all mixed. They passed between a red double-decker bus and a cement transporter and the bus-driver and the truck-driver had clasped their hands and were leaning on the steering wheel and looking down at the children and smiling. The two T.A.'s, an elderly woman from, perhaps, Kerula, and a young woman from, I should say, Somalia, both beautifully costumed, were in among the children who were local and exotic, each of them distinctive and all, hand in hand, moving as a body, with a noise like a brook. They crossed over with a babbling, their language ran like a small clear river. I closed my eyes for a few seconds, just to listen, and as I listened I saw the living waters, I saw the streams of my childhood in the country of my heart. And when I looked again, there in the sunlight the children were crossing, hand in hand, safely, and people had halted on the pavements either side and were watching, all manner of people, all the mix of those streets, had halted to watch. The teachers and the teaching assistants, looking anxious, ushered their charges across and people stood to watch and were smiling. Then it was done. The teachers waved to the drivers, the traffic started up, and the children passed two by two, with the merriment of a stream, towards their school.

# Afterword: April-May, 1968

## Prof. Stephen Constantine
University of Lancaster

THE MAY DAY MARCH in Oxford in 1968, which my brother David joined, was a protest against Enoch Powell's notorious 'Rivers of Blood' speech, delivered in Birmingham on 20th April and widely publicised in national newspapers. In it, among many scurrilous assertions, he had predicted that racial conflict would be the result of allowing so many 'coloured' immigrants to enter the UK. But the Oxford march was not the most representative reaction. True, there were demonstrations and letters of protest by staff and students in other university towns (for example, Nottingham, Cambridge, Sheffield and London). Christian churches also in more sober fashion condemned Powell's comments, and it is important to record that representatives of Sikhs and other immigrant communities themselves objected publicly to Powell's inflammatory remarks and the discrimination they were experiencing. An editorial in *The Times* condemned his 'Evil Speech', and Edward Heath, the Conservative party leader, dismissed him from his shadow cabinet.

Nevertheless, demonstrations, petitions and letters *in support* of Powell by Smithfield market porters, London dockers, steelworkers, immigration officers, many trade unionists, and several national and local political representatives made more conspicuous headline news. Opinion polls calculated that around 70 per cent of the nation agreed with Powell. He claimed to have received over a 100,000 letters of support (and a mere 800 or so of dissent). In his home patch, 700 members of the North Wolverhampton Working Men's Club agreed unanimously to continue its ten-year-old colour bar. There were predictable responses from Oswald Mosley (founder of the British Union of Fascists), Colin Jordan (leader of the National Socialist Movement) and other right-wing organisations, including the National Front (formed the previous year). Student members of York University Conservative Association added their pennyworth of support.

Historically there had been few formal restrictions on immigrants from any source wishing to settle in the UK. Indeed, literally for centuries, migrants had usually been free to enter a Britain which acquired a largely justified reputation as a haven of liberty and a land of opportunity for all, including the politically and economically oppressed. More pertinently, by the legal doctrine of *jus soli*, all those born in crown territories, whether in the UK or in the overseas Empire and irrespective of ethnicity, were regarded as equal subjects of the crown. By that privileged status they were all supposedly free to enter and live on equal terms in the UK, or in any other British territory (though this was an entitlement denied increasingly to those with unacceptable skin colour seeking to enter white settler societies like Australia). However, an Act of 1905, particularly targeting Jews fleeing poverty and pogroms in continental Europe, had made the entry of aliens into the UK a discretionary rather than automatic right. These constraints were tightened by an Act in 1919 and subsequent Aliens Orders. Under their cover, and by other administrative devices, official efforts were also made, discreetly, to discourage the permanent settlement in the UK not just of aliens but of black and Asian British subjects from overseas, especially seamen, and, later, even those who had come to Britain and had served the 'mother country' during the Second World War. The covert aim was to keep Britain 'white' – and therefore 'British'.

Post-war, as the country stepped towards decolonisation, the British Nationality Act of 1948 distinguished for the first time between 'Commonwealth Citizens', that is those belonging to independent states within the Commonwealth, and 'Citizens of the UK and Colonies', therefore including the many millions of British subjects in the still very numerous British colonial territories. This distinction was not intended to affect rights of entry, and did not. The UK remained open to immigration by both classes of citizens – and even from the Republic of Ireland. Indeed, initially after 1945, most new arrivals were from Ireland, as so often in the past, or were resettled Poles and displaced persons from continental Europe, not always locally welcomed it should be said. However, immigrants were soon arriving from Commonwealth and colonial territories in the West Indies, Africa and South Asia. This movement had by the 1950s begun to make the arrival of 'coloured' immigrants into a still almost entirely 'white' society a political issue. The country was being obliged to address the consequences of its imperial past and consider its post-imperial future.

As commonly with migrants there were 'push factors'. Under-investment and unemployment in the British Caribbean, one of the slum areas of Britain's proud empire, prompted many to escape to the UK. Political, demographic and economic instabilities caused by the 1947 break-up of the Raj into independent India and Pakistan, coupled with localised population growth and land hunger, spurred others to migrate. Decolonisation was also unsettling for the Asian communities displaced by the Africanisation policies of newly independent East African states. Among the 'pull factors' were the experiences of those from the Empire overseas who had been in Britain during the war in the armed services or in war work, and were keen to return. A few immigrants, especially from the West Indies, were also officially recruited to meet a post-war labour shortage, particularly in public sector jobs (London Transport and the NHS). Others were attracted by career opportunities in education, the arts, entertainment and sport. (As an example, unrelated to David and myself, Learie Constantine, born in Trinidad, arrived and played cricket for Lancashire, and later served on the Race Relations Board.) Some arrived and opened restaurants and liberated the UK from a regime of 'meat and two veg'. (There were 1,200 Indian restaurants in Britain by 1970, 8,000 by the end of the century.) Moreover, as so often with transnational migration, information about opportunities flowing back from pioneers encouraged family and friends to follow, in the process known as chain migration. Naturally, and again in common with transnational migrants elsewhere, new arrivals were drawn to the culturally familiar, in food, fashion and values, and formed or joined immigrant communities in which they could also get advice and secure practical support in finding accommodation, in raising their families (for most were young), in accessing public services, in obtaining employment and in setting up enterprises (for many were energetic and ambitious). In such communities they were also more protected from the hostility often encountered and were more able to cope with disappointed hopes. And once settled, again in common with other transnational migrants, the established often funded the immigration of other family members (spouses, children, siblings, parents), thus accelerating the effect of chain migration.

Exact numbers are unknown, but Home Office figures suggest net immigration between 1955 and 1960 of 160,000 West Indians, 33,000 Indians and 17,000 Pakistanis. So-called 'coloured' people – immigrants and their descendants – probably numbered fewer than 50,000 in 1951, but rising nearer to 500,000 by 1961, though still forming less than 1 per cent of the UK's population. By 1980, with more arrivals and the birth of children in the UK, the proportion had risen to just over 4 per cent, around 2.2 million. Within those aggregated national figures were the far higher proportions in particular places, another natural consequence of the process of chain migration which had precedents in the earlier formation of, for example, Jewish, Irish and German communities in UK cities. By 1971, three-quarters of the West Indian-born, two-thirds of the Pakistani-born and over half of the Indian-born population, but only one-third of the British-born, were living in the seven officially defined conurbations of London, Manchester, Birmingham, Leeds-Bradford, Liverpool, Newcastle and Glasgow. Concentrations in particular districts and streets were of course even more apparent.

Too little attention was paid in public discourse to the contribution which disproportionately young and enterprising migrants were making to the UK's economy, as workers, entrepreneurs and in the professions; to how they were offsetting the ageing of a host population in which the birth rate from the 1950s was generally falling, while life expectancy among the elderly and retired was increasing; and to how additional 'stock' was contributing positively to the nation's cultural awakening and diversity. Of course, young immigrants and families needed homes and school places and sometimes the assistance of social services, although mainly being young they drew proportionately less than the UK-born on the NHS (except for maternity services), in which indeed some of them worked as doctors and nurses.

The prejudice and outright hostility which black and Asian immigrants encountered was not without precedent in the UK (or in other countries), as Jewish, Irish, Italian and German immigrants had experienced in their time. But racial animosity directed at 'coloured' immigrants ran deeper. The letters which Powell received in such huge numbers in 1968 and public utterances in his support expose a resentment at the ending of Empire and the unmooring of notions of white supremacy and of racial hierarchy entrenched in indigenous British culture. Assumptions long nourished in popular literature, in the press, in music halls, in films (including Hollywood imports), in commercial advertising (soaps that made even the 'nigger' white), and, with an Empire bias, in the teaching of history and geography in schools were being assaulted. 'Over there' was the 'other' which helped define who 'we' are; and now the 'other' was here, the culturally 'alien'. Particularly provocative in that context was the sight of black guys dating or worse still marrying white girls, to which Kit de Waal's story in this volume so powerfully attests.

Many white families in marginalised districts of big cities had reasonable complaints about low wages, poor housing, high rents and over-strained (in reality under-funded) public services including their kids' schools. But black and Asian immigrants as intruders were seen as responsible. Some, already disturbed by the 'permissive society' and white British youth culture, deplored the cultural impact of 'these people', with their strange dress, discordant music, 'smelly' food, supposed criminal tendencies and imagined infectious diseases, and the alien religious practices which seemed to be central to their communities. Moreover, all that was apparently destabilising of traditional white British working-class communities had been imposed upon them from above without consultation, consent, advice or support, and this was resented. 'They' had done this to 'us', and only Enoch was speaking up.

As noted, post-war governments had been endeavouring covertly to limit 'coloured' immigration. Anything more transparent had been resisted by some Whitehall departments and government ministers sensitive to much still prevailing liberal sentiment in the UK, and concerned also about the effect of restrictive legislation on political relations with the multiracial Commonwealth, to which the UK purported still to provide moral as well as political leadership. There was also the complex practical problem of how to limit undesirable 'coloured' immigrants while allowing entry to citizens from the 'white' Commonwealth and to the still far larger numbers arriving from the Irish Republic. It was not in the end any evidence of public disorder, not even the riots provoked by white youths in Nottingham and Notting Hill in 1958, which prompted restrictive legislation. It was, rather, the failure of administrative measures to prevent a sudden increase in immigrant numbers from the West Indies and South Asia, rising to 136,000 in 1961, and exaggerated concerns about the potential effect of (only) such immigrants on housing, employment and social order, which prompted government at last to legislate.

Overt racial discrimination was still to be avoided, but such was the administrative intention behind the Conservative government's Commonwealth Immigration Act of 1962. It required immigrants from the Commonwealth and colonies to have obtained an employment voucher, issued either because they had the promise of a job, or had desirable skills, or had secured one of the vouchers available to some of the unskilled; or had evidence that they could support themselves, or were students. In 1965 the Labour government reduced the number of vouchers for the skilled, abolished vouchers for the unskilled, and tightened regulations on the admission of dependants. When Asians with UK passports faced discrimination and later expulsion by post-colonial governments in East Africa, Labour's response in 1968 was to restrict their entry by imposing quotas, unless they, a parent or grandparent had been born in the UK. Then, in 1971, the Conservative government finally scrapped the distinction between 'aliens' and 'British subjects', and restricted automatic entry to 'patrials' – to British or Commonwealth citizens who could prove, especially, that they, their parents or their grandparents had been born in the UK. The bias in all this legislation towards admitting people of 'white' origins was thinly disguised. Nevertheless, the generation of a multiracial UK continued, helped by the continuing admission (though increasingly restricted) of family dependants. The 1971 Act came into force on 1$^{st}$ January 1973, when, by coincidence, the UK joined the European Economic Community and thereby accepted unrestricted entry into the UK of citizens of what came to be called the EU. The UK had finally turned its back on Empire.

But it was not immigration as such which prompted Powell to speak out in 1968. Indeed, in public, he had been subdued about immigration, even though in his Wolverhampton constituency a substantial immigrant community had been forming. He became more articulate when out of government office following the 1964 election. Thereafter in speeches critical of what he saw as insufficient legislative constraints on immigration, Powell expressed a hostility to black and Asian immigration redolent of popular prejudices but also indicative of his own personal political history. Stationed in India during the war, he may once have aspired to be the Viceroy of India (he had learned Urdu in preparation). But decolonisation, the replacement of Empire with Commonwealth, and the too evident signs of Britain's decline as a great power, subordinated to the USA, turned Powell into a 'little Englander'. English political traditions and cultural values were to be resolutely defended, against the dilution and corruption which he saw as the inevitable consequences of unchecked immigration and, worse still, of an enforcing on the British people of a doctrine of multiculturalism. An extreme free market ideologue (except with respect to the free movement of labour), Powell objected to state legislation which constrained a citizen's right to choose with whom to do business, though his language and his target were informed by something even more virulent. Integration, he insisted, was not just impossible: it was undesirable. Hence Powell was objecting in 1968 to the Labour government's Race Relations Bill which was to make racial discrimination a criminal offence, not only in public places as had a rather toothless Act in 1965, but more generally in employment, housing and public services. Implicitly, multicultural diversity was to be accepted, and integration and mutual tolerance were to be required by law. It was this bill which provoked Powell, filled his postbag, divided political parties – and prompted Oxford's May Day march in its support.

Subsequently, though with rumbling dissent, too much institutionalised racism, and bad lapses, the UK seemed to mature into a post-imperial, multicultural, and outwardly more tolerant society. I defy anyone not to be moved by the celebration of diversity contained in the image of the children crossing Oxford's Cowley Road on the last page of David's story. However, while that image reflects the reality of many local communities in this country, we must record with dismay the anti-immigrant feeling and racial abuse whipped up by the lies and rhetoric of some of the anti-EU 'Leave' campaigners in the UK referendum in June 2016, some of it targeted not at EU citizens from continental Europe but at British-born descendants of post-war Commonwealth immigrants and other 'people of colour'. It leads to the painful sense that my brother's inspirational image remains as yet an aspiration. One is left hoping that a later generation will see fit to make it a reality.

# May Hobbs

## Maggie Gee

### I.

ANNA IS READING A tattered *Vogue* which has a feature about travel-writing. Something has enraptured her, a paragraph about the last remaining virgin forest in Siberia. '…Human foot never trod', she whispers. Birch, larch, shivering poplar. White. No-one had ever seen it, but in her mind she stands there, silent.

Her mother is going on from the kitchen. 'May Hobbs. She's like a watchword for me.'

'I've heard enough about May Hobbs,' sighs Anna, as the white leaves shiver.

'Everyone should know about May Hobbs. She said we had rights just like the blimmin' men.'

Anna leaves the Siberian *taiga*. In a second, she's back in Seabridge, on the old battleground with her mother. 'What did she go to prison for?'

This was a sore point, with Ma.

'Nothing, really. It was a stitch-up. Like the FBI and Hillary Clinton. This was Hoxton, remember, last century. They were always in and out of each other's houses. A feller dumped those coats on May… She was innocent, like Hillary is. Property is theft, in any case.'

'You should leave our front door open, then.'

Anna likes to have the last word. Her mother has got

237

worse since she started doing a politics degree for the Open University. All information makes her indignant: the weather, the gap between rich and poor, the growing lack of respect for education 'before I've had a chance to finish mine', and now Trump standing for president. Anna's ears burn. She longs for quiet, or anything that would stop Ma talking. Besides, it's influencing Kim, who is only ten, but getting stroppy. 'Let's put the TV on.' Anna grabs the remote.

But there he is, the yellow-gold quiff, the unsmiling face staring down at the crowd as if he is picking out tomorrow's dinner.

'That man's a wolf,' her mother says. 'You think he's funny, but mark my words...'

'Come on, he's a joke.'

'We won't be laughing.'

Sometimes Anna swam back in time, as the beloved, relentless voice went on, to twelve years ago, when she had left home 'for ever'. For ever turned out to be a couple of years. Just after the millennium. She was twenty-one. Everything... shone. She was going to be a poet, then.

The best thing about the flat Anna shared with Sven had been the shower. New, expensively imported from Sweden, with slats of pale wood transfigured by the light, the white, pure light from the frosted sun on the long window on the left. The rush of bright water, which was easy and ceaseless, stopped her hearing any noise the child made. In the first year of little Kim's life, Anna and Sven were going to get married. At first Anna's life with him was heaven: she had escaped the muddle of home, the stress of exams, Ma's expectations, she had her own child and her wealthy lover, though her mother disliked him on principle, for being Swedish and having money. The water poured down her straight pale limbs. She never wanted to leave that lit space, just stood there staring at her shrinking belly rinsed clean by the silvery sound of the water, and she was still a girl and Sven would stop shouting and start to call her his princess again, and her life would continue, a pure strong line with the power to go anywhere and everywhere.

Now, ten years after Kim was born, she and Sven have long parted, and Anna is heavier and slightly sadder, though she laughs a lot more, with a dry bright sound, and she is a woman in her thirties, no longer sure what to dream about.

Anna still writes poems, and lives with her mother – she never meant to, but 'It makes sense, Ma.' Her mother helps out with Kim, of course. But Ma has lots of course-work to do for her Open University degree, which she reminds Anna is 'no joke'. 'Politics, philosophy and economics'. Ma likes to say the words, with their clicking consonants and polysyllables and soft, important, brainy 'S'es. Her essay this month is on 'Politics of Protest'. May Hobbs is going to get dragged in. Anna laughed out loud when Ma told her the title: 'You'll get a distinction, you're always protesting.'

Ma will have a degree before her daughter does, for which Ma blames Sven, who was 'a middle-class wanker' who 'effed up your life because you had no sense.'

'He was the father of my child.' They bicker gently, mother and daughter, and sometimes savagely about Kim (Ma thinks Anna could make more effort), or bitterly about politics.

At the moment, it's the US Election. 'Stop going on,' Anna begs her. '*Obviously* Trump won't win.'

But Ma believes her daughter is 'clueless' about the way the world is run. 'He's going to win because he's a celebrity. Not that he's ever done anything. I'm ashamed of you. You just don't care. Your whole generation. You don't know you're born.'

'Have you changed the world, Ma?'

'At least we tried. I haven't given up, and nor should you.'

'Could I change the world?' Kim asks from the sofa where she is trying to do her homework.

'No,' says Anna.

'Yes,' says Ma.

The house they share is a Georgian terrace which one day might sell for decent money – 'silly money', Ma likes to say, though she has no evidence it's true. The house was gutted by the council in the eighties, with most of the original features removed: the Georgian banisters, the panelled doors. Ma bought it cheap as a sitting tenant from the life insurance when her husband died, though they still have a mortgage to repay which never seems to get much smaller. What is it now, twenty, thirty? There is no garden, just a yard, which Anna complains about: she loves flowers, and brings back a succession of pots which most of the time she forgets to water. She loves the names: amaryllis, lily. The stairs are too steep for Ma's arthritic knees and weren't easy for Anna when Kim was a toddler but they're used to it, all of them, though Ma and Anna both always say: 'It's just temporary.'

It was Anna who Ma had expected to move, her clever daughter, away and upwards, not into a flat with an 'effing Swede', but away, overseas, on her own account, flying, flying, far from Seabridge, with jobs, doctorates, fame, riches, the glittering prizes her daughter deserves as the second cleverest girl in the class – the cleverest one, Wendy, had gone off to Oxford and now makes millions in the City.

Ma reminds Anna about Wendy sometimes, and Anna is always quick to reply. 'Well you wouldn't want me to do that, because then I'd be an exploiter, right?'

'A few millions might come in handy.'

But Anna is dreamy, and a cleaner, like Ma, or as Ma was before her elbow got bad and she had to claim disability benefit (she still earns a bit as an Avon lady – walking's OK – and she likes the women to whom she sells cosmetics and 'affordable perfume' door to door, Sparkly Citrus Eau de Toilette or Rare Amethyst Eau de Parfum; she could sell more if she'd only pretend she used some of the goods herself.)

Ma isn't happy that Anna is cleaning but that's because she is 'old-fashioned,' as Anna kindly explains to her. 'It's a normal thing. Lots of my other friends do it, who could have *good jobs*, but they prefer this, they like the freedom. I'm not like you, it's not for ever.'

And yet, Anna is thirty-three. Day by day can turn into 'for ever'. Not all Anna's claims are to be trusted. What are those 'good jobs' her friends decline?

Anna still has plans, but they are as misty as the sea-view at the end of the road. It's October, and today she's off for an interview with 'this new lady' as Ma calls her, scornfully, a woman recently moved 'Down From London', a 'DFL', as Seabridge calls them.

2.

Irina Nemirovska is indeed a lady. Her great grandparents came to England after the Russian Revolution, having survived a long, expensive, zigzag flight through Europe during which they were forced to spend a lot of their money, so her great-grandfather hated Bolsheviks. His children rebelled by voting Labour and kicking out Churchill after the war, so *their* children, naturally, voted Tory, while Irina, by the blind logic of opposites, is a left-leaning former academic and writer. She would 'rather not have a cleaner', but she's 'lazy', she laughs, though she 'works all the time' – (she expects her friends to deny she's lazy) – and she can afford one, so why not? Besides, she likes to spread money around. That's how society should function, she thinks. Irina likes to help things along.

So far, she hasn't had a good morning. She's writing an article about 1970s activism. She knows her stuff, she used to teach it, she's assembled all her materials, but the voice to write it in – that eludes her. She's watched, once again, *Nightcleaners*, the black and white film about the office-cleaners who came out on strike in 1972. A little too 'arty', she thought, at first, but the more she watches it, the more it haunts her: the tired, wise faces of the women workers, or their figures, in long-shot, framed in lit office windows as they dusted other people's desks or emptied other people's waste-bins: moments of geometric beauty. She re-reads the transcript of what they said. One particular exchange burrows inward, unsettling.

*Voice Over: What would socialism mean to you?*

*Cleaner: …it's a life for the people. Yeah, it's a life for the working-class people. If that was possible, but that wouldn't be, could it? It couldn't be.*

*Voice Over: Why not?*

*Cleaner: Ohhh, it's asking for the moon, isn't it?…*

*Voice of shop steward: If people are strong enough, this is the thing.*

The way they talked. The way they hoped. Irina knows she can't catch that. And maybe she feels, obscurely, excluded. She copies the paragraph on to some paper and stares at it, shaken, stirred. What would socialism mean to you? It's a life for the people. Yes, it's a life for the working-class people. Ohhh, it's asking for the moon…

She walks around the house with the piece of paper, restless. Maybe Irina needs someone to talk to, but Seabridge is hardly likely to supply that. Not that she's lonely: or is she, actually? No, but she'd like – a kindred spirit.

History. It is so hard to catch. Looking backwards, it all looks obvious, the way the workers won their rights. But at the time, everything hung in the balance. Even the women didn't know it would happen. No, it was asking for the moon. And now, she thought. Brexit, Trump. Brexit happened, so maybe Trump…? No, impossible. Of course not. Is she getting old? She doesn't feel strong enough. Maybe the human race is doomed.

It's a relief when the doorbell rings. She opens it: there is a pale, dark girl. Oh yes, of course, the girl for the job. Irina has felt naked without a cleaner. What if one of her friends came down from London?

'Hello, I'm Anna' – the girl's shaking off rain. Intelligent face. A bit round-shouldered.

'Come in to the warm,' Irina says.

'Oh yes thanks, I'll just change my shoes. I wouldn't like to dirty your carpet –' but somehow, a leaf blows into the hallway.

Soon Anna's balanced on a gilt *fauteuil*.

'Do you have children?' Irina asks. She herself is the last in her family. The house is full of gold-framed photos, recently unpacked, thick on the surfaces as gleaming scales on butterflies' wings. She hopes the cleaner won't knock them over.

'One girl. Ten. That's why I'm doing this. So I can be there for her.' Anna smiles a virtuous smile, but secretly knows it's not true any more – Kim comes home and goes straight to her bedroom and stays on her phone until supper-time. She is putting on weight, and looks secretive, but Anna can't worry about everything, she will leave it to Ma, who worries for Britain.

'Good, of course.' Irina's sizing Anna up. Should she ask about her education? You didn't need it, though, to clean. 'I have a lot of books. I don't expect you to dust them – the most important thing is not to touch the ones I'm actually working on.'

'Are you a writer? I like books. And writers.'

'Do you? Why? A lot of them are ghastly,' Irina laughs, but thinking *Good*. 'I do write things. Articles mostly. A few books of political history.'

'Mum's always saying I should have been a writer. I did come top of English at school. But I didn't go to university.'

'You don't need to go to university to be a writer.'

'I still write poems, and other bits and pieces.' Anna can see Irina has lost interest. The old lady might have been a beauty, once. Under short white hair, her dark eyes slant upwards. High cheekbones and red lipstick. Gold chain, gold necklace. Anna's mother never wears lipstick, despite selling it to others for Avon.

'If you want to write, just go for it,' Irina says, with an air of finality, and puts her reading glasses back on.

Easy enough for you to say, Anna thinks, concealing irritation with a grateful smile. *You want me to be your cleaner, not a writer. You want to keep writing while I clean your loo, and I don't blame you, but don't pretend.*

'This woman,' adds Irina, indicating the paperback lying face down on the walnut table with a smiling, sturdy woman on the cover, 'wrote a brilliant book about her life, and she had no education to speak of. She was a cleaner, like you, but she became a writer...' (Her voice tails off. The girl's face was almost... hostile. None of her generation cared about history.)

'Ummm.' Anna's only half listening. 'My mother's into politics. But –'

'What does she do?'

'Well, she used to clean. Now she works for Avon.' Anna feels obscurely ashamed. 'But she's doing an OU degree in politics.'

'The Avon Foundation?' says Irina, smiling, though somehow the name doesn't sound quite right. 'They run creative writing courses, don't they? Several of my former pupils have been.'

'Do they? Ma never mentioned that.'

'They are a splendid institution.'

'Ma's more on the selling side.'

Something Irina said earlier has got under Anna's skin. About the woman who was 'a cleaner, like you'.

'I think of myself as someone who cleans,' she says, with a spurt of animation.

'Yes?' says Irina, not understanding.

'Not – a cleaner,' Anna explains. 'I don't define myself as a cleaner. I do lots of things. We're all, you know, players in the gig economy.'

(It is a phrase she has only just learned. It caused an argument with her mother, who shouted 'No, you're wrong, you're WORKERS. You have forgotten you are all WORKERS. You're not just, like, separate molecules.' Later she heard Kim shouting in the bath, just trying it out: 'I'm a WORKER, right? I am a WORKER.')

'So I'm not, you know, just a cleaner.'

'No, I see.' A longer pause. After all, a cleaner was what Irina wanted, someone who would really do the work. 'You do like cleaning, though?' she probes. There's something dreamy about the girl. Also, an edge of discontent.

*It's not a fucking hobby,* Anna thinks. But 'Of course,' she replies, 'I like to do a good job.' There's some truth in that. It's nice when it's done and the whole house smells of synthetic citrus. Summer breeze: lemon trees.

'That's reassuring,' says Irina drily, and laughs to show she has a sense of humour, then tries to cover her face with her hand.

Beautiful ring, Anna notices. Heavy gold, with a ruby-red stone. 'How much do you pay?' she blurts, slightly rudely, but the woman doesn't look offended and, after an infinitesimal pause, names a sum one third above the going rate. 'That'll be fine,' Anna says quickly.

Of course, she thinks, she is a DFL, they are all mad, but she can afford it.

In fact, this isn't strictly true. Guilty that the girl's a would-be writer, Irina has added over a pound to the hourly rate she had meant to offer. It's a hefty slice from her academic pension.

Not that she has to live on that, but her father told her, 'Never touch your investments.' The new house is another investment – Seabridge is said to be coming up. But she has kept the house in Chiswick.

'When could you start?' Irina asks. 'I do like a really clean kitchen and bathroom.' She knows she should have said that before she made the offer.

'Course,' says Anna. 'I'm really clean. Have you read my references?'

In fact, she hasn't sent any. Not all employers are reasonable… occasionally there have been disputes. 'I posted them first class,' she adds. 'But you know, the post is hopeless here.'

'Oh, I don't tend to bother with references,' Irina says. 'I follow my instincts.'

(Does she? In fact, she is questioning her instincts, which are to say 'Yes' and get this over. There's a glint of hunger and recognition in the way the girl looks around the room, at the polished wood and the wall-to-floor bookshelves Irina has built at great expense.)

She would like the tables to be turned, Irina guesses: she should be writing, and I should be cleaning. Her generation want to inherit. They hate the baby boomers, clinging on. She doesn't understand I'm *Russian*, so I'm not part of all that nonsense. I grew up in Chiswick, 'little Russia'.

'So I'll start Wednesday,' Anna says as she leaves, and gives a specially dazzling smile.

'Er, wonderful. But no sprays,' says Irina. 'And nothing that turns the loo orange.'

'Course,' says Anna, though all her stuff is sprays (so much faster, and they scent the air, giving the clients the 'feel-good' factor. Irina will never know the details: most of Anna's clients, embarrassed, stay well out of the way while the cleaning happens.)

'Did you see that monstrous thing Trump said?' Irina asks, as Anna dallies on the doorstep, putting on her outdoor shoes. 'About molesting women?'

'Oh him. He's nuts,' Anna says happily. 'See you soon! Have a great weekend!'

That was an odd thing to say, her new employer muses, because it's only Thursday. Some of us work harder than others, she thinks.

She closes her front door on the November rain and goes back to reading May Hobbs's *Born to Struggle*. Such a brilliant memoir! Such a splendid story! Yet the young woman seemed to have no interest.

3.

'What's she like?' Ma asks, when she and Anna are unwinding over a property programme on TV (*Escape to the Country*: they both love it, because for once they feel they are ahead, both of them live in the country already, and it's fun to watch clapped-out bankers from the City who are gagging to live in places like Seabridge. Though is Southwold, Suffolk, *entirely* like Seabridge? – Ma has a momentary twinge of unease.)

'What's *who* like?'

'The DFL? Your interview?'

'Oh. All right. Good money. Feels guilty.'

'I know the type. Can't be bothered with them.'

'She was OK. The house was lovely.' Anna is gazing at the screen, where a beautiful Victorian gothic tower is going for a million pounds even though it is falling into the sea. *I might never have a home of my own.* She pushes this desolate truth away. 'Lots of books. Political.'

'Political? Do you mean UKIP?'

'Socialist. Doesn't like Trump.'

Ma chokes on her pizza, personally affronted. *She* is the political one. How could someone employing her daughter as a cleaner claim to be a socialist?

'Hypocrite,' she says, her mouth open, tomato on her upper lip, and Anna, repelled, looks back at the screen.

'Well I like her,' she says, untruthfully. 'Maybe we'll be friends,' she adds for good measure.

'Pigs might fly,' Ma says, with finality, but stung with jealousy, as Anna intends.

Three weeks went by, which meant nine hours of cleaning. Everything was going smoothly. It was always best to make an effort at first, so clients were favourably impressed.

Besides, Irina seemed nice. So far there had been no complaints. She offered Anna coffee on arriving and leaving, and thanked her profusely when she left.

Last week she'd been about to throw away a red leather coat, only slightly worn but too small for her, beautifully cut, with a red leather hood, and she offered it to Anna, instead. 'It looks so much better on someone young and lovely,' Irina said, and her eyes were happy. 'By the way, I liked what you did with the cushions.' Anna had sloped the cushions on the bed in gentle, graduated mounds of cream, whereas Irina just piled them on at random.

'I like to make a room look pretty,' said Anna. She'd have liked her own bedroom to look like that, with everything creamy, and soft lighting, and orchids growing, palest pink and vanilla. Whereas her own bedroom was still painted the purple she'd demanded as a teenager. Ma had insisted they do Kim's room first. Sometimes Anna fears Ma loves Kim best. They have identical, determined jaw-lines.

'You have an artist's eye,' said Irina, remembering the girl wanted to write. She thought, on the whole, the arrangement was working, but one slightly odd thing had happened that morning. She'd found Anna sitting on the striped chair on the landing, holding a piece of paper in her hand. It was the sheet on which Irena had written the haunting paragraph from the transcript: '... a new life for the working-class people. But it wouldn't be, could it. It couldn't be.'

The girl had jumped like a guilty rabbit. 'Just having a tiny rest,' she said. 'I was reading this. I like the words.'

'Really? Well, you could copy it out. I mean, as soon as you've finished the cleaning.'

Yes, the girl was a dreamer, and slow. By the time she had finished, it was long gone lunch-time, but Irina still offered her a drink, and Anna seemed keen to sit and talk. Eventually Irina had to say something.

'Have you finished your coffee? I've got to get on.'

'OK if I copy that bit of paper?'

'Yes, but do it now, I've got a deadline.'

'What kind of deadline?' Anna asked, miffed. She wasn't quite ready to go back to Kim, who had been acting up at school, but she swallowed her coffee, burning her throat, and started to put on the leather coat.

'Oh, I have an article to write about this woman. She was, you know, an activist —' Irina briefly wondered, would she know the word?

Anna was pulling the hood over her head, admiring herself in the heavy gilt mirror. She'd been thinking of selling the coat in the market. But it did suit her. She thought, *I'll keep it.* Yes, it was a fairy-tale coat.

'See you next Wednesday.' She smiled her best smile.

'Thank you so much. That'll be US Election Day... No, the day we get the results. Honestly, I really am nervous.'

'Americans aren't lunatics,' Anna asserted. 'It'll be fine. Have a lovely weekend.'

'Oh. Yes... But it's only Wednesday.'

4.

As Irina closes the heavy front door, she notices she's not wearing her ring, the beautiful, high-carat ruby ring she inherited from her great-grandmother. It is the creation of a jeweller famous for making tiaras for the Romanovs. She isn't worried: she often slips it off when she's writing, because sometimes her fingers swell and stiffen, and she longs to take everything off that confines her. Where did she leave it though? A moment of panic. Of course it will be by her laptop.

But the ring isn't by her laptop. Irina doesn't want to start worrying, so she goes on writing for half an hour. May Hobbs's face, dauntless, ruddy, firm jaw, bright eyes and regular features, gives a half-smile from the cover of the book.

'May Hobbs's role in the politicisation of the 'night cleaners' of the 1970s cannot be understood without reference to Hoxton, the working-class district of East London where she was brought up by a series of substitutes for her parents, ending up, after getting into trouble with the police, with a foster mother, Jenny, she adored. This seems to have given her an undying belief in the community life of that part of London, where "no-one had much, but what you had, you

shared." "We were always in and out of each other's houses…"
When at one point in her peripatetic existence (she often had
to flee her debts and struggled to keep a roof over the heads
of her six children) May managed to get a large flat for them
all far from her roots, she became depressed and pined so
much for home that after only three weeks she went back to
Hoxton. "One person's slum is another person's community,"
as she wrote in *Born to Struggle*. The feminists from "Women's
Liberation" who took up the cause of the night cleaners when
the male trades unionists failed to help them, came from a
different social background…'

And so do I, Irina thinks. And so did my parents, and
grandparents. I can't imagine what it would be like to have
people always coming and going, helping themselves to food
from the kitchen.

Do I believe in the common people? I am a socialist, I
ought to. (*Am I a socialist? Of course I am.*)

Then she notices, again, her empty finger. With a sigh, she
goes off to search for the ring, looking, at first, quite light-
heartedly. She wears her jewellery every day – a pair of gold
earrings, this ring, her chain – and not infrequently mislays the
ring because of those urges to take it off. When she was younger,
it didn't happen. Maybe she's worn it all too long.

But the ring is worth tens of thousands of pounds: 18 carat
gold, exquisitely worked with a coiled snake and lotus flowers,
the ruby cradled in a dew of small diamonds. Five years ago
she'd asked a jeweller, a former lover, what he'd value it at, and
he'd got out his watch-glass and turned it, squinted, turned it
again, squinted, sighed. 'I'd buy it off you for twenty-five, even
thirty, *daragaya*. But you'd get more if you went to auction.'
£30,000! But she'd never sell it. It means that she is still
someone special with a history that stretches from St Petersburg
like a trail of stars near the north pole (she'd flown over it, once,
on the way to a conference), not just an outsider in an English
resort where most of the inhabitants supported Brexit. The ring

is proof she is European; to her Russia means Greater Europe, the land of Pushkin and Nabokov, although she's been exiled for several life-times. But no, she is Russian, her soul is Russian, and like the ring, she is one of a kind.

After three hours of searching, she is desperate. It is seven o'clock. On the radio, Trump is farting out rage against liberals and praising Putin's leadership. How hateful to hear her country's name on his lips! She switches him off so hard she hurts her hand. She's looked everywhere. In her handbag, in her pockets, in the kitchen, in every one of her three bathrooms, on the book-shelves, under the book-shelves.

Without it, she can't settle to writing. In the next few seconds she will certainly find it. But the regular rushes of hope grow weaker.

At 8pm, without prior thought, Irina rings the new cleaner's number, which Anna had written on the telephone pad. Midway, she has doubts, but continues dialling.

'Hello?' Anna sounds sleepy and surprised.

'Did I wake you up? I do hope not.'

'No, we were watching *The Apprentice*. Everything all right?' Anna asks.

'Yes. Er, no. Not exactly. It's nothing, really – I just wondered…'

The pause extends. Anna starts sweating. Has she left a tap on, and flooded the house?

'I've mislaid a ring. I'm, well, fond of it, it was handed down from my great-grandmother. I just wondered if you'd happened to spot it? It's quite… striking. With a red stone.' Irina becomes bolder as she goes on. After all, this isn't an accusation.

Oh God she believes I stole it, thinks Anna. 'No,' she says, 'sorry. I wish I had.' She racks her brain. Has she seen any jewellery? 'I think I know the one you mean. I saw it on your finger when I came for the interview.'

'Oh well, don't worry, it will turn up,' says Irina gallantly. 'Sorry to bother you.'

MAGGIE GEE

'No, I'm sorry,' Anna says. Her mother is listening. 'I'll come Wednesday. Bye, Irina. Hope you find it.'

'What's up with her?' Ma asks at once.

'Oh, nothing.'

'You don't look happy.'

And it all comes out, the missing ring, her embarrassment. Predictably, Ma is enraged. 'How dare she ask you? How dare she?'

'Look, Irina wasn't accusing me. I expect she will have found it by Wednesday.'

By the time they've finished rowing *The Apprentice* is over and Trump is on the news again. The BBC has photos from inside Trump Tower. The doors are made of solid gold. Everything gleams golden-yellow. And Trump has ruffled a lot of feathers by praising Putin's actions in Syria. 'Switch it off!' Ma shouts, scornful. 'He's a murderer!'

'What's wrong with him being friends with Putin? I don't want Kim to get blown up.'

'Why would I get blown up?' It's Kim's voice, anxious. They have forgotten she's in the room. 'Is Donna really a murderer?'

'Take no notice of your grandma,' says Anna. 'Stop eating sweets and go to bed.'

'She should know about Putin. And Trump,' Ma asserts.

'No she shouldn't. What's the point?'

This time the row deteriorates, even though Kim is listening. 'It's not *appropriate*', Anna shouts. She rarely shouts, so this is quite shocking.

'But she should know things,' Ma insists. 'We've got the American election next week.'

'She's a LITTLE GIRL,' Anna screeches.

'I'm not a little girl,' Kim says stoutly.

'Why do you always take your grandma's side!'

They stare at each other, the three of them, stuck, till Kim, unbearably torn between the two people she loves most, starts to sniffle, and clutches Ma's hand.

That's the last straw for Anna, who now feels like a bad mother. 'I won't be ganged up on, I won't! We need our own place, we need our own place! I'm going out,' she cries, and leaves, snatching up the red coat, slamming the front door.

Ma hugs Kim. 'Never mind,' she says. 'I shouldn't have annoyed Mummy, should I?'

'Will she come back?' Kim asks, afraid. Once her mum had run away for a week. 'Is it my fault?'

'No, course not. I expect she's just gone down the street,' Ma says. Together, they go and peer between the curtains, through the first floor window, at the misty night and the street dwindling into nothingness, and they glimpse her in the distance, in her red hooded coat, flying along the white treeline of street-lights.

Kim thinks, my mummy is beautiful and special, as she vanishes beyond the last moon of white mist. 'Will she be all right?'

'Course she will. I expect she's gone to write one of her poems.'

But Ma doesn't sleep till she hears her come in.

## 5.

When Wednesday arrives, Anna gets up early to make herself a cup of tea and finds Kim crying in the bathroom. The truth comes out: she is being bullied. A boy stuck his pencil in the back of her neck during maths, which Kim is very good at, Kim protested and actually thumped him, and ended up in the headteacher's office.

'I don't want to go to school,' she sobs. 'Can I stay home? I've got a pain.' They sit and cuddle on the landing. Anna is counting the stains on the carpet, which Ma has steam-cleaned without success. She kisses the hot, greasy top of Kim's head. Ma must have been too busy to wash it.

Before Anna can point this out, Ma bursts from her bedroom with a bright red face, clutching a blaring radio. 'You won't believe it. You won't believe it!' – and stomps into the bathroom, slamming the door.

Kim almost stops crying. 'What's the matter with Grandma?'

'I don't know. She's got an essay to write. And I've got to clean for the new lady. I think you'll have to go to school.' Kim starts crying loudly again. Anna stands up to go downstairs. As she does, the door of the bathroom opens and her mother yells, 'Trump's bloody won!!!'

Anna looks over her shoulder and misses a step, the shoddy 1980s banisters crumple and she plunges headlong with an unearthly scream, landing on her right shoulder. The pain is unbelievable.

'I've got to go to work,' she keeps wailing as the paramedics check her over. 'My boss will think I've done a runner.'

The young man is focused on her collar-bone. His eyes are kind. 'We'll have to take you in, all the same. I'm afraid it's broken in two places.'

As they help Anna towards the door, Kim is torn between crying in case her mother, being broken, dies in hospital, and crying in case she has to go to school.

'Kim, you're going, it's EDUCATION,' Ma insists, at the end of her tether. 'Otherwise you'll be a cleaner, like her.' She loves her daughter; she hates her daughter.

'But what about the ring,' Anna wails. 'She'll think I've done a runner with...' But the door closes with finality, and they hear the ambulance drive away.

'It isn't education, it's Own Clothes Day for charity. None of mine fits,' Kim sniffs and sobs. 'And I haven't had any breakfast. And I hate Coco Pops, in any case. I told Mum, but she never listens.'

'Right,' says Ma. 'Good girl for saying. I'll do toast, then you come with me. You'll learn a few things by the time I've finished.'

And this is why, when at 10am Irina opens her front door, headachey from staying up for the misery of the US election, and sure the loud doorbell is the cleaner, she's surprised to see a hot-eyed old woman and a fat, pretty child standing on her doorstep. Jehovah's Witnesses? 'Yes?' she snaps.

But it's Ma, who leaves Irina in no doubt. 'I've come to clean in place of my daughter. She's fell downstairs and broke her collarbone. This one's off school' – indicating Kim – 'but she hasn't got anything infectious, OK?'

'Oh,' says Irina. Her headache sharpens. 'So sorry to hear about…' Her mind goes blank. She gestures vaguely in the air.

'My daughter's name is Anna,' roars Ma.

'But it won't be necessary for you to clean. I mean, very kind of you, but honestly…'

However Ma has screeched over the threshold – 'I'll get on with it. I've brought my kit. Have you got a telly for her to watch?' – pulling Kim in after her willy-nilly. Irina follows them, twisting her hands, her helpless hands with the naked fingers: her Russian ring has not turned up. She wishes she had never come to live in Seabridge, and soon she wishes it even more, because Ma has something on her mind, and offloads it in the drawing-room, which says to her, loud and clear, 'money'.

'I know about your ring, we've heard all about it, I know you rang up and asked my daughter, I can tell you straight away SHE HASN'T NICKED IT, I've brought my daughter up to be honest, but I'm going to have a look for it, OK? And I've got GOOD EYES' – Ma shoots a glance of scorn at Irina's rimless reading glasses – 'so I'll probably find it.' This is delivered at very high volume. Irina starts speaking, but Ma has gone, finding the vacuum as if by instinct and dragging it, deafeningly, into the room. 'Behave,' she yells at Kim. 'Say PLEASE and THANK YOU.'

Kim and Irina stare at each other. Finally Kim, impressed and emboldened by her grandmother's frontal assault, says in a rush: 'Where's your telly, please?' Irina, speechless, leads her next door, and Kim sinks down on the leather sofa and flicks, flicks, from channel to channel, a bewildering succession of hideous sounds. She has sunk so far down into the sofa that only her feet are visible, and her plump pale legs like small Fairtrade bananas, the only ones Irina will have in the house.

'Do you want…?' Irina tries. But what could she give her? Anyway, Kim's in a world of her own.

6.

Three hours of fear ensue for Irina. Is it even true, that Anna's had an accident? Have they just come to rob her home? She can't call the police, too embarrassing.

*That lazy young woman stole your ring*, whispers a small, furious voice in her ear. *You saw her face. You knew she wanted it. And now the others have come like vultures. They will take everything away.*

*No, I refuse to think that thought,* another voice counters, adult, rational.

Irina moves her laptop up into her study, but because there is never any room on her desk, she leaves May Hobbs's book on the drawing-toom table. She closes the door upon her visitors and goes back to her article.

She'd been writing about Chapter 6 of May's book, which was titled, 'Cleaners of the World, Unite'. With that termagant down below, Irina finds the slogan galling, though of course there's really no connection. She flicks back through her box of file-cards, looking for quotes from May to insert, but the first card she settles on makes her feel empty. 'The community was united against the world outside it. It was as if you were all relations – and we probably were through intermarriage… No-one was pulling forelocks to anyone else… No-one even locked their doors – not that anyone had anything worth nicking.'

Irina feels alone in the world.

She can't work, she can't settle, and she switches on the

radio to hear post-election pundits, stupid with sleep, whipping themselves into self-righteous frenzy about the likely end of the world now Donald Trump has been elected. The old woman is banging about on the staircase, then the vacuum roars on below.

Irina decides she must go downstairs. Otherwise they might stay for ever. The stair carpet is very clean, and Ma has polished the brass stair rods. But when she opens the drawing room door, she sees Ma standing motionless, outlined against the light through the lace curtains, for the rain has stopped, and there is thin sunlight.

'This book,' Ma says. She sounds puzzled and accusing. 'This book was on the table. How did you get hold of it?' It sounds as though she thinks Irina stole it.

'I bought it, obviously,' Irina says stiffly.

'Did May Hobbs... did she actually write it?' Ma is cautious. She is out of her depth.

'Yes. It's her autobiography.'

'Autobiography. Is that fiction?'

'No, of course, it's about her life. Why are you interested in May Hobbs?'

'I knew her, didn't I.'

'What, in person? I don't think it can be the same one.'

'It is the same one. Who led the strike. It says so here. Against the government. Ministry of Defence, for one. I did know her. She was all right. May would have a laugh with you...'

'You actually knew her?' Irina can't believe it. 'The same May Hobbs that led the cleaners' strike?'

Ma realises she has an advantage. Irina is staring as if Ma is Jesus. 'Yes, I was in it. I was part of it, I don't know if she put our names, but I was one of them, the night cleaners, I cleaned with May, I went to her meetings.'

'Well, this is extraordinary.'

There is a pause in which they gaze at each other, seeing each other for the first time. The ornate Russian clock on the mantelpiece ticks loudly in the silence between them. Time has just changed, and space, and power. For a few seconds, it's all up for grabs.

Ma starts talking, and can't stop.

'We had no time, we worked from 10pm till 7am, then we all went home, got the kids off to school and did the housework, maybe two hours' sleep before we picked up the kids and soon it was evening and off we went to work again. For that they paid us less than the daytime cleaners. But somehow or other we got to May's meetings, they would have gone on treating us like dirt for ever.' It's wonderful for Ma to have an audience; Anna never listens to her.

'Would you like to sit down?' Irina interrupts her, but deferentially, and tries to take her duster.

'I haven't finished dusting.'

'No, please, I insist.' Irina tugs away the duster and points Ma ceremoniously towards the *chaise longue*. Ma inspects it with care before sitting down.

'We once had one of these, I got it in a junk yard, but then it turned out to have woodworm –' She blushes deep red, then tries to recover, she has always prided herself on good manners. 'Of course, yours wouldn't have come from a junkyard.'

'It actually belonged to my grandmother,' Irina says. 'We were very fortunate. My family was Russian.' She waves apologetically around the room.

'The Russian Revolution! Brilliant country!'

'Quite,' says Irina, awkwardly.

Kim rushes in from the room next door, shouting 'Grandma, the murderer is on the television!'

Both of them gape, not understanding. 'The mad man you said about! Donna Something! With the scary yellow hair! The one who's going to blow up the world! With his scary son! Don't you want to see him?'

'Oh him,' says Ma. 'No, we're busy.' After a short pause, she continues. 'Nobody told me May had written a book. I wish I'd known, I would have read it!' Her voice is wistful. Why wasn't she told? The educated kept good things to themselves.

'It was a great victory, wasn't it?'

'Was it?' Now it all spills out, Ma's memories, not in order. 'It seemed like a victory at the time. The women were earning £12.50 a week, and that went up to £16.50, with 50p extra for 'unsocial hours' – that bit did feel like a victory.'

'Don't say another word, I have to get us coffee.' Irina practically runs to the kitchen and makes coffee with the door open, calling through 'Filter or *cafetière*?'

'I like a latte really,' says Ma, keeping her end up, feeling happy. Irina comes back in while the kettle boils, and Ma continues, 'Was it a victory? I don't know. See the cleaning industry was all contractors. So first we got the workforce unionised, well I say "we", but really it was May. She persuaded us we could hope for better. But soon as we got a place unionised, the employer just goes with another contractor. So the worker never even met the employer. Well we never really HAD an employer. It's the same thing, isn't it, this "gig economy" my daughter goes on about as if it's cool. The profit goes to the parasites who set themselves up between the workers and the payers… In the end we ran a strike against the civil service. They gave in because everyone supported us, the post office unions, the electricians. The postmen wouldn't deliver any letters, and the GPO engineers blocked the phones. I've loved postmen ever since! That's what happens when people, you know, stand together.'

Irina delivers her attempt at a latte and watches Ma anxiously to see if she likes it. This is so exciting! She must take notes. Seabridge has wonderful characters, she realises. A friend of May Hobbs – she is in luck. Ma skims off the wrinkled milk skin from her coffee, smiles forgivingly, and drinks it. 'Very nice, thank you.'

'Good! You stood together and it worked,' says Irina, gazing lovingly at Ma. 'May Hobbs must have been so happy.'

'Maybe on the day. We all went and got drunk. But in the long run – I don't know. They only got in different contractors. May Hobbs got driven out of the country. The powers that be threatened her, 'You'll never get a job in this country again.' She'd caused a row in too many places. She already had to dye her hair whenever she went for a job interview…'

Irina keeps nodding her crest of white curls as the marvellous revelations continue. Kim is listening intently. Every now and then she taps Ma's hand, but Ma doesn't feel like being interrupted.

'So what happened to May in the end?' asks Irina.

'She went to Australia, believe it or not. The whole family took off and left. I stayed in touch with her son for a bit. He said they didn't ever settle, not really. But then, she was always a bit of a gypsy. They don't have possessions, do they, gypsies? When they die they burn the caravans with everything in it, they don't pass stuff on. So the gypsy world doesn't get all cluttered – '

Ma catches herself back. This room is cluttered with lamps, books, photographs. 'She ended up reading tarot cards, would you believe it? For money, I mean. I saw her just before she left the country. I said, "May, you ought to be a politician." She wasn't interested. She said, "It's not me. They all make compromises, don't they? I'm not going to play the political game." People courted her. May turned them down. Which is all very well, but we needed her. We need some decent politicians…'

Kim has been waiting patiently for her grandmother to run out of steam. At last she draws breath, and Kim tugs her arm, then whispers something in her ear. Ma pushes her away, frowning, then freezes as she understands. 'WELL, GIVE IT HER BACK THEN!' she shouts, stentorian. Kim jumps up meekly, goes over to Irina and holds a round plump hand out towards her, facing downwards, closed like a nutshell.

'It was under the cushions on the sofa,' she said. 'Grandma said you lost it. *I* found it!' And she drops the gold ring on to Irina's lap, proud. Irina stares, then smiles and smiles, clasping her old white hands around it. 'This is a happy, happy day,' she says. She has forgotten about the election, it's far away, and *carpe diem*.

Seabridge is no longer lonely. May Hobbs's friend! And now this blessing! It lifts her up, a great wave of emotion, shining gold, like beauty, fairness, her long-lost Russia, and love itself, glowing at the ring's red heart, and as she soars along the crest, she decides to give the poor child the ring – she has others, and this one hurts her hand. It's always been too big and heavy. And it will be a magnificent gesture!

At last, she can be part of it all.

And yet, there's history, and common sense. 'It's very special. My great-grandmother's.' And she is so attached to it. This is the moment: but the wave ebbs, leaving her back on her feet in the shallows. The child must be rewarded, though.

'Can we go home now? Will Mum be home?' Kim asks. She has always known she must look after her mother, and now bits of her are actually broken.

'We'll go and see her at the hospital,' says Ma.

'I will get you a taxi,' Irina offers. 'And you, little girl, you should have a reward.' She bustles upstairs to her bag in the bedroom and unfolds two twenty pound notes. Reward people for honesty, that is what her mother taught her. But then she thinks, she can't be more than eleven. Forty pounds would be too much for her. Money can corrupt you, she thinks, sadly. She re-folds a twenty and takes out a ten. Thirty pounds seems… appropriate. And then, of course, there are the wages, though it seems impolite to pay someone she knows.

She gives Kim the reward, and Ma looks contented, and takes Anna's wages without comment. 'I'll call you a cab now,' Irina says. 'But I hope you'll come back for a coffee soon.'

'We could go on the bus,' says Ma, half-heartedly, more from politeness than anything else, and is taken aback when Irina agrees 'If you're sure, darling. I know it's not far.'

They look back at her as they reach the pavement. She stands in the doorway with the light behind her. Quite tiny really. Getting smaller.

7.

It's cold at the bus stop and Kim feels low, but Ma is happy and boisterous, remembering how she impressed Irina.

'What are carrot cards?' Kim asks her gran.

'Carrot cards? What are you on about? – oh, TAROT cards. They're nonsense, really.'

'Why did that May woman have them, then?'

'Because people want to know the future. Tarot cards are supposed to tell you.'

'Can I have some?'

'No.'

'Why not? I want to know about Donna Trump.'

'You can change your own future, Kim, you know. You don't have to look at a pack of cards. May was just tired, I expect. She'd fought so much she had a right to be. You're not tired. You've got your life ahead.'

The bus arrives with its golden windows, each one framing a pair of passengers, and lifts them out of the rainy afternoon which is just beginning to get dark. They are back in a world of warmth and people. Someone gets up so they can sit down. Some language students sing, badly, in English, a song they learned this afternoon. When they hit a duff note, people groan and laugh.

'Why did I have to give the ring back?' Kim asks, suddenly. 'You said Rinna was a thief.'

'What?'

'You said, "Property is theft." When we were walking to the house. You said, rich people are all thieves.'

'That was before I knew her, though.'

'Why is it different when you know people?'

'Well it just is.' Ma is slightly impatient. Her elbow, unused to polishing, is gip. Why had she tried so hard with those stair-rods? Pride, really. She needn't have bothered. Then she makes an effort to be nice to Kim. 'Irina's Russian, any way. She gave you thirty quid, didn't she?'

'How much did the ring cost?' Kim asks her. 'Was it, like, you know, a hundred pounds? I wish she'd given me a hundred pounds.'

'Ungrateful…' But Ma is pleased, and laughs. 'You're a bright one. You'll do well.' She thinks about it. 'Probably more. Maybe a thousand, two thousand.'

'She should have given me two thousand pounds.'

'That's enough talk about money. We've got enough, more or less.' Unless interest rates go up, Ma thinks. And if they do, how will we pay the mortgage?

'But you said it was good to get more money. You did a strike to get more money. One day I'll do a strike, too.' Kim isn't quite sure what a strike entails, but she wants to be brave, like Grandma was. She's going to buy a house for her mother.

'Good girl. You do that. Now we'll go and see Mum.'

8.

In hospital, the sheets are white and clean. They have kept Anna in in case she has concussion, but she will be allowed to go home soon. However, Anna is in no hurry. She loves the hospital's antiseptic smell. It's quiet until visiting hours begin. She is dreaming of never having to clean again.

It's a very strange job, really, she thinks. I do things other people shrink from doing. Things they prefer not to think about. What they want from me is magic. She gets out her notebook and thinks about writing.

*What is it we do? It's…*

She has to pause. And then she knows. *It's miraculous…*

A woman comes slowly into the ward with a big spray, and starts spraying the surfaces. She is small, and bowed, in her overall, and looks as though a million years ago she came from China, or the Philippines – somewhere a long way away, in any case – and has been here for another million. Nobody looks her in the eye, or says 'Hello', or 'Please' or 'Thank you'. She works methodically, and sees no-one. Her progress is infinitely slow. She is bowed so low, she is almost on the floor.

Anna's looking down from her high, hard bed. Something suddenly grows from her centre, unfurls like the tongue of an amaryllis towards the woman, who never looks up: a green-gold thread, a magical tendril. Anna floats round the room beside her.

I am like you, Anna thinks. All of us women, cleaning and cleaning. And everyone looks down on us. I pretend they don't but I know they do.

'Thank you,' she whispers to the woman, who flinches, and frowns, craning up to hear. 'I'm a cleaner, too,' Anna says, louder, and the tiny woman gives a tiny nod. Anna returns to the thread in her head.

*What is it we do? It's miraculous. We make time run backwards, that's what we do. The kids' sticky fingers didn't touch the banisters. The dying man didn't piss on the floor, just floated peacefully out of the window. The drunk dad didn't spill his beer. That's what we do, we undo touch. We're special people, time travellers. We're here to make the world new again.*

*There are thousands of us. Hundreds of thousands. All over the world, there must be millions. If we all stood together in one place, we'd make a whole country. A continent. All standing up like trees in the sunlight. Birch trees, yes, all white and clean, birch trees, aspens, trees like that. Like the trees in that Siberian forest. Thousands of miles of birch forest, untouched by anyone, untrodden.*

*No-one could get to us, all together. And it would be cold and fresh and bright. Nothing dirty anywhere near us. Just standing in the sunlight all together.*

*All the cleaners in the world. The straightest, now, in the light. The cleanest. And there would be a life for us. A better life. Could it be? Could it?*

Kim comes sprinting down the ward.

# Afterword: Women's Liberation in London in the 1970s

## Prof. Sally Alexander
Goldsmiths, University of London

IN 1971-2 EVERY THURSDAY evening for over a year, I left home for Shell Mex House on London's South Bank, opposite Waterloo Station, to leaflet night cleaners as they arrived for work on the night shift at 10pm. The underground entrance was next door to Shell. Some women came up the steps from the darkness, others arrived by bus or car – driven to work by husband or lover. We – there were always two of us, members of the London Women's Liberation Workshop (WLW) – would accost weary looking women, clutching their belongings, just before they entered the buildings. Some politely took leaflets, others rushed past. Within a few weeks we knew most by sight, some very well. May Hobbs, a former cleaner, blacklisted by employers for urging cleaners to join a union, sometimes came with us too, but Shell was only one of several buildings across London to leaflet. Vital, charismatic, a natural orator – May's presence lifted everyone's spirits.

May formed the Cleaners Action Group (CAG) in 1971, determined to improve the pay and working conditions of all cleaners, especially night cleaners, across London and beyond. Her dream was a trade union branch of their own in the Transport and General Workers Union (TGWU), run by the women themselves. She approached feminists for help, first some women in International Socialists (IS), then her local

265

women's liberation group in Hackney, where she lived. News travelled fast by word of mouth. Sheila Rowbotham, historian and a close friend, told me about the campaign and introduced me to May; I took the idea back to my local group in Pimlico and before long several WLW groups supported the campaign.

Night cleaners needed all the help they could get. Isolated, the work invisible, cleaners worked through the night – from 10pm until 6am – in most cases returning home in time to wake children and husband for school or work. They grabbed a couple of hours sleep if they could during the day. Cleaners worked one or two to a floor, a supervisor over them, with perhaps one break for a cup of tea and sandwich. May's complaints about the square footage of floor space each cleaner had to clean within a certain time had earned her the sack. Dusting, emptying waste paper baskets, hoovering, scrubbing lavatories – this was 'women's work', its rhythms documented in a haunting interrogative film, *Nightcleaners*, made by the Berwick Street Film Collective during the campaign.[1] Asked by the filmmakers why they did nightwork, the replies were repetitive: my husband's pay is not enough, my children need me during the day, we do it for the children.

We knew little of either the work or lives of the women we wanted to help. But May knew everything and everyone – cleaners, supervisors, union officers and many of the employers, and she recognised the energy that women's liberation unleashed, she knew how to inspire and direct us. We were to leaflet the buildings regularly, talk to those brave enough to listen. Tens of thousands of night cleaners were employed across London in 1970, about 40 or 45 on the Shell building. Most were white working-class women, some were Caribbean and Asian, and there was also a handful of men.[2] Some only worked intermittently, relied on social security, or had overstayed their work permits. Shell Mex House contracted out its cleaning to a firm named Office Cleaning Services (OCS) which seemed to operate from a small white van, only appearing if there was trouble as news of the campaign spread. Cleaning companies, then as now, were often small businesses, some run by ex-cleaners who knew the conditions and hours and pay in minute detail and could undercut, and bargain with the women, knowing there were plenty seeking work.

I quickly learned how to catch the women's attention, talk to supervisors, persuade union officers to a meeting. We handed out questionnaires, huddled together on the pavement to discuss them. Why do night cleaners get lower pay than day cleaners, how much cover money do you receive, are you understaffed, do you receive Sunday bonus, can you be sacked without notice? We drew up a list of demands. Shell cleaners wanted a minimum hourly rate, over-time and cover pay. Efficient equipment, ventilation in the offices, proper cover and adequate supervision mattered almost as much to them as pay. Supervision was a contentious issue. Some supervisors were fair and good to the 'girls' as they called themselves. A sympathetic supervisor could make all the difference – re-adjusting a shift when someone was off sick, dovetailing working hours with childcare. Others were hostile, had favourites, or lived in the pockets of the employers.

Through the autumn and winter, we counted the list of members, added up the dues (we only needed 30 or 40 members for a separate branch) and tried to arrange meetings between the women and union officials. This took all our powers of persuasion. Union officers never tired of telling us that the cleaners' case was hopeless. A key scene in *Nightcleaners* shows a packed meeting of women in a pub close to Waterloo Station, being addressed by Mr. Churchouse, the local Transport and General (T&G) union officer, who explains why the women would not succeed: no skill, overcrowded labour market – women made poor trade unionists, seldom earned enough to pay their weekly dues and, anyway, employers would not listen to them. Always the emphasis was on the obstacles in their way.

Meanwhile, the campaign was gaining support. Ken Gill, President of the Draughtsmen's and Allied Technicians' Association, and a communist, agreed to meet us informally, to offer us advice. He was married to Tess Gill, a lawyer in the London WLW. Brian

Nicolson of the London Trades Council came too. Gill listened carefully to everything we told him. No sign of impatience. Then told us what we already knew – subliminally. The basis of trade union organisation was to establish a skill, to demonstrate to the employer the value of the particular group of workers in their employ. Trade union recognition in the workplace depended on this skill, its value and scarcity. Cleaners, especially night cleaners, were vulnerable because anyone could do their job. Although, as he acknowledged, a good, reliable cleaner was hard to find, there were hundreds queuing up to take her place should she leave or get the sack. Moreover, he told us, May's position was a difficult one. No longer working as a cleaner (she was blacklisted), she could not be the shop floor representative, she had no authority to speak to either employer or union on the cleaners' behalf, and a union would be unlikely to by-pass its own officials to make a place for her.

The cleaners' branch in the T&G did not materialise, despite a steady recruitment of 25 or 30 from the Shell building alone. May took to phoning General Secretary Jack Jones at home. When the Civil Service Union (CSU) showed an interest, May switched her allegiance from private to the public sector. In the summer of 1972, cleaners working in the Ministry of Defence buildings came out on strike. The CSU official, young and keen, drove up to the picket line in his white sports car. After a few weeks the cleaners, supported by the lorry drivers, the Post Office and a 24 hour picket organised by the Women's Liberation Workshop, won a £2.50 per week rise for a 45 hour week, putting the weekly wage up to £14, rates which were lost when, a few months later, the cleaning contract was not renewed. The campaign revived intermittently during the mid-to-late 1970s, though without May, who moved to Australia (disappearing as suddenly as she had appeared, from our point of view), the campaign lacked direction and focus. By the end of the 1970s it had died out completely.

May scarcely mentions the Women's Liberation Movement in her 1973 memoir, *Born to Struggle*. A new movement, born in the aftermath of 1968, women's liberation was democratic, utopian, favouring small groups and direct action. We set up women's centres, feminist law centres, Women's Aid (for protection from domestic violence). We created publishing groups; we taught, made films, joined study groups, and more. We believed in trade unions, in collective action. The night cleaners campaign was part of a wider struggle of working women in London in the 1970s, beginning with the Dagenham Ford machinists' strike for equal pay in 1968, encompassing the Trico women's unsuccessful two-year strike beginning in the summer of 1976, followed two months later by the migrant women's strike at Grunwick's photo processing factory, led by Jesaben Desai. These struggles changed the face of British trade unionism. The Working Women's Charter drawn up in 1974 by the London Trades Council symbolised that transformation. Its demands included nurseries, free contraception and equal human rights, as well as a national minimum wage, equal training and maternity provision. 'We were a thorn in the side of the TUC,' remembered Chris Coates, then TUC librarian, a couple of years ago. The relationship between domestic life and working conditions has to be re-negotiated anew with every generation, every culture and place, if women workers' lives are to improve.

Differences between us and the night cleaners were both apparent and real. Their faces were etched with exhaustion; we wore long hair, dressed and spoke differently. Education and income made the significant difference. But as we got to know each other, some of us became close friends. Some of us had children, we laughed at the same things, we learned to trust each other. For months, May, her husband Chris and their three children, were in and out of the house that my partner, my daughter and I shared with others, including one of the film-makers, Mary Kelly. Many feminists lived collectively in the run-down inner suburbs of London. We went to meetings and demos together, as many as would fit into Chris's car. My diaries for those years are filled with meetings, demonstrations, adult education teaching, and so on. The children in our house could not distinguish between a meeting and a party. Some cleaners came to hear Bernadette Devlin from Northern Ireland speak about British rule in 1972. Jean Moremont, whose fine, thoughtful face is one of the most eloquent images of *Nightcleaners*, became a good friend. Jean, one of 18 children, had always loved reading and writing, and had wanted further education but her parents needed her earnings. Her husband was a postman, in the Post Office union; they had seven children, he looked after their much-loved youngest while Jean cleaned. Respectful and supportive of Jean's actions, he eyed me sceptically whenever I arrived to pick her up in Battersea. Trade union officials, he pointed out, would not stand around on street corners leafleting like us, or get up at one in the morning to speak to cleaners during their break.

I often look up at the windows of London's tall buildings at night to see whether the lights are on, and imagine the cleaners at work inside. Several hundred thousand night cleaners work across the city, only today most are immigrant or migrant workers, often illegal, and their wages are lower, relatively, than they were at the end of the 20th century. Marc Karlin, when making the film *Nightcleaners*, asked two women, including Jean Moremont, what socialism meant to them, 'a better life for the working-class people' both said. 'Only,' Ann added, 'that couldn't be, couldn't be...', 'Why not?' Marc asked. 'It's like asking for the moon,' Ann replied.

# Notes

1. *Nightcleaners*, 1975, Lux; the Berwick Street Collective comprised Marc Karlin, Mary Kelly, James Scott, Humphry Trevelyan.
2. In 2005 there were 250,000 night cleaners employed in Greater London, many of them illegal immigrants, BBC News, 19 September 2005, http://news.bbc.co.uk/1/hi/magazine/
4259608.stm

# The Opposite of Drowning

## Francesca Rhydderch

THERE WAS ONLY ONE Englishman living in Capel Celyn in 1965, and because he left the village on the same day as everyone else there was no reason to think his intentions were any different. His was the last van to scramble up the track into the neighbouring valley, its engine jumping and knocking in the new quiet. Like those who had left ahead of him, he pressed his foot down hard on the accelerator, pulling against the uphill strain of the farmhouse furniture roped together in the back, a wife and daughter in the passenger seats beside him.

My grandfather's name was Danny Inman, but the villagers had come to know him as *gŵr* Manon (Manon's husband) and later as Danny Manon (Manon's Danny). It wasn't that anyone had ever told him he had to speak Welsh. He just did, until they forgot he had been English to begin with. No-one mentioned him by name after he left, but that was because by then there was no village and no villagers. The people of Capel Celyn had become the people of other places, apart from at odd moments when they might see a report in the papers, or on the television. A decade later the national news ran a feature about it again, this time because of the drought. A technicolour film that made everything look unreal homed in on what was left of door frames and gateways, a single chimney breast low down, and on higher land blunt copses of tree stumps, remnants of ash and elm.

Danny had called it a resettlement. Manon – my grandmother – said it was an evacuation. My mother Kate, who was fifteen years old when they left, painted the word 'EVICTION' on posters and banners and joined the marches. In the end all the words for it merged into one. Eight hundred acres, twelve farms, one post office, one school, one chapel and a cemetery were emptied out so the valley could be filled with water.

It took years to shift the living, but it was the dead who proved the most troublesome. They couldn't be sold like the soil in which they were buried, or told to take compensation. It was decided that surviving relatives could say for themselves what they wanted to do about the graves. Manon's mother had loved swimming, had lived for her Sunday school outings to the seaside at Harlech, even after she stepped into a smack of jellyfish. The purple stinging marks all the way up her legs never faded. When the corporation wrote to Manon saying this was her final opportunity to make her wishes known regarding her mother's remains, Manon decided to leave her where she was. Two weeks on she changed her mind, but by then it was too late: the headstones had been taken up and loose earth covered with layers of sand and concrete, ready to take the weight of a reservoir.

★

When I look at the pictures my grandmother cut out of the newspapers and glued into a scrapbook, my skin prickles with her stories. Heat rash, she used to call it, but it feels like something else. A local minister said that the days between the villagers trickling out and the water rushing in had felt to him like that long moment when a soul leaves a body; my grandmother shivered as she repeated it. What is it? I asked each time, tasting the deliciousness of feeling scared. Ugh, she said, shaking her shoulders as if to get rid of something caught on her jumper, a flying insect, or a spider. Someone must be stepping over my grave.

At the new house, my grandfather had spent four hours unloading everything, not stopping, determined to finish before it got dark. Why? my grandmother asked afterwards. We could have left it in the van, finished off the next day.

He found spaces for the furniture in the most unpromising places: he put the standing clock at the turn in the stairs, and the tallboy in the porch. The house being brand new, the paintwork was fresh; at least there were no chips or shadows to contend with, he said, signs of other lives which he would have had to disguise with the larger pieces – the dresser, or the upright piano. My grandmother made him a cup of tea while he went to wash the dust off his hands. When she came back into the living room with two cups in saucers on a tray and a plate of pink wafer biscuits (and this was exactly how she described it to the next-door neighbour afterwards, in her faulty English): he'd vanished into the air. Did she mean thin air? I asked when she told me the story. Oh yes, she said every time. That's what I meant.

★

But the air soon thickened out again, because there was me filling it with my cries for milk while my grandmother and my mother bumped around the kitchen late at night boiling bottles and teats. The midwife told my mother to let me cry, otherwise I'd never leave her alone, so she did, until I became used to it, waiting instead for my grandmother to slip quietly into the room and lift me from my cot. It was a pattern the three of us got used to, and I knew it would do no good to make a fuss, even when I reached primary school, and my mother was away in Carmarthen more often than she was at home, in court for criminal damage – climbing public television transmitters and making sure the police knew about it.

Why? I'd asked her that morning, watching her dress.

Because unless we stand up to them they will make us

listen only to English, she said, brushing her hair over her shoulders and adjusting her silver pendant. It will keep on pouring into our ears, filling us up, giving us no choice.

But I don't want to stay here with Mam-gu.

Why not?

I didn't know exactly how to put it: Mam-gu wasn't how she used to be. She would go off in the mornings, saying she was going to catch the bus into town to do some shopping, but she'd come back with her string bag empty and mud on her shoes. I never said anything about it; instead I'd talk to her about things that might remind me of the Mam-gu I liked better: When would dinner be ready? Could I have custard with my apple tart? I wanted to go to the park. I was tired of lying in the garden, reading.

Oh, I don't like this muggy weather, she said, standing over me, undoing her apron and pegging it to the line.

Nor me, I said, not taking my eyes off my book, the brightness of the words on the page. My mother had bought me a collection of folk stories with a soft cover and black-and-white pictures inside, and I was reading the tale of the Lady of the Lake, whose husband knows that if he strikes her three times she will return deep into the waters, taking her livestock with her. In the line drawing across the middle pages the Lady of Llyn y Fan Fach watches her animals following her out of the lake towards her husband-to-be, Gwyn, haunches rippling, their cow eyes almost human.

I was stretched out on my stomach on an old blanket, propped up on my elbows. I heard the click of the radio on the kitchen windowsill as Mam-gu switched it on for the lunchtime bulletin. I knew that if I listened for long enough I would hear my mother's name. Everyone said she was the saviour of the language, a poster girl for the campaign. When she stormed meetings, led rallies and spoke into a hand-held loudspeaker, the papers always ran pictures of her on their front pages the next day.

I'm going up to run myself a bath, Mam-gu mouthed through the window over the cheerful voices. I nodded, and went back to my book.

Mam-gu had cultivated every corner of the garden, apart from the lawn where I'd spread out my blanket. She grew tomatoes against the back wall of the house, and fruit bushes along the crazy paving that led to the washing line. Sometimes she gave me an empty ice-cream tub and told me to fill it with gooseberries so she could make fool for pudding. It was a task I liked to linger over, feeling the papery husks against my fingers as I pulled the fruit away from the plant.

The murmur of wood pigeons was making my eyelids droop. I glanced up at the bathroom window and saw Mam-gu standing naked, looking out at the farmland behind the house. Her breasts dangled comfortably without a bra, and the crumpling skin around her neck was pink where she'd caught the sun. She was staring out across the cornfields beyond the garden hedge. The council had put in for planning permission to build thirty new homes there – they'd already been up to stake out the land with levels and tape measures. That'll be the next thing, she'd said. I wondered what my mother would do then, if she'd climb trees and telegraph poles.

Perhaps Mam-gu was thinking the same as me. Her lips were moving as if she was having a conversation with someone as she opened the window wide, letting the metal handle hang down.

A cloud ran across the sun, and I shivered as I remembered that my mother might not be back this time, if they found her guilty.

I read on to the end of the story as the sun came out again, its heat rushing through me. The poor husband of the Lady of Llyn y Fan Fach can do nothing except stand at the shores of the lake wondering if he should just follow his wife and her livestock back into the water, knowing that if he does, being mortal, he will drown. Going towards Esgair Llaethdy, the Lady calls the cattle by name: *Mu wlfrech, Moelfrech, / Mu olfrech, Gwynfrech/* Hump-brindled, Hornless-brindled, / Rump-brindled, White-freckled... And the little black calf/ Which is on the hook,/ Do thou also come home quite sound!/ *Dere dithe, yn iach adre!*

Somewhere far off through the depths of the story came a ringing, an electric buzzing that shook the pigeons from their nests.

Mam-gu? I called up at the open window. She didn't answer.

The doorbell buzzed again. I closed my book and left it on the blanket. I ran past the homely burble of the radio in the kitchen to the hall. It was dark inside after the sunny garden, and the outlines of ordinary things – the umbrella stand, the little table with the cream phone on it, the tallboy – seemed to swell, then recede into the shadows.

Mam-gu? I said, louder this time.

There was a shape that looked like a man on the other side of the front door's rainbow glass. I reached up to open the latch. I had never done it before. It was easy.

When I saw him, the words that came into my head were Danny Inman. His face was the same as it was in the newsprint photographs in the scrapbook, but his hair had turned from black to white.

Where's Manon? he said.

Mam-gu!

I waited for her to sigh, get out of the bath and tread her heavy way downstairs, but the only sound that reached us was the sucking of the overflow. I closed my eyes and put my fingers in my ears. I waited for him to go away as everyone said he had the last time: in silence.

He didn't. Instead, he reached out and unfastened my fingers from each side of my head, one at a time. Then he bent down and whispered in my ear, holding on to my arm until I stopped pulling away from him. I stood still, keeping my eyes closed, listening to his voice. It was a not unpleasant sound, like the soft rush of running water, and I wanted it to carry on.

# Afterword: From Capel Celyn to S4C, 1965-1979

## Ned Thomas

FRANCESCA'S STORY IS FRAMED by two episodes in the late twentieth-century history of Wales which relate to each other in several ways within a wider culture of language protest.

The first is the drowning of the valley of Tryweryn to provide water for the population and industries of Liverpool. This involved the removal of the village community of Capel Celyn which was made possible through a private bill sponsored by Liverpool City Council which allowed compulsory purchase of the land. This passed through Parliament in 1957 though opposed by 35 of the 36 Welsh MPs (the thirty-sixth abstained). Eight years later in 1965, in the face of widespread and continuing opposition, the valley was drowned, and the fact that the village was a Welsh-speaking community lent a wider symbolic and national significance to the event. Welsh was being wiped out and Wales itself was perceived to be helpless.

The Welsh Nationalist Party, Plaid Cymru, had led the opposition but its leader Gwynfor Evans, a strong pacifist and believer in constitutional methods, had resisted calls for direct action and faced criticism from a younger generation when those methods proved ineffectual. There were attempts at minor sabotage as the dam was being built; a new organisation calling itself the Free Wales Army turned up at the opening ceremony, and some years later other pipelines carrying water to England were attacked with explosives, but the main focus of Welsh protest from now on was to be linguistic, and the methods adopted would be non-violent and eventually much broader-based.

In 1962, when Parliament had already passed the Tryweryn Bill, Gwynfor Evans's predecessor, the critic and dramatist Saunders Lewis, broadcast a radio lecture entitled *Tynged yr Iaith* ('The Fate of the Language') which called for a movement which would engage in non-violent direct action in defence of the right of Welsh-speakers to use their own language when dealing with the public authorities. It led to the foundation by university students of the *Cymdeithas yr Iaith Gymraeg* ('Welsh Language Society') which has remained to this day a movement largely (though not exclusively) made up of young people.

The Society's campaigns have been many and various, and have often involved direct action, when constitutional methods have failed, in which the law-breakers declare their responsibility for their actions and are taken to court which they use as a platform to persuade their fellow citizens of the justice of their cause. An early and very visible campaign involved the painting out of road signs when the authorities resisted the demand for bilingualism: to have Abertawe and Aberteifi (the names used every day by Welsh-speakers) alongside the English forms Swansea and Cardigan. The authorities initially refused on the alleged grounds of public safety, but this argument collapsed when the accident statistics of bilingual countries showed there to be no such danger. When members of the Welsh Language Society were prosecuted for defacing road signs, other members removed further signs and dumped them outside the courts and police stations. Court proceedings in turn became the occasion for language protests, and when some of those convicted of language offences were sent to prisons and remand centres outside of Wales and denied correspondence in Welsh, the ripples of protest spread wider still.

The other event which frames Francesca's story is an episode from the Welsh Language Society's campaign for a separate Welsh-language TV Channel. This started in the early 1970s with the giving of evidence to various committees on the future of broadcasting and culminated, a decade later, in eventual victory. *Sianel Pedwar Cymru* (S4C) started broadcasting on 1ˢᵗ November 1982. But in the interim, hundreds of people had been taken to court for the non-payment of TV licenses as part of the campaign, studios had been invaded and expensive equipment damaged, students had swung by their hands from the gallery of the House of Commons, and several TV transmitters in England, as well as in Wales, had been switched off. Young women were prominent among the activists who served prison sentences.

I saw this campaign at close quarters, at first as a journalist reporting on Welsh affairs for the London press; at the same time as a TV columnist who followed the developments in television in some detail and understood the technological possibilities; and finally as a Welsh-speaker drawn into the protest movement myself, becoming briefly a member of the Welsh Language Society's governing body. At a late stage in the campaign, when the newly elected Thatcher government reneged on its election manifesto promise to establish a Welsh-language channel, I switched off the Pencarreg TV transmitter in the company of two very respectable figures: Pennar Davies, the principal of a theological college, and Meredydd Evans, a former head of light entertainment for the BBC in Wales who had also taught philosophy at Bangor, Princeton and Cardiff.

I have told the story elsewhere of how students helped us break in, how the friendly Welsh-speaking constables were rather perplexed as to what they should do with us, and how the authorities then took nine months to decide on the charges, allowing us in the meantime to tour the country, speaking to meetings and getting valuable media coverage for our cause. We were eventually tried by the Crown Court in Carmarthen and given a substantial fine by a judge who had decided not to hand out prison sentences and risk making martyrs of us. But this should not allow people to think that interaction with the courts and the police was always as civilised. Students were often treated very roughly by the police and in one of the conspiracy trials against officers of the Welsh Language Society the jury was undoubtedly rigged.

But although this decade of protest prepared the ground in the sense that it forged a consensus in public opinion, it would not have been enough to produce the Thatcher government's u-turn had not Gwynfor Evans, the by now ageing leader of Plaid Cymru, in 1980 stated that he was prepared to go on hunger strike – unto death if necessary – if the government did not honour its manifesto pledge. This announcement met with initial unbelief, but those who knew Gwynfor well did not doubt that he was in earnest, and gradually prominent Welsh people of all parties and persuasions united to bring pressure on the government. Many of those like myself who had been active in the campaign were not just pleased but intensely relieved when the government relented since we felt that a hunger strike would have taken the campaign into uncharted territory. It was in many ways an unexpected initiative from a man whose political career had been marked by a strict adherence to constitutional methods. Some thought that he may have been compensating for that earlier unwillingness to go beyond constitutional protest at the time of Tryweryn.

The direct action but non-violent campaigns of the Welsh Language Society did not at first command support in the wider Welsh-speaking population – indeed there was considerable hostility fanned by the English-language press. But gradually the dedication of the young generation, the protest songs of Dafydd Iwan and the Welsh pop movement, the support given by prominent Nonconformist ministers who took Martin Luther King as their model, all spread the message wider and wider. Some magistrates refused to convict language offenders and we now know that within the higher judiciary there were people who behind the scenes were arguing for linguistic rights within the legal system. Not only did a consensus on the question of the TV channel emerge but one saw a wider emergence from the inferiority complexes which are internalised when people's own language is repressed over time. Also a solidarity emerged with other movements of the same period, notably feminism and the peace movement. This can be observed in the novels of Meg Elis and Angharad Tomos (who both spent time in prison for language offences) and the poetry of Menna Elfyn (whose husband was imprisoned). There is a continuity from the mid-1970s to the mid-1980s, and some overlap between militant Welsh-language protests, the Greenham Common camp (first set up by the 'Women for Life on Earth Group' from Cardiff), and the support groups for the 1984-85 miners' strike in Wales.

How does the period framed by Francesca's story appear at this distance in time? In 2005 Liverpool City Council issued an official apology for the drowning of Tryweryn. So that is all right, is it? While it is no doubt to be welcomed I can't help but recall Auden's lines:

History to the defeated
May say Alas but cannot help or pardon.

In Wales, the fiftieth anniversary of Tryweryn was commemorated in 2015 with cries of 'never again' now that we have our own devolved government. But there are signs that events which are still alive in social memory may become institutionalised with time. The well-known graffiti south of Aberystwyth which read 'COFIWCH DRYWERYN' ('Remember Tryweryn') have recently been repainted and preserved with a grant from Cadw, the historic monuments agency for Wales. Every nation, I suppose, must have its official symbols. These can be a comfort zone you can retreat into or, alternatively, an inspiration to future action, and I should prefer our main emphasis to be on today's problems. Throughout the world far larger dam projects with massive forcible relocations of population continue to occur, for example in India and the Kurdish areas of Turkey. And here at home, as others have pointed out, had the Welsh-speaking valley of Tryweryn been spared it would very probably, like similar scenic areas, today be full of holiday homes and English-speaking retirees from the English cities, financed by the gross regional imbalances in purchasing power which exist within late-capitalist Britain – a much more complex problem to solve.

The Welsh language protests of this period can be set in a wider international context of rising post-Second World War expectations: the civil rights movements in Northern Ireland and the United States, the process of decolonisation, and the re-emergence of repressed nationalities and languages within the Spanish state after Franco's death in 1976. 'Awakening' is a word that could be applied in all these cases – or in Welsh '*Y Deffro*' – and it implies a growing understanding of their own condition not just by a few leading figures but by whole communities and generations, as in Francesca's story.

# THE NEW CROSS FIRE &
# THE BRIXTON RIOTS

# Bed 45

## Jacob Ross

SHE WAS FIGURING OUT what to do about her Intern, Leah, when the police pulled her over. She'd been thinking that the red-haired, pale-skinned Yorkshire girl – small and almost timid by the look of her – had been with her for nine months; had just got the Residency she wanted; now, she was about to drop everything and return home. Leah had mumbled something about her father's worsening condition, and pit closures.

The police had parked their white van half way across the street. The arm that waved her down directed her towards the barricaded side of the road.

She pulled up, hand-braked, cut the engine and watched two uniforms approach – a tall male, his elbows angled away from his sides, face shadowed by his peaked cap; and on his left, about half a step behind him, a bowler-hatted female, stiff in her skirt and tunic.

Further down the street, her gaze halted on a knot of men, their black tunics streaked red by the glow of the Abbey National sign overhead.

A tap on her roof pulled her attention back. She rolled down the glass; looked up into the face of the woman – large eyes, a soft young mouth, cheeks drawn white by the cold out there. 'Is this your vehicle, Mam?'

Mavis nodded.

'Can I see your license, please?'

Mavis dragged her bag from the passenger seat, settled it on her lap and fished out the card.

With her eyes still on the bunch of uniforms, she did as she was told. She stepped out of her car, unlocked her boot, and dropped her keys in the outstretched palm of the man. He raised an arm; another left the van, strolled over, plucked her license from his fingers and walked back to the vehicle.

She glanced at her watch. It was eight past six – a chill mid-January morning, stiff with frost. She pulled the collar of her pea jacket closer to her throat.

A transit van approached, slowed down and was abruptly waved on, its tail-lights disappearing in a streak of yellow.

There was a shuffling among the tightly packed uniforms down the street, a sudden adjustment of the pack, then a voice rising from their midst, pitched high with agitation and something else that stiffened her spine and made her turn to face the young woman.

'What's happening? What's all this about?'

A policeman had pushed his head into her boot; a woman had her knees on the passenger seat, her hand busy in the glove compartment. The tight bun that sat on the nape of her neck, silvery under the spillage from the street lamp overhead.

The young woman who'd asked for her license followed her gaze up the street. The electronic chatter of her radio came in fits and starts. 'Can I ask you where you're coming from?'

'Work – I'm on my way home.'

'And where is work?'

'Lewisham hospital. I'm a doctor there.'

'Do you have...'

'It's in my bag.' Mavis slipped her hand into the side pocket of her bag and retrieved her name tag. The man took it from her and headed for the van. He leaned into the driver's window.

Mavis eyed the young woman – early twenties, if that. In training – obviously. 'I'd like to know why you stopped me.'

'We're interested in a vehicle that fits the description of

this one: white Austin Princess...'

'Sorry, Miss MacPhail. Police business...'

'Doctor,' Mavis said. She hadn't realised the man had returned. She pointed at the press of men. 'That boy you've got against the bank, what are you doing to him?'

'Police business, Miss MacPhail.'

'Doctor,' she said again, raising her head at him.

The man sketched a smile, lifted his shoulders and dropped them. 'What time did you leave work, Miss?'

'You phoned the hospital. I'm sure they told you. I'd like to go home now.'

'Here,' he said. He'd settled her keys and cards in his outspread palm, his elbow tucked tight against his side. She would have to step very close to him to retrieve them. She held his gaze and did not move.

The young woman took them from the policeman's hand and passed them to her.

★

Mavis shouldered her front door shut and strode to the kitchen. She lit a couple of candles, then made herself a cup of chamomile tea.

She unhooked the phone and dialled Bergette. When husbands and boyfriends were allowed in the delivery wards, her friend had retrained and moved from Maternity to presiding over bodies in the morgue.

'Berg, it's me,' she said.

'Mavis, sweetheart, what time is it?'

'Sorry, Bergette, I'm just off work. Are you in later?'

'Yes, what's the bother, Pet?'

'Would you let me know if a young man is brought in by the police. He's around eighteen, nineteen. Tallish, short hair. He's wearing a chequered shirt. No coat.'

For a moment she thought they'd lost the line. Then Bergette's voice came, soft and tentative: 'Mavis, are you alright?

Is he... is it troubling you again?

'Not at all, Bergette, I'm talking about something I just saw less than twenty minutes ago, on New Cross Road.' She hadn't felt this pressure in her head for a long while – things crowding her mind and pushing against her skull. 'They... they bring them in and there's not a mark on them, yet we have to rush them straight to ICU. How many cases, what's the...'

She became aware of the Irish woman's silence at the other end of the line – of herself talking too loud and too fast. Mavis took a breath and stopped herself.

'A coloured boy, you said?' Bergette cut in.

She almost said, of course. Instead, she heard herself breathing an apology before replacing the handset.

The untouched cup of tea sat cold against her elbow on the marble worktop. Sleep never came easily. She would drift around its edges until it sucked her in. Always before that, there was the limbo of not knowing what to do with herself.

Through the wide south-facing kitchen window, past the black grid-work of railway pylons, the A2 was streaked with traffic heading south to London Bridge. Here and there among them, pinpricks of flashing blue.

*Is he troubling you again?...*

Bergette's gentle query; her own quick denial came back to her. She pushed herself to her feet, took the stairs for the room she rarely visited, and never tidied.

On the door, in dark brown letters: DARREN'S DEN.

His books were still there; LPs stacked on the chair beside the clothes cupboard; on the shelf, below the north facing window, rare edition EPs of Jackie Opel, Gaylads and Prince Buster. Above that, a poster of Bob Marley – the singer's hair rooted in the earth – fisting the air.

She'd left a single picture of her boy on the wall above the bed, the only one she could bring herself to look at now.

It is night and the single light from a streetlamp is falling on him. A shoulder is propped against the lamppost. He's brought a struck match to a reefer between his lips, the flame lighting up his lower face, the curve of his jawline, his right eye and the arc of his brow. Beyond him, the diminishing procession of streetlights on Streatham Road.

She could not find him in the picture he'd pasted on his door – a murky 12x14 print of his night-world. Of basement raves, subterranean sound systems and faces so smeared by the coloured lights they looked like apparitions. It was from one of those *bashments*, they said, on his way home on the night bus, that she'd lost him to the uniforms.

★

The cheeping of her pager pulled her out of her doze. As she reached for it, the phone began to ring. The clock said eight thirty seven.

'Doctor MacPhail?' Anna, their fast-talking receptionist was on the line. 'Sorry about this. We, we're obliged to call you in. As you know, Consultant Khan's in Oslo.' Mavis could hear the young woman's breathing on the phone.

'What's happening, Anna?'

'It's the fire this morning, they've been bringing them in.' Anna sounded different – choked. 'We're sending Keith, on blue.' Anna clicked off.

Keith, their best driver. *On Blue.* Mavis hurried to the shower.

★

Above the shrill of the siren, Keith, the small Welshman, filled her in. 'Coloured kids,' he said. 'Party at one of them houses on New Cross Road – was it? Neighbours not happy with the noise. Fire bomb through the window. There was talk of a white car speeding away. It's a new year, for God's sake – what a way to start it off. *Ofnadwy.*'

'White car, you said?' She narrowed her eyes at Keith.

The driver shrugged, blew air through his lips. 'S'what I heard from the paras.'

Mavis pressed her back against the seat, closed her eyes and said nothing more.

They were waiting for her at the entrance of Accident and Emergency – a cluster of nurses, ambulance men and junior doctors at the side of the rotating doors, arms folded against the cold, held together by a silence she'd recognise in any hospital anywhere.

The tall Romanian care nurse she knew as Nelu broke from the group, strode ahead and stood at the open door of the lift.

She heard her name, looked past Nelu to see Leah skimming across the tiles, a clipboard against her chest. The Intern ducked under Nelu's arm and positioned herself beside her.

'Bed 45,' she said, handing over the clipboard.

'Anna called you in too?'

Leah shook her head. 'I had some catching up to do, Doctor.' She pointed at the clipboard in Mavis's hand. 'Female, about fifteen, not yet identified.'

Mavis looked up from the papers. 'Just one? Keith said thirteen.'

The girl raised pale blue eyes at her, then lowered her head. 'The others are with Bergette. Keith said how it happened.'

'Yes,' Mavis said. 'He told me too.' She shook the sheaf of papers. 'Eighty per cent burns?'

'Rule of nines,' the girl said. 'That's how I calculated.'

The Intern and Nelu had already done some preliminary interventions. They'd checked the patient's airway breathing and her arterial pressure, administered a tetanus shot, and Ringer's lactate solution. They now had her on 100 per cent oxygen. It was as far as Leah dared to go.

'You did well, Leah.' And Mavis saw the flush of pleasure on the young woman's face.

The lift hissed to a halt. 'I want Nelu up here again, and

two of his staff. I'll be needing Hartmann's solution, a couple of large bore cannulae, catheters, a nasogastric tube – you know the rest. I'll go change. Meet me there in five.'

They were all in the room when she walked in. 'Alright,' she said. 'We'll adjust the bed first. Then I'll talk you through the procedure as we go. It's going to be invasive work.'

She spoke to them in the low flat tones she'd picked up from Consultant Khan. It protected her, placed her at the necessary distance to maintain a steady hand – a voice leeched of everything but the exacting logic of procedure.

When she pulled herself out of it, the clock at the back of the room said 4:30.

She thanked the team and took Leah's elbow. 'Let's change and get some coffee.'

She felt the stiffness in the young woman's arm, looked at her and saw that her lower lip was trembling. 'People should see this,' Leah whispered. 'People should see what they've done to her.'

Mavis urged her out of the room.

Outside, the frost hadn't left the roofs of the outbuildings. Steam rose up from the bright metal chimney of the incinerator a couple of blocks away. The usual throb and hum of voices; and beneath that, the low, almost tidal murmurs of bodies in distress. After fifteen years, she still hadn't got used to it.

In the hospital cafe, Leah sat facing her, both hands around a Styrofoam cup of coffee while Mavis pushed a withered pain au chocolat around her plastic plate. From time to time, the Intern raised her head at the padding of feet on the tiles, and the chirpy banter of the woman at the coffee counter.

Mavis pushed aside the untouched food. 'Leah,' she said, her voice thick with a conviction that surprised her. 'Your family would want you to stay and complete what you came to London for. You said you're the first to get this far?'

If the young woman heard her, she showed no sign. 'People should see, Doctor – what they did to that girl.'

'Your father – how is he?'

Leah looked down at her hands and frowned.

'How's he?' Mavis insisted.

'Black lung disease. It's...'

'Coal Workers' Pneumoconiosis – I know. I'm sorry to hear that. As I said, they'd want you to stay and complete what you came here to do. I recommended you for the Residency and I happen to know you'll get it. After that you're through.'

Leah was stirring the black liquid with a finger. 'Bed 45 – she has a ten per cent chance of survival. Do you think?'

'Comes a point when the maths don't count anymore, Leah.'

'People should see...'

'You keep saying that. It will be in the newspapers. They'll change the facts of course – no mention of the firebomb, no white car driving away. The children – they'll have brought it on themselves. A fight perhaps. And, of course, the parents won't believe it.' She eased aside the plastic plate with an elbow. 'They'll want to know what really happened to their child, and why.

One morning, a policeman will knock on their door. He'll talk nicely – look as if he understands. But when he's gone...' She rubbed her face, pressed her back against the chair. 'All they'll get from that conversation is that it was their fault – something they didn't do.'

'I'm sorry,' Leah said.

'About?'

'Keith told us about your son.'

'That man talks too much.'

Leah's gaze had shifted past Mavis's shoulders, a new alertness in her eyes. Mavis heard the clatter of footsteps behind her, then her name.

'Keep out of this, Leah,' she muttered.

Carol, the Senior Clerk, halted beside their table. The usual fuschia-red shoes, matching lipstick, black skirt straining against her bony thighs. 'I'm so relieved to find you, Doctor MacPhail. I thought I'd missed you. Erm, would you mind having a conversation with the parents, now that we've identified Bed 45 – that is, when they arrive?'

Mavis leaned back in the chair. 'Can't do it, Carol, I'm sorry.'

The slate grey eyes widened. 'Can't? But Doctor... We thought that...'

*You're one of them, it's better if you do it.* She almost finished the sentence for Carol; thought she'd said the words, but Carol was still smiling down at her.

'I'm not talking to the parents, Carol. That's what you're asking, isn't it?'

'Doctor MacPhail, are you... are you declining?'

'I am, Carol. I am. Thank you.'

'Shall I speak to Consultant Khan about this then?

Mavis lifted her shoulders and dropped them. 'If you wish. Of course.'

She listened to the diminishing clatter of Carol's heels on the tiles.

With Carol gone, she turned to face Leah. 'I want you to look at me while I speak, Leah. I want you to hear what I have to say. And when I'm done talking, I want you to give me your word. You keep saying people should see Bed 45, and I know you don't mean the newspapers.'

'Leon's right,' the girl cut in. 'He said it's getting worse out there.'

Mavis conjured a picture in her mind of a lean young man, standing just outside the main doors, his braided hair pulled back in a bun. She'd seen Leah stepping out the door, hooking an arm in his, and striding off with him. Used to be an orderly – from Brixton, she'd heard – with the most direct gaze she'd ever seen from a young black man. A couple of months in the wards, then he was no longer there.

There was something sullen, almost accusatory in Leah's eyes. The young woman was fingering the small necklace of green, yellow and black beads around her throat. Darren wore one of those; his girlfriend too.

'What exactly do you have in mind, Leah?'

Leah held her gaze, said nothing.

'Your boyfriend, why'd he leave the job?'

'What he's doing now is more important. Like he said, it's getting worse, and people need to know.'

Mavis planted her elbows on the table and leaned into the girl. 'That would be a breach of everything you learned in here, from me, from the others, from this profession. You understand? A doctor does a doctor's job. That's all. I want a promise from you, Leah – right now, that you wouldn't be so stupid.'

Leah sat red-faced but calm, her head down, her small hands folded around each other in her lap. She nodded and looked away.

★

Leah went silent on her, but the Intern didn't drop the conversation. She left newspapers on Mavis's desk, the headlines underlined in pencil. 'THIRTEEN PERISH IN FRONT-ROOM FIRE – NO EVIDENCE OF ARSON', 'BRAWLING BLACKS BURN…'

Mavis's elbows were on one of the pages of *The Sun* newspaper, a pencil in her hand, when Consultant Khan called and suggested a coffee. He had the thick eyelashes and luminous night-dark eyes she'd only seen in Indian men – the grey moustache as meticulously kept as his hands were. Fifteen years beside him in the operating theatre and she thought she knew his mind. Khan rarely wasted words.

She was the best Intensivist they had, he said. The three-month break they'd given her last year – for understandable reasons – had been good for her. She'd recovered well, been doing an impeccable job till now. The hospital couldn't afford to lose her, which was why –

'I've been doing my job,' she said.

'It's not just the job, Mavis. It's your state of mind.' His voice remained low but there was a new edge to it. 'Not much to do now anyway. Nothing that Nelu, myself and your Intern can't handle, until the parents decide what happens next, of course.'

He tapped the table, then spread his fingers, the dark eyes turned inward. 'Technically, Bed 45 should not be with us. Why Mavis – why is she still holding on?'

'She hasn't seen herself; she doesn't know what she looks like now.' Mavis stood up. 'Effective from? The time off, I mean. And for how long this time?'

Khan rested a hand on her arm. 'Sorry about this, Mavis. Carol will handle the details.'

'I'll finish off the week – that's three days. Would you mind saying that to her for me?

*

She left the afternoon the father switched off the ventilator of Bed 45. He'd come in on his own – an exhausted, broad-shouldered man, with a calmness of voice, and an expression they could not read. He did not look at them; addressed instead the space above the bed. Said his daughter's name after every sentence. The man left them with a picture of a soft-spoken child who was quick to laugh, and was always on the phone to friends. He talked as if he regretted they hadn't known her as she used to be.

Wanting to spare herself the numbing finality of that silence when the machine stopped, Mavis left before he turned the switch.

She'd asked Carol for three extra days before she left, when all she'd really needed was fifteen minutes on her own with the girl in Bed 45. And as she slipped the camera into her bag, cleared her desk and pulled the door behind her, she told herself that letting her off last year had been a mistake. They should have worked her even harder. They should have worked her till she died. They shouldn't have sent her home into a silence which unmoored her from the only thing she had left, that felt worthwhile to her.

She cleared out Darren's room, stripped the wall of his picture and set about painting over the smudges. She brought his music records downstairs; spent the first day working out the wires and connections of his record player, then began listening to the night-world music that he danced to with his friends.

She was almost at the end of them – the crisp bite of January having given way to the soggier, cloudier days of late February – when she came upon a large brown envelope. She paused over her son's careless scrawl in green ink, LKJ, then slipped out the glistening disk.

On the sleeve, a black and white picture of a young man in the doorway of a police station, flanked by uniforms, facing the street with a megaphone to his mouth. She imagined him mouthing the title of the album to the small crowd facing him: *Dread Beat an' Blood.* The voice that rose up from the vinyl had no rage in it. But the rhythm and the words were heavy with attrition.

It was all she listened to from then, kept returning to the third song – 'All we Doin' is Defendin'' – because it brought home to her the extent of her self-deception. She'd tried to teach her boy how *not to be.* To wear no puffer jackets, no trainers or tracksuits in public. No hoods. Nothing that would turn the eyes of the uniforms on him. The fact was, out there, her boy had been naked, regardless of what she'd made him wear. Naked, from the time he'd left her body.

Tonight, an anchorman is sitting behind a curved blue desk, in a green silk tie and crisp white shirt.

The TV headline is the 8-hour march from Fordham Park to Hyde Park. A man in a pressed blue shirt faces the camera and is talking on behalf of the uniforms about the inconvenience of disrupted traffic, the clampdown on criminality and lawlessness. The TV flashes a newspaper headline – The Day the Blacks Ran Riot – then takes her to the rain-slicked streets of

Brixton. It pauses on the backs of hatted West Indian women in closely buttoned coats, shoulders folded against the drizzle, carrier bags dangling from their fists.

The camera slides over the blurry shapes of youths in beanie hats, hands stuffed down their trouser pockets, leaning cross-legged against a music record shop and the wide glass frontage of British Home Stores. It is a tour; selective, she thinks, but fascinating nonetheless. She's seeing the way they see.

A short pause on the graffiti along the railway bridge – *Thirteen Dead and Nothing Said… Blood Ah Go Run in '81 If Justice No Come.* White vans parked in shadowed side-streets; uniforms in tight formation at street corners. And now, the camera closes on a dreadlock, hair sticking from his head like horns, a matchstick in his mouth. He is staring straight into the lens at her. 'Like, is still winter, yunno, but it hot out here. Real hot! All Man got to do is put a match to it, den boom! Cor Babylon harassing and downpressing bredrens fuh nuthing. And Man tired ah dem raas claat SUS.'

The camera follows him up the street, his walk – something between a shuffle and a bounce – then it cuts back to the crisp white shirt.

Trust them to pick a face that frightens them, she thinks.

★

It is the 8th April – two months and three weeks since she'd left work. She'd been counting, perhaps as a way to measure her days at home until they called her back. She'd barely left her house. She lit candles and listened to LKJ. Outside, the daffodils that had begun to stipple the small garden yellow, had been promptly bitten back by the frost. Unreadable weather: warm one day, wintry the next. Flat grey days that segued into short periods of hard light skimming across the roofs and lighting up the whitewashed walls of the bungalow next door.

She decided that, this morning, she would strip the sign from Darren's door and get rid of his clothes. The phone rang and she ignored it, fearing the distraction might change her mind. It rang again. This time the caller wouldn't hang up.

She dropped the bin bag on the floor, unhooked the handset and put it to her ear. Leah's voice — squashed to a whimper. 'They took him, Doctor. They took Leon last night. And they're not telling us where he is. They said I'm not his next-of-kin. They won't tell me what they've done with him. They keep saying...' Leah broke off, and the oddness of the sound of this quiet young woman keening in her ears raised the hairs on Mavis' arms.

'Leah,' she said. 'Where are you? Tell me where you are. I'll come over now.' Leah uttered something fast and breathless, then hung up.

Mavis shook herself out of the numbness, swallowed on the lump in her throat and reached for the phone. The uniforms *had* told Leah; she just wasn't ready to hear it.

Bergette answered on the first ring. 'They said he choked on his vomit.' Bergette's voice was the softest she'd ever heard it.

'They said the same about my son. Remember?' Mavis told her, and hung up.

★

She woke from a dream of multi-horned, dark-skinned men glaring through the window at Bed 45. She dressed for the cold, made herself a cup of coffee, but found she could not drink it. She parked her car at New Cross Gate and took the train to London Bridge.

At Boots, the chemists, the young man at the machine rewound the roll of film in her Kodak Instamatic and retrieved it from the camera.

'One hour service, please' she said.

She stood outside the doorway of the shop, her head an echo chamber to the rush of footsteps on the station concourse, the bang and clatter of the gates, the bedlam of arriving and departing trains.

Forty-five minutes later, the technician handed her the stuffed envelope with something between curiosity and avoidance on his face. 'I'm a doctor,' she said, offering him a smile. 'Routine stuff.'

She phoned Leah from the station. The Intern's answerphone kicked in.

'Leah, I have the pictures you wanted – of Bed 45.'

A clatter at the other end, then Leah's querulous, 'hello?'

'The entrance of the tube station. Meet me there,' Mavis said.

She took the train to Brixton. Leah's back was against the metal grid-work of the gates, a dripping umbrella held stiffly down her side. The girl looked different with her head tied in the style of the old Caribbean women who walked past them. Her eyes were swollen and bleary. Through the fog of rain, Mavis watched small groups of young men drifting along the pavement on the other side of the road, submitting themselves from time to time, with an almost sleepy indifference to the riffling hands of the uniforms before they were moved on. Even from here, having just arrived, she felt the electricity in the wet air: the unhurried walk of those young men, their hands shoved deep into puffer jackets. That very long, backward gaze from lowered heads.

She handed Leah the small bag. 'How... what will you do with them?'

'Make copies,' Leah said. 'Pass them around.' The young woman fixed her with a frank, red-eyed stare, then swung an arm at the youths across the road.

'Why don't you stay with me a while, Leah. I have room.'

Leah shook her head. 'I want to be here when it blows, Doctor.' Her Intern glanced at the bag. 'I think this will do it. Soon.'

Mavis was about to ask her how soon, but Leah had already pressed the bag of photos to her chest, ducked into the rain and was gone.

# Afterword: From New Cross to Brixton, January to April, 1981

## Prof. Stephen Reicher
University of St. Andrews

I REMEMBER THE NEW Cross fire well. At the time I was doing my PhD on crowds in Bristol, but most of my time was spent in London. I was a member of the Executive of the National Union of Students. I had responsibility for the Anti-Apartheid and Anti-Racism campaigns. My girlfriend, a black activist, lived just up the road from New Cross in Peckham, so we closely followed the twists and turns of the case. Exactly what did happen on the night of 17th January 1981 at 439 New Cross Road is still unclear. But what is quite certain is that the police, the coroner and the media viewed events through the racist prism of black danger. They fixated on the idea that the fire was not the outcome of an attack or even an accident, but rather arose out of a fight between the partygoers themselves. In this way the victims were turned into perpetrators. Parents, friends and the community were left to grieve their loss without the powers that be making even a gesture of sympathy. Eventually, some two months later, Margaret Thatcher did write a belated letter of condolence, but even then it was not addressed to the parents but to a local community worker who had been awarded an MBE.

There was nothing new here – the original insult being compounded by the reactions of a society that ignored black experience and held black lives cheap. But this time – perhaps because of the number of deaths, the poignancy of so many young lives lost in the midst of a birthday celebration – the reaction was different. One week later, a thousand people attended a meeting at the Moonshot Club, itself victim of an arson attack a few years earlier by the National Front. The New Cross Massacre Action Committee (NCMAC) was formed and they then called for a 'Black People's Day of Action' on the 2nd March.

For many, the day proved a turning point in the self-organisation of black people in Britain. Between 15,000 and 25,000 people (depending on which source you trust), mostly black, took time on a working day to march 17 miles over eight hours through the streets of London. That event I also remember well. It articulated a shared sense, so powerfully conveyed in 'Bed 45', that black people stand beleaguered – at best ignored, at worst assailed, by police, press and Parliament.

This sense was made clear in NCMAC's 'Declaration of New Cross'. The declaration starts by describing the massacre as 'an unparalleled act of savagery'. It continues: 'The national authorities in Parliament and government, in a further act of barbarism, ignored the tragedy of the families of the dead and injured.'

This sense was also made clear in the banners and placards and chants on the march: 'Murder, Murder'; 'Police Cover Up'; and so on. Menelik Shabazz's documentary of the day shows this vividly.[1] Part of the soundtrack is a song by Johnny Osbourne: 'Thirteen dead and nothing said; oh, what are we gonna do?' The answer to Osbourne's question is given in the title of the documentary: 'Blood Ah Go Run'. This was chanted throughout the march, sometimes in this abbreviated form, sometimes expanded to 'Blood Ah Go Run in '81 Unless Justice Come.'

Justice didn't come. The press covered the march in terms that compounded the original offence: 'Day the Blacks Ran Riot in London'; 'Black Day in Blackfriars'; 'Rampage of a Mob'. Just more representations of black people as dangerous.

An Inquest came to no conclusions about the deaths. The coroner's summary was inaccurate according to the High Court, but the verdict was not changed.

The NCMAC protested to Parliament about the police response to the fire. Parliament did not respond.

Just over a month later, on 11th April, the Brixton riots erupted, fuelled by rumours that Michael Bailey, a young black man, had been killed in police custody.

The connection between New Cross and Brixton seems obvious. It is the message of Jacob Ross's story. And he is quite right to remind us that there is a connection. The riots of the 1980s didn't just 'happen': they were not random eruptions of primitive violence in a civilised world. Rather they were responses to constant racist experiences in which the police played a pivotal role. As the Institute of Race Relations concluded in their submission to the Royal Commission on Criminal Procedure in 1979: 'to put it at its least, the failure of the police to protect the black community leaves it exposed to racist violence. At its worst police practice reinforces that violence.'

But when it comes to exactly how New Cross is connected to Brixton, I am less convinced by Jacob's tale. For the path to Brixton was not paved by hidden acts of agitation. Nor did it depend primarily upon stoking horror and outrage at the consequences of racism. People in the black community were well aware of racism, and they had daily experience of its consequences. What was critical was precisely that individuals came together as a community. And that was precisely what was achieved on the 2nd March 1981.

Marches, demonstrations, crowds in general are often portrayed as affairs of the heart rather than of the head – as the venting of pent-up frustrations. But they are so much more than that. On the 'Day of Action', British black people could look around and see that they did not stand alone, nor did they have to take their daily slights alone. 'I' became 'we'; individual identity became a shared social identity.

People did not share an identity, they shared a common narrative concerning the nature of their world – a world in which they were confronted not only by the thugs of the National Front but also by the indifference, or even the hostility, of media, police and politicians. Individual opinions concerning the illegitimacy of 'the system' was thereby transformed into a social fact.

Most importantly, perhaps, people felt empowered to express and to assert their viewpoint. When I watch the images of that day, I see that it was raining. In my memory it was sunny on the march. Perhaps that is because of the warmth of the occasion. For sure, the event was sombre. For sure, it was angry. But it was also celebratory. In pictures and films you can see that people are smiling and laughing. For on that day, the streets of London belonged to the black community. The pictures of the 13 victims were held aloft. They had been made visible. And when the march passed through Fleet Street, the black voice for once effaced the press rather than vice-versa. Moreover, when officers tried to divide the march at Blackfriars, protesters refused to let this happen and confronted the police. 'Black people united will never be defeated' read some of the placards. For once this was more than an aspiration.

So, a sense of *identity* (through a shared narrative), *illegitimacy* (of 'the system'), and *empowerment* (through collective demonstration) – that is what was created in the 8 hours and 17 miles of the 2nd March demonstration. Identity, illegitimacy, empowerment. Those are the conditions which are critical to collective action. Identity, illegitimacy, empowerment. That is the path from New Cross to Brixton – which itself was no simple venting of frustrations.

But that is another story.

# Notes

1. *Blood Ah Go Run*, 1982: http://player.bfi.org.uk/film/watch-blood-ah-go-run-1982/

# The Stars are in the Sky

## Joanna Quinn

AT GREENHAM, WE ONLY do the chores we want to do. There's no expectation, no rota, no list. No-one feels put upon or guilty. There's no simmering resentment. I wish my husband Stephen could see how well it works, but I can just imagine him saying, 'Don't be ridiculous, Ann. It won't get done by itself.' And his mother, taking the jay cloth from his hands, 'Here, let me do it, Stephen. Stephen, tell me, do you know when Ann will be coming back from that funny camp?'

Something else that's different: when I'm home, I loathe mornings. I loll about in bed as long as I can, feeling immobile and persecuted, while the kids shriek dementedly about the place, but at Greenham, that 'funny camp', I love waking up. Soon as I open my eyes, I swish back my tarpaulin shelter to see the sky. It's perishing cold first thing and your bones ache from sleeping on the ground, but your face is poking out your sleeping bag into the fresh air and there's something wonderful about that. I pull my duffle coat on over the clothes I've slept in, lace up my muddy boots, and do a bit of washing up – usually scrubbing saucepans encrusted with the sediment of last night's lentils. It's not easy keeping stuff clean here. We string our belongings up in trees to keep them out of the mud – soggy socks and tin mugs and blankets stinking of wood smoke. Our camp is surrounded by our own domestic detritus, our bits and pieces.

After the washing up, I usually have toast by the campfire with Theresa. She'll have been up since dawn poking the cinders, keeping the fire smouldering, sitting wrapped in a shawl like a Navajo squaw. Theresa's fifty-something, a sculptor from Dagenham, got four kids. Says she's been getting up at the crack for years, and can't get out of the habit now, so she may as well be useful. Says it's the task and the privilege of the crone to tend the fire.

Today, Theresa hands me a cuppa and says she's been praying to the goddess Athena since she saw the first light in the sky.

'Is Athena listening?' my friend Nic calls from her tent. 'Christ, it's freezing.'

'She always listens, duck,' says Theresa, 'but she hasn't done anything about moving your tent away from mine as yet. I'm going to keep asking though. Can't keep listening to you snore.'

'Love you, Theresa,' says Nic, in the stiff voice of someone trying to light a fag lying down.

'And I you, my dear.'

Both Nic and I know why Theresa was praying this morning. Last night, the missiles arrived.

But I don't want to think about that. I slosh back my tea and head into the bedraggled trees to collect firewood. I meander about, piling up branches on a bit of plastic sheeting to drag back. When I'm doing this, half my brain goes over what we discussed round the campfire the night before. Some of these women know so much. History. Politics. The Miners' Strike. Nicaragua. When they turn to me, I can never think what to say. But I talk to them in my head afterwards, and that feels like a natural continuation of the conversation, albeit one in which I'm a bit chattier. The other half of my brain scuttles off on its usual worrisome course, thinking about my Fi and my Danny getting up and having their Rice Crispies – and how Stephen always gets irked by their mess, his annoyance hanging over the breakfast table before they've even spilt anything.

Mornings in our house. An unending pile-up of

claustrophobia and irritation. Me hiding by the kitchen sink like a terrible hostess on the gin.

I was lurking in the kitchen when I opened the letter Nic sent me, the one that made me come to Greenham for the first time. December 1982. Nearly a year ago now. I was standing at the sink in my tatty dressing gown waiting for the kettle to boil, while Fi and Danny squabbled over their new advent calendar. The kitchen full of steam and condensation, dense as a swamp.

Fi was shouting: 'It's my turn today, Mum, tell him.'

'I had it first,' whined Danny.

'You have to share it,' I said, opening the envelope to find a page ripped from a wire-bound notebook, the top edge a ragged line of little circles torn open. Nic's biro handwriting exactly the same as it was at school – all zig-zags and exclamation marks.

The letter said: 'Ann, I miss you!! Why do I never see you? Are you still reading? Still painting? You bloody better be. When do we get to go to the pub and solve the world again? But anyway, this is important –'

'Mum!' shrieked Fi. 'He's pushing me!'

'You have to share,' I said, pouring hot water onto a teabag without looking up from the letter. 'It's important to share.'

Nic wrote: 'You've got to come to Greenham. You've seen the news, right? They're putting 96 American nuclear weapons in fucking BERKSHIRE!!! There's a mass action planned for next weekend. Bring waterproofs. Bring something to leave behind on the fence. If you really want to, you can bring Stephen (but you can't leave him behind on the fence – ha ha! Joke!), he just can't be involved in the action – he can help sort out food & childcare. You could involve the kids though (sorry – forgotten names again!!).'

Stephen appeared then, in his pyjamas, rubbing his head, as if unexpectedly summoned like a genie. 'What's all this shouting about?' he said, and rushed at the kids, tickling them until they were hysterical.

'They need to get dressed. You're not helping,' I muttered, narked by his jollity.

Nic's letter ended: 'If every woman copies this letter & sends it to ten friends & they each send it to ten others, then we shall be hundreds, thousands!!! Each woman is a spring that can become a stream, a river, an ocean. Ann. We need you.'

Stephen came into the kitchen, looking for his tea. It's a tiny kitchen – a galley kitchen the estate agent called it, as if it were something romantic and swaying on a wooden ship. It's just two lines of work tops looking at each other with a narrow trench in between where I pivot between sink and fridge, oven and bin, cupboard and cupboard. Stephen said: 'Why have the kids only got one advent calendar? They need one each or they'll fight every morning.'

I tucked Nic's letter into my dressing gown pocket. 'You can get them another one, if you want.'

'No time today, love. Up to my eyeballs. They'll have some at the corner shop.'

I was trying to think if I had ten friends I could send Ann's letter to. Trying to think if I even had ten friends anymore. The mums I chatted to at the school gate. My next door neighbour. The woman who worked at the corner shop. Not really friends. All of them always busy and scattered and doing something that screened off their attention – consoling little kids, picking up shopping, counting out change.

Stephen turned the radio on and a blast of music filled the kitchen. Bouncy electronic pop with big-haired harmonies over the top. Bucks Fizz. In the front room, Fi started dancing like she'd seen on the telly, jutting her hips, making her eyes wide.

Stephen picked up my mug. 'Is this mine?'

'Does it look like yours?'

'Hey, Mrs. Grumpy-in-the-Mornings,' he said, hands up as if I were going to shoot him. Then he sang along with the song, pointing his fingers like pistols: '*If you can't stand the heat, get out of the kitchen.*'

'I can't stand Buck's Fizz. They're just a shit Abba,' I said, clattering about in the cupboard for another mug for him. 'A shitter Abba.'

'No language in front of the kids, Mummy,' he said, frowning like the school teacher he was, and he danced into the front room with my mug, singing: '*If you can't stand the cold, don't sleep on the floor.*'

'Look at me, Daddy!' shouted Fi.

'Beautiful, sweetheart,' said Stephen. 'You'll be shaking your stuff on *Top of the Pops* in no time.'

I came to the conclusion I didn't have any friends I could send Nic's letter to. Not one. 'Well, I'm going to go,' I said to the mugs in the cupboard. Then I shut the cupboard door, turned round and tried it again, over the tinny blare of Radio 1: 'Stephen, I'm going to Greenham Common this weekend.' He was dancing with Fi, but paused to put a hand behind one ear and cock his head, wincing and flinching in the way we do when we mean *what? What did you say?*

The following Saturday, Stephen dropped me off at Leigh Delamere services, saying, 'I thought your bra-burning days were behind you,' with a smile so I couldn't take offence.

'So you don't think nuclear war is something to worry about?'

'Course I bloody do. It's just all this — it's not helping.' His 'all this' was an airy wave at a coachload of women heading into the service station. Their coach had signs propped up in the windows saying, 'WE SAY NO TO CRUISE MISSILES' and 'WOMEN FOR LIFE ON EARTH' and 'GRANDMOTHERS AGAINST THE BOMB'.

'I've done a casserole,' I said. 'There's loads of food in the freezer for the kids. You won't need to go to the chippy.'

'I know how to feed them.'

Two young women with shaved heads walked past then, arms round each other's waists, hands tucked into each other's back pockets, strides perfectly matched.

Stephen laughed, shook his head. 'That sort of stuff isn't going to help the cause, is it?'

'You're quite right. We should keep the lesbians inside.'

'Don't be facetious, Ann. I'm trying to discuss this with you. You're always saying we should talk about politics more.'

'I am discussing it.'

'Just makes it an easy target for the tabloids.'

'But it's not their fault, is it? What the press do.'

'The problem is, Ann, when they banned men from Greenham, they made it all about themselves.'

'What do you mean "they"?'

'You can't cut yourself off from the real world. I can see you're going to get upset again. Let's leave it there.' He leaned into the dashboard, peered at the clock, tapped the petrol gauge, twisted the heating knob right then left – a little litany of empty checks.

'I'll say hi to Nic for you,' I said, opening the car door, and he laughed again. I thought of the few times they've been in a room together. How much I wanted them to like each other, my oldest friend and my husband, and the awful strain of it – a tight skin of awkwardness pulling across everything, like I couldn't find a way to be myself enough for either of them. The echoing, audible gulps of wine. The pained smiles.

'She doesn't like me,' he said, and there's a little pleasure in how he says it, as if he's been proved right in something. 'She never has.'

'You're very different people,' I said, getting out of the car. I didn't want to hear him go on about Nic again. He always talks about her in a sort of wry, knowing way, as if she were a problem student at his school. Says she's a hopeless idealist. For Stephen, the words 'hopeless' and 'idealist' are inextricably linked. There isn't any other kind.

'Kiss Fi and Danny for me,' I said, as he reached across to pull the passenger door shut, drove away.

Standing there in my wellies, holding a rucksack and a sleeping bag, it was like I'd been dropped off by my parents at Guide Camp. I felt weirdly nervous. Nic had instructed me to meet a friend of hers in the Little Chef. Kathleen. Sixty-something in a wool coat with grey hair frizzing out from under a crocheted beret. 'Ann?' she said, in a loud laughing voice, with a thick Scouse accent. 'Nic's friend, Ann? This way, pet. I've got seats saved for us.'

'You're from Liverpool,' I said. 'Nic and I were at university there. We loved it.'

'Why would you go anywhere else? God's own city,' she said, shepherding me to one of the coaches with pats from her wide veined hands. Two seats left at the front for us and the passengers were already singing as we climbed on board, a song about spirits and mountains that went cheerfully round and round like a carousel.

Kathleen sat next to me, her comfortable bulk resting against my side. She opened a Tupperware box to offer tuna paste sandwiches to me and the two older women sitting across the aisle, both with tight perms battened down beneath headscarves and pale eyes smiling behind thick glasses. 'We're from the same church,' explained Kathleen. 'We do as many of these as we comfortably can. Most of us lost people we loved in the last war. Don't want another one, do we?'

A punky teenager with a pierced nose suddenly loomed over our seats: 'Got a light?'

Kathleen reached into her coat pocket and pulled out a lighter. 'I don't smoke meself, but these youngsters are always losing theirs,' she said, leaning on me confidingly. The teenager shuffled her pack of fags to offer me one, and I was reaching up to take it when I glanced out of the coach window and saw that another coach full of women and banners was over-taking us and they were all waving at us like they knew us. It made me laugh out loud. And behind them, a few cars back, there was another one gaining on us, all full of waving arms and grinning open faces behind the glass, and behind that, another one, and another, and another. And it suddenly felt that there were hundreds of us, a phalanx of coaches coasting down the motorway, all full of women waving at each other across the oblivious car drivers, high up and silent and delighted and on our way.

Nic was waiting for me when I got off the coach at Greenham. We'd had the odd phone call but I hadn't actually seen her for over a year. She was always travelling to exciting places, campaigning about things, doing stuff with Greenpeace; I was always stuck with the kids. She rushed towards me, looking a bit mad in a poncho and muddy jeans with plastic bags tied over her shoes, and hugged me in a rolling side to side way, hissing in my ear: 'You came. I bloody knew you would.' Her hair was shaved up the sides, there was a new crinkling of lines around her eyes, and she had a walkie-talkie shoved in her pocket, but she was still Nic. Nic who sat beside me on our first day at secondary school in 1962 and was my best friend before the bell rang at the end of class.

A steady stream of women wove around us as we hugged, hundreds pouring out of coaches and cars, while press photographers snapped away, helicopters buzzed overhead, and a moustachioed policeman in a helmet and long coat shouted: 'Keep moving, ladies – save the romance for your dirty little tents.'

I looked up over Nic's shoulder and saw the fence that surrounded RAF Greenham Common: thick wire mesh, ten foot high, held up by cement pylons and topped with rolled barbed wire. Beyond that, the banality of a carpark. Empty roads. Hedges. And then a blank treeless area made up of concrete runways and small bunker-like buildings – those mysterious locked-up structures you only ever see at military places. Windowless. Anonymous. No clear purpose. Which, of course, means they must have a very specific purpose.

The women's camp, or what I could see of it, was ramshackle and improvised: a cluster of tents squished onto a narrow strip of grass between the fence and a busy main road. There were bits of plastic sheeting propped up on sticks to create shelters; stacks of wooden pallets covered by grubby sleeping bags; decrepit floral armchairs; a couple of deck chairs; buckets of sand filled with fag-ends, and an old-fashioned pram now used as a flower bed for delicate snowdrops. Middle-aged women in bobble hats were sitting on hay bales sharing a hipflask, while teenage anarchists with loud-hailers boiled a kettle over an open fire. It was like the bomb had already been dropped and this was the ad-hoc world afterwards; people making a place from a flat nothing.

'How long have these women been here?' I asked, my chin still resting on Nic's shoulder.

'Some have been here for more than a year. When the first protesters arrived, the camp guards thought they were cleaners. Can you imagine? Walking all the way here from Wales and, when you arrive, there's a soldier handing you a mop and bucket.'

'I didn't know it was like this.'

'You're here now too,' and she pulled away to look at me. 'Great to see you, my oldest and bestest.'

'It's been ages, hasn't it? I'm sorry I haven't seen you for so long.'

'Did Kathleen tell you what we're doing? We're calling it "Embrace the Base". We're going to surround the base – a massive chain of women holding hands.'

'Holding hands?'

'In the best spirit of passive resistance. We're meeting violence with love, baby. You remember Ghandi?'

'I've forgotten most things. Having kids turns your brain to porridge.'

Nic pointed at two women passing with waddling toddlers in snowsuits: 'They managed to find their way here, even with their porridge brains.'

'Do you think I should have brought Fi and Danny?' I asked and felt again the guilt of having them – which was also the guilt of having left them behind.

'Don't worry about it,' she said, pulling me forward. 'Let's find a place on the fence.'

One year later, and that perimeter fence is the backdrop to my life. I walk around it every day with Nic. After Embrace the

Base, people left things hanging on it, to show they'd been there. Scarves, toys, poems, flowers, teapots, bracelets, nappies, photographs of parents, husbands, boyfriends, girlfriends and children. Every woman who came along was asked to bring a gift for the base – things to represent the many loves of our lives. I saw a couple of wedding dresses tied onto the fence and, in one spot, an entire dinner service set, carefully strung up, piece by piece. 30,000 women turned up that day. We were all over the news. It blew my mind. I never knew there were so many women willing to stand up and be counted. It was like we'd all been hidden away somewhere.

Since then, we keep adding stuff to the fence. Keeping it going. Pairs of tights, knitted babies' booties, Christmas decorations, postcards sent from well-wishers all over the world. It looks like something from the Glastonbury CND Festival. Last week, I put up a drawing Danny did of me as a superhero, one giant hand crushing a flaming rocket. The fence itself has been patched up multiple times. We've taught ourselves to use bolt-cutters so we're able to keep cutting our way in, opening windows and doors into the base again and again, just to show we can. Let's get some air in here. Let's get some light on the subject. There's even an old bit of fence back at our camp that we use to cook food over the fire.

My daily Greenham routine is largely dependent on the time Nic gets up, which is determined by whether she's had company in her tent the night before, but she usually surfaces by nine – then we grab some plastic containers and go to get fresh water. It's a couple of miles, following the fence around the base, passing close by the missile silos – great concrete storage towers that look like they're emerging from the ground. It's bonkers how quickly you get used to being within spitting distance of stuff purposely designed to end lots and lots of lives. The two of us stroll arm-in-arm, like how we used to walk to school together, smoking cheap fags, singing 'Ticket to Ride' and planning our epic futures.

There's a total of nine miles of fence round RAF Greenham,

interspersed with big metal gates, which have been named after the colours of the rainbow by the women camping near each one. Each camp has its own character. Nic and I are at Green Gate – a peaceful, Robin Hood hide-out tucked away in the woods – but every day we make our way to Yellow Gate, which was the first and original. The one I arrived at. The water pump is there and our post goes there too, along with the donations people send to support us. The soldiers behind the fence usually ignore us as we pass, though there's a couple that nod half-heartedly.

They're busy today. Distracted. Behind them, we can see a huge white aeroplane marked 'US AIR FORCE', which arrived in the small hours, waking us all up. It came into land with a juddering roar that shook the mugs hanging in the trees. The plane is gaping open at one end. There are military vehicles clustered round this open end and armed paratroopers standing with their backs to it. Nothing has come out of the plane yet. It's all very quiet. A curious still life. A stage set.

'Morning troops,' Nic shouts cheerfully, as if we were on a country ramble and not walking past a plane full of nuclear warheads that Nic says are 16 times more powerful than the bomb they dropped on Hiroshima.

'A beautiful winter's day,' says one of the soldiers, and he's got one of those radio smooth American voices.

'Be even nicer if you went back home, eh? Rather than guarding missiles that could end the human race,' says Nic.

'And there was me, thinking we were going to have a half-way decent conversation.' He turns away, bored by us. You never know what you'll get with the soldiers. They're so young, some of them, you wouldn't think they would have the nerve to treat us like they do.

But it is a beautiful day. Clear and crisp. The tree branches are silvered with frost and clumps of frozen grass stick up like stiff wire filaments. The sky is a thin pale blue, as if cold air was seeping through from space.

Yellow Gate is frenetic, full of reporters who have pitched up en masse with their cameras and microphones so they can put to us – with am-dram incredulity – that *surely* the arrival of US missiles at Greenham today means that the women protesters have *failed*. *Surely* all their *efforts* have been in *vain*. *Surely,* they say. *Surely.* As if it were something so blindingly obvious it pains them to ask the question. As if they were begging us to put them out of their misery by agreeing with them.

A local councillor is there, eager to answer the journalists' questions, all suit-straining belly and bustling officialdom. His eyelids flutter as he expounds at length on why Secretary of State Michael Heseltine was right to say women may be shot if they enter the base. The councillor has a booming oratory of repeated phrases: hard-working rate-payers; unsavoury illegal encampments; council by-laws. He never glances behind himself, to where real women are living and breathing. Like the soldiers, he rarely looks at us.

The reporters call out: 'Councillor, how are the women breaking into the camp? Isn't this place meant to be high-security?'

'High security my arse,' shouts Nic. Women around us laugh and jeer. The camp is twitchy today. I can feel it rising. The bobbies can too. They're exchanging glances, tightening helmet straps, shifting themselves into lines. They've got policemen on horses. They've never had horses before. I suppose they don't want the Americans to have any unpleasantness on their special missile day.

The council man proclaims: 'Even RAF Greenham, with all necessary measures taken, cannot be entirely woman-proof.' How the reporters laugh, only to be told by the councillor that national security is not a laughing matter. It is important we remember, he chides, that a properly defended Western Europe is more likely to remain at peace than one whose weakness tempts an aggressor to strike.

Weakness, as it turns out, is very tempting indeed. Whenever they have military convoys travelling out of the camp, we organise women to lie down in the road in front of them. We always know when they're planning a convoy because the wife of an American soldier who lives near the camp washes his uniform specially and hangs it out on the line so we can all see. We put ourselves in front of their vehicles and we chant – *We are women, we are women, we are strong, we are strong, we say no, we say no, to the bomb, to the bomb* – and the policemen that come charging in to drag us out the way don't hold back. They get pretty bloody angry with a group of women doing nothing but lying down. They dislocate our arms and break our fingers. All so a big American lorry can drive round Wiltshire for a few hours, pretending it's fighting a war, like little boys do.

Policemen are muttering into walkie-talkies; their horses stamping and snickering. 'This won't be pretty,' says Nic, her voice low and quiet. She's put our water containers down without me noticing. She's scanning the camp, catching gazes, pulling people in.

Having taken their fill of the man from the council, the reporters ask for a Greenham spokeswoman. Nic tells them we don't have any spokeswomen because all of us have an equal voice. We even have a wooden post back at Green Gate, painted with the words 'The stars are in the sky' to remind us there's no stars here.

'No-one's extra special – not even you, sweetheart,' says Nic to a glamorous woman reporter, struggling in the mud in her heels. To her, we must look like feral creatures. Stigs of the Dump. Nic with her tufty hair, knitted leg-warmers and massive waterproof poncho. Me in my muddy duffle coat and my dad's old army gaiters.

'I'd get out of here if I were you,' I say.

'I've got a job to do, thanks,' she snaps. 'And the quicker you find me a spokeswoman, the more likely it is you'll get on the news.'

One of the journalists shouts: 'Come on ladies, don't you think you should be with your families this Christmas?'

'You're spot on, lad – I should,' replies Kathleen, my travelling companion on the coach, now an old hand based at Violet Gate. 'I'll do that once these missiles have gone and my grandchildren are safe.'

315

There's cheering at this, and the camp women start to move together, chanting – *which side are you on? I ask you, which side are you on?* – their tone accusatory, aggressive.

Nic and I link arms automatically, shifting back to join the women who are becoming a crowd, who are becoming a movement, and we add our voices to theirs: *Are you on the side that don't like life? Are you on the side that beats your wife? Which side are you on?* I see the faces of the policemen in their black uniforms lining up against us: one just a spotty youth, looking terrified, and an older man to his right, shaking his head very slowly like a disappointed headmaster, a slight smile on his face, and I know he will be the one to come at us the hardest, the one that hates us the most. You learn to recognise it.

Nic hisses in my ear: 'Ann, remember, when they grab you, go totally limp.'

They come at us quicker than I expect. Men on foot and on horseback. For a second, I think of *Henry V*, that battle speech I studied at school, and as the group of us linked together fall back, I'm whispering to myself: 'Once more unto the breach, dear friends.'

'Sit down, sit down,' shouts Nic, and we sink to the floor, which is the hardest most unnatural thing to do, when there's men with truncheons and massive horses in front of you. To lower yourself. Not to run. Not to put your arms up. Not to shield your face. *Cry God*, I think, *Cry God for fucking England*, and then the police move in and one is reaching down to pull a woman away by her hair and she's still chanting – *Are you on the side who locks the door? Are you on the side who loves the law?* – with her eyes screwed shut in pain. Two policemen drag away a woman just in front of me. She's ululating, the noise high and primal, as they chuck her to the side like a sack of rubbish. When one woman is taken away, another dashes in to take her place. I see Kathleen heaved off by two coppers young enough to be her grandsons – one has his leather-gloved hand over her mouth to stop her chanting, as if that were an offence – and I try to catch her eye to tell her I am here with her, but she's been hauled behind a police van and is gone.

Nic and I are in the front line now. Our turn next. Her strong arm is linked in mine and I hear her saying over and over: 'Go limp, Ann. It'll hurt less. You're a floppy rag doll. Leave yourself behind.'

In this noise, and in this fear, I think of my kids, their faces. My boy. My girl. I wonder what they're doing now.

Before I came to Greenham, Stephen and I had watched this QED documentary about what would happen if a nuclear bomb was dropped on London. Parts of it had wedged in my head. Little shrapnel shards. Whenever I gave the kids a bath, I would hear the words *water instantaneously boiling*. When I cooked their tea, I heard *human flesh, like all animal fats, will melt and burn*.

On the programme, they showed cheering crowds at Charles and Di's wedding and said all those people, plus another quarter of a million, would die immediately from the blast. They used a pumpkin to show what happens to human flesh caught in flying glass and it was shredded to pulp in beautiful slow-mo with sound effects like something off *Dr. Who*. Then they cut to a real couple in Shepherd's Bush trying to build a nuclear shelter in their garden.

'Our garden isn't really big enough,' I'd said.

'It is. I could do that,' said Stephen. And I knew that would be the last I'd see of him – a confident figure walking out the back door with a set of printed instructions and a spade, determined to build a shelter when all around him the sky burned and howled. A man sure of his purpose, even as he was wiped from existence.

*'You may be the only one in your area with a shelter, are you prepared to use force to keep others out?'* asked Ludovic Kennedy, the narrator.

'What kind of question is that?' I'd said.

'Turn it off if it upsets you,' said Stephen. So we did and the image of the Shepherd's Bush couple sitting miserably smoking in their shelter shrank to a pin-prick, and there we were, in our quiet front room with the tiled fireplace and the sconce lights and the wood pigeons cooing outside. 'There,' said Stephen, ruffling my hair. 'All better now.'

But Ludovic Kennedy was insistent. All that night, he kept asking me: *Would you be able to find all your family in time? Would you be able to find all your family in time?*

The policeman who drags me away from Yellow Gate is a big bloke. He's sweating and swearing. 'If I wasn't getting so much fucking over-time, I wouldn't be bothering with you, love,' he says, depositing me in a ditch at the side of the road. 'Do me a favour and stay there for now, would you?'

'We've a right to protest,' I say, getting to my feet.

'You have, darlin'. My wife's right behind you. But I'm knackered. And if you go back there, I'll just have to bring you right back here again.'

Nic appears behind him, a graze on her forehead. 'We're calling it a day,' she says, putting an arm round me. 'People are getting hurt. Let's go back to Green Gate.'

'Sensible girls,' says the policeman, smiling and brushing himself down. 'Get back, have a cuppa.'

Theresa greets us when we arrive back at our camp. 'The warriors return. Nip of Baileys?'

Nic's quiet. I can tell she feels defeated, as if we'd fought a real battle. She takes things to heart. Always has. The other women leave her be and she skulks off into the trees to dig a new shitpit. I'd never dug a shitpit before I came to Greenham. Didn't know that's what you did. Never camped outside. Never cooked over an open fire. When I was little, I loved exploring the woods near our house, but as I got older, they became dangerous places, where trench-coated strangers might lurk, their hands shifting in their pockets, so I stayed inside in front of the telly, or hung about at the youth centre, watching the boys play pool.

In the evening, we Green Gaters gather together for a meal. The darkness is different outside. The trees creak. Leaves skitter about. It feels elemental and right to huddle round the fire. There's no men allowed at Green Gate ever, but at other gates they can visit in the day time, and then, when night falls, they all have to go. You hear the car engines starting up, the headlights striping through the trees like torch beams, then the sounds diminish as they head back to cosy suburbia, leaving us women out here in the wild, open dark.

I think of my faraway kids then. Our bedtime rituals. Bath, pyjamas, warm milk, stories. *Charlie and the Chocolate Factory*. *Paddington Bear*. *The Lorax*. I remember how it feels to carry their warm little bodies up the stairs. I used to try to get home at least once a week but it was always hard to get a lift back from the camp, and Stephen didn't want me hitching, and the kids would get so excited by me turning up. Too excited really. It would always end in tears. Theirs or mine or both.

So now the gaps between my visits get longer. Stephen has different ways of doing things and I don't know what they are so I get them wrong and then he gets cross. He says I put them back or put them out or something like that. I put them somewhere they shouldn't be. It seemed to work all right when I was the solid centre and Stephen was the one to come and go, staying late at work, missing bedtimes. But when it's me who comes and goes, it creates a disruption. Or that's what Stephen says. He says I upset them. I wonder if Fi and Danny remember the thousands of bedtimes I did before. All the nights they were ill. All the nappy changes. Or maybe they're like cats — maybe they just remember the person who fed them last. No. No, that can't be true.

Tonight, one of the women here is serving up veggie curry. As she's sharing it out, she says: 'It used to drive me crackers when my husband would come home and say, "What have you been up to then?" as if he couldn't see the food I'd cooked sitting on the table.' There's knowing laughter round the campfire.

Theresa says: 'I was a full-blown hippy. Still am. But goodness, I spent a lot of time cooking for men.'

'Thank god I never had anything to do with them,' says Nic, and she doesn't look at me, but I can tell by a certain set focus in her eyes that she's thinking about it. She reaches forward to stroke the hair of a woman sitting at her feet and I feel a thorny prickle of exclusion in my chest.

There's a pause and I try to say something I've been pondering on my wood-collecting trips. 'But food does have to be cooked. My kids do have to be looked after. They're only little. Three and six.'

'Who's looking after them now?' says a woman opposite me.

'Their dad. Their grandparents. I'm lucky.'

'Shouldn't be a question of luck, my dear,' says Theresa, her face in the firelight a latticework of lines. 'Men have a responsibility too. A relationship must nourish both those in it.'

'But what if it doesn't?' says Nic, and all the flickering faces turn to her. 'For every woman here with a supportive partner, there are ten more made to feel guilty for not being at home.' There are nods, murmurs of agreement. 'Why do women have to seek permission to do what they want? Ann, you came here to make the world safer for your children. How can you feel guilty about that?'

I don't know what to say. That is why I came here, but it's not the whole of it. I do worry about the missiles, of course I do, but you can't think about them all the time. The apocalypse is too big a concept to lug around with you all day. Mainly I think about firewood and lentils and mud and squalor and hugs and direct action and cups of tea. But then there's the other bit of my split brain, which circles my kids endlessly, like a dumb moth round a lightbulb. I don't know if Fi and Danny consider the threat of nuclear escalation more important than having a mum waiting at the school gates. And I wish Nic was sitting with me, her leg resting against mine, so we could be on the same side again, and I could be sure of things.

If we have an issue at Greenham, we always have a meeting. Every big decision has to be a collective camp decision;

everyone has a turn to speak. It can go on a bit and I can hear Stephen's voice in my head saying, 'Hundreds of women trying to make a single decision? Jesus, you're going to be at that bloody camp till the end of time. Our children will have forgotten they ever had a mother.'

But I always look forward to Nic talking. She has this definiteness about her. When we first became friends, my mother kept saying, 'I'm not sure about that Nicola Gardener,' and I was baffled because Nic was the surest person I had ever met. She saw things in a bright, clear light. She knew what was wrong and how it should change. Even at school, she was organising protests about the lowly rates of pay for pupils working in the tuck shop. I was hopelessly hormonal. Emotional driftwood. Covering my exercise books with drawings of George Harrison and doodled flowers and different versions of my name – *Ann Harrison, Ann McCartney, Ann Harrison, Ann McCartney* – over and over in a squiggly mass.

Nic was only in our school for a year before she got in trouble for bunking off and her parents sent her to boarding school, but we wrote to each other every week. Told each other everything. I was funnier and bolder in those letters than I ever was in reality. (The real me was loitering on the edge of dancefloors with hair so tightly done it was painful to smile.) Nic's handwriting on an envelope lying in the hall could lift the whole day right up because there I was again, the better version of me. 'I'm a terrible fool for romance,' I would write to her, all verbosity and extravagance, 'Oh woe, oh woe, I'm an insufferable doormat.' And I would draw tiny wailing cartoons of myself down the margin. 'That's just like you, Ann,' she'd write back, in her firm angular hand, 'you do yourself down so much!! But you've got a good heart.' And I would think – oh, so that's what I'm like. There I am.

That night at Greenham, we talk about whether we should break into the camp and occupy the air traffic control tower.

'Would it be a criminal offence?' I ask.

'Loads of us have been up in court,' says a woman from Blue Gate, sipping a can of lager. 'Doesn't mean anything. Gets us great publicity.'

'Don't we lose the moral high ground if we break the law?' I say.

She laughs. 'The Americans dump their weapons in our country and we sit about debating the pros and cons of touching a control tower?'

Suddenly Nic says: 'Where do your parents live, Ann? Woolhampton, isn't it? If the Russians aim a missile at this site, are they in the fall-out zone? I know you know your fall-out zones. We talked about it often enough. All those nights down the student union.' There's something sharp and light in her voice then, something flashing past.

'How many revolutions have been unarmed?' says Blue Gate.

'Greenham is a peaceful protest,' says Theresa.

'Protest can't always be peaceful,' says Nic.

Blue Gate adds: 'You're just doing what men want you to do. Fitting in around them. Fuck that shit.'

'I'll drink to that,' says Nic.

I look down at my muddy gaiters – my dad's muddy gaiters. Ones he wore in France fighting the Germans. I feel daft all of a sudden, like I've been playing dress up. I'm grateful for Theresa's warm voice, reminding us that we're all on the same side, that we're all Greenham women. I glance up at Nic but she's turned away talking to her latest squeeze, who's called Julie or Julia or Jules or something like that.

After we've talked and eaten, I pull my bobble hat on to walk to the phone box to call Stephen. It's starting to rain. It's miserable when it rains. You feel like you're pointlessly camped on a filthy roadside verge, while everyone normal is driving past you, going home for a nice long bath.

As I walk the fence, I hear a British squaddie call out to me: 'I'll see you in your tent later, darling. Better be waiting, yeah?'

'The chubby little one?' says his mate. 'I couldn't shag her sober.' Hilarity ensues.

I grit my teeth and try to remember what Theresa says about softness being a strength, about women's bodies being the sacred source of life, but I still want to cry. I keep going, one foot after the other, following the wobbly light of my torch, praying they don't come after me like they did Nic last week. They threw a skinned rabbit at her. Red and raw. Its black bead eyes wide open. When she told us about it, she looked at me, as if to say 'See? This is what they're like.'

A policeman swaying on his feet like a bored park-keeper glances at me as I pass Yellow Gate, his radio crackling with robotic voices, then returns his full attention to the padlocked metal gate he is guarding. I used to think policemen were there to protect me.

Standing in the piss-stinking phone box, I dial the number of my house, letting the numbers spin back round one by one. I think of Stephen putting the kids to bed and I love him then. I miss him. I often do when I'm waiting to speak to him, imagining him pottering about, very distant and unaware. Then his actual voice comes on the phone.

'That you, Ann?'

'You sound tired. Everything okay?'

'Busy. Danny's been a pain in the arse all day. I was about to sit down with a beer.'

'Did he sleep all right last night?'

'I don't know, love. Sort of. I don't know.'

There's a pause, some clicking on the line. Nic says the phone's tapped but I can't believe anyone would want to listen to me talking to my husband.

'Did you get his nativity costume sorted? I thought you could use Fi's old nightie.'

'Your mum's doing something. I don't have to do everything, do I?'

'Course not. He will need one though.'

'Have you rung me up just to berate me? I've had a bloody long day.'

'It's been a tough day for me too. The missiles arrived. There were policemen on horses –'

'For god's sake, Ann. I just told you I'm tired. Now is not the time for another tirade about the indignities suffered by the women of Greenham. If you want to stay there, stay there, but don't inflict it on the rest of us.'

'A tirade?'

'Can we just leave it?'

I can never seem to say it to him. How it really is here. There's a poster in the Quaker Meeting House in Newbury where we go to have hot showers that Nic pointed out. It says, 'LET YOUR LIFE SPEAK'. I hope mine does a better job than I do.

Someone taps on the phone box door. I look out of the cracked glass and see a queue of women standing under umbrellas waiting to call their families. They're all lined up, tightly holding their important unimportant questions about nativity costumes and PE kits and bedtimes and mealtimes and the whereabouts of special blankets.

'Stephen,' I say.

'Hang on, someone's out of bed,' he says and there's a clatter, and footsteps and I hear him bellowing up the stairs and, far away, very tiny, Danny's high little voice asking for milk, asking for stories, asking for Mummy.

Stephen comes back to the phone, and he's almost vicious with annoyance: 'He asks for you every night. Every bloody night.'

'He does that even when I'm there,' I say. 'I'll be holding his hand and he'll still be shouting that he wants his mummy. It's just something he says.' This is what I tell myself. That mummy is just an interchangeable shout of need, like asking for a biscuit or a teddy. Not something specific. And certainly not that, even when he has me, he still wants more of me, because my son's need is that vast and that never-ending.

I hear a gulp that tells me Stephen has brought a beer with him to the phone. '*The Two Ronnies* is on in a minute,' he says.

'Remember to take the camera to Danny's nativity.'

'It'll be the same as last year. A hideous free-for-all.' Then his voice softens. 'It's nearly Christmas, Ann. When are you coming back? When do I get my wife back?'

I watch the women outside tapping their toes, their faces absent as their minds go running over all the little things they need to remember to ask their husbands because they don't trust their husbands to remember. A sort of unconscious constant rumination, like the way blind people seem to look at nothing but their hands are busy reading Braille, minuscule lumps and bumps, tiny but vital. And behind them, I can see the fence and the base and the black silhouettes of guards patrolling with dogs and I can hear the giant arc lamps sizzling in the rain, and the raindrops, as they are lit up by the lamps, are a molten stream of amber pouring from the sky. Who will do this apart from us?

'Ann,' he says. 'Are you still there? Say something.'

I say: 'Stephen, why aren't you proud of me?'

I don't really say that. I say: 'The bleeps are going. I'm going back to the others. Kiss my babies for me,' and I put the phone down.


On the day of Embrace the Base, when the daylight started to fade, everyone began to slowly drift away, hugging like old friends, and leaving behind them thousands of little candles, flickering will-o-the-wisps, tilted and melting.

Nic was watching me watching the women leaving in the dusk. 'Are you going home now, Ann?'

'Yeah,' I said. 'But I'll come back.'

She raised her eyebrows. Gave me a tight hug. Exhaled in my ear then let me go. 'Say hello to Stephen for me. If he can bear to hear my name.'

'You're very different people,' I said.

She half-smiled, looked at me with a tired and fond exasperation, then waved me off.

A woman I'd never met before gave me a lift home that night and we talked non-stop like we'd known each other for years. When I crept through my front door into the silence of a house full of sleepers, it was like I'd come back from another planet. I stared about a bit. There were the usual bits of Lego scattered about the front room, a couple of lights left on, a vinegary smell of chips.

I turned the lights off and headed up to Fi and Danny's bedroom. Their arms and legs were dramatically flung out across their beds, as if they had fallen into sleep from a great height. I tucked Danny's Action Man in next to him and sat there on the floor for a while, thinking about the women at Greenham.

Nic didn't believe I would go back. I could imagine her quick voice chivvying me like she did when I was trying to get out of cross-country running at school. 'What are you going to do, Ann? Are you not even going to try?' She always told me to be brave. She even encouraged me to go on my first date with Stephen when I met him in the last year of uni. Then he and I got serious, and I couldn't talk to her about him, because she would know what it meant. It would mean the end of me and her. The end of us sharing a flat, going on holiday together, spending all our free time together, just hanging out, being ridiculous, solving the world.

She'd told me herself: 'Married men take their friendships with them; married women leave theirs behind.' We'd laughed about it – how our respective dads were jollying it up at their respective golf clubs, while our mums stayed home, stirring food in saucepans, with a phone tucked between chin and shoulder, the twisty wire stretching back into the hall, pulled as far as it would go, saying to women they missed: 'We must meet up one of these days. We must meet up.'

But back then, Stephen was all cherubic curls and long limbs in a bed-sit in Freehold Street with a stack of Hendrix LPs and a gas-fire that hissed as he undid my shirt. He had this kind of cocksure certainty. 'I'm going to have to marry you,' he said, pulling me down onto his bed, and it was such a relief to have someone state it like that, as simple and straightforward as a fact. It felt like he was telling me a story I had always wanted to hear.

I didn't have any bridesmaids because I couldn't have Nic up there with me when I said my vows. When I left Miss Ann Mulligan behind and went off as Mrs. Ann Kingston, waving from the car in my big white dress.

Stephen Kingston. Nic Gardener. When I think of them, I see Nic pulling me out the door behind her and I see Stephen patting the space next to him on the sofa, and I know each of them loves me and is entirely certain of my place and I envy them that.

After my phone call to Stephen, I walk back round the fence to Green Gate, feeling a bit glum about missing Danny's nativity play. As I slosh along in the slippery mud, I keep asking myself: 'What are you going to do, Ann?' Because this camp – squashed in the gap between fence and road – is only temporary. We have made Greenham feel like our permanent place, decorated it with pictures of the loves of our lives, but the council have started discussing bailiffs and forced evictions. I don't know where we go from here. How do you go back once you've left?

('Don't anticipate the blow,' says Nic, when we lie down in front of the convoys and the police come for us. 'Just let it happen. Leave yourself behind.')

At Green Gate, I find Nic so we can start our night watch duty. Night watch means we stay up till dawn, guarding the camp. Shepherds watching over our flock. We sit there with our torches, looking out for soldiers trying to put cans of maggots in our sleeping bags or random men following women into the bushes trying to intimidate them.

The two of us sit huddled beneath a tree, where we've got a clear line of sight over both camp and perimeter fence. We've strung up a bit of canvas to give us some shelter but it's still cold, with spiteful little splatterings of rain.

'Know what I learned today?' says Nic. 'That massive plane that carried the missiles in – it's called a Starlifter.'

'Really?'

'Incredible, isn't it? Think about some man designing an

aeroplane that will carry nuclear weapons – then deciding to give it a pretty name.'

I tuck my arm into Nic's. She's shivering like a child. 'They're wrong, aren't they?' I say, because sometimes it doesn't seem possible that so many powerful people could all believe the wrong thing. Stephen says I take them too seriously. He says they don't really believe what they say – that it's brinksmanship, a war of words – as if the politicians were blokes down the pub, winding each other up. I think you should never make threats you aren't prepared to carry out – every mother learns that.

'Yes,' says Nic. 'They're wrong.'

It's dark and cold. Looking up at the cloud-covered sky is like looking at the underbelly of a bridge – black and starless. We can hear the never-ending humming of the generator inside the camp. Nic rummages in her pockets for her baccy tin. Rolls us each a fag, puts one in my mouth, one in hers. The damp paper sticks to my cracked lips. 'That's the last of it,' she says, rattling the empty tin. I nod, reach my lighter from my pocket, spark it up with one hand cupped protectively round the wavering flame, and we lean in together, inhale quickly, suck them alight.

# Afterword: Yellow Gate, NVDA, and Carrying Greenham On, 1983-1987

## Lyn Barlow

JOANNA'S STORY OFFERS US a glimpse into the vibrant early days of life at Greenham. Her protagonist Ann, like so many other women, myself included, came to Greenham for a specific event, in her case 'Embrace the Base', and were so overwhelmed by the experience that they couldn't return to their former lives. Greenham was powerful, and life affirming, even in the midst of the nuclear missile base committed to destruction. Being, from the start, a women-only camp and one committed to non-violence, it gave women a rare opportunity to not only 'speak out', to dare to raise our voices against patriarchy and the war machine, but also an opportunity to 'act out' by taking part in creative, symbolic, supportive, acts of disobedience. It empowered women, from all classes, races, sexualities and religions. For many women this was their first taste of liberation, for many, like me, their 'university'.

I lived at Yellow Gate for nearly four years. I came from a working-class, male-dominated, community in the North of England, slightly 'politicised' in that I'd spent a number of years in care, rebelled against a system that 'gave up' on its charges, and got involved in the start of 'Who Cares?', a fledgling campaigning group trying to promote and highlight the rights and lack of opportunities for children in care.

I came to Greenham pretty naive, with little political awareness. I knew I had a need to do something, not only to make my views, particularly about nuclear weapons and war, heard but also to make my fears, especially of a possible nuclear holocaust, manageable. Like so many I had recurring nightmares which left me feeling powerless and afraid, the only way I could live with such fear was to face it and try to do something about it.

I chose to live at Yellow Gate because it was the first camp I'd visited and an American woman, Arlene, had spoken to me and made me feel welcome. At that time Yellow Gate was made up of an eclectic bunch — radical young women, mainly from London, alongside older, predominantly middle-class women, well educated and articulate, and a number of lost souls, like myself. Over time the camp changed, many of the younger women effectively burnt out and left and the camp struggled with its own identity. At one point there were three separate sub-camps, or 'fires' as we called them; one made up of the few remaining younger 'anarchists', one made up of older, predominantly middle-class stalwarts and one, mine, for those stragglers who didn't know where they belonged. In time, we came together as one. Although I loved Yellow Gate, it wasn't always easy, or comfortable. I lacked confidence, I didn't know how to articulate my ideas, to make myself heard, I was pretty much in the shadows, on the periphery, intimidated by other, much larger-than-life characters. Eventually I found my strength, through taking non-violent direct action (NVDA). Many of those early actions and events weren't spontaneous, they were well organised and planned, the result of many brainstorming meetings where women from all the different camps came together with one focus. I became involved with the 'ten days' of action which was to start on 20th September 1984, and was aimed at bringing women from far and wide, to take part in NVDA and also hopefully bolster the number of women actually living at camp. I have fond memories of the build up to those 10 days, I remember the excitement growing around the camps and particularly the creativity it inspired:

> September 20th for 10 days
> Women come together to find new ways
> Of living, loving, taking care
> A miracle is happening here
>
> We'll break the law, we'll go on strike,
> We'll do exactly what we like,
> Uprising women day and night
> A miracle is happening here
>
> — *Jane Dennett of Yellow Gate.*

Once I'd taken part in my first instance of NVDA, which was cutting a hole in the perimeter fence, I realised this was my way to 'articulate' myself, to feel empowered. From that point onwards I was unstoppable, not always in a constructive, or even healthy way. I had boundless energy for taking action. I soon had my first experience of prison, and remembered how social workers in the past had prophesied my ending up there — though in entirely different circumstances! Eventually this realisation led to me feeling alienated from other Greenham women I was imprisoned with, that I felt a closer affinity to women imprisoned as a result of their childhoods, backgrounds, experiences of abuse, their lack of 'choices'. It also eventually led to a sense of disillusionment with many other aspects of camp life.

It seemed to me that a small number of those who lived at Yellow Gate considered themselves superior, even over other Greenham women living at different camps. They considered Yellow Gate as not only the 'main' camp in terms of it's location — directly outside the main entrance to the base — but 'main' as in terms of importance and integrity. I'm sure I was guilty of that on occasion too. But all these feelings of disillusionment took years to germinate, overall I was very happy living there and towards the end I'd formed relationships with women from the other camps, especially Orange.

I left Greenham at the end of 1987, along with many others, with little choice in the end, a result of an awful and highly choreographed 'split' that turned woman against woman and effectively heralded the end of Greenham, though the predominantly younger, more close-knit women of Blue Gate continued until after the Cruise missiles finally left.

Greenham gave me a strength that enabled me to achieve more than I'd ever dreamed of. I went on to work for investigative journalist, Duncan Campbell, at *The New Statesman*, a relationship formed as a result of my actions at Greenham, through our need to engage with the media and expose the workings of governments, military and intelligence agencies, areas he was extremely knowledgeable about. After leaving the *Statesman* I returned to education. I'd left school with no qualifications, not uncommon for children in care. I excelled as a mature student and eventually gained a place at New Hall women's college at Cambridge, something no-one prophesied. Whilst I had always had a healthy disregard for elites I succumbed and became one of them. The irony wasn't lost on me.

Greenham changed the lives of so many women and, I believe, influenced and shaped future forms of protest. The Aldermaston Women's Campaign, initiated by women living at the camp, was formed to alert the public to the secret workings of the Aldermaston Weapons Research Establishment where Trident and future generations of nuclear weapons are still being designed and developed.

Cruisewatch, a mixed group, which collaborated with Greenham women, successfully tracked and disrupted Cruise missile convoys, from the moment they left Greenham till they reached a destination, usually on Salisbury Plain, where, claimed the American's, the convoys would 'melt into the countryside'. Another similar group Polaris Watch/Nuke Watch followed warheads, or nuclear components, regularly transported from

Faslane Naval Base in Scotland to the Royal Ordinance Factory at Burghfield where they were serviced.

A number of peace camps, both women-only and mixed, were established in the UK, such as Molesworth, Upper Heyford, Menwith Hill and Faslane, as well as in other countries: Holland, Germany, Australia and the Seneca women's peace camp in the US. Most of these devolved practices from Greenham, and used NVDA methods that were to a great extent influenced by Greenham.

Similarly, in 1996, the daring sabotage of a Hawk warplane bound for Indonesia by the Seeds of Hope East Timor Ploughshares movement took the bravery of the Greenham women one step further. Increasingly in the late 90s, new protests, against building and development work, such as new runways and the destruction of woodland, organised by warriors, borrowed from Greenham's live-in tactics, with protesters living in canopies, and tunnels, and using NVDA to prevent or hinder land reclamation or environmental destruction. Likewise traces of Greenham can also be seen in the Occupy Movement of 2008 onwards. These are just some examples of how the essence of Greenham continues to live on in the creativity behind so many new forms of protest.

## THE BATTLE OF ORGREAVE

# Withen

## Martyn Bedford

2014

Everyone filed out of the chapel to gather by the wreaths, which were arranged in front of the stand bearing Dad's name, sharpening the air with their scent. We stood in the September sunshine, too warm in our formal clothes. People said what a lovely service it had been. My sister-in-law, Tanya, told me how much she'd liked my speech.

'You did Don proud.'

The note cards were still in my fist, bent into a tube and damp with sweat. I thanked her. Slipped the cards into the pocket of my suit jacket. Suzy caught my eye through the crowd of mourners and mouthed, *You okay?* I nodded. She was with Mam, stooping to retrieve the cellophane-wrapped messages and reading them out to her. The dutiful daughter-in-law. Not that my mother would have had more than the vaguest idea who Suzy was.

Rich nudged my elbow. 'What the fuck's he doing here?' he said, under his breath.

I looked where he was looking. A figure stood at the top of the steps that climbed a grass embankment above the chapel. The thick brows, the great dome of his head. Uncle Peter. Thirty years older than the last time I'd set eyes on him, but unmistakeable.

It should have fallen to me to take charge of the situation. But ever since the two of us were big enough to fight, the age difference between me and Rich had seemed notional. I was the kid brother, I just happened to have been born first. That's how it had been when I was a boy; I felt no different now, aged fifty-three.

'We just pretend we haven't seen him?' Rich said, as if I'd suggested exactly that.

Tanya must have cottoned on that something was wrong. 'Who is it?'

'Dad's brother,' I told her.

She hadn't met Uncle Peter but it was clear she knew all about him. She laid a hand on my brother's sleeve. 'Don't make a scene, Rich. Not today, not here.'

Richard freed his arm and, before we could stop him, made his way over to the steps.

1984

When the footage came on, Chinese subtitles scrolling down one side of the screen, I didn't realise what I was watching at first. Becca sat beside me on the bed. We were drinking beer and swapping stories from our day, half an eye on the news. The TV was parked on a chest of drawers across the room. In an 8th-floor bedsit of a 17-storey block in Tsim Sha Tsui, huddled among the high-rises of Kowloon, the violence played out through a fuzz of interference:

Missiles arcing down on the police lines.

Close-up of a cop, blood staining his blond sideburn bright red.

Long-haired guy in a T-shirt and jeans, aiming a kung-fu kick.

Police in riot gear, scattering people across a scrubby, dusty field.

Mounted cops in formation, riding – cantering – right at the men as they fled.

It was only when I heard 'Orgreave' that I finally caught on. I gestured at the TV with my beer bottle. 'Fucking hell, that's just a few miles from where my folks live.'

We'd arrived in Hong Kong four weeks earlier. You could pick up work as an English tutor – no qualifications required, or teaching experience; they just wanted native English speakers for one-to-one conversation. By the day of Orgreave, I'd been travelling for nine months: the US, Canada, Australia, Papua New Guinea, Indonesia. I celebrated my 23rd birthday in the March, in a bar in Singapore with a few others from the backpackers' hostel.

That week, in the UK, the miners' strike had started.

'Your dad's out,' Mam announced, when I phoned so that she could wish me a happy birthday. 'Rich as well, and Uncle Peter.' I'd read about Corton Wood and the other pits in the *Straits Times*, so I wasn't surprised the walkouts had spread to Withen Main. It was more than that, though. 'Arthur's called out the whole country,' Mam said.

She always referred to Scargill by his first name, as if he was a friend of the family.

'Should I come home?'

'What good would that do, love?'

That remark still niggled me later, in the bar. I drank too much, too quickly, and wound up in an argument with the only other Brit. Branwell. Twenty, on a gap year.

'The miners are already paid heaps, aren't they?'

'They're not striking for more money.'

'Why then?' What other reason *could* there be?, his expression said.

'To save the pits from closing. To save their jobs, their families.'

'How does that work?' Branwell laughed through his nose. 'They close a pit by going on strike to stop the pit from closing. Genius.'

'If the government shuts a mine,' I said, 'it might as well shut down the whole community. But you wouldn't know about that, would you, living in Hampshire.'

He studied me through the cigarette smoke. 'I mean, who'd even want to work down a coal mine anyway?'

'My dad. My brother. My uncle. Most of the lads I were at school with.' *Were*. I hadn't said 'were' instead of 'was' in about five years.

'Not you, though. And remind me, Matt, where is it you live now?'

I took a slug of beer to stop myself from calling him a *Tory wanker* right there in front of everyone. We'd become a spectator sport, me and Branwell.

The table jolted, spilling someone's drink, as I stood up and headed for the toilets.

Branwell hit one nail on the head. I'd been backpacking since September but I'd been away for years. Since going to journalism college in Harlow. There was an identical course at Sheffield, a bus-ride from Withen, but I'd wanted to be near London to pick up shifts on the nationals. That's why, when I graduated, I took a job on the *South London Press* instead of applying to the papers back home. Dad had asked if I was trying to tell them something. It was his way of letting me know I would be missed, while also reminding me where I was from. Rich had put it more bluntly. *Matt's too clever for Withen, Dad.* Three and a bit years I worked at the *SLP*, sharing a rented house in Gipsy Hill with a vegan motorcycle courier who said *Ay oop lad* every time I entered a room.

After I'd finished skulking in the toilets, I went to buy another drink, delaying the moment when I'd have to rejoin the others.

'You're very cute when you're angry.'

It was one of the Kiwis, standing beside me at the counter. She'd only arrived at the hostel that morning. Blonde, freckly, pretty. She looked like she enjoyed making mischief.

'Sorry about that,' I said.

'About what?'

'Souring the mood. Pooping the party.'

'It's your party, birthday boy.'

'And I'll cry if I want to.'

'Besides, that guy's a total dick.' She pronounced it 'duck'.

I laughed. Sade was playing. *Shady*, Mam called her; not *Sharday*. 'What's that?' I asked, pointing to what looked like a dried-out chilli on a cord round the Kiwi girl's throat.

'A Maori aphrodisiac charm. Makes me irresistible to men.'

'Does it work?'

She laughed and gave me a thump on the arm.

'Can I get you a drink?' I asked.

'At *last*, he gets the whole point of the conversation. I'm Becca, by the way.'

We travelled together after that night. Malaysia, Thailand, Burma. Now there we were in Kowloon, watching Orgreave.

'Is that the pit where your lot work?'

'No. And Orgreave's not a pit, it's a coking plant.' I explained about turning coal into coke for use in steel-making. 'The miners are trying to blockade it.'

'Would any of your folks have been there today?'

On the TV, a car had been set alight. 'Rich, maybe,' I said. 'Not Dad or Uncle Peter, I wouldn't have thought. They're a bit old for scrapping with the plods.'

The footage ended. The bulletin cut to the studio and a No. 3 typhoon warning.

2014

Once they'd finished talking, Uncle Peter turned away and walked stiffly along the path that led to the car park. My brother rejoined us, tugging his tie loose.

'Said he'd come to pay his *respects*.' Rich ran a hand over the lower half of his face, as if checking whether he needed a shave. In fact, his skin was perfectly smooth, still pink in places with razor burn. 'I told him he were about thirty year too fucking late for that.'

I glanced back up at the path but Uncle Peter was already

lost from view.

My brother and his wife joined Mam in the funeral car, along with their kids. It eased away so quietly you wouldn't have known the engine was running. I told Suzy about Rich confronting Uncle Peter. If she had an opinion about that, she kept it to herself. Laura and Ben stood with us, both on their phones, messaging. We headed away from the chapel along the wooded path, the last of the mourners. This year's leaves had yet to fall but last autumn's still lay on the ground in places, dry as paper underfoot.

'Thanks for looking after Mam back there,' I said.

'She kept asking where your dad was.'

'What did you say?'

'That Don had probably snuck off somewhere for a smoke.' When I didn't respond, Suzy added, 'I didn't know what to say for the best. I mean—'

'No, I'd have most likely said the same. Anyway, he would've, wouldn't he? If Dad was here, he'd have been having a crafty fag.' I checked that Laura and Ben weren't lagging too far behind. 'Remember the first time you came home? He was so stressed at meeting you he got through about thirty Woodbines that afternoon. I've never known him pronounce so many aitches.'

'They kept calling you *Matthew*.'

'Did they?' I let out a laugh. 'I'd forgotten that.'

'Actually,' Suzy said, 'I think they were as nervous of you as they were of me. In case they let you down in front of your new London girlfriend.'

That evening, we'd gone down to the Welfare with Mam and Dad for a drink and to introduce Suzy to my brother and Tanya, who was his fiancée then. Rich had just finished a shift and was telling us about a runaway tub which had nearly wiped someone out.

'The work must be *so* dangerous,' Suzy said. 'I can't imagine how you guys do it.'

There was a pause. I saw Rich and Dad exchange glances;

they could decide to feel patronised by this poshly-spoken southerner, or they could let it go.

I cut in. 'Tell Suzy about your accident, Dad.'

Dad looked at me. He saw right away what I was doing. He wasn't one for talking all that much, since he'd developed his stammer — but he told her the story. Told it the way he always used to, for people hearing it for the first time, punctuated with sips from his pint.

'This w-were a few year ago,' he began. 'I were cu-cu-cutting wi' me mate, Ralph, when there were this almighty gruh-great crack. D-dint 'ave time to dive out way or owt. Buried up to me chest, like. It were right quiet at first and me lamp 'ad gone out, so it were puh-puh-pitch black. Then I heard Danny Rudge go, "No, Ralph — Don's gone." Well, I th-th-thought they were just going to leave me there. So I managed to get me 'ands fuh-free — there were these two w-w-wooden props holding most of weight off me — and I'm banging about and shoutin', "I'm all reet!" And then Ralph and Der-Danny come scrambling over this gu-gu-great slurry heap and start pulling me out.'

'Were you hurt?' Suzy asked. She'd been hanging on every word.

'Me-me legs w-w-were stuck, see.' He fell quiet, staring at his beer.

'Tell her, Dad,' Rich said. I loved him for saying that. For playing along.

Dad shook his head, blinked away the moistness in his eyes. 'You tell 'er, son.'

Rich pointed at Dad's legs. 'He lost them both,' he told Suzy.

Silence around the table.

'My *God*, I had no *idea*,' Suzy said, her own eyes welling up. 'You lost *both* your legs?' she asked Dad.

After a moment, he said, 'Nuh-nuh-nuh-not me legs, no. Me boots.'

'Your *boots*?'

'Aye, brand new they w-w-were. I paid a flamin' fortune for them boots.'

We all fell about laughing. When Suzy called us a *bunch of bastards*, we laughed harder still – and she was laughing loudest of all.

We emerged from the shade of the trees into the car park, bright as an over-exposed photograph. Suzy aimed the fob at our VW and popped the locks. It was only as I shrugged off my suit jacket and opened the front passenger door that I spotted him, sitting on a bench in the small water-garden below the parking area.

From the back, it might've been Dad. A plume of cigarette smoke feathered in the air above his bald head. I remembered my uncle as broad, stocky, barrel-chested – like one of the wrestlers on World of Sport. Mick McManus. Although Rich reckoned he looked more like the baddie in Thunderbirds. We used to pretend to hypnotise each other behind his back whenever he, Aunt Sylvia and our cousins came round. Sitting there, smoking, he appeared stooped and round-shouldered. Shrunken.

1984

On the way back from the international telephone exchange, I spotted one of the COAL NOT DOLE stickers on the subway. Rich had sent several sheets of them, *post restante*, and Becca and I stuck them wherever we could. I've no idea what the local people made of them. The few of my students who knew of the strike were bemused by what they'd seen on TV.

'Why police not have water guns?' one had asked me. Leon. All of our students chose Anglicised names for themselves, in addition to their Chinese ones. Cindy, Peggy, Irene, Flora, Charles, Marvin. Mercedes, in one case.

'Cannon,' I corrected Leon. 'Water *cannon*.'

'Yes, water cans and crying gas and rubber bullet. Why England police not have?' He sounded puzzled but also indignant, as if some natural law had been breached.

Kowloon-side, Becca was waiting for me in the cafe in the basement of our building, sitting at one of the Formica-topped tables, a fat teapot and two small cups set out. Steam rose off her tea; when she saw me, she smiled and began pouring mine. The place was full. We were the only non-Chinese.

'I've ordered congee,' she said, as I sat down opposite her. 'That okay?'

I would have preferred toast and eggs but I said, 'Yeah, that's good.'

Billy Joel was playing on the radio. Uptown Girl. The Hong Kong stations had run a continuous loop of his songs since we'd arrived. When they weren't playing Two Tribes.

'How're things at home?' Her tone was bright; it was just a regular phone call – the weekly check-in with my folks – so she had no reason to suppose anything was wrong. Then, as she set the teapot back down, she must've taken a proper look at my face. 'Matt?'

I was so tremulous I couldn't believe the cups didn't rattle as I placed my palms on the table. The sour fumes from the tea made my eyes water. 'Dad's... in hospital.'

'Your *dad*? No.' Her chin puckered. 'What... I mean, how is he? Is he okay?'

'Yeah, the hospitals are full of people who are okay.' I don't know where that came from, or what she'd done to deserve it. I waved a hand as if to erase the words. 'Sorry.'

The waitress appeared. She was about ten years old, in blue dungarees and wearing a Beatles haircut. She set down the bowls and plates: thick rice-and-fish porridge and tubes of spongy bread. In our first week in Hong Kong, after months of Southeast Asian food, we ate McDonald's every day. More recently, we'd been conditioning ourselves for mainland China.

The girl told us to *enjoy*, looking delighted to have spoken this one word of English.

After she'd gone, I said, 'There was a swelling on the brain, but it's come down.' I couldn't meet Becca's gaze. 'Mam thinks he might be out by the weekend.'

I drew two pairs of chopsticks from the dispenser and handed one to her, still in its paper sheath. It was noisy in the cafe: clatter, conversation, music.

'What happened?' she asked.

'He went to Orgreave with Rich. My uncle as well.' I popped my chopsticks from their wrapper. 'Dad got separated from the other two.' I took a breath. 'Apparently, the cop hit him three times – once to knock him down, then two more whacks while he was on the ground. Two that Dad can remember, anyway.'

'Jesus.'

'They're going to charge him.'

'Good. Too bloody right.'

'Not the cop, my dad.'

'*No.*'

'They're just waiting for the doctors to say he's well enough to be questioned.'

'Charge him with what?'

'With whatever they like. Just *being* there is enough.'

As we picked at the food, I recounted what Mam had said. How things had become too lairy for Dad's liking on the field and how he and Uncle Peter had retreated to the village, *out of harm's way*. How the rest of the pickets were eventually forced back there, too – across the railway line, or over the bridge – and how the police had gone after them, hunting them down. Dad *was in wrong place at wrong time*, as Mam put it.

I couldn't understand what he was doing at Orgreave in the first place. Rich was the flying picket. He went wherever he was needed – down to Nottinghamshire, if he could sneak past the roadblocks. Dad stuck closer to home, at Withen Main, standing outside the pit where he'd worked since he was sixteen. 'It's only a token,' he'd said, one time, when Mam passed him the phone. 'It's a hundred per cent, here. Other morning, a pigeon flew over gates and me and your uncle shouted *Scab!* for sake of summat to shout "scab" at. Even the coppers laughed.' Dad was a veteran of the '72 and '74 strikes. He was in his thirties, back then; at 48, he no longer needed to prove himself on the lines. Picketing was just something you did. *Tha gets less macho wi' age.* He pronounced it 'macko'. Rich was 21. Him and the other young lads were going for it, according to Dad. *Like bloody football hooligans, some of 'em.*

I pushed the bowl away. For a moment I thought I might be sick. I saw Becca sneak a glance at the clock on the wall. Eight-forty. Our first tutorials were at nine.

'What are you going to do?' she asked.

'I'll go in. I can't just not turn up.'

'I didn't mean that.'

The Longest Time came on the radio. 'Billy fucking Joel,' I muttered, but she paid no notice. She was waiting for me to answer her question. The actual question. I'd never known Becca look at me like that – as if she didn't recognise me.

'I don't know,' I said.

'Yes you do, you just can't say it to me.'

2014

'Now then,' I said, sitting down beside him. After thirty years, 'Hello Uncle Peter' would've sounded too juvenile, and calling him plain 'Peter' didn't seem appropriate either.

He must have heard me approach because he showed no sign of being startled; a brief glance, that was all, as if to check which one of us it was.

'Matt,' he said, with a slight nod.

The bench faced a perfectly oval pond fringed with ornamental grasses, encircled by a brick path and a margin of neatly laid pebbles. Like a water feature in a Japanese garden. For a moment I was put in mind of Becca; the faintest of blasts from the past.

'You're just about the last person I expected to see today,' I said.

'Aye, Rich said much the same back there. Only wi' more effin and jeffin.'

'I can't believe my brother swore. You sure it was him?'

Uncle Peter let out something that might have been a laugh. 'Anyhow, I don't need telling twice, Matt. So, I'll finish this,' he raised the cigarette, 'and be on me way.'

I gazed out across the valley, the sweep of pasture and woodland.

'There are worse spots to sit,' I said.

The last time we'd seen one another, he was several years younger than I am now, his face looming at a bedroom window of his darkened house. Below, in the garden, I'd stood with my brother. We'd already thrown two half-bricks through the downstairs windows but Rich insisted we stay so that our uncle saw who'd done it.

I pointed to a sapling close to the pond, a plaque planted in the soil at its base and blue-and-white ribbons fluttering from the spindly trunk. 'Wednesday fan, d'you think?'

Uncle Peter nodded. 'Well, his suffering is over now.' I couldn't help smiling. He'd always been the joker of the family. 'I can see their ground from my house,' he added.

'You're in Sheffield these days?'

'Walkley Bank, aye.' He paused. 'You still follow Leeds?'

'Not really. I watch them when they're playing in London, that's all.'

He took another draw on his cigarette. 'Never knew how you could support that lot.'

'Broke Dad's heart, me being Leeds.'

Every other Saturday, we'd stand on the Lowfields terrace – arriving an hour before kick-off, so I could bag a place at the front of the middle tier. Dad would watch the game with his little radio pressed to his ear, to find out how Rotherham were getting on. That radio – one of its successors, anyway, held together by two rubber bands – was in the bedside cabinet at the hospital when Rich and I cleared out his personal effects.

'When he was ill,' I said, 'even quite near the end, he always got me to read out the football stories from the paper, if I was visiting.'

I would feed him, too: spooning yoghurt into his mouth, or tinned peaches cut up small for him to swallow. I shaved him. Trimmed his toenails. When Dad soiled himself, I washed him and replaced his incontinence pad. I didn't tell Uncle Peter any of this.

'Cancer, wor it?' he asked.

'Leukaemia.'

'It were bowel, wi' your aunt.'

'Aunt Sylvia died?'

'Two year ago.'

We'd reached this point, where people died – *family* – and we didn't know, or even know where they lived, or anything about their lives any more.

'How did you hear about Dad?'

'I still get *Advertiser* sent over. Saw it in funeral notices.' Uncle Peter had finished his cigarette. He pinched the tip between his thumb and middle finger, as Dad used to, and slipped the stub in his jacket pocket. 'I weren't going to come,' he said. 'But...' he let the sentence trail off with a shrug.

I finished it for him. 'He was your brother.'

'Aye, he was. When all's said and done, we were brothers.'

He stood up, with difficulty, one hand holding the back of the bench for support. *New hip*, he explained. Looking in the direction of the car park, he asked, 'That your missus?'

I stood as well. 'Yeah, Suzy. Those are our kids in the back: Ben and Laura.'

Their faces were towards us, hologrammed by the sunlight on the glass.

That night in the winter of 1984, our uncle hadn't come downstairs; he'd remained at his bedroom window, motionless – watching us, watching him – until Rich and I turned away, let ourselves out of his garden and headed off down the silent street.

'Will you come back?' I said. 'To the wake.'

'I don't think that's a good idea, do you?'

'I'm asking you. I'd like you to be there.'

Uncle Peter turned towards me. 'You don't half have a look of him, you know.'

'I was thinking the same about you.'

After a moment, he said, 'What about Rich? The old lags from pit?' He still held on to the bench, standing at an awkward angle, as if one leg was longer than the other. A sheen of sweat had formed in the greyish stubble above his top lip. 'What about your mother?'

'It's Dad's funeral,' I said. 'Not theirs.'

1984

It was Saturday before I could get a flight out of Hong Kong; Sunday, when I stepped off the bus at Withen. Dad had been discharged the day before. He was lying in bed with the curtains shut when Mam took me up. The light gave him headaches, she explained. The room smelled of stale sweat and the lemon barley water which stood in a jug on the bedside table.

'Matt's here, love.'

But Dad was dozing. I set the dressing-table stool beside the bed and watched him sleep while Mam went downstairs to make a brew. In the gloom, the gauze patch on his head might have been a scrap of paper that had blown in through the window and landed there. Dad looked as if he'd aged about ten years in the ten months since I'd last seen him.

He woke before Mam reappeared, rolling his head to one side and blinking at me as if he suspected I might be a figment of his imagination.

'Hello Dad.'

'W-wuh-wuh-what're you doing here?'

'Nice to see you, too.'

'You should've st-stayed in Hong Kong.'

'That whack on the head has made you less grumpy, then.'

'I told her you'd do this.' Mam, he meant. 'Told her nuh-nuh-not to say owt to you.'

Mam was in the doorway, carrying a tray of tea and

biscuits. The logo on one of the mugs read: *NUM – Support the Miners*. 'Who's "her"?' she said. 'The cat's mother?'

Dad pushed himself up into a sitting position while I repositioned the pillows at his back. 'How long have you had the ponytail?' he asked.

'Couple of months,' I said.

'Don't start on him, Don. He's just flown half-way round world to see you.'

When Rich came in later, he gave the ponytail a flick. 'You Matt's girlfriend?'

'Very funny,' I said.

'Hey, Dad, what d'you reckon?' My brother half-turned me towards the bed. 'Is it just me, or does Matt look like the back end of a police horse?'

The ponytail had been Becca's idea. My hair was already collar length when I left England and I'd decided not to cut it the whole time I was away.

'You know what would really suit you?' she said, trailing her fingers through my hair after the first time we'd made love.

So, by the time we left Singapore, I was a ponytailed man.

We'd been politely awkward with each other during my last three days in Kowloon; as if preparing for, or protecting ourselves from, the other's absence. We revised our plans: I would somehow scrape together enough cash to fly out and rejoin her, when Dad was fully recovered. If I couldn't, she'd travel to Europe anyway. To England.

I'd been home two weeks when I received a blue airmail envelope. It contained a long, lovely letter which ended with Becca saying she'd decided to go to Japan.

The editor at the *South London Press* agreed to rehire me as a features writer. I moved back down to London. Anything spare from my wages, I sent to Mam and Dad. The strike was four months old by then and Mam was the only one bringing any money into the house, from the little she earned as a school dinner lady and the part-time cleaning job she'd taken on.

They'd sold the car, Rich's drum kit and hi-fi system, the bone-china crockery and walnut sideboard Mam had inherited from Gran. Most of their food came from donations to Withen Women Against Pit Closures, which the committee divvied up between the striking families.

When she wasn't working, or making sandwiches at the Welfare, or shaking a collection bucket in Rotherham for the WWAPC, Mam toured the country with some of the other women to give talks and raise funds. I'd even set up a visit to South London, to address the local trades council. To see her before a room full of strangers – nerveless, articulate, informed – was a revelation. At home, the sole woman in a house of opinionated men, she was usually more of an observer than a participant whenever politics cropped up. But there she was, at Lambeth Town Hall, bringing a hundred people to their feet in applause. I recorded every word for the piece we ran in the paper.

'Make no mistake, this dispute isn't just about coal mines, or the mining industry, or miners. It's about all of us. All of *you*. What we're witnessing is nowt less than a planned attack on the British working class and our communities. Mr. Ridley, Mr. MacGregor, Mrs. Thatcher – they hate us. And, if we let them, they will destroy us.'

When the clapping finally subsided...

'The prime minister didn't batter my husband at Orgreave. She didn't put him in hospital. You won't find her fingerprints on that truncheon.' Mam paused. 'But when I look at my husband – my Don – and see what he's become since that day, Mrs. Thatcher's shadow hangs over him as surely as if she were standing right there in the room.'

The police didn't charge Dad in the end. They might as well have banged him up in a cell, though, because he'd more or less imprisoned himself in his own home. He spent most of his waking hours watching television, filling the living room with cigarette smoke. He no longer picketed. Seldom left the house at all, except to sit in the back yard with the *Daily Mirror* or the *Rotherham Advertiser*, if the weather was fine.

The doctors couldn't tell if the speech impediment was physical or psychosomatic.

'He's lost confidence in himself,' Mam said, when I was home one weekend and we were alone in the kitchen. 'A cupboard door bangs and he jumps like he's been shot.'

'He looks as if he's lost weight,' I said.

'Well, he would do. There aren't many calories in Woodbines and PG Tips.'

I tried to piece together what happened to him at Orgreave. But Dad was reticent about it and Rich had become separated from him in the chaos and so didn't witness the incident. According to Uncle Peter, Dad was hiding behind an ice-cream van when he got hit.

'An *ice-cream* van?'

'Aye, *Rock on Tommy* it were called.' He, Aunt Sylvia and our cousins had come round for Sunday dinner because it was cheaper to use one oven than two. 'I'd gone on to Asda to buy some sarnies and left your dad queuing for 99s.'

'Blimey,' Rich said, 'you two aren't exactly Fidel Castro and Che fucking Guevera, are you?'

We all laughed around the table; even Mam, despite the language. Even Dad.

'When I headed back from supermarket,' Uncle Peter went on, 'the street were swarming wi' coppers, chasing our lads all over place. Running into folks' gardens and everywhere. You were already on ground by then, Don. This feller from Thurcroft had taken his T-shirt off and were using it to stop blood from where you'd been clobbered.'

'D'you remember any of that, Dad?' I asked.

'I remember p-payin' for 99s. But I don't remember gettin' any ch-chuh-change.'

The thing from that day that sticks in Dad's mind above all else is the vibration from the police horses' hooves as they cantered across the field. *You could feel it in your feet and right up your legs.* I've lost count of the times he's told me that in the years since.

In the film footage and photos which I've trawled through, I've only ever found one shot of my father at Orgreave. It's in a video clip of pickets rolling a tractor tyre down the slope towards the police lines. You can make out Dad, Uncle Peter and my brother in the background. Dad throws his head back, amused by something Uncle Peter says. They look happy, drenched in sunshine, shirtless in Rich's case – like three men on a works outing to the seaside. I've asked, but none of them can recall what my uncle said to make Dad laugh.

2014

'You'd never know it had been there, would you?' Uncle Peter said.

We were in his little green Corsa, following Suzy along the road that passed the industrial estate where Withen Main had once stood. The wheel from the winding gear had been installed like a piece of modern sculpture in a small park at the bottom of the high street but, otherwise, there was no trace of the colliery in the village. Even the air was fresh, these days, the once seemingly indelible acrid stench from the coke ovens long since dispersed.

'I remember Mam phoning me,' I said, 'the day they announced it was closing.'

I was on *The Guardian* by then. The features editor packed me off to Withen with a photographer to put together a colour piece, a *personal reflection* on the village where I'd grown up and the death of its coal mine. Eight hundred words.

'Never seen a site cleared so quick,' my uncle said.

'You came back in '92?' He had already been gone seven years by then.

'Just to see it one last time. Only it were nowt but a big wasteland wi' a JCB levelling it off.' He steered into a turn. 'Christ, when I think of the years I spent under there.'

'What did you do?' I asked. 'After you left.'

We were heading up the high street, with its pound shops and charity shops, betting offices and loan dealers. People were eating at tables on the pavement outside the chippy.

'Bit of labouring,' he said. 'Cab driving, this and that. Last few year, before I retired, I were a car-park attendant at Sheffield Hallam Uni. *Professor of Parking*, my girls called me.' The gears crunched as he shifted up. 'How about you? You still on papers?'

'No, I'm a journalism lecturer, now. At Goldsmiths.'

'Funny how we both ended up working in Higher Education,' he said, and I laughed.

Then he asked if I was still *a union man*. I told him I was, for all the good it did, seeing as the management paid us little or no attention. 'Hardly anyone turns up to branch meetings, anyway,' I said. Me included, I might have added. 'We have a one-day strike, they dock us a day's pay, then we all carry on as if nothing had happened.'

Uncle Peter asked if Dad found work when the pit closed.

Not then, I tell him. For the next nine years Dad was on benefits, then – just as he hit retirement age – Asda took him on part-time: rounding up the trolleys, emptying the waste bins, tidying the delivery bay and recycling area, that sort of thing. It affected his pension but he was just glad to be doing something. It was apparent that Uncle Peter knew none of this.

By the time we followed Suzy into the restaurant car park, we'd gone quiet. His knuckles, misshapen by arthritis, were white where he gripped the steering wheel.

'Didn't this used to be The Kestrel?'

'It changed hands about ten years ago,' I said.

'What is it – Chinese?'

'Thai. They serve English food as well, though. They'd have to, round here – keep the UKIP voters happy.' We'd parked. I unclipped my seatbelt. 'We'd have had the do at the Welfare but it's all boarded up,' I said. 'Has been for years.'

Neither of us made a move to get out. Uncle Peter still had one hand on the wheel.

'I'll be with you in there,' I said. 'You'll be all right.'

Without turning to look at me, he said, 'I only went to crem to pay my respects, Matt. Say goodbye to him. That's all. I weren't planning on any of this.'

'I know. Me neither.'

A few bays along, Suzy, Ben and Laura had climbed out of the VW. My suit jacket was draped over Suzy's arm. She looked hesitant, as if unsure whether to come over.

'Julie and Fiona were dead set against me coming at all,' Uncle Peter said. *Julie and Fiona*. My cousins. Teenagers, the last time I'd seen them; they would both be pushing fifty, now. 'What you did that night, you and your brother...' He trailed off, shook his head. 'The girls have never forgiven you for that. Sylvia never did, either.'

'That was us, not Dad.'

'He knew you'd done it, though.'

I nodded. 'Yeah.'

'Aye, I thought so.' After a pause, he asked, 'I don't suppose he ever mentioned me – when he were near end?'

I considered lying but just said, 'No. He didn't.' It came out harder than I'd intended.

Suzy was at the passenger door. My uncle pressed the button to lower the window and a gust of heat entered the air-conditioned interior, along with traffic noise and cooking smells.

'Hello,' she said, dipping her head to the window. Smiley, breezy.

I introduced them and she reached awkwardly across me to shake Uncle Peter's hand.

'Do you mind taking Ben and Laura in?' I said. 'We won't be long.'

'Okay.' She didn't look pleased about it.

'Nice lass,' Uncle Peter said, after she'd gone.

'Dad was always asking me if I knew how lucky I was. *Don't blow it*, he used to say. *Tha won't find another one as good, Matt.*' As I spoke his words I heard him saying them. My jaw tightened and it was all I could do not to cry right there in front of my uncle. I took a couple of breaths. 'She doesn't know about that night. Or Ben and Laura.'

'You never told them?' He sounds surprised enough not to believe me.

'I didn't want them to know that about me.'

Uncle Peter sat with his hands in his lap. Smashing his window was such a small matter, set against thirty years of cutting him, and our aunt and cousins, out of our lives.

'Do you ever regret going back?' I asked.

'In Ninety-two?'

'No, Eighty-four.'

He took so long to answer I wondered if he would. Finally, he said, 'There hasn't been a day when I don't. Not one day.'

1984

From her tone of voice, Mam might have been calling with news that someone had died.

'Your uncle has gone back,' she said, just like that.

'Uncle *Peter*?'

'How many other uncles have you got?'

'He can't have.'

'Rich and his mates saw him go past on scab bus not half-hour since.'

I stared at the half-written feature sticking out of my typewriter, as if the meaning of what Mam had said might be encrypted among the words there. 'Are they sure it was him?' With those grilles at the windows, and the speed...I left this thought unspoken. They were sure. You didn't name someone unless you were certain.

'I just phoned Sylvia,' Mam said.

'What did she say?'

'She hung up on me.'

There was a metallic taste in my mouth. 'Have you told Dad?'

'Rich is with him now.'

It was mid-December. The strike had entered its tenth month and, although support was weakening in some areas, around 95 per cent of South Yorkshire was still out. At Withen Main you could count the strike-breakers on one hand. Each day, under police escort, the bus ran the gauntlet, trailing cries of *Scab!*, the meshed glass spattered with phlegm. As I set the phone in its cradle, I pictured Uncle Peter's face at one of those windows – the thick, black brows drawn taut over eyes that stared dead ahead. He wouldn't so much as flick a glance at the pickets jostling with the cordon of police just a few feet from the side of the bus as it sped past. He wouldn't spot my brother, spotting him. But he would know he was there.

My uncle had stood side by side with the men; with Rich, with my dad.

Now he was one of the scabs.

'How can he see his own brother beaten to ground – see him, way he is now?' Mam had said on the phone. 'How can he see *that* and go back to work?'

She blamed Aunt Sylvia. While most of the women in the village had united behind the strike, Sylvia had distanced herself from all of that. At that Sunday dinner, not long after I'd returned from Hong Kong, my aunt had criticised Scargill for not calling a ballot.

'There were a ballot at every pit,' Rich said. 'We voted with us feet.'

'A proper one,' Aunt Sylvia said. 'A national one.'

'And let those cunts in Nottingham vote to shut down our coalfield?'

Mam rapped the table. 'Richard Marron, don't you dare use that word in this house.'

'What, *Nottingham*?' my brother replied. Mam glowered at him, staring him down.

'We'd have got more support from other unions. And from public.' This was Uncle Peter. He shrugged. 'All I'm saying is we gave press and Tories chance to say strike's not valid – to make us out to be nowt but a bunch of yobboes.'

'Arthur knows what he's doing,' Mam said.

'Calling a strike in spring?' Aunt Sylvia asked. 'After NCB had built up coal stocks – after you'd all worked overtime for months to build up stocks for them.'

The argument continued. I took a back seat, not entitled to join in. I'd moved away, I didn't work down the mine. I wasn't going short of food, or struggling to pay bills, or being battered by the police on the picket lines. Away from Withen, though, my semi-detachment made me more radical. At work, whenever I entered the newsroom the other journos would chant *Maggie, Maggie, Maggie – Out, Out, Out!* Aged 23, I was elected Father of Chapel and proposed a motion at the next NUJ branch meeting that we should come out on strike in support of our comrades in the National Union of Mineworkers. The motion was defeated.

Looking back, I can see that I was seeking to assuage my guilt; like a man who has escaped from a sinking ship. That I was seeking, albeit unconsciously, some kind of acceptance – from my brother, from Mam and Dad, from myself – that I was still one of them. That I wasn't too clever for Withen.

By the time I went home for Christmas, Uncle Peter had been back at work two weeks.

'Have you spoken to him?' I asked Dad.

'Why would I d-d-do that?'

'To ask why he's gone back.'

'I know wuh-why – cos they're skint,' he said.

Mam said my uncle's and aunt's electricity and gas had been cut off, and my cousins were going to school in clothes and shoes they'd outgrown, and that the younger one, Fiona, had been diagnosed by the doctor as malnourished. 'Like no other family in Withen is in same boat,' she said. 'Or rest of Yorkshire, or South Wales, or Durham, or Scotland.'

'Puh-puh-Peter's m-made his choice.'

'Or had it made for 'im by Sylvia.'

It was the worst of choices. We aren't a religious family but it carried the weight of a commandment in our house and throughout the mining communities:

*Thou shalt not scab.*

On Christmas Eve, Rich and I went round to my uncle's house and did what we did.

I'd like to blame it on the beer, but we weren't too drunk to know what we were up to.

I'd like to say I tried to dissuade my brother. But I didn't.

Once the village got wind of what we'd done to one of our own, it was open season on Uncle Peter. In the following weeks, other windows were smashed, dog shit was pushed through the letterbox, the shed in the back yard was set alight, SCAB and SCUM were daubed on the front door and on the chipboard panels he'd fixed over the windows. If they ventured into the village, my uncle, aunt and cousins were sworn at, spat at. Julie and Fiona were frozen out at school; friendless. In the shops, no-one would serve Aunt Sylvia. One evening, when he went to the end of the street to post a letter, Uncle Peter was set upon by three men and beaten so badly he spent nearly as long in hospital as Dad had done.

I can't say whether my brother was responsible for some or any of these incidents. He insisted, has always insisted, that he wasn't.

'I said all I had to say when I stood in his garden after we'd done his windows.'

From that night on, they were dead to us.

2014

In the lobby of the Emerald Buddha sat a wooden Buddha, painted green – a serene, slimline Siddhartha Gautama, not the fat, jolly version. He was in the lotus position, hands configured in a symbolic gesture that I might once have been able to interpret. I ushered my uncle into the bar area, expecting a scene from a western, where a crowded saloon falls silent. But there were a few turned heads, that was all. I couldn't immediately spot my brother.

'Beer?' I asked Uncle Peter.

'Not when I'm driving.'

'It spills going round bends,' I said, supplying the punchline to one of his gags.

'You remember my jokes, then?'

'They're all in the British Museum, now.'

He gave a wheezy laugh. We were passing through the throng, Uncle Peter struggling due to his hip. I muttered *excuse me* and *thanks* as people made way for us.

'I'll come to bar with you,' he said, sticking close to me.

'It's all right.' I pointed. 'Suzy and our two are over there.'

As I steered him in their direction, we came upon Mam, sitting with a neighbour from the sheltered housing. They had glasses of sherry in front of them. We both paused, as if it had been our purpose all along to approach her table. Her semi-vacant gaze settled on each of us in turn and I heard her murmur to the woman beside her, 'Who's that chap with my Don?'

'It's me, Mam. Matt.'

She smiled at me as if I'd said something silly.

'Mam, this is Uncle Peter.'

'What did he say?' she asked her companion.

'Uncle Peter,' I repeated. 'He came to pay his respects to Dad.'

'You had a brother called Peter,' she said, addressing my uncle. Then, to her friend, 'I were a bridesmaid at their wedding. Don were best man.' She looked up at Uncle Peter. 'What were her name, love – Peter's wife?'

'Sylvia,' Uncle Peter said, quietly.

Mam frowned. Took a sip of sherry. 'No, that weren't it.'

She lost interest in us. We stood there pointlessly for a moment before moving on.

'Poor bloody woman,' my uncle said. 'When you think how she used to be.'

On my way to order drinks, I passed a seating plan at the

entrance to the dining area: twenty tables, four on each. Me, Suzy, Ben and Laura had been put together at one of the top tables.

'We'll be calling everyone through in a few minutes, sir.'

It was the *maitre d'*. Indicating our table on the plan, I said, 'Sorry to be a nuisance, but could you lay an extra place at No. 2, please?'

I was at the bar when Rich drew up beside me. He gazed straight ahead at the spirit optics. 'What you doing, Matt?' Casual. He might've been asking me to recommend a whisky.

'Buying our uncle an orange juice.'

My brother gave me a sidelong look.

'It's been thirty years,' I said.

'Once a scab—'

'Christ, Rich, spare me the fucking clichés.'

'Cliché. Right.' He placed his hands on the edge of the counter, as if about to perform a set of bench-presses. 'You going to *announce* him? Make another of your speeches?'

I let that go. 'We don't have the right to turn a man away from his brother's funeral.'

'There. Jot it down on one of them fucking cards of yours so you don't forget it.'

The barmaid set an orange juice and a pint in front of me. If she'd heard what we'd said, you wouldn't have known. She'd smiled, before, when I greeted her with *sawat dee* – but politely, as if humouring me. I was glad Rich hadn't been there to witness that.

'Or are you going to flog a piece to *Guardian*?' my brother asked, when she'd moved away to serve someone else. '*The uncle who came in from the cold.*'

'D'you remember him making a set of battery operated floodlights for your Subbuteo pitch?' I said. 'Or when he used to take us tobogganing at Rother Valley? Or him stopping Dad from giving you a belting that time you—'

'I remember him crossing picket line,' Rich cut in. 'Going

back to work when Dad were still having blackouts from where that bastard copper had knacked him.'

'You can't blame Uncle Peter for what happened to Dad.'

'We lost strike cos of cunts like him.'

I shook my head. 'The strike was already lost by the time he went back.'

'Oh aye? Were that the word on street, then, Matt, down in fucking London?'

Our raised voices had drawn the attention of some of those standing nearby. We fell quiet for a moment. I sipped my pint. The beer was sharp and hoppy.

We *had* blamed our uncle. Me included. After he'd turned scab, we came to hold him responsible for the way Dad was after Orgreave. Uncle Peter left Withen Main – left mining – in May '85, two months after the end of the strike. The men wouldn't work with him. He left the village, then, as well – him, Aunt Sylvia, the two girls. They didn't tell anyone, they just went. Dad, meanwhile, stayed on at the colliery until it closed. But he wasn't able to do the same work as before; they took him off the face and put him above ground, on to the screens, sifting waste material from the coal that other men had mined. It was a job usually allocated to lads or old-timers, or miners with disabilities. If he'd lost confidence after his head injury, the switch to unskilled work brought him lower still.

None of it was Uncle Peter's fault. But we made a correlation between our father's decline and our uncle's absence. His betrayal. Dad never admitted as much but, with the loss of his brother, he'd lost another vital piece of himself.

'What d'you think Dad would've made of this place?' I asked.

Rich frowned, as if taking a moment to adjust to the change of subject. 'They used to come here for Sunday lunch, sometimes – him and Mam.'

'Seriously?' I took in the black-and-gold decor, the diffused lighting, the low-slung, furniture, the wall-prints of seated, standing and reclining Buddhas. Bangkok meets Ikea.

'They do a proper carvery,' Rich said. 'Special rate for OAPs.'

'Dad was always one for a carvery. *Pile it high and shovel it down.*'

Rich didn't have anything to say to that. We lapsed into another, briefer silence.

'I'm going to take his drink over,' I said, finally.

'Leave it where it is,' my brother said, 'and take him back to his car.'

'No, Rich. I'm not doing that.'

We were eight and ten, kicking a ball in the back lane; twelve and fourteen, in the school playground. We were 21 and 23, in Uncle Peter's garden on Christmas Eve, 1984.

Rich stared at the glass of orange juice, as if debating whether to send it crashing to the floor. But his hands remained braced against the bar. His shoulders relaxed.

Looking me square in the face, he said, 'Dad wouldn't have wanted him here.'

'Probably not, no.'

Rich nodded. 'You always were a selfish fucker, Matt.'

In the corner, Suzy had managed to snaffle a seat for Uncle Peter. He sat with one leg bent, the other straight out in front of him. She was squatting beside his chair, showing him the photos she kept in her purse of Ben and Laura when they were little.

I handed my uncle his drink.

'All right?' Suzy asked. She must have seen me talking to Rich.

'Yeah,' I said. 'Everything's sorted.'

18th JUNE 1984

I can only piece this together from the fragments I've been told and from my imagination:

They leave Withen after first light in Uncle Peter's brown

Allegro (the one with the boot that won't shut when it's open and won't open when it's shut.) My uncle drives, Dad sits in the front passenger seat, my brother is in the back. Rich has joined the picket at the coking plant several times in the preceding weeks but this is the first time for Dad and Uncle Peter. They're in a convoy streaming out of the village. A glorious day is forecast but the sun has yet to dissolve the slicks of mist in the fields. The men's breaths steam up the windows and my uncle steers one-handed as he wipes the windscreen with a grubby yellow chammy. Dad will be craving a cigarette but smoking isn't allowed in the car, by order of Aunt Sylvia. Rich rubs his palms on his thighs, the way he does when he's nervous. Dad hums under his breath: Tom Jones, 'The Green, Green Grass of Home'. He doesn't even realise he's doing it.

Half a world away, in Kowloon, it's lunchtime; Becca and I are grabbing a bite to eat between tutorials. I doubt I'll be giving my dad, my brother, my uncle, a moment's thought.

'Let's have some music,' Uncle Peter says, turning on the radio.

Over whichever song is playing, he asks if they've brought packed lunches – *snap*, he calls it – and Dad snorts and says, 'What is this, Pete – a fucking school trip?'

They all laugh.

'Hey, Richard.' My uncle glances in the rearview mirror. 'Nice perm by the way.'

'It's not a perm,' my brother says.

'I thought it were Kevin Keegan in back for a minute there.'

'It's *not* a fucking perm.'

'Looks like one from where I'm sat.'

Rich doesn't say anything. Just scowls out of the car window.

'Well I reckon it suits him,' Dad says. 'All he needs is a spandex suit and he could enter Eurovision.'

'It's not a *perm*, all right,' Rich says, 'it's a fucking *demi-wave*.'

There's a brief pause, then all three of them are laughing

like it's the funniest thing they've ever heard.

They're still laughing when the news comes on. Uncle Peter shushes the other two. The newsreader refers to the strike, *entering its 16th week*. Perhaps in relation to this item, or a different one, the prime minister's husky, carefully modulated tones issue from the speaker. Rich leans forward between the front seats, intending to turn off the radio. But my uncle has beaten him to it.

Thatcher falls abruptly silent.

'That fucking woman.' This will be Dad. He can't hear her voice, or see her face, without calling her *that fucking woman*. Or *that woman*, if Mam's around.

I picture him, glaring at the dial, as if the radio is responsible for Thatcher; or as if Thatcher herself is hidden behind the black, plastic fascia and might start speaking again.

'Even wi' radio off, I can still hear that voice,' Rich says.

'She could be dead in her grave,' Uncle Peter says, 'and we'd still not shut her up.'

The convoy crests a hill, opening up a sweeping view towards Sheffield: the motorway, the twin cooling towers at Tinsley. And, there, the coking plant – glinting beneath the risen sun like a space station from the cover of a sci-fi magazine.

'Here we go, boys,' my uncle says.

Rich takes it up, quietly at first. 'Here we go, here we go, here we go...'

Uncle Peter joins in, '... here we go, here we go, here we go-o...'

Then Dad, '... here we go, here we go, here we go, here we go-o-o, *here we go*.'

Rich is beating out the rhythm on his knee, Dad is rapping the dashboard, Uncle Peter thumping the steering wheel with the heel of his hand, three voices united as one: 'HERE WE GO, HERE WE GO, HERE WE GO, HERE WE GO, HERE WE GO, HERE WE GO-O; HERE WE GO, HERE WE GO, HERE WE GO, HERE WE GO-O-O, *HERE WE GO!*'

2014

The *maitre d'* banged a small gong and invited us all to take our seats for lunch. Our corner of the bar was farthest away, so most of the other mourners had already gone through by the time the five of us filed into to the restaurant.

The top tables stood beneath the far windows. Sunshine streamed in, brilliant against the white walls and tablecloths. The Withen Main Lodge banner hung from a wall – huge, dominant – its reds, yellows and purples shimmering, the portrayed figures so etched with brightness they were translucent, ghostlike. The last time I'd seen it was on 3rd March 1985, swaying on poles at the head of the procession through the village, as the men – my father and brother among them – returned to work at the end of the strike. They marched behind Withen's colliery band, heads held so high you would think they had won.

'We *have* wuh-wuh-won,' Dad said, that day. 'You only l-lose if you don't fight.'

As we approached the top tables, I was peripherally aware of Mam, and Rich, Tanya and their kids, already in their seats. Watching us. I led the way, then Uncle Peter, with Suzy at his side, helping him, followed by Ben and Laura.

So I was the first to see what had been done.

The table was stripped.

No chairs arranged around it, no tablecloth draped over it. No place mats, no plates, no knives and forks, no spoons, no wine glasses, no water glasses, no napkins, no jug of water, no basket of bread rolls, no butter dish, no salt, no pepper, no small vase of flowers. No name cards. Just a number 2 clipped to a stand in the centre of the bare wooden table.

# Afterword: The Miners vs. the South Yorkshire Police, June 1984

## Prof. David Waddington
Sheffield Hallam University

I HAD BEEN TOLD to expect something of a 'cushy number' during the interview which led to my appointment as postdoctoral research assistant on a project called 'Communication processes within and around flashpoints of public disorder', which was due to be carried out by a small research team at what was then known as Sheffield City Polytechnic. My eventual colleagues (Chas Critcher and Karen Jones) had made it apparent from the outset that one major reason given by the Economic and Social Research Council (ESRC) for funding this research, as part of its 'Crowd in Contemporary Britain' initiative, was that, unlike other major English cities, Sheffield had been virtually unaffected by the nationwide urban disorders of 1981. The remit we were given was, not only to uncover possible reasons for this variation, but also to explain the absence of any tradition of collective violence in the city and its surrounding communities. Thus, on taking up my post on 1st March 1983, I spent the first twelve months of my contract trying to discover why, with the exception of a handful of local confrontations during the 1980 steel strike, and a small town-centre fracas involving the police and Afro-Caribbean youths one year later, ours was such a politically vibrant, yet essentially placid, place in which to live.

This somewhat cosy and predictable form of academic existence was suddenly undermined by the onset of the year-long miners' strike. Starting in March 1984, I defied ESRC advice to 'steer well clear' of any possible conflict by spending virtually every day on some form of picket line, march or demonstration. The data deriving from this process of participant observation was used alongside interviews with pickets, police and other 'key informants' (e.g. local politicians and journalists) as the basis of several published case studies of 'set piece' confrontations, such as the 'Battle of Orgreave', and community disorders occurring in South Yorkshire pit villages, like Grimethorpe and Maltby.[1] As you can imagine, this constituted an extremely enriching and illuminating experience, which gave me an unrivalled insight, both into the nature and causation of the strike, and the disfiguring and destructive long-term impact it had on community and family life.

Martyn Bedford's story focuses, not surprisingly, on this fundamentally divisive nature of the strike: of the tragic way in which it created lasting social schisms, not only in the 'split' communities of areas like North Derbyshire, but also in the solidly pro-strike coalfields of Scotland, Yorkshire and South Wales. The roots of such divisions were primarily ideological. Very few strikers and their wives or partners would have contested the popular notion (subscribed to by the members of Matt's immediate family) that the Conservative government under Margaret Thatcher had provoked the strike with the deliberate intention of 'smashing' the National Union of Mineworkers (NUM). However, there were countless opponents of strike action who shared with Matt's Aunt Sylvia the conviction that Arthur Scargill had been too blinded by personal vanity or reckless political ambition to resist leading the miners into a conflict in which the odds were so patently and insurmountably stacked against them.

It is now evident with the benefit of twenty-twenty hindsight that the reality of the situation was actually far more complicated than it might have seemed back then. Evidence has since emerged that, whilst the Thatcher government was undoubtedly well-prepared for a possible showdown with the miners, the strike was not intentionally provoked in the manner presumed by the popular conspiracy theory of the day.[2] Rather, it was a bungled and unauthorised decision by the management of the Yorkshire Area of the National Coal Board (NCB) to announce the closure of the Cortonwood colliery in South Yorkshire which acted as the trigger for the ensuing year-long struggle. Far from seeking to engineer or encourage immediate strike action, Mr. Scargill's NUM National Executive tried, albeit in vain, to strategically contain the momentum already being generated among the rank-and-file within the increasingly irate Scottish and Yorkshire Areas of the union. It must also be remembered that the 'flying pickets' who poured over the border from Yorkshire into Nottinghamshire the instant that strike action was formally authorised (thus setting the scene for confrontations between police and pickets and strikers and working miners) did so in contravention of official NUM directives.

The controversial issue of strikebreaking (or 'scabbing', to employ the more emotive parlance of the day) is handled with particularly commendable sensitivity in Bedford's story. The type of violence meted out by Matt and Rich to Uncle Peter and his family was seldom undertaken lightly or in any arbitrary manner. Indeed, this particular example exemplifies the fact that there were invariably additional emotional factors involved which made the perceived betrayal of one's fellow workers seem all the more reprehensible and unforgivable.

An actual example of this kind concerns the well-publicised sequence of events which unfolded in the small pit village of Fryston, in my home town of Castleford, West Yorkshire, when convoys of heavily-protected police vehicles became involved in the daily ritual of escorting a solitary 'super scab' back into work – presumably in the hope that this would provide the catalyst for a much wider abandonment of strike action. Local residents and strike supporters eventually responded to this tactic by bombarding the police convoys with bricks, and by vandalising the colliery's management office block, and then setting it alight – all under the cover of early morning darkness. When this deterrent activity failed to have the desired effect, a dozen or more strikers forced their way into the strikebreaker's home and gave him a savage beating, a crime for which they were all later imprisoned.

The NCB Chairperson, Mr. Ian MacGregor, subsequently visited the victim of this violence to 'thank him' in full view of national television reporters and proclaim him as a hero.[3] One thing that Mr. MacGregor was either unaware of at the time or just 'strategically failed' to mention was that, prior to the strike, the so-called super scab had been on the verge of being sacked because of repeated absenteeism, and that it was only due to the intervention of local NUM officials that he had been able to continue in his job. It was this additional piece of local knowledge which had inspired so much hostility towards him.

'Withen' also trains an extremely illuminating spotlight on the plight and anguish of those miners and their families who suffered torturous crises of conscience, relating to the possibility of going back to work in order to deal with increasing levels of poverty, ill-health or the fear of losing one's job. In Bedford's story, we saw how Uncle Peter returns to work (much to his eternal suffering and regret) primarily because he is 'skint', the gas and electricity has been cut off, the kids have outgrown their school clothes, and one of them (Fiona) has become clinically malnourished. The potency of this dilemma was explicitly recognised in 'split' communities, such as those of North Derbyshire, where miners who held out to the last adopted a relatively forgiving attitude to 'hunger scabs' – i.e. those men perceived to have been 'driven back' out of unbearable necessity. Perhaps one of the most moving sights of the entire dispute coincided with what the NUM referred to as the 'orderly return' to work, on the morning of 5th March 1985, when returning strikers at some Derbyshire mines not only clapped but also invited those colleagues whose resolve had been worn down in this way to walk alongside them back into the pit.

Bedford's account of Orgreave is sprinkled with important details that I can personally verify (such as the presence of the ice-cream van, the youths rolling the tractor tyre towards police lines, and the sinister reverberation of the horses' hooves as they close in on the pickets), all of which further imbue his story with such a satisfying flavour of authenticity.

For perfectly understandable reasons, Bedford's narrative lacks the requisite legroom in which to convey the predominantly quiescent nature of a conflict episode which actually began as a brief confrontation between handfuls of police and pickets on the 23rd May, and was marked by various peaks and troughs in the ensuing violence, which concluded in the cataclysmic encounter of 18th June. Most of the day-to-day picket-line encounters at Orgreave consisted of angry, but largely ritualistic, bouts of pushing and shoving which coincided with the twice-daily arrival of the convoys of lorries which were responsible for collecting coke for the Scunthorpe steel works. Such was their almost instinctive grasp of the relevant 'rules of engagement' that the pickets and police invariably backed off from one another whenever the cry of 'Man down!' rang out; and both sides would break into mutual bouts of laughter at the shout (for example) of 'Hands up! Who's lost a brown brogue, size 9?'

It is perhaps misleading to suggest that the large numbers of pickets gathering at Orgreave on the 18th June did so as part of a carefully planned trade union exercise. True, in the early hours of that morning, two dozen or more NUM activists from nearby Doncaster had succeeded in wrong-footing the token police presence and entered the plant virtually unopposed in an attempt to appeal to the coke workers for a show of solidarity. However, many of those pickets arriving later in the day claimed that they had originally been despatched to the Nottinghamshire coalfield, only to find all access roads blocked off by the police. Such men were therefore directed to fall back on Orgreave, a destination to which all roads remained relatively accessible (suspiciously so, in fact) – fuelling subsequent conspiracy theories that it was the police, and not the miners, who were intent on a set-piece 'showdown' that day.

Certainly, there can be no disputing that what happened on the 18th June could be justifiably described as a 'police riot', insofar as the officers concerned clearly chased down pickets with the avowed intention of vengefully meting out the type of 'punishment' exacted on the likes of Matt's father, and of indiscriminately arresting anyone too slow or unsuspecting to evade them. In one particularly memorable instance, I saw a mounted police officer chase a group of pickets right up to the entrance of the nearby Asda supermarket. As the latter were about to disappear through the automatic sliding doors, the mounted policeman ducked down with the apparent intention of pursuing them into the busy shopping area. Following two more abortive attempts, he clearly thought better of it, turned and cantered off in search of easier forms of quarry. Other miners were not so lucky. At one point, I stopped to sympathise with a picket who was standing on a grass verge, supporting with his own hand an injured arm that was clearly dislocated at the elbow. 'It's alright, cock,' he responded to my expression of concern. 'Our First Aid lads are on their way. They should be arriving anytime now.'

Afterwards, while in the process of fleeing from charging police officers, I found myself suddenly propelled ten yards forward by what I had first taken to be an almighty push from behind. An eye-witness later pointed out that a police officer had used his short shield to club me in the back. My instinct for self-preservation being already paramount, I carried on running into the nearby Handsworth housing estate and eventually took refuge alongside a miner from North Derbyshire in the passageway separating two houses. A makeshift barricade, comprising two dustbins and some empty Ikea-like cardboard packaging, was all that stood between us and the menacing glare and intentions of marauding police 'infantrymen' who looked (and, frankly, acted) like something out of Star Wars.

We must be careful not to underestimate the extent of the psychological trauma induced by the experience of being assaulted and/or arrested at Orgreave, and later tried in court. The distressing range of psychological symptoms continuing to affect Matt's father, decades after he was assaulted and taken into custody simply for being present on the Orgreave picket line, approximate to those actually associated with one particular Yorkshire miner (Russell Broomhead) who developed a nervous stammer and chronic agoraphobia as a result of being repeatedly beaten about the head by a police officer (in an incident appearing on that night's television news) and subsequently brought to court on the extremely serious charge of 'riot'.

TV evening news broadcasts on the 18th June projected a deliberately misleading representation of the day's events, in that they falsely indicated that the police had only been *reacting* (in what was portrayed as a highly controlled and well-disciplined manner) to the intense violence and provocation they had been subjected to by the miners. The credibility of this generalised media account was fatally undermined at the subsequent trial (and acquittal) of 15 miners who had been brought to court on charges of riot. It was during these proceedings that defence lawyers produced evidence – in the form of an unedited police video – which showed that the day's violence had been both instigated and prolonged as a result of *unprovoked police aggression*. Officers called as witnesses admitted under oath that they had behaved indiscriminately in beating or arresting anyone who just happened to be in their way. They also conceded that they had signed specially prepared, incriminating statements of encounters they had witnessed and/or been involved in – in some cases, several weeks after the 'incident' in question had supposedly taken place.[4]

South Yorkshire Police (SYP) experienced a second, self-inflicted public relations disgrace four years later when the mishandling by their officers of a sudden build-up of crowd congestion just before the kick-off of the 1989 FA Cup semi-final between Liverpool and Nottingham Forest at Sheffield Wednesday's Hillsborough stadium resulted in the deaths of 96 football fans. Senior SYP spokespersons wasted no time in disingenuously attributing the fatal crushing to the collective impatience of scores of Liverpool supporters who had allegedly forced their way through a forbidden exit gate. However, a subsequent judicial inquiry chaired by Lord Justice Taylor laid the blame for the disaster squarely at the feet of the match-day commanders, who were said to have 'frozen' to such a degree that their decision-making capacity was correspondingly paralysed.[5]

The ongoing repercussions of Orgreave and Hillsborough remain potent enough to ensure that SYP are still striving, decades later, to recover the loss of public confidence and perceived legitimacy resulting from these infamies. The onset of social media and rise of citizen journalism are helping to ensure that the police now occupy a societal goldfish bowl in which any possible atrocities committed during public protest will be closely scrutinised and brought to public attention. Had the Battle of Orgreave occurred only yesterday, it is unlikely that the police would have dared to engage in such openly aggressive and repressive behaviour. As things stand, the events which Martyn Bedford has re-imagined in such eloquent and compelling fashion will continue to reverberate for many decades to come.

# Notes

1. For relevant examples of our work see: Waddington, D. P., Jones, K. and Critcher, C. *Flashpoints: Studies in Public Disorder.* (London: Routledge, 1989).
2. See, for example: Beckett, F. and Hencke, D. *Marching to the Fault Line: The 1984 Miners' Strike and the Death of Industrial Britain.* (London: Constable, 2009).

3. Mr. MacGregor refers to this incident in his memoirs: *MacGregor, I. The Enemies Within: The Story of the Miners' Strike, 1984-5.* (London: Collins, 1986), p. 334.

4. A first-hand account of these trials is available in: Jackson, B. with Wardle, T. *The Battle for Orgreave.* (Brighton: Vanson Wardle Productions Ltd, 1987).

5. For a fuller discussion of the nature and implications of South Yorkshire Police's handling of Orgreave and Hillsborough see my own article: Waddington, D. P. 'Public Order Policing in South Yorkshire, 1984-2011: The Case for a Permissive Approach to Crowd Control', *Contemporary Social Science: Journal of the Academy of Social Sciences,* (2011), 6(3), pp309-24.

# Never Going Underground

## Juliet Jacques

Albert Square, July, 2000

Amidst the bears and dykes, queers and straights who had crowded Albert Square – not as packed, nor as passionate as it was back in '88, but heart-warming nonetheless – I recognised him before he recognised me. Perhaps, though, that wasn't surprising.

'Johnny?'

'Oh my God... Martin?'

'Marina.'

'Of course – Marina. Sorry, darling.' He introduced me to the man by his side, although I struggled to catch his name over the hullaballoo as a drag queen, dressed like someone from a John Waters film, daubed '28' over a Stagecoach bus windscreen in red paint. After several attempts, I heard that he was called Stuart. He kissed me on both cheeks, then asked Johnny: 'Is that the guy you used to go out with?'

'Less of the "guy", please,' I replied, trying to make a joke of it.

'He – sorry, she's – my ex, yeah,' said Johnny. 'We met when we were fighting the Tories. The first time round.' He scanned me over. 'You look well.'

'Thanks.'

'When did you...'

'Back in the mid-nineties.'

'Congratulations,' Johnny offered. 'I hope you're happier now?'

'In some ways. My parents won't talk to me. Nor will my brother. Don't miss him, mind.'

'Seeing anyone at the moment?' he asked.

'No, I'm single,' I told him. 'I'm always single.'

'God, it's been ages,' Johnny said. 'Why don't we wander into the Village and catch up over a beer? It's on me.'

'Yeah, sounds nice.'

We walked across Piccadilly Gardens, still a construction site after the IRA bomb had torn it apart, four years before. Johnny still held his 'SCRAP SECTION 28' sign, and knocked on a window as we passed the coach station.

'The twat who owns Stagecoach gave a million quid to the "Keep the Clause" campaign,' Johnny snarled. 'Fuckin' Evangelicals – God can't call 'em back soon enough.'

As we headed towards Canal Street, Johnny asked: 'When was the last time you were here?'

'I moved to Bristol after my surgery. The clinic thought it'd be best to start again somewhere else. I'm not sure if they were right, but I've made some new friends. I had to come back for the protest, though, if just for old time's sake.' Johnny smiled. 'You still here, then?'

'I'm a Northerner and I'm proud!' Johnny put his hand on his heart. 'I was in London for a while, working for Labour, and that's how I met Stuart. But I'm a Manc in my heart, so I came back after we smashed the election.'

'Christ, it's changed around here. For one thing, the sign reading "Anal Treet" is gone.'

'Long gone,' Johnny lamented. 'It's quiet now, but at the weekends it's full of hen dos wanting strip-o-grams. The shiny bars with the fancy salads are all for the straights. It's got even worse since *Queer as Folk* – so many tourists, and they're not all on our side. Some of the old guard are clinging on though – Stuart and I went for a drink in the Rembrandt last night.'

'That's still here?'

'Napoleon's and the New Union too.'

'Do they still have the same drag queens?' I asked.

'Yep. Different millennium, same songs, some of the same punters. The ones who survived.'

'Ah – bless them. I guess they enjoy it...'

'Hey – you'll like this place,' Johnny told me, pointing at Manhattan Show Bar. 'It's run by that woman from that BBC *Sex Change* documentary.'

'Oh God, she's from round here, isn't it?' I replied. 'Scared the life out of me as a kid, that.'

Johnny said hi to the 7ft drag queen on the door, both the least intimidating and the most terrifying bouncer I'd ever seen – someone who would just as easily spike you with her tongue as with her stilettos. 'That's Truly Scrumptious,' Johnny told me. 'Or Ken to his mates.' Inside, there were all these young bar staff – 'trannies', Johnny called them – pulling pints. The one who served us looked about 19, she seemed so at ease in her pretty pink top, long brown hair (which might be a wig), short skirt and fishnets, and immediately I wished that Manhattan's had been around in my day. None of the tables were free, so we propped up the bar, and Stuart asked me to tell him about how Johnny and I met...

FALLOWFIELD, MANCHESTER, JANUARY 1988

We'd driven all the way from Reading in silence, Dad and me. I always thought he'd guessed, the way he didn't invite me to the football or the cinema like with Mark. But he'd never talk about it, not even uttered that ghastly line, *it's just a phase...*

He helped me unpack at Oak House, but he was off back to Reading as soon as my stuff was in my room. I was the first to arrive, so he wouldn't have met any of my new flatmates anyway. They put me in all-male halls because I got my forms in late. Not my fault – they never gave me any – but I ended up with some absolute wreckheads. They did every drug under the sun – dope, pills, E's, whizz, you name it – and liked their lager too; Athletics Union social on Wednesday, Haçienda on Saturday. It wasn't like that down south: the guys with crew cuts got wasted down their local, and the gays who spent twenty quid on their hair went to London. Anyway, this lot reckoned they were hard enough to hold their own at the clubs, even in the so-called 'Gunchester' days.

Immediately, I realised that the only privacy I'd get was when I locked my door, and even then, I'd be expected to hang out a lot – so none of the secret cross-dressing that I'd done at home. In any case, I'd only brought my make-up. I wore bits of it – nail polish, eyeliner, mascara – just to test the water. Mostly, they ignored it. Rob would ask if I was into Bowie. He liked the Berlin albums as much as all that house and rave stuff, and made me feel a little less alone. Otherwise, it wasn't great – I thought uni would be talking about books, joining a band, getting into politics, but they weren't up for protests or even much discussion, and a couple voted for Thatcher in '87. *Maybe it was those Tory billboards saying that Labour would make straights go to camps with gay sports days, as if that would ever happen – bollocks to sport and bollocks to all the fucking tossers who like it…*

So, first thing I did at Freshers' Week was join the Gay & Lesbian Society. Not that I really thought I *was* gay, but I liked men. Some men. Maybe I was bisexual. Maybe I was a transvestite, and that made me gay, I didn't know. I just didn't like being a guy, and thought someone there might understand… But I went on the first social and didn't click with anyone, so I tried to make friends with the other English Literature students. That didn't work either, so when I got back after Christmas, I tried again. I found a flyer at the Union, and a couple of nights later, put on my make-up and got the 42 into town. I kept my head down as some scally on the top deck kept yelling 'Eh! Pete Burns!' at me. When I got to the top of Oxford Road, I asked a woman how to get to Canal Street, and she stared at me like something a cat had dragged out of the gutter. Then I saw these guys, some with bleached hair and crop tops, and others with skinheads and leather trousers.

- *Excuse me… do you know where the Rembrandt is?*

- *'Excuse me!'* one of them said, taking the piss out of my accent. *Welcome to the North, babe! We know where it is – but wouldn't you rather come with us?*

- *Well…* I said, checking them out. *Let's see.*

I walked with them, and they asked me how old I was, where I was from, the usual. They were going to Napoleon's, but I decided to stick with the Rembrandt. I'd never been anywhere like this before: I stood outside, trying to peer at the punters to figure out what they might be like, but you couldn't see through the windows. I stepped inside and cast my eye around. It was like the pubs in Reading – except with posters for drag queens instead of covers bands, pop instead of rock on the jukebox, staff who *didn't* stare at you like you'd come round at Christmas and pissed on their kids. They were playing Dead or Alive, 'You Spin Me Round', and as I went to the bar, these older men gave me the eye. I can't lie: it was intimidating but in a way they made me feel sexy, a little more than ever before, even though I didn't fancy them…

There was only one gang that could've been students – twenty years younger than everyone else. It was called the Gay & Lesbian Society, but something was missing.

– *Is this just for guys?*

– *The girls split,* I was told. *They prefer the dyke bars.*

– *And they're more into politics.*

– *Maybe I should join them,* I joked. Well, half-joked.

– *I wouldn't try that, duck.*

– *They're women-only.*

– *Why?*

– *Some of them hate men, a few of them* really *have it in for trannies.*

– *Seriously? What's the problem?*

– *I don't know. Apparently, the most male thing you can do is cut your dick off.*

– *SIMON!* said someone. *That's* not *what happens, and even if it was, that's bloody insensitive.*

– *Sorry, Joanie,* replied Simon. *I just can't think of* anything *worse.*

– *Don't do it, then.* He turned to me. *Sorry about that. One Bacardi Breezer and he's a fucking 'mare. Just ignore him. Like we do.* Simon glared at him, and he smiled back. *I'm Johnny.*

No airs or graces, no sense that he had some preconception of what gay men were meant to be like. Just a smart, funny, friendly lad. And *dreamy,* with his blond hair and blue eyes... When everyone else was dancing, we got talking. About how his parents never gave up on him 'coming home with a lass', how he split with his first long-term boyfriend who'd voted Tory. *One of those self-hating queers,* Johnny said. And about how he'd been with his little sister in the only gay pub in Rochdale when it got firebombed.

Johnny gave me this leaflet. It had little bombs round the edges – his idea, he said, after *Capital Gay*'s offices got burned down and the Conservative MP for Lancaster proclaimed that it was 'right that there should be an intolerance of evil.' It said, 'STOP THE CLAUSE' in foreboding letters, above: 'FIGHT FOR GAY AND LESBIAN RIGHTS'.

– *It's not just that the Tories want us to die,* said Johnny. *They want us never to live at all.*

– *What do you mean?*

– *They're trying to pass a law making it illegal to talk about being gay in schools. Or even have books about it in libraries. You're not gonna let them – are you?*

Thatcher's plummy, fingernail-on-blackboard voice rang in my ears. *Children who need to be taught to respect traditional moral values are being taught that they have an inalienable right to be gay.* I pictured my parents, and maybe Johnny's, nodding along. All her talk of what children were *denied,* and she would snatch even the prospect of education from us.

– *Of course I'm not going to fucking let them.*

– *Come to the meeting,* he insisted. *I'll introduce you to everyone.*

★

I loitered outside the Students' Union in this velvet blouse and a little mascara. Johnny jumped off the bus, beaming as he saw how many people were entering. I went to shake his hand.

— *Oh, for fuck's sake, darling — gimme a hug.* He smiled. *If this lot don't all hate Thatcher yet, they will soon,* he guessed, and we went inside.

All the boys were on the left, and the girls on the right. No butches or femmes. Then I realised that the only time I'd seen lesbians was in *The Killing of Sister George,* and that was twenty years old. These were all T-shirts and trousers (but not dungarees, like in *Daily Mail* cartoons), badges with slogans, short hair, no make-up. The guys looked mainly 'straight-acting'.

— *Watch out for the older ones,* warned Johnny. *They might be PIE.*

— *PIE?*

— *Paedophile Information Exchange. They were big in the seventies, but a few are still skulking around.* He paused. *Or they might be the Socialist Workers' Party.*

— *How can you tell?*

— *Wait for them to offer you a newspaper.*

As we laughed, two blokes piped up behind us.

— *All the dykes keeping to themselves as usual.*

— *Can still smell the fish though.*

Johnny turned.

— *Mate! Fuckin' 'ell! Did you learn nothing from Lesbians and Gays Support the Miners?*

— *Minors?* The bloke replied. *You're not PIE 'n' all, are ya?*

— *They've shown solidarity by coming,* Johnny told them. *You should do the same.*

Johnny turned back, shaking his head. Luckily, Hugh — the Secretary of the North West Council for Lesbian & Gay Equality — started the meeting. There was dead silence as he talked about how one in five gay people had attempted suicide; about how Manchester's notoriously Evangelical chief of police, James Anderton, had described gay people, drug addicts and prostitutes who had AIDS as 'swirling in a human cesspit of their own making'; about Lord Denning, who boasted about personally sending gay men to prison before decriminalisation; about there being no mainstream gay press to counter this, and that Jack Cunningham, Labour's Shadow Home Secretary, supported the clause, even though it was part of a Local Government Act that would strengthen the Tories by persuading bigots that public services should be cut.

Johnny got up.

*– The Tories have moved the goalposts,* he said. *London councils are trying to provide positive images of gay couples, and Thatcher calls it 'promotion of homosexuality'. If Labour won't fight her – we will!*

There was applause: he returned my smile, and then a woman shared a story about her friend with mental health problems.

*– He had a breakdown and checked into his local clinic. They asked him some basic questions, but as soon as he mentioned his boyfriend, they packed him off to Wythenshawe Hospital, slung him in a room on his own and told the staff not to touch him. When I went to see him, they made me wear a gown, like he had the bloody plague. And Thatcher thinks kids are learning too much about gay people.*

*– Say something about school,* Johnny nudged me.

*– We got told* nothing *about sexuality,* I said. *Every day, kids at my comprehensive in Reading called me 'faggot' or 'bender', gave me no end of shit for liking books more than football, chucked things at me because I wasn't into girls. People die of the ignorance this breeds, and no-one – gay, straight, whatever – should stand for it.*

And there were cheers all around the room! *Whoa,* I thought. Johnny took my hand as I sat down: *That was fuckin' brilliant!* Hugh told us how we could support the campaign – flyering, writing to the Lords, getting friends involved. There would be a march into town, a rally, and a festival with bands and speeches.

*– Let's do this!* Johnny cried as we left.

*– Can we talk at yours?*

*— Sorry luv, I'm back at my mam's at the moment. Only way I can do my MA. What about yours?*

*— My flatmates might be around, not sure they're cool with it.*

*— What are they going to do? Hold a Straight Pride march? Come on, it'll be fine.*

So we got the bus together to Oak House. I told him about how my flatmates would say things like *Nothing against gays, but I hate the ones who mince about*, and thought that *The camp ones were a put-on.* He took my hand again, subtly, and said that he didn't really get on with the *ultra-gays,* and that like my flatmates, he liked his E's and went to footy occasionally, Rochdale or Man City, but that their comments sounded like textbook homophobia.

*— I think everyone's out,* I said as we opened the door, to silence and darkness. We grinned at each other, went to my room and shut the door. Finally, we could be intimate with each other, and Johnny put his hands on my shoulders...

*— You know I'm a transvestite,* I told him.

*— I knew you liked a bit of glam,* he replied. *I didn't realise you were that into it.*

*— When I was 14, my older brother caught me wearing my mum's dress. I thought he was out and I was putting on her lipstick. The fucker took a photo and told me that if I didn't give him my pocket money every week, he'd show everyone we knew.*

*— Jesus,* he sighed, sitting on my bed. *Still — you're here now.*

*— Yeah... I like guys. It's just, I've never said this to anyone before...* I sat next to him. *I think I'd feel sexier... as a woman...*

*— You want to dress up?* I nodded. *Well... first time for everything...*

I put some black tights over my shaved legs and boxers. Johnny helped me put on a cheap bra, which I filled with socks. Then he helped me pull a purple dress over my body, and I stood in front of the mirror and fitted a long brown wig from Affleck's Palace.

*— Will you do my lips?* I asked.

*— What's the point?* He kissed me, and then picked up my

lipstick and did it anyway. *Gorgeous, darling. Now, what's your name?*

– *Mesmerelda,* I told him, laughing awkwardly as he practically doubled up.

– *Mesme-RELDA!* He screamed. *Are you angling for a slot at Napoleon's?*

– *It's a funny name, but I'm not a drag queen. I'm not even sure if I'm gay.*

– *Really?* Johnny asked, looking at my crotch.

Then he kissed me, and I thought: *Oh God, my chance has come at last...* But just as I took off his jeans, I heard the door. My flatmates were back from some club, wankered, screaming and shouting. *Just ignore them,* Johnny told me, and we carried on, but they started fighting outside my room – I couldn't tell if they were playing or not. One of them shoved this guy, Barry, and the lumbering oaf crashed through my door, which we'd forgotten to fucking lock. He collapsed onto my floor, looked up and me and went:

– *Fuck me! That's sick!*

– *What?*

– *Look!* Barry yelled, pointing at me giving Johnny a BJ.

– *Dressed as a fucking slapper, too!*

I froze. Johnny shot flaming daggers at them.

– *Whatever, I'm out now,* I whispered to Johnny.

– *Not getting up, Bazza?*

Barry muttered something and stormed out. Then I locked the door, and got back to Johnny.

★

That Saturday, we planned to go clubbing together. Johnny helped me pick out a new outfit in the Northern Quarter – black cocktail dress, bag and purse, size 7 heels. You should have seen the looks on the little old ladies' faces when we got those! Especially when they asked *Are these for your girlfriend* and Johnny said *No, it's for her,* pointing at me.

We went back to Oak House as I didn't want to get changed in town.

– *What do you think of the pearls?*

– *They make you look like me Nan!* Johnny laughed. *If you want to be a drag queen, camp it up, but if you wanna blend in, calm it down.*

– *Alright, I'll leave the pearls. What about the lippy?*

– *Hmm… maybe a touch,* he said, dabbing my lips with some bog roll.

I didn't try to hide it from my flatmates – there was no point now. They'd stopped talking to me anyway, apart from Rob, so Johnny called a gay-friendly cabbie, and we decided to wait outside. As we got onto the streets, these lads outside Gaffs started hooting and wolf-whistling at me. But it was worth it – we kissed for most of the journey.

*Watch out for Anderton's foot-soldiers,* said Johnny as we walked towards Canal Street. When we got there, it was packed – the bars had 'STOP THE CLAUSE' posters up, people were out drinking and if the cops had tried to nick anyone, they'd have started another Stonewall. There were more women than I expected, and no caustic remarks about *trannies.* So we chinwagged with the drinkers, downed a few in Napoleon's and went back to mine, spending the Sunday in my room, door open, with lots of pens and card.

Rob asked what we were plotting. I explained about Clause 28. *I know, it's fuckin' disgustin',* he replied, so we told him to come to the rally. *See?* Johnny shouted. *That woman's gone too far – the straights won't stand for it.*

– *Well, some of them,* I said.

– *It'll grow,* Johnny replied. *Trust me.*

The next evening, Johnny and I attended a second meeting. There were scores of people going into the Town Hall – *Told you,* said Johnny – and it took ages for Hugh to get us to sit down and shut up, it was buzzing. Hugh mentioned celebrities who were supporting us – not just the usual ones like Ken Livingstone and Peter Tatchell (*Both good Labour men,* Johnny whispered) but soap stars, musicians, actors – Ian McKellen had come out in response to the Bill, we were informed to rapturous cheers, and he probably wouldn't be the last.

The first vote concerned Viraj Mendes – an asylum seeker in Hulme, whom the government planned to deport. The radicals – mainly the SWP – wanted us to campaign on his behalf, to *build more solidarity,* like with the miners. To my surprise, Johnny voted against. *We don't want to confuse things,* he said, as I abstained. *More people will back us if it's just about the Clause.* So, the meeting decided not to campaign for Mendes.

The next item? I knew what a palaver this was going to be when Hugh uttered the words *Clone Zone advert* and Johnny threw his head back, sighing. Immediately, the room felt heavier; something had to break. As soon as Hugh spoke about how much money the shop had given to the campaign, I heard a woman's voice cry out:

- *He looks like he's got a bleedin' pineapple down his knickers!*

Loud guffaws from the right-hand side of the room. Which was where, I clocked, all the lesbians were. A few guys let out a giggle, soon stifled by disapproving glances from the more 'serious' activists.

– *There were separate meetings about this,* Johnny said.

– *And you didn't tell me?*

He looked apologetic. *I only found out afterwards.*

They displayed the advert on an overhead projector. Now, the room was dominated by a huge image of a bloke in his Y-fronts, with a boner the size of the Free Trade Hall, scheduled to feature prominently in the Festival programme. You couldn't help but laugh, except that it nearly tanked our movement – a cacophony of voices screaming things like:

– *They've given us so much support!*

– *They can support us without waving their giant dicks in everyone's faces!*

– *It's about having a right to our sexuality!*

– Your *sexuality! What about ours?*

*– This is supposed to be about gay and lesbian rights, not bloody porn!*

*– All the banners say* GAY AND LESBIAN, *what more d'ya want?*

A man stood up.

*– Christl Everyone calm down! Fuck me!* The projector was turned off and the sniping fell silent. *I remember before 1967,* he said. *Before decriminalisation. People thought that gay men were predators, potential rapists, obsessed with sex. Lots still think that – listen to what's coming out of the Tory party, or the flamin' Manchester police. I know we need to stand up to them, but this sort of thing will only give them ammunition.*

Hugh banged the table.

*– We need to settle this democratically. All those in favour of keeping the Clone Zone advert, put up your hands.*

Johnny's arm shot up.

*– We need to be able to celebrate our sexuality,* said Johnny. *Otherwise, why are we here?*

*– And those against?*

Tentatively, I raised my hand – along with everyone on the right-hand side, and a few on ours.

*– If the women don't feel welcome, it's not their movement,* I whispered. *And I don't think it's worth alienating them over this.*

A voice behind me interjected: *You what?*

*– I can see his point,* Johnny told him. *We can't be divided right now. And maybe we do need to be 'respectable'.*

*– If only a bit,* I added.

Hugh asked for abstentions, and then announced that the advert would not be used. There were cheers from the women, and a few murmurs from the men. Johnny gave me a half-smile, eyebrows raised. I took his hand, and we moved on to the final item.

*– Andy Bell and Jimmy Somerville wish to perform at the Festival in drag. Some on the Committee feel this could confuse the issues around sexuality, and these sort of drag shows are demeaning to women. We are sure that they'll accept our invitation even if we would prefer–*

— *If we pulled the advert on grounds of taste,* someone butted in, *we should pull this too.*

— *Wait!* Hugh continued. *Others felt that we shouldn't censor anyone's sexuality, however they want to express it — otherwise we're as bad as they are.*

— *But the tabloids will have a field day!*

I stood up.

— *Look, it's simple. We respected the women's opinion on the advert, and we should respect the transsexuals' opinion on this.*

— *There* aren't *any bloody transsexuals,* a bloke yelled.

— *Why not?* I asked.

— *Maybe they're just not interested,* a woman answered.

— *If there are any here, please raise your hands,* came a voice from in front of us.

— *For fuck's sake,* shouted Johnny. *It's not a sodding witch hunt.*

- *All those who think Bell and Somerville should* not *perform in drag, please raise your hands.*

Most of the room put up their arms. I didn't, and nor did Johnny. I slumped into my chair.

— *Sorry, darling. But if we respected the decision on everything else…*

I sighed as Hugh passed the motion and concluded the meeting. As we left, a woman came up to me. She was a bit older than most people there, slightly dowdy, softly spoken.

— *Hi, I'm Philippa. I just wanted to thank you for speaking up.* There was an awkward silence. *If you're interested, our group meets every other Thursday. Maybe I'll see you there.*

She handed me a card, headed 'TV/TS Support Centre', with a P.O. Box address and a phone number. I thanked her, and she walked away. I kissed Johnny on the cheek and got the bus back to Oak House, alone, trying not to cry.

★

We found each other outside Jilly's Rockworld, Philippa and I, slightly ahead of time. As the marchers strode into view, some time after we heard the claps, cheers, whistles, even drummers and saxophonists on the horizon, the chants of 'We're here! We're queer! We're not going shopping!' she asked if we were waiting for my *boyfriend*.

– *We decided not to meet for the festival*, I told her.

– *Oh... what's up?*

– *The last meeting. I don't think he got why I was so upset about the Bell and Somerville thing.*

– *Why? You're not a drag queen, are you?*

– *Well... no... But I thought he'd understand why I didn't think it was fair...*

– *Maybe it's for the best,* sighed Philippa. *Maybe they'd make us look ridiculous.*

– *Yeah, they probably would.*

We let ourselves be sucked into the surging crowd, seeing men hold hands in the street, lesbian couples with children, handwritten signs demanding EQUAL RIGHTS NOW, or declaring that LESBIAN AND GAY RIGHTS ARE HUMAN RIGHTS, that WE'RE OUT AND WE'RE STAYING OUT, SWP placards and banners of groups from Bradford, London, Newcastle that had joined us. I held up my NEVER GOING UNDERGROUND logo and walked along the fringes, earnestly.

– *Giv' us a smile, luv!* A stranger accosted me. *I know it's a protest but you can still have fun!*

I struggled to turn my lips upwards, unconvincingly, and then turned to Philippa.

– *Johnny doesn't fancy me as a woman. He said it was fun once but it doesn't turn him on.*

– *He's a gay man – what do you expect?*

– *This is more important to him right now.* I waved my hand across the crowd. *He says he can't concentrate on a relationship. Maybe we'll work things out, but...*

I couldn't help but join in the chant: *What do we want? Equal rights! When do we want them? Now!* We turned onto Albert Square, just as one of the organisers, Kürşad Karamanoğlu, stoked up the audience: *If London is New York, then welcome to San Francisco!*

— *Christ alive,* said Philippa, *look!*

It was astounding, pulsating crowds as far as the eye could see, some listening attentively, others cheering and whooping as a man with a megaphone proudly told us that twenty thousand had attended. I clapped along as we were told that this was the largest national demonstration in Manchester in the last twenty years, and that the police *were not the most numerate* as they had planned for fifteen. *Stick* this *in your stupid pipe and suck it, Anderton!* I heard as Philippa and I tried to push towards the front. Then, under the Manchester University Gay & Lesbians Students banner, a familiar voice: *I tried to tell this kid in my Maths class that I fancied him when I was 14, but I bottled it. Probably would've got my head kicked in anyway—*

I tapped his shoulder.

— *Mesmerelda?*

— *Marina.*

— *I'm* so *glad to see you!*

To my surprise, he gave me a massive hug, but I knew from the way that he kissed my cheek that things weren't quite the same.

— *This is incredible! We even got a Labour councillor to stick his neck out!*

He joined the applause as Michael Cashman from *EastEnders* came on and shouted *I'm here… because I'm proud!* He was jumping up and down, embracing everyone around him, almost hyperventilating – I'd never seen anyone so ecstatic. So we stayed together as Cashman talked about *ordinary men and women made extraordinary by society's focus on what we do in bed,* and it was inspirational, really, to see so many people agreeing with him, all of whom fell quiet as he talked about how people could gas or shoot us, but that as long as people continued to procreate, homosexuality would exist. Then, two actors from *Brookside* came on, well received being Scouse icons: Sue Johnston compared the clause to the Nazi book-burning, before Steve Parry screamed: *Who the hell is going to get a closet big enough for all of us!*

— *There bloody well ain't n'all,* beamed Johnny, putting his arm around me.

— *Not once most of you are out,* I said.

— *What do you mean?* I hesitated. *You're out now, aren't you?*

— *I don't feel* out, I replied. *Not really.*

— *Do you want to be a woman?*

— *Maybe. I don't know. Perhaps we should talk about it later.*

From his silence, I knew that we would never survive something that colossal; it might be best that we try to be friends now, rather than tear ourselves apart further down the line. After Philippa had gone, we spent the evening together, but I found it impossible to enjoy the Communards or Erasure as much as everyone around me seemed to, and Ian McKellen's recital of Thomas More, beautiful as it was, didn't quite strike me in the same way as it did Johnny. At the end, we kissed, but it just wasn't like the old days any more, and I went home alone – seeing Rob with his girlfriend when I got in, hearing him say that they both had a brilliant time at the protest, just made it feel even more bittersweet...

★

'So that's it,' I told Stuart. I noticed that Manhattan's had cleared out, and that the barmaid (who, she told me, was called Marlene) had been listening to most of my story. 'I guess things are better now.'

'Yeah, but it's still not great,' Marlene interjected. 'Some kids in a car chucked a load of eggs at Truly a while back. They missed, but you can still see it out the front.'

'And the local rag are still at it,' said Johnny. 'They picked out a photo of a couple of leather queens that Marketing Manchester had put in a brochure and ran a headline saying, "Is this how we want to promote our city?" Of course, they encouraged everyone to say no. People are getting scared to hold hands again.'

'Tony will sort it,' replied Stuart, and Johnny put his arm

around him. 'The Loony Left might not have stopped the Clause, but we will.'

'Perhaps, but we did the groundwork,' I sigh. 'It's weird how these things pan out.'

'What do you mean?' asked Marlene.

I explained how the Clause, introduced to silence and separate us, had brought us all together, and how the campaign had led me somewhere entirely different to most of my comrades. I told Johnny, Stuart and Marlene about how I'd gone to Philippa's TV/TS group, which had met in Canal Street, until I moved away, and how they had supported me when my parents disowned me, and when old friends like Rob from halls turned their backs on me.

Marlene in particular looked apprehensive, and I didn't want to leave her on that note.

'Now, things are...' I hesitated. 'I don't know if they're better, but they're not getting worse. I guess they're just different.'

'And they'll change more once we finally get rid of that objectionable law.'

Johnny smiled, and hugged me nearly as hard as he had when we'd first met outside the Student Union. 'It's been so wonderful seeing you again. Keep in touch, yeah? Stuart and I have bought a flat just round the corner – come and stay whenever you like.'

'Absolutely. And if you're ever in Bristol – feel free to do the same.'

I watched Johnny and Stuart leave, hand in hand, and then saw that Marlene had brought over another gin and tonic. I asked if it was for me: she said it was, and shook her head, smiling, when I reached into my handbag. 'You're very sweet, but I should really go,' I told her. I left my email address, kissed her on both cheeks and then headed towards Manchester Piccadilly, boarding the train back to Bristol with more hope than I had since... well, I can't remember.

# Afterword: Before the Act, 1988

## Dr. Em Temple-Malt
### Staffordshire University

SECTION 28 HOLDS A CERTAIN mythical, symbolic power for sexual minorities of all generations. There are different stories to be told about Section 28 depending not just on who is telling the tale, but when the story is being told. Those living and writing about their lives during the 1980s recall decades of public moral censure which forced many to lead hidden lives to avoid the spotlight of stigma. Others joined political groups and critical communities which allowed them to confidently and unapologetically display their non-hetero sexuality in public. For some though, this carried the risk of becoming estranged from one's family of origin. Living under a Thatcher-controlled Conservative government was especially grim. People's memories include a moral panic about the demise of 'the (nuclear) family', the HIV/AIDS epidemic that was decimating huge swathes of the gay community, mothers and fathers who could no longer pretend to be heterosexual, leaving opposite-sex partners to set up homes with someone of the same sex, risking the loss of their children. Stories told in later decades, with hindsight, are more optimistic in tone. The 1980s is the era where things began to more visibly change. Having to endure decades of stigma and ill-treatment was what seemed to galvanise and mobilise certain members of the lesbian and gay community to campaign for equality of opportunity and relational rights.

In 1986, the Labour-led Haringey Council produced a manifesto that sought to prioritise 'equality of opportunity' and included a section on lesbian and gay rights.[1] The idea of 'positive images', referred to the need for all sections of the community to have access to a series of successful role models for young people, which would go some way to counter societal prejudices and derogatory stereotypes. Education was seen as a way of communicating positive messages about lesbian and gay individuals to ensure future generations of adults would know there were options other than heterosexuality, and to help end discrimination against lesbians and gay men.[2] The Lesbian and Gay Unit within Haringey, wrote to local head teachers in the summer of 1986 to remind them of the commitment to 'equality of opportunity', and to include positive images as part of their education provision. This letter was leaked to the local press and government.[3] Given the way social attitudes are *these days* towards LGBT people in the UK, you could be forgiven for wondering how on earth this seemingly simple act caused such controversy.

Some sections of society (academics, parents' rights groups, etc.) interpreted the 'positive images' policy and the suggestion that schools might teach young people about alternative ways of conducting adult relationships as a real threat to morality and the heterosexual family.[4] In the 1980s, there was a sense of moral panic about the stability of 'the family'; it was thought to be in crisis. The family wasn't in crisis. Instead, the Conservative's ideological perception that the family should be independent from state intervention and self-sufficient[5] was at risk.[6] Over two decades, easier access to contraception and the availability of 'no fault' divorce in 1971 had altered people's attitudes towards, and the way they were conducting, family relationships. This change in attitudes led to greater diversity of family relationship types. Alongside the familiar nuclear family there were also divorced and reconstituted families with step-children and lone mothers,[7] as well as more couples cohabiting outside of marriage (i.e. living together as a way of testing the strength of their relationship). A rising divorce rate intimated that the taboo on ending marriages was disappearing; women were less willing to endure unhappy marriages.[8] That the family, as a social unit, was undergoing a transformation, meant that more people might temporarily need support from the Welfare State; an issue which alarmed the Conservative government.[9]

The Section 28 bill emerged as a way to respond to the specific anxiety that the heterosexual family was under threat from the 'positive images' policy.[10] It was thought that introducing this legislation would curb the actions of Labour-controlled local authorities' (e.g. Haringey, Brent, Lambeth, Manchester) plans for the introduction of 'positive images' in education. The bill was drafted by Lord Halsbury and submitted to the House of Lords in December 1986. A year later, Conservative MP David Wilshire introduced Section 28 in the House of Commons in the final stages of the preparation of the Local Government Act. It was during parliamentary debates about Clause 28 that some Conservative MPs grossly distorted the actions of Labour-controlled local authorities characterising their 'positive images' policy as *promoting* homosexuality, accusing them of giving lesbian and gay individuals 'special treatment', and misusing ratepayers money. David Wilshire for instance, specifically accused the Greater London Council (GLC) of misusing rate-payers' money by funding the publication of books such as Susanne Bosche's *Jenny Lives with Eric and Martin* (1983).

Opposition to the introduction of the bill was taken up by Labour and some Liberal Democrat MPs. They tried to challenge the notion that schools were *promoting* homosexuality. An example can be seen in the parliamentary speech made by Mr. Ken Livingstone in 1987:

> The survey showed that children who were homosexual felt that they had had no assistance at school. So talk of promotion is nonsense [...].
> Much of what has been said has been deeply offensive to millions of lesbians and gay men in this country. It is

particularly obscene to hear their relationships dismissed as pretending. I know several lesbian mothers who have struggled to come to terms with the discovery of their lesbianism after marrying and having had children. They have had to face the problems of the divorce that follows, and have had to fight to keep their children, because they loved them. [...] To dismiss those relationships as pretence is incredibly unhelpful to the thousands of women who struggle to continue to be able to raise and care for their children.

The leadership of the Labour Party were criticised for not adequately challenging the Conservative government's characterisation of the 'positive images' policy as promotion of homosexuality.[11] Outside of Parliament, lesbian and gay men came together in various ways to oppose the introduction of the clause. Examples included lesbians and gay men creating political alliances in an effort to oppose the introduction of the clause.[12] Negotiating and agreeing on which issues to campaign about was often fraught,[13] as many gay men and lesbians were influenced by different political ideologies (e.g. socialism, feminism). We are given a glimpse of the tense atmosphere of these negotiations in Jacques' story where the women activists ridicule the Clone Zone advert featuring the man with the 'pineapple down his knickers'. Their particular problem was the explicit and seemingly flaunting display of gay men's sexuality. A resolution of sorts was reached, where the groups would only campaign against issues that affected both lesbians and gay men. Despite this, a number of campaigns were criticised because they seemed to be 'elitist', focusing on access to theatre, literature, the arts and charities which meant less visible groups' issues were neglected (e.g. LGBT parents).[14] Other enduring examples that have entered LGBT folklore are the stories of lesbian protesters who abseiled into the House of Lords when the House voted in favour of including the clause in the Local Government Act. And the now infamous invasion of the BBC's

Six O' Clock news, during which one protester managed to chain herself to Sue Lawley's desk and was sat on by Nicholas Witchell. The impending threat of the introduction of Section 28 encouraged many previously unpoliticised LGBT individuals to come together in mass opposition rallies all over the UK.[15]

Despite the great efforts and enthusiasm of LGBT activists, Section became law on 24th May 1988:

*28 Prohibition on promoting homosexuality by teaching or publishing material*

(1) The following section shall be inserted after section 2 of the [1986 c.10] Local Government Act 1986 (prohibition of political publicity) –

'*2A Prohibition on promoting homosexuality by teaching or by publishing material*

1) A local authority shall not –

(a) Intentionally promote homosexuality or publish material with the intention of promoting homosexuality;

(b) Promoting the teaching in any maintained school of the acceptability of homosexuality as a pretended family relationship.

2) Nothing in subsection (1) above shall be taken to prohibit the doing of anything for the purpose of treating or preventing the spread of disease.'

Contentiously, the law that was designed to prevent local authorities introducing 'positive images' into education had little practical effect in that regard. Instead, the clause had a major impact on the everyday lives of lesbian and gay individuals, making people more cautious about displaying their non-heterosexual identities and funding for lesbian and gay services was dramatically reduced.[16]

The ending of Jacques' story is compelling, in particular its pragmatic ambivalence. It took a further 15 years to repeal the law. It is unlikely that the repeal *itself* led to change. In fact, the reverse is more likely. It became possible to repeal the legislation *because* social attitudes towards sexual minorities in the UK had transformed profoundly over the previous 15 years. Traditionally, same-sex relationships had been cast as illegitimate, inferior and a threat to the heterosexual family. However, in the decade after Section 28 was introduced, the public profile of lesbians and gay people became more visible.[17] LGBT organisations like Stonewall (founded in 1989 in reaction to the introduction of Section 28) were instrumental in bringing the private stories of lesbian and gay individuals into the public domain. Stonewall's strategy was to give visibility to particular lesbian and gay issues with their equal rights agenda, and sought incremental change on the grounds of equality with heterosexuals.[18]

During their first-term, the New Labour government initiated the repeal of Section 28 in 1999. It was finally repealed in 2003. Reasons for repealing the legislation included a wider commitment to ending 'unjustifiable discrimination', and the perception that the original legislation was both offensive to lesbian and gay individuals, and redundant.[19]

The repeal of Section 28, in comparison to its introduction in the late 1980s, was notable for the lack of any sustained public opposition. It received very little coverage in the mainstream press, partly because the media were preoccupied with Iraq, and the allegations that it had weapons of mass destruction. Parliamentary debates where MPs supported the repeal were replete with examples of the routine everyday discrimination that lesbian and gay people faced. For example, in his 2003 parliamentary speech, Chris Bryant MP spoke of gay men and lesbians having to 'think twice before booking a hotel room', or 'taking out a mortgage', and think 'three, four or five times' when writing a will, out of fear of how others might react.[20]

Bryant's ability to talk openly and compassionately about the daily lives of sexual minorities in Parliament was indicative that attitudes towards them had changed. Also indicative of this change is the series of 'equality' measures introduced by the Labour government, designed to reduce discrimination and injustice (for instance, the Children and Adoption Act 2002, the Civil Partnership Act 2004, Gender Recognition Act 2004, and the Equality Act 2010).

In the 14 years since the repeal of Section 28, there's been a seeming shift in the way sexual minorities are represented in popular culture. Lesbian and gay people's experiences are increasingly ubiquitous, becoming part of the wallpaper of everyday life, feeling less tokenistic and more 'ordinary'.[21] Nowadays, we have popular soaps on the telly all featuring LGBT people, and the story-lines in which they feature tend to be about regular issues rather than specific, sensationalist issues around sexuality. Some of our best loved talk show hosts and radio presenters just happen to be gay. Pop songs and music videos in a similar way feel inclusive, portraying the everyday lives of sexual minorities such as Carly Rae Jepson's 'Call me Maybe' (2012) where she pursues a boy she has a crush on, only to discover he is attracted to men. More recently, Clean Bandit and Zara Larsson's 'Symphony' (2017), depicts one man's grief because he has lost his male lover. We are also seeing sexual minorities being recognised and equally targeted as consumers in advertising. In March 2016, a TV advert for Lloyds TSB titled, *Taking that Next Step* depicted key phases of their customer's everyday lives such as birth of a child, first days at school, first teen kiss, a surprise marriage proposal and grieving relatives at a funeral. In the months after this advert aired, giant billboard adverts followed up with stills from the advert, as well as variants on its theme: one version featured a man on bended knee proposing to his male partner; another showed the outcome of this proposal, with the tag-line: 'He said 'Yes''. I noticed these particular versions on certain sites: on the London underground, on Princess Parkway in Hulme, Manchester, and so on. While these developments are cause for celebration and markers of inclusivity and progress, we shouldn't be naïve about their impact. The representations of sexual minorities that are available for other's consumption are not inclusive and are providing uneven opportunities for display. They only include people who fit strictly prescribed parameters of homonormativity.

Whilst people in the UK may now be enjoying an 'era of equality' where non-heterosexual people no longer feel compelled to censor their sexual orientation in public, in other parts of the world this equality is still a long way off. Let's consider just two examples. In Russia, in June 2013, an act of Parliament was passed that was designed 'for the purpose of protecting children from informal advocating for a denial of traditional family values' – in common parlance 'The Gay Propoganda Law'. Sound familiar? Since the passing of this law, the Western media have been keenly reporting the plight of sexual minorities living in Russia. Liz MacKean's Channel 4 Dispatches documentary *Hunted: Gay and Afraid* (2014), for example, draws connections between the passing of this law and the increasing instances of gay people being 'hunted' and persecuted for their sexual orientation. Presently, a lot of UK media coverage is focusing on the use of concentration camps for sexual minorities in Chechnya. There are also the accounts emerging from researchers studying the everyday lives of Polish sexual minorities (as well as Russian).[22] Common experiences, their participants report, include the difficulties of daily life without recourse to legal and social protections, the threat of estrangement from families-of-origin, and a strong sense that same-sex desires and relationships should not be publicly displayed for fear of psychological, physical or sexual violence. The experiences of these Russian and Polish participants bear striking similarities to the stories that emerged in the studies carried out in the 1990s about the everyday lives of sexual minorities in the UK.[23]

Telling stories to different audiences about the everyday lives of sexual minorities over the last half century has played an important role in eliciting change. Indeed it remains a vital tool for disrupting heteronormative thinking and facilitating greater awareness about sexual minorities' daily lives.

# Notes

1. Cooper, D., 'Positive Images in Haringey: A Struggle for Identity' in: Jones, C., and Mahony, P., (eds.), *Learning Our Lines. Sexuality and Social Control in Education* (London: Women's Press, 1989). p50.

2. Ibid, p47. See also: Weeks, J., *Against Nature: Essays on History, Sexuality and Identity* (London: Oram Rivers Press, 1991), pp.137-138.

3. Cooper, 1989, op. cit., p.50.

4. Durham, M., *Sex and Politics: The Family Morality in the Thatcher Years.* (Basingstoke: MacMillan, 1991). Morgan, P., 'An Endangered Species?': in David, M. E., (ed.) *The Fragmenting Family: Does It Matter?* (London. IEA Health and Welfare Unit, 1998). Haskey, J., 'Families: Their Historical Context, and Recent Trends in the Factors Influencing Their Formation and Dissolution': in David, M. E., (ed.) *The Fragmenting Family: Does It Matter?* (London: IEA Health and Welfare Unit, 1998).

5. Segal, L., 'The Heat in the Kitchen': in Hall, S., and Jacques, M., (eds.) *The Politics of Thatcherism* (London: Lawrence and Wishart, 1983), p209.

6. Reinhold, S., 'Through the Parliamentary Looking Glass: Real and Pretend Families in Contemporary British Politics': *Feminist Review 48* (1994), p.61.

7. Evans, D. T., *Sexual Citizenship; The Material Construction of Sexualities* (London: Routledge, 1993), p.71.

8. Beck, U., and Beck-Gernsheim, E., *The Normal Chaos of Love.* Translated by Ritter, M., and Wiebel, J., (Oxford: Polity Press, 1995).

9. Silva, E. B., Smart, C., (eds). *The New Family?* (London: Sage, 2009). Jamieson, L., 'Intimacy Transformed? A critical Look at the 'Pure Relationship': *Sociology 33* (1999), (3).

10. Levidow, L., 'Witches and Seducers, Moral Panics for Our Time' in: Richards, B., (ed.) *Crises of the Self, Further Essays on Psychoanalysis and Politics.* (London: Free Association Books, 1989). Reinhold, S., (1994), op. cit. p.62.

11. Thorp, A., 'The Local Government Bill [HL]: The 'Section 28' Debate.' (Research Paper, 2000) 00/47. p.87. Weeks, J., 'Clause for Concern': *Marxism Today 78* (February, 1988). Sanders S., and Spraggs, G., 'Section 28 and Education' in Jones, C., Mahony, P., (eds.) *Learning Our Lines, Sexuality and Social Control in Education* (London: The Women's Press, 1989).

12. Healey, E., 'Getting Active: Lesbians Leave the Well of Loneliness'. In Healey, E., and Mason, A., (eds.). *Stonewall 25, The Making of the Lesbian and Gay Community in Britain* (London: Virago Press, 1994), p.95.

13. Cooper 1989, op. cit. p.70.

14. Thorp 2000, op. cit. p10; Sanders and Spraggs 1989, *op. cit.* p102; Healey, op. cit. p95.

15. Smith, C., 'The Politics of Pride': in Healey, E., and Mason, A., (eds.). *The Making of the Lesbian and Gay Community in Britain* (London: Virago Press, 1994).

16. Weeks, 1988, op. cit. pp.2-3.

17. Cruikshank, M., *The Gay and Lesbian Liberation Movement* (London: Routledge, 1992), p172.

18. Stonewall, *The Case for Equality* (London: Stonewall, 1998). Stonewall, *Repealing Section 28 Parliamentary Briefing.* (London: Stonewall, 2003). See also: Rahman, M., 'The Shape of Equality: Discursive Deployments during the Section 28 Repeal in Scotland': *Sexualities* 7 (2004), (2), and Bamforth, N., *Sexuality, Morals and Justice, a Theory of Lesbian and Gay Rights Law.* (London: Cassell, 1997)

19. Hansard. HC–Deb–10–March–2003–c65.

20. Ibid, HC–Deb–10–March–2003–c64.

21. We haven't quite reached that same level with bisexual and trans' people's experiences. See: Heaphy, B., Smart, C., and Einarsdottir, A., *Same-sex Marriages, New Generations, New Relationships.* (Houndsmill: Palgrave MacMillan, 2013).

22. Stella, F., 'The Politics of In/visibility: carving out queer space in Ul'yanovsk': *Europe-Asia Studies.* (May, 2012). Ambramowicz, M (ed). *Situation of Bisexual and Homosexual Persons in Poland 2005 and 2006* Report. (Warsaw: Lambda, 2007). Mizielińska, J., 'Between Silencing and Ignorance: Families of Choice in Poland' in *Dialogue and Universalism* (2010), 5/6. Mizielińska, J., Abramowicz, M., and Stasińska, A., *Families of Choice in Poland: Family Life of Non-heterosexual Persons.* Report. (Accessed 5.9.2015), available at: http://rodzinyzwyboru.pl/wp-content/uploads/
2015/03/Families-Of-Choice_Report.pdf

23. Weeks, J., Heaphy, B., and Donovan, C., *Same-Sex Intimacies, Families of Choice and Other Life Experiments.* (London: Routledge,

2001). Dunne, G., 'A Passion for "Sameness"? Sexuality and Gender Accountability' in: Silva, E.B., Smart, C., (eds). op. cit..

# That Right to be There

## Courttia Newland

THAT MORNING HE NOTICED Maxi liked to sleep on the edge of his bed. One arm beneath her ear, close to falling. The sheets had gathered by their waists. She was warm, a shiny new penny. Chris rubbed the curve of her hip, inhaled.

'So, what d'you think?'

Sleep deepened her voice. She shifted, cleared her throat.

'We should go.'

'Really?'

'We should.' He buried his nose in the crest of her spine, hoping she wouldn't mind. The tiny lump of bone felt good.

'OK. Shall we get up then?'

'I'll try,' Chris said. He stretched and groaned.

They showered, dressed, ate a hard-boiled egg each, and walked to the park hand-in-hand. Her fingers were tiny; he liked their feel. She smelt of something he recalled but couldn't place. Sunlight warmed the day. The streets were already livening, parents wheeling slack-limbed children in skeletal buggies like sagging deckchairs, teenagers pressing two litre blimps of cheap alcohol to their lips. A gathering of people jammed the flow through the park gates so they had to wait before going in. He tried to avoid looking at Maxi, taking sideways glances trying not to be caught, but she seemed not to notice, eyes forever on the distance, perhaps seeing something Chris couldn't find.

Her cut off dungaree shorts, loose rag of a white T-shirt and worn trainers had thrown him the night before. Too casual for a first date, leaving him wondering if he'd been shunted, unwilling, into the friend zone. Yet in tentative sunshine they seemed perfect. He'd worried about her being cold as they sat in the noisy beer garden. He was after all, and he'd worn a jacket, yet she never even shivered, just stared into his eyes as they talked over pints. She'd wrapped loose strands of hair around her first finger, cupped her chin in a palm and leant her head to the left. Chris found it both enticing and intense.

'Dirty Cash' echoed and rolled from council block walls at the south end of the park. There were easily thousands of people. Close to huge speakers, crusties danced a stamping, fitful march, blonde locks whipping air, bangled arms high. A thin goth with kohl rimmed eyes stood beside a bin filled with black and white placards, smoking a flattened roll up with hurried drags. A sweet cloud of Red Seal enveloped them. Maxi took two placards from the bin, handing one to Chris. It was slightly heavy as he raised it, and the flat paddle of cardboard caught the breeze. He almost couldn't keep it straight, using both hands to lift it. The slogan said, 'DON'T PAY! *FIGHT!*' He rested splintered wood against one shoulder.

The park heaved with locals and out of towners. People standing around the squat ice-cream truck, sitting in picnic-sized groups, kicking footballs. Whistles and foghorns blasted, Chris shielding his eyes against the ever-present mist of drifting smoke. Maxi tugged at him, and he lowered his head.

'Fuck me, it's more like a party,' she yelled in his ear.

'I did think there'd be speeches.'

'Nah, it's good,' she said, grinning, starting to move. Chris felt stiff, unable to respond. His feet were mired in the grass. Legs useless.

'Yeah, it's good.'

A passing bloke handed Chris a flyer. He took it without looking, showing it to her. *Class War*, the headline said, and beneath a picture of a guy thrusting two fingers at the reader:

*You can count on 2 fingers how much poll tax to pay.* They sniggered like school children.

'Nice,' she said. 'You're keepin that.'

'I am.'

He slipped his fingers beneath the twin straps of her dungarees, pulled her near. Maxi rested easily against him. She felt right, a snug fit.

Speeches came after the music and when they were finished, the crowd pushed out of the park like overflow. No-one said it would happen, or told him what direction to go in. People seemed driven by instinct, or prior information Chris hadn't been told. They found themselves pressed intimately against strangers as they were forced out of park gates onto the main road, waving placards, careful not to bash anyone, chanting at pale blue sky. The crowd was solemn, focused. A group of drummers pounded instruments, mouths taut, cigarettes protruding, puffing blue smoke. More frantic dancing took place in front of them, men and women resembling the squatters he'd seen around Rushcroft Road as a child. Marchers stepped around their convulsing bodies, trying not to smile.

The tarmac felt hot underfoot. Maxi and Chris dolly stepped, stopping when the crowd stopped, responding to calls to lift their voices, walking again. It felt strange to march where cars normally took precedence, to make this part of the road their own. It made him anxious, fully aware of the police shadowing them on both sides. They seemed amiable enough though, pausing to listen to a protester once in a while, nod, or point, or make suggestions. Many more walked in step with the marchers, ignoring them. He studied their eyes to see some recognition of their presence and what they were doing together, but after a while he gave up.

On occasion, Maxi accidentally bumped him. She'd smile, or place an arm around his waist, placard thrust upwards, both of them walking like three-legged racers until it got awkward. She'd let him go to bound along the wide road with even more rigour, fist pumping, loud enough to make other marchers turn, wondering who she was and what the hell was going on. He gave her that joy, Chris felt it. He wasn't sure if she knew that, although it was obvious to him, the instant surge of energy, a continuation. Seeing her push herself into the air on tiptoes and bounce high, stride amongst people or bend so she could talk to a protester's kid, reminded Chris of what had changed between them, making him smile and momentarily stop mouthing voiceless chants he had no feel for, lowering his placard until a whistle jolted him back to where he was, why he was supposed to be there.

Small and compact she was. Strong. A glowing brown that put him in mind of rich, damp earth. Vital. Not fat, not skinny either. Curvaceous, that was more like it. A wide mouth, teeth that refused collective definition, demanding individuality; canines, incisors, molars. Important in their own right. Lips that brought to mind licking, before he closed his eyes and banished raw carnality too base for the likes of her. Shallow dimples. A perfect smile that won over everyone, and of course she was smart in class, creative, even making her own clothes. Best of all, she was fun. Before the blue hours of early morning, whenever he'd seen her enter the uni cafeteria she'd made him tense as silent flashing lights, a sharp whisper of radios, firm hands on his elbow. Not fear exactly, although close. Hesitance. Expectation. She made him think of moments that hadn't arrived, lay waiting. Perhaps around the corner, maybe never, present like a build of pressure in the air. Even though she'd only nodded or smiled when she saw him sitting alone, ignoring his uneaten lunch, after all those weeks the close, solid feel of their mutual atmosphere was impossible to deny.

She came back, slipping a hand into his. So natural, like an action they'd performed forever. Without knowing, Chris succumbed. Over Lambeth Bridge, along Millbank and Abingdon Street, onto Westminster in a marching trance, revived only when the chants of *Maggie, Maggie, Maggie*, and *Out, Out, Out* fell into temporary, muttered silence, then evolved into something newer, louder. And they were under again, blinded by a continuous swell of bobbing heads behind, in front and on all sides, no trace of the road beneath them, nothing but everyone. Men wore plastic smiling Maggie masks, waggling their fingers in a pantomime wave. Tambourines shivered close in his ear. Nurses beat empty tin cans or upturned plastic buckets alongside pristine suited pensioners, medals at their chests. A family of tourists stood outside the Houses of Parliament as they passed, all-weather windcheaters bulging swollen sails, father snapping photos with concentrated determination, mother pointing, motioning to her son, blonde daughter off to one side, eyes darting. Photographers wove in and about, never still, Chris turning whenever they came near. The tendons in Maxi's neck stretched taut as she raised her chin, a small fist pounding air with every *Out, Out, Out,* so hard he heard the strain of her voice, saw the red flush of her cheeks. Chris felt proud, knew it was foolish. One night, that was all. One special night. Yet he couldn't find a way to dispel those foreign emotions. He needed to have a word with himself. His mates would laugh, Mum would shake her head. Of course she'd never approve of Maxi, it would all be in her eyes.

Past the tube station, up Whitehall. Police behind metal barricades on one side, protesters roaring, chanting, dancing, beating instruments on the other. Faces pressed against stranger's backs, strides shorter, stopping more often. At Downing Street the marchers gathered outside tall gates and sat. Whooping, placards raised, immobile. Yellow high-vis jackets were a field of bright flowers before them, at least two hundred or more. Police clutched the barricades with both hands, blankly staring into the crowd, or wandered, oblivious to the thousands of them yards away. Something in their demeanour made Chris cold. He'd seen it before, years ago, so he motioned his placard towards a patch of grass over by the M.o.D., where groups ate sandwiches, cling film dangling like loose, transparent skin. They went and sat amongst them.

'Look at that,' Maxi said with infant delight. An unseen protester with a giant Mekon head on broad shoulders wandered by, nodding at police and marchers alike, touching people's hair with what looked like genuine affection.

'You're loving this, innit?'

'It's so good. Like white people's carnival.' Her eyes wandered, she clutched his hand in hers. 'Thanks for comin, Chris.'

'That's alright. I'm enjoying it.'

'Sure?'

'Yeah, course. I am.'

'I'm not like, weirdin you out?

'Nah. Not at all.'

She leaned closer. Her hair was gloss black, so dark it shone. He placed her smell, cinnamon. Wondered how that was possible.

'You got the nicest eyes.'

Sweat prickled on his forehead, miniature needles of pain. He wished for a breeze and turned towards the people.

'You do, honest.'

'They're just black.'

'But deep black. And I like the shape, so nice.'

He turned back. She was staring again, only he couldn't hold her gaze.

'You have very kissable eyes you know.'

They laughed, Chris forced to take her all in. The chestnut round cheeks, bright teeth, the thick smears of eyebrows.

'You are weird. It's a north London thing, I swear,' Chris said.

'Shut up you. I said so anyway. An you're shy.'

'True,' he said, watching a lone ant scurry across a blade of grass, falling when it couldn't take her weight, continuing. A short, dark-haired steward close to their age, thin voice amplified by a megaphone and handheld mic with a pig's tail black wire, started asking people to vacate the area. Those on the grass swapped looks.

'It's different,' she said.

'That makes us similar.'

'Doesn't it?' She leant back, tilting her head. Gave a big sigh. 'I told Tariq an them we'd meet at Traf Square.'

'*We?*'

He tried not to deflate the word, considered his attempt a failure.

'*I*, really. There was no "we" yesterday.' She kept her head tilted so he couldn't read her. 'There is now.'

He didn't get it, or any of this. Much as she was there before him, talking that way, it all seemed as unreal as being on the march, a placard at rest by his feet. For two whole years he'd watched her traverse campus knowing he'd never make a move. So painful; she invaded all his thoughts. In the past they'd talked a little, though nothing like the last three weeks. Class work, dissertation deadlines, all studies. Then she suggested they go and see a film at Prince Charles, the new Batman. A steaming pile of shit, but it was funny. He smiled again, facing the crowd in case Maxi thought he was laughing at her. A shrivelled old man in a wheelchair, placard slotted by his side, wheeled by a young woman in a black tracksuit jacket and leggings. Chris tried to read his sign, couldn't catch it. A tidy group of eight nuns drifted past, black swans floating upstream to Trafalgar Square.

'Unbelievable. Real solidarity that is.'

'Yeah. I can't believe how many people are out here.'

'Nuts innit?'

'Proper nuts.'

He squinted as the sun emerged, tugging a handful of grass.

'D'you know Tariq an them?'

'Not really.' Chris threw the grass to one side, reaching for more. 'I keep to myself at uni, mostly.'

'Yeah,' she said, jiggling her red Converse. 'Best way.'

He studied his own sensible shoes, scuffed and nondescript as himself. He searched the grass for the ant. It was gone.

'Huh?'

'Best way. To get work done. You're sensible.'

'Not great with people more like.'

'An honest.' Maxi tore her own wad of grass, extracting a blade and pointing it at him. 'Not many honest men, trust.'

She grinned again, eyes sparkling. Heat rose. She bit her bottom lip, edging over to him until they touched.

'We don't have to meet Tariq you know.'

'I was hoping you'd say that.'

Maxi frowned into the distance. Others on the grass looked that way. A few police were arguing with some tall blokes by the barricade. The blokes were pulling the fencing towards them, a big officer was tugging it back. They looked like oversized toddlers fighting over a toy. Three officers joined the tug of war. People peeled off from the march to help. The police ducked, letting go as empty soft drink cans and a placard or two fell from the sky like the sporadic first spots of rain. The tall blokes wrenched the barricade away.

On the grass, a heavy man with the circular, balding head of a friar gathered his thin wife and two knobble-kneed boys. When Chris looked again, they'd disappeared.

'That's not good,' he muttered. Maxi didn't hear him.

The short, dark-haired steward came back, repeating his request for people to leave. His cheeks were flushed. Some families and couples packed up, the majority stayed. Maxi turned behind them to speak with a wiry young guy in rainbow-coloured McDonald's sunglasses and a floppy white sun hat. He'd just come from the top end of Whitehall, where the police had blocked all access to Trafalgar Square. You had to go along Embankment. The guy spoke in a drawl, and kept dragging his sibilants. He seemed high on something. It wasn't life.

'Cheers, mate,' Maxi said. Her expression flattened and she kept frowning, trying not to. Seated protesters began to stand. The knot of marchers opposite Downing Street was bigger, surging to and from the gates like lapping water. They couldn't see any police. There were too many people.

'What d'you reckon?'

'I don't know.'

'Maybe we should move. Those police aren't gonna stand around forever.'

'Yeah,' she said, getting up, brushing grass from her legs and bottom. Chris had an insane urge to help, unable to stop feeling that if they moved from their place there'd be no going back. And yet the mounting tension across the road worried him. He was anxious by nature, but this time it seemed justified. Drums emanating from the thick of the knot grew more intense. There was shouting, not unified and orderly like their chants, but firecracker bursts exploding from unseen places, swearing, name-calling, wordless, raw anger. Maxi peered on her tiptoes, arms wrapped around her own body even though springtime heat brightened the sky. Someone sang, 'We shall not be moved,' but it petered out when a handful of earnest stewards arrived and implored they do exactly that. He was thankful Maxi hadn't gone over to where the cans were raining more heavily, and the shouting erupted with greater violence. He tried to see what was happening, unsure what to do or say. She seemed quiet. Chris worried she might be afraid.

'Maxi,' he said, 'I really think —'

A roar, drowning his words, overpowering the consistent whistles and drums. It rose above all, hung in the air. He held Maxi by both shoulders as a sea of dark blue poured into the crowd. Chants transformed into high-pitched whoops, became screams. A tide of marchers came running by, bumping them, knocking them sideways right and left. A man appeared from the crowd, a small child's face pressed into his neck. Eyes alarmed, a rictus expression, screaming, 'Get the kids out of the way, they're going to charge!' In his wake, Chris saw the rise and fall of unified truncheons split people in all directions. The thud of falling rocks and masonry, a tinkle of broken glass. Picnickers got up, unsure. The guy with the multicoloured glasses couldn't be seen.

He grabbed Maxi, pulling. She stood firm until a second rush of people came moments after, dark uniforms penetrating the shifting crowd beyond. They ran as best as they could towards Trafalgar Square, his hands tight on her shoulders, shouting: 'Stay with me, stay with me.' Many refused to run. The M.o.D. windows shattered with a sound like crystal rain.

They bumped into a wave of marchers coming the other way, from the square no doubt. At once there was nowhere to go, and they were pushed together, sharp sweat and cigarette smoke spinning Chris's head. There was nothing to see in front or behind, just bodies. A voice sang: 'We won't pay our poll tax! We won't pay our poll tax, la, la, la, *la*! La, la, la *la*!' and it was taken up like a terrace song. Chris pressed his mouth shut. Maxi's shoulders heaved, although he couldn't hear anything she said, couldn't even hear his own voice as he leaned over, shouting reassurances. Her skin was hot and slippery. She trembled like Chris feared she might the previous night. He rubbed her shoulders and tried to push forwards with her, but they were stuck, crushed tight until she gasped.

A scream. It got louder, the pressure of the crush stronger, people crying in real terrified fear, released as uniforms appeared on all sides. Truncheons swung. The mute thud of contact, grunts of officers. Maxi shouted, only he couldn't make out the words. A long-haired, bearded man appeared on his left like a sudden apparition, covering his head as he was repeatedly hit, then grabbed by his arms and legs by four policemen, lifted and sometimes dragged from the road. The man fought, kicking, so they put him down and hit him again. Limp, he was carried away, blood streaming from his head, peppering his faded T-shirt, leaving ten pence droplets on white lines.

Maxi bent forward, hands clenched. Screaming 'Fuck off! Leave him alone,' shaking with force. Chris put his arm around her again, trying to get her away. A riot policeman materialised. His eyes were blue, heavily lashed, narrowed. His face red, teeth gritted, yellow. He pushed Maxi hard with his rounded transparent shield, full in the body and face, and when she stepped back, he swung at Chris with his truncheon. White light exploded on his head. Skin split, warmth gushed into his ear. He fell back, clutching. Maxi screamed. He hit the floor. It was rough, inviting, a hard mattress. Feet kicked and stepped all over him. He was stifled by people. The roar was loader, an intense throb that made him want to vomit. Hands pulled. They were pulling and he didn't want to get up. He was jostled on all sides and the pulling grew stronger, so he rose on one knee quick, fearful of being trampled. He got to his feet, right arm keeping balance, left hand splayed, holding back blood.

A group of men had piled onto the riot policeman who'd attacked him, ten at least. The policeman tried to beat them back with wild swings, only they were too many. They ripped and pounded him with white rocks in clenched fists. He screamed, disappearing beneath their feet. Their knees pumped with precise, vicious stamps and Maxi was at his side saying, 'Come babe, come.' A war cry, an advancing wall of dark blue and riot shields. They ran.

He had no idea where they might head, just away. Fingers stuck together, glued by his own blood. It trickled down his forearm, beneath his elbow and into his T-shirt, ending by his underarms but he couldn't take his hand away. Chris smelt metal. He could barely stand, leaning his tall body on Maxi for help, forcing her to stumble. They turned back towards Westminster, finding themselves at Downing Street to see the stutter steps of mounted police horses high above the scattered marchers, forwards and stop, forwards and stop. People booing. Marchers being arrested. A man having his trousers and shirt pulled from him by police tugging at his limbs, left only in his boxers, and still they continued. A young girl in her mother's arms cried and cried. The mother's eyes were red, vague. She swayed with the crowd.

Some marchers tried to confront the police and were pushed away, or beaten back. Horses lined the far end of the road, blocking escape via Parliament. Barricades were removed. The crowd, who had stood and watched for the most part, began to panic; Chris felt it through his pain. In an instant, they were amongst them. A mounted policeman on the far side of the road shouted, 'Get on the pavement you stupid bitch,' yet Chris couldn't see who they were talking to. The horses turned in circles, riders hitting the people below with thin white sticks. They rode back to the Parliament end and waited. Maxi stepped from one foot to another, distant though composed, the strands of hair she'd curled around her finger lying flat against her sweaty temples. '*Shit*,' she said, '*shit, shit, shit.*'

Sharp pain shot through him; he bowed, clutching his head with both hands. 'Babe,' she said, and something cool touched his right temple. Possibly her lips, Chris couldn't tell. She wrapped her arms around him, raised him up. 'It's OK,' she said, 'We're goin home.' He stood, closed his eyes tight. Colours swirled in darkness. It hurt, it hurt. He opened them and the horses ran full pelt into the crowd, close in a tight team. People jumped, lashed out, were beaten with the long sticks, or were trampled. Chris saw at least one person run down by four horses or more.

'What the fuck?' he whispered. He tasted tears, mixed with sweat. 'What the fuck, Maxine?'

'Let's go, yeah?' she said, turning Chris around and leading him. 'We're goin now.'

They went back the other way again, walking fast. When they got to Horse Guard's Parade they saw fallen, grey barricades and people wandering stunned. Nurses, nuns, crusties. Women in saris waving huge banners. Groups of Black boys in baggy T-shirts and dark glasses. Protestors crouched over tending the injured, leisurely arrests. 'Go home,' a flat-capped policeman with a megaphone blasted at the roadside, 'Please go home.' A Black kid, lithe and handsome, cupped a hand around his mouth, and shouted; 'We've got no homes to go to mate!' Despite everything, people laughed. They kept on northwards, Chris stumbling over feet, sometimes his own, shrill whistles making his head pound, drums beating back his thoughts, an earthy stench of horse manure he never forgot saturating everything, craning their necks over their shoulders so they wouldn't be trampled by mounted police.

Without realising they reached Trafalgar Square. Every metre of space seemed occupied; every step, every statue, every plinth. Marchers lined the stairs to the underground, or perched on the ornate fencing above like birds. Lions and war heroes obscured by a collage of bright T-shirts and jeans. The noise was greater than anything they'd heard all afternoon. Banners waved and songs were filled with collective power. Chris's heart fluttered. He gulped back something solid. An almost religious pride came over him; Maxi's eyes glistened. They stumbled across the road and up the steps onto the main concourse in time to see a swell of people burst from Northumberland Avenue, yelling and thundering the police into a swift retreat, back into the square and eventually Whitehall, with its champing horses and solid construction of riot police. Wrenched by Maxi, Chris climbed the steps, bleeding head forgotten, fists clenched and teeth gritted. He stopped her, looking back from higher ground. Marchers flooded the square, outnumbering those tasked to stop them.

'Yeeeessss!' he roared. 'Yeeesssss!'

He was clapped on the shoulder, so forceful it stung. He spun, enveloped by a smell of musty clothes and roll ups. It took him a moment to understand he was being hugged.

'Nice one brother,' a man said, breath warming his ear. 'Nice one.'

The man let go – a pixie-like bloke with no facial hair and startling blue eyes, cheeks and forehead smeared with black dirt. Another pushed a bottle of water into his hand. He drank until they took it from him, pouring it over his wound. He yelled, threw back his head, relishing the release. Bloody water dripped from his clothes and chin. Beside him, Maxi trembled. He drew her to him so he could feel her heartbeat against his. She shuddered, and he rocked her side to side until they almost fell. They laughed, singing with the people.

Stark white police transit vans appeared below, three in single file, grilled windscreens, headlights flashing. He watched the vans accelerate through narrowed eyes, saying nothing, squeezing Maxi harder. Protestors leapt onto pavements. Some were clipped as they dived, rolling into low walls and fencing, clutching their ankles, rocking with pain. Marchers streamed from steps and statues, blocking the road with their sheer weight of numbers, looking like unkempt soldiers. They taunted the drivers and their colleagues, threw placards at the windows. Chris couldn't hear what was said, but their arms were gesturing, and he could feel their rage. The vans couldn't go further. They backed off, whining reversal until they'd disappeared.

'That's right, fuck off!' Pixie bloke screamed.

'Bastards,' Maxi yelled, over and over.

Chris couldn't move, couldn't speak. He saw night, a sparkler glow of orange sodium lights, the thick smell of burning petrol, a distant, rhythmic crunch of glass. The open door his sister's friends hadn't bothered to shut as they piled out into chilled night, high with lust and excitement, leaving the echo of her voice for company. 'Listen,' she'd said, face close and severe. 'Move an it's licks, y'hear?'

Silence inside, clamour and sirens out. Mum on night shift as usual, but this was different. The squeak of the door, driven by breeze, waving open a crack, wandering to, yet open. Young Chris edging down the empty corridor to click the latch and step onto the balcony. Down stairs, onto barren streets. Only a short walk to Coldharbour where the fighting was battle loud and the heat of flaming cars prickled his face and hands, and masked people ran, arms arced as they stopped, leant, threw. Swearing, cries of exhilaration, loss. The crackle and buckle of warped metal. Walking until, before the barricade of smashed cars and upturned supermarket trollies, that dark blue rushed from black van doors. Pistoning truncheons, the Rasta whose screams never died, tripped by a gleaming boot, rolling, raised by grasping hands pulling at his clothes, his locks, until both were ripped from his body. The howls of fear, the sight of all that blood, the policeman who turned, a thick lock in his fist, dripping at one end, grinning at young Chris even as he ran for their empty flat, breath scraping his raw throat like grit.

The flash of white. A rising growl of engines as the vans returned, accelerating, at speed.

'Jesus,' he said, 'Jesus, look!'

He moved. Feeling Maxi's hand on his back without registering her, running down concrete stairs, almost slipping on patches of fountain water, regaining balance to push through teaming bodies in silence, focused on his goal, teeth clenched, fists bunched. There, in the midst of the people surrounding the van, he saw red-faces of rage, vivid white circles of the driver's eyes, even as the thought flashed through his mind; trapped. Trapped. There were many more protesters than the first time, encircling the vehicles, rocking the van between them, pounding at windows, stabbing at tyres, smashing headlights, sometimes even with their fists. He stumbled on something. Bending, he realised what it was; a fist sized lump of black rock, possibly tarmac, solid and glittering, rough edges. He pushed closer, someone slipping under his arm as he raised his fist. Maxi, not seeing him, running forwards, kicking at the remaining lights. A swarm of hands reached for the grille, wrenching it from the windscreen. Behind their van, the same was happening to the vehicle that followed, and the next after. Chris launched himself onto the bonnet, raised his hand and brought it down. The burly driver and woman next to him flinched, covering their heads, mouths frightened screams. The windscreen starred into a tiny pulsar map before his eyes, then he did it again, and it became a larger spider's web on the driver's side. He reached his arm back for a third go but he was sliding, falling off the bonnet, feet touching road. Maxi dragged him away as the driver slammed down his boot and the van shot backwards, following its already retreating transit siblings. Marchers hung from the driver's side door, smashing the window with placard sticks, chanting 'Fuck off, fuck off.' They fell, covering their heads, helped up by their comrades. Chris dropped his tarmac weapon to the littered ground.

Without a word they fell back just as another wave of riot police entered from Westminster, fingers clasped, sprinting to their former high point on Trafalgar Square. They were panting, hands on knees. His head began to throb; Chris had forgotten his injury. He sat on a damp step, surrounded by the legs of marchers.

'You OK?'

He nodded, wincing at the pain. There was a glistening bruise on Maxi's forehead.

'You?'

She did the same and held him. A clash of fighting echoed below.

'Not comin out with you again. Next time you ring I'm fuckin well avoidin it mate,' she said.

They laughed. Maxi carefully put her head on his shoulder. She kissed his cheek and wrapped her arms around him.

After the riot squad, more horses, driving a wide avenue through the marchers until they packed the road, rather than protesters. A lost woman wandered yards from them, expression contorted. A young boy led her from the road. The horses charged again and again, oblivious to the banks of people on each side, their whoops and yells and condemnation. Maxi stood to watch. Soon, Chris joined her. The third time they stormed the crowd, missiles began to fly. Empty cans, placard sticks, litter.

At first he thought the smoke was an echo of '81, his nightmare reformed, forever taunting. It came from high on blue portocabins opposite the square, protesters swinging from the latticework of scaffolding to the street, even as flames billowed from open windows, and the riot police who'd climbed to get them leapt down as carefully as they could manage. Maxi shouted 'South Africa House, *woy!*' Fist pumping, gleeful. 'Come on!' She leapt the steps, back into the concentrated thick of the crowd.

It was eerie in the midst of it. A strange, almost reverent silence fell. Something ancient, tribal. Another echo, their connected pasts. Unified by spectacle, police and protesters all turned to look at the blazing cabins as flames spat over the crowd. Black smoke disgorged above them. A lacklustre, tired voice yelled, 'Fire,' hardly caring. An engine, sirens blasting, edged through the crowd, turning towards the cabins, tentative as an animal spooked by humankind. They cheered. A man in a white coat and white cowboy hat held his arms aloft, making a victory sign with both hands. Although peaceful, the feeling was still charged. The pressure hadn't dissipated, only lulled.

Maxi tugged, nodding to the right. Two punks kissing furiously before an uncertain row of riot police, truncheons held limp, shields low. The police tried not to look but as they couldn't move from their hastily-assembled front line, the punks were impossible to ignore. What made it worse, the lovers were oblivious to the police presence. Their abandon was complete, unaffected. Their hands roamed each other. Eyes shut tight, blind.

'What d'you reckon?' Maxi said. She couldn't stop looking. Chris shrugged.

'Sure.'

They walked towards the line of averting eyes, a wall of blue. He wanted to cover his mouth and nose from the smoke, but didn't want to give them the satisfaction. She turned in his arms, hips solid beneath his fingers, more real than breathing. Their lips touched. He tasted blood and didn't care. For the gift of that moment, Chris forgot everything – the '81 screams, the rotten stench of the day, and the reality of being there, together.

# Afterword: From Peaceful Protest to Riot, 31 March 1990

## Dr. John Drury
University of Sussex

THE POLL TAX — OFFICIALLY known as the community charge — was a local taxation system designed to replace council rates. Whereas rates were based on the value of property, the poll tax was a standard charge for all individuals, and so was widely seen as regressive. The national demonstration against the poll tax — the subject of Courttia's story — took place on 31st March 1990, the weekend before the new tax was to be introduced. Yet only a few months later, it was announced that this new tax — a 'flagship' policy for the Conservative government — was to be abolished. This failure was ultimately one of the main factors that led to Margaret Thatcher's decision to resign as prime minister (alongside other divisions in her cabinet over Europe). The widespread campaign of non-payment, protests in courts, and resistance against bailiffs put paid to the whole scheme: it had quickly become completely unworkable. The poll tax riot described in the story has also been directly linked to the resignation of Thatcher. Causal connections are hard to prove. What is clear is that the riot was not just a shock for the wider public, but a disaster for the government, who were made to appear unable to govern.

The riot was presented in much of the news coverage afterwards as an 'unprovoked attack' by protesters on police, which had been planned by 'criminals' and anarchists.

Conservative government ministers and Labour politicians said the same thing, and supported 'examplary punishments' for all those found guilty.[1]

Among some of those defending the protest there was a critical counterpart to this 'anarchist conspiracy' explanation: the idea that there was a *police* conspiracy, orchestrated by the government, to discredit the anti-poll tax movement. This 'police conspiracy' theory was expressed, for example, by some members of Militant Tendency, the organisation that set up the All Britain Anti-Poll Tax Federation, when they referred to the role of police *agents provocateurs*.[2]

What these competing accounts sought to explain was how a peaceful protest ended in widespread conflict. The question is an important one, but there are better explanations than conspiracy.

In the month leading up to the national demonstration, local anti-poll tax unions held demonstrations at town halls in England and Wales[3] where councils were setting the rates for the new tax.[4]

Many of these protests involved trying to disrupt council business – by invading town hall chambers, shouting down council discussions, and even throwing food at councillors.[5] A number of these events involved conflict with police.

Despite these disorderly precedents, the riot at the national demonstration was unpredicted and unexpected. When marchers assembled in Kennington Park there was a symbolic vote for a peaceful protest, which was overwhelmingly supported in the crowd. Most of those who attended the demonstration had not been involved in the town hall protests. Indeed, many were people who had not been on demonstrations before, or who were not regular 'political' people – as in the case of Chris, the protagonist of this story. Alongside these numerous neophytes there were also more experienced people who had been on many demonstrations in the 1980s. This mixed composition of the crowd – united by opposition to the poll tax, but diverse in other ways – is important in understanding some of the dynamics that are captured in Courttia's story.

One of the problems with the 'anarchist conspiracy' explanation is that it wrongly assumes that crowds are inherently gullible, and therefore that people in crowds are easily swayed towards mindless violence by powerful 'agitators'. On the contrary, decades of research by social psychologists supports the view that behaviour in crowds is shaped and limited by shared definitions of identity, and that only those seen as consistent with that identity are able to exert influence.[6] At the anti-poll tax demonstration, while there was a minority calling for confrontation with the police, they were initially rejected and ignored by other protesters.[7]

Yet research in social psychology has also shown that a peaceful crowd may well come to align itself with the confrontational minority – in particular when *police* act upon the assumption that the crowd is easily swayed to mindless violence. And this is precisely what happened on 31st March 1990.

At the time of the demonstration, police riot training and public order manuals reproduced the old myth from nineteenth-century 'crowd science' that 'submergence' in a crowd leads to suggestibility and contagion; in this account, law-abiding individuals are liable to lose their reason in crowds; they will regress to a primitive state, and will engage in indiscriminate violence.[8] These beliefs about crowd psychology were certainly evident in the case of senior police officers on duty that day in London.[9] This meant that when anti-poll tax protesters sat down in Whitehall opposite Downing Street, police understood it as indicative of incipient danger and disorder – in contrast to the protesters' own view that their actions were simply a 'traditional' and hence legitimate form of protest.

There was a further contrast in perceptions in that while many in the crowd saw those who initially threw missiles at the police near Downing Street as 'unrepresentative' and saw the missile-throwing as 'sporadic', police saw the same group as *representative* of, and influential within, the crowd, and their behaviour as 'a concerted attack'. The police's ill-judged decision to ride horses into the crowd in Whitehall was not motivated by desire to create disorder (as the 'police conspiracy' theory has it) but rather by *fear* of the crowd.

The police's other misjudgement, of course, was that people in the crowd would not fight back. The police's interventions (not only the use of horses and riot police charges but also the creation of dangerous crushes) were experienced by protesters as *illegitimate* (since they were peaceful protesters), which served to legitimise confrontation with them – initially as self-defence and subsequently as retaliation.

The police's interventions were also experienced by protesters as *indiscriminate* – they could affect everyone, and they therefore created a sense of common fate. This served to unite people who previously saw themselves as diverse and disparate. This unity in turn created expectations of social support within the crowd for action against the police.[10] Hence conflict became collective. Around 5,000 people actively confronted the police in the riot. What is more, they were widely supported in the rest of the crowd, with those not directly involved often cheering on the 'rioters'.

As people were pushed into the West End, there were numerous attacks on property, especially luxury shops and cars. While this part of the riot has been less examined in research studies and was not included in the short story, it is worth mentioning for two reasons. The first is that urban riots have often displayed a pattern similar to this: the initial conflict and confrontation is with the police; this then develops into an attack on certain property targets.[11] (The Brixton Riot of 1981, referenced in the story, also took this form.)[12]

The second reason that the attacks on property in the West End are worth mentioning is that they illustrate a central theme of the story – that of change. Chris changed from peaceful protester to someone prepared to confront the police. He felt a new rage towards the police, but he also felt a new capacity within himself to take on the police. Others changed not just from protester to attacker of police, but from attacker of police to attacker of 'wealth'.

Of course, most crowd events are routine and predictable, not dramatic and life-changing; and most protest demonstrations involve a relatively predictable march from A to B, ending in nothing more than a peaceful rally. Crowd events very often reproduce and reinforce existing relations and beliefs. But occasionally participation in a crowd event leaves indelible social and psychological marks. The literature on protest contains many examples of psychological transformation, especially various kinds of politicisation.[13]

In the poll tax riot, as in those others where psychological change has occurred, the underlying process was a shift in *power-relations*. At the beginning of the conflict, power was located with the police: they were able to close off roads, to determine the route of the crowd, to move against the crowd and push people back – to impose themselves. But they inadvertently created a common identity in the crowd around an anti-police feeling, which served to shift power away from themselves and to the crowd.[14] Once that power-shift has taken place, the retreat of the police serves as evidence to crowd participants of their new-found collective agency. In these situations, attacks on new targets – luxury shops, cars, banks, the M.o.D. – express not a descent into mindless violence but collective conceptions of legitimacy and illegitimacy that are usually hidden from view in everyday life.

## Notes

1. *Battle of Trafalgar* (Despite TV):
https://www.youtube.com/watch?v=Mala4_ElCcE&t=31s
See also Burns, D. *Poll Tax Rebellion* (London: AK/Attack International, 1992).
2. See *Battle of Trafalgar* (op. cit.) and BBC Radio 4, *In Living Memory*,

Series 7: Episode 2, '1990 Poll Tax Riots'. See also: http://www.bbc.co.uk/programmes/b0093ws4

3. The tax had been introduced to Scotland the year before.

4. Burns, D., op. cit..

5. Drury, J. and Reicher, S., 'The intergroup dynamics of collective empowerment: Substantiating the social identity model.' *Group Processes and Intergroup Relations, 2* (1999) 381-402.

6. Reicher, S., 'Crowd psychology' in: V. S. Ramachandran (ed.), *The Encyclopedia of Human Behaviour* (London: Elsevier, 2012), 2nd ed., pp631-637.

7. Stott, C., & Drury, J. 'Crowds, context and identity: Dynamic categorization processes in the 'Poll Tax Riot'.' *Human Relations, 53* (2000), pp247-273.

8. Hoggett, J., & Stott, C., 'Crowd psychology, public order police training and the policing of football crowds.' *Policing: An International Journal of Police Strategies & Management 33* (2010), (2), pp218-235.

9. Stott, C., & Reicher, S., 'Crowd action as inter-group process: Introducing the police perspective.' *European Journal of Social Psychology, 28*, (1998) pp509-529.

10. Stott, C. & Drury, J., 'The intergroup dynamics of empowerment: A social identity model.' In P. Bagguley & J. Hearn (eds.), *Transforming politics: Power and resistance* (London: Macmillan, 1999), pp32-45.

11. Reicher, S., & Stott, C., *Mad Mobs and Englishmen? Myths and Realities of the 2011 Riots.* (London: Constable & Robinson, 2011).

12. Waddington, D., *Contemporary Issues in Public Disorder: A Comparative and Historical Approach* (London: Routledge, 1992).

13. Vestergren, S., Drury, J., & Hammar Chiriac, E., 'The biographical consequences of protest and activism: A systematic review and a new typology', *Social Movement Studies, 16* (2017), (2) pp203–221.

14. Stott & Drury, 1999, op. cit..

# The Turd Tree

## Kate Clanchy

BUT LUKE SAID SHE should definitely come to the demo. They should go together. Time had moved on and so should they. No, three months was quite a lot when you actually thought about it. There were people he wanted her to meet.

Also, she should bring Lennie. Why not? Loads of the mums from the commune were bringing their kids. Loads of the *parents*, he should say, because most people in the commune didn't have Victorian family models, unlike Melissa. It was really liberating the way no-one went on about naps and food, and fathers mucked in with their kids. Oven chips were vegan, had she thought of that? Jammie Dodgers were vegan. That was the way to bring up a child, thinking of the whole world not just yourself and Gina Ford.

'Lennie's not vegan,' said Melissa, baffled. Neither was Luke, last she saw of him. That was surely an omelette he'd been eating in their little kitchen in Bow on their last evening together, gooey in the middle, golden with yolk. He'd wiped the pan with the bread, told her he was leaving, left. And that was certainly butter on his crescent of crust, butter she'd bought, bread she'd sliced, his teeth marks still in it.

'Who's vegan?' she said, annoyed with herself for crying. Big tears in the round plastic cup of her parent's phone. Ridiculous. As Luke said, their problems went back *years*, not

429

just since Lennie. Melissa had just had her head in the sand. In the nappy bucket. Bread bin. Omelette pan.

'No-one's vegan,' said Luke. 'What are you talking about?'

'I can't bring Lennie on the demo,' she said. 'It will be cold.' And she waited tensely to hear about Iraqi babies who might get incinerated, never mind cold, and whatever had happened to Melissa's consciousness, as well as the rest of it since the baby, and didn't she realise this was the biggest issue not just of now but of their entire lives probably, a pivot in the course of world history which would probably result in unending war and terrorism and crusades and God knows what until, like, 2050? Couldn't she see that?

But: 'Oh,' said Luke, 'Honey, don't worry. We'll wrap him up warm.'

It was appalling, the way she softened at the least sign of tenderness. She said, milking it, using her little voice: 'There will be so many people. He's only two and three-quarters.'

'But his mummy and daddy will be there,' said Luke, using his special, cosy voice too. 'We'll take care of him.'

'Will you come here, then? Hemel Hempsted? Come with us?' begged Melissa.

'Come to your parents' place?' said Luke.

'My parents are going to this one,' she said. 'They've actually got a parish bus.' And there was a silence and Melissa realised she had gone too far, as she always did.

'But if you came,' she said, 'obviously we wouldn't have to go on it. We'd go on the train.'

'Even the Tories are going on this demo,' said Luke. 'Even the Tories see this war is wrong. I guess that's good.'

Which was stalling. And an insult. Melissa's parents weren't Tories. They were soggy green liberals who lived in a house full of Nicaraguan coffee and books about God and climate change and proportional representation. 'Lost causes,' Luke used to say. Jeff and Linda, the patron saints of dead stuff and Fairtrade. But these days Melissa's politics were gravitating towards her parents'. Like sand in an egg timer, she could feel it seep from her toes. Because where had being too Marxist to get married got her? Bankrupt in her parents' basement, that was where. And anyway, she thought, wasn't this Iraq business a lost cause? Blair would do what he wanted, regardless of demos, really, so her parents and Luke were definitely on the same side.

'No,' said Luke, 'definitely not the parish bus. And not the train either. I'll meet you there. At the demo. Hyde Park.'

'We'll never find you,' she said. 'There'll be thousands of people. Thousands and thousands —'

'Of course we can find each other,' said Luke. 'It's 2003. We can use our mobiles.'

Mean. He knew Melissa didn't like her mobile, and also that she felt bad about not liking it. Luke was ever the early adopter, Apple Mac, email, Windows, iMac, and Melissa was ever the stick in the mud. Luke had said, 'What sort of self-employed picture researcher doesn't have a phone these days?' An unemployed one. And he'd made her buy one, a little Nokia brick which mostly sat silently in its charger, letting her know how unemployed she was. Luke's own latest Nokia had a tiny camera inside it. Melissa could not see how that would ever be of any use to anyone. Her own camera was still film: the grand, hefty, Canon with an even heftier detachable zoom lens which she was once going to make her living from, and now only used to stalk Lennie in the playground. She took close-ups of him on the swings or on the climbing frame when he didn't know she was doing it. They came out like wildlife photos of deer: Lennie's tiny nose and pointy eyelashes, the tip of his profile, enclosed in the fold of his hood or the cage of a swing, and everything behind him indistinct, blurred, swept with bright lines like worn rock, or the Northern Lights, time.

Luke caught her thought. He was good at that: that had always been the trouble. 'Lissa!' he cried. 'Come on. It'll be a grand thing,' he said. 'Something really right about it. You know. Lennie on his first demo. Come on, how many demos did we go on, eh? It's how we met. More or less.'

According to Luke, they had met at the Poll Tax Riot of

1990. But Melissa knew that they had been to all the same meetings that term, when she was in her first year and he was in his third. They had been on the same bus, three times, they had worked on the same paper. Melissa knew, she had set her cap at his cap, and her cap was a Breton one, with badges. She had bought it specially, and a donkey jacket, for the Poll Tax demo. She had packed up her camera, brand new then, and Luke had actually nodded at her on the bus, said it was important to document the whole thing, an important job. And when they got to London, he had stuck by her, and when they arrived in the Strand, late, and realised that the tide of people was running backwards, already, at terrifying speed, away from something with thunder and horses, Luke had pulled her up on the base of a lamppost, and clasped her round the waist with both arms. 'Take the pictures,' he had cried, 'Go on, it's what we're here for,' and she had clicked and clicked, turning in the circle of his arms, image after image of the hot river of the crowd.

'Remember how you sold those photos,' said Luke. 'Maybe you can do that today. It'll never get any more important than this, Lissa. Iraq! This could ruin the world till 2050. More than that. We're talking the whole Middle East, Lissa. We're talking the future of humanity. That's why we've got to do things like this together. The demo. We've got to be a family. Show Lennie we still belong together. You bring him on the train, I'll meet you in Hyde Park. It'll be a healing thing.'

And she yielded, the way she always did.

Because she was pathetic. She really was. Oh, Melissa might not be globally, wholly pathetic – she had friends, still, she used to have a job, she surely would again, just as soon as she got out of her parents' basement in Hemel Hempstead and back to London – but she had an inner frozen island of patheticness on which flew a white flag of surrender to Luke. It was patheticness, not politics, that had brought her now to another frozen island, a narrow raised bed of roots under the third tree from the Achilles Way entrance to Hyde Park in the middle of the largest crowd she had ever seen or imagined, a crowd huge and slow as a frozen sea of grinding icebergs. And Luke, of course, was not there.

Yes, she was early. She had done the whole thing early because she didn't see how else it was going to be done, not with a push chair. She was on the Hemel Hempstead train at seven sharp, and processing along Piccadilly well before ten o'clock, but even then the crowd was so dense you could walk only at funeral pace. They were funereally quiet too, murmuring to each other almost spookily in the traffic-free, Christmas-holiday-feeling, hungover street. No-one seemed to know quite what to shout. 'Bliar' didn't work very well, it was a sight-pun really, you couldn't pronounce it, and no-one had found a rhyme for 'WMD'. At one point, someone started shouting *Maggie Maggie Maggie*, a seagull cry, and got a laugh and an *Out Out Out* from the crowd.

People were still quiet now, in fact, even a whole Hyde Park full. There were yells and music, and on the distant stage, there were megaphoned echoes of speeches, but somehow it all got sucked up into the giant quiet, the anxious, shivering and muttering quiet. As if they were all at an immense train station, far away, perhaps in a Soviet Republic, in the past. As if they were all queuing outside it in the cold, fleeing a disaster, stamping their feet under this enormous, over-coated sky.

The problem, imaginary Melissa said to imaginary Luke, was that Melissa didn't know what to shout either. It might shock Luke to hear it, but she wouldn't be surprised if Saddam Hussein did have nuclear weapons somewhere, he was an evil dictator after all. Supporting him wasn't the same as CND, actually. Saddam Hussein would never paint a peace sign on his face like the green faced group rearranging their sign against the fence. He really wouldn't! And even Blair. He was the leader of the Labour Party! They had campaigned for him, Luke and Melissa! And he had told the truth about Kosovo. A sort of truth. No, Kosovo was quite bad, and it was right to invade. Melissa wasn't sure he was a Bliar. Maybe just an over-righteous church person, a bit like her dad: sincere, primarily, but a little misguided. The imaginary Luke shuddered, a cold thought in a cold air, and she wished desperately that he would actually turn up, warmer and more vivid than other people, with his bright cheeks and eager mouth, his quiff of shiny black hair. Because he would know what to shout, and she would agree with him, that was how they were.

But Luke couldn't find them now if he wanted to. It was impossible. When she had first got to their island, two hours ago, there was room around them and the park still looked like a park, with trees and paths and people streaming down the paths to the gathering in the middle where the barking stage was, and Lennie had been asleep. Now, Lennie was awake and peering over the furry pouch of the pushchair and the whole park was packed like rice in a jar. People were still streaming in, pressing in, circling around Melissa's island like walrus. The island was tiny now. Three of them on it, raised up just a foot or so above the crowd. Melissa, Lennie in the pushchair, and a girl with rainbow hair who had nothing to do with them.

Melissa had called Luke, twice, to give their position, once calmly two hours ago, and once in panic, two minutes ago. Both times they got cut off. She had also sent a text message giving their position carefully calibrated from the park entrance. Typing the message had taken her nearly twenty minutes, with all that twiddling on the keys, and said 'turd tree' at the end of it despite her best efforts.

It wasn't a turd tree, yet, but it could be, soon. Lennie had had prunes for breakfast, borrowed from Granny who soaked them carefully overnight to keep her aged bowels working. Melissa had a supply of wipes with her but it could still be a nasty business if Lennie suddenly asked if he could have a poo in a potty which he sometimes did and which Melissa had to encourage. They didn't have a potty. She'd have to get him to do it in the Tupperware sandwich box, now empty of sandwiches, then seal it carefully and wrap it all up in a nappy bag and carry it home under the push chair, where, with any luck, it might freeze.

'Where's Granny?' said Lennie again.

'She's somewhere here,' said Melissa, summoning herself. 'With Grandad. With the church people.'

'They went on the bus,' said Lennie, 'we went on the train. Why Mummy?'

Melissa had given many answers to this question over the last six hours. Why she had got on the train in the frozen dark and stood by the pushchair next to the door for the rattling hour from Hemel Hempstead instead of getting on the warm bus with her parents and a crowd of decent well-meaning Methodists she had known all her life. Why she had crawled here in the impossible cold, through the impossible crowd, on her own, instead of walking under her parents' banner, the one which said, after much consultation, 'GOD IS LOVE ST MARY'S HEMEL HEMPSTEAD' and which belonged really to the revival rallies.

'Why Mummy? said Lenny again.

'We wanted to meet Daddy,' said Melissa, and added, truthfully, 'And Daddy wanted you all to himself.' Lennie had had his nappy on since Charing Cross. Eventually, if she just left it, it would leak, everything would get wet and then all the careful layers of his clothing would freeze, like a frosty millefeuille dessert. But if she pulled him out, and pushed him through a change, the rainbow girl would see, and she might have strong views on disposable nappies, the way Luke did. She looked the type, in her DMs and her rolled dungarees and vintage donkey jacket. The type to suddenly talk to you, ask you if you knew something and if not, why? She might even know that toilet training at three was too late, and Melissa would be unable to tell her that Lennie had been two months early and his development was fine considering, great, and it wasn't actually Melissa's fault at all, but Luke's because the child had regressed in so many ways since his daddy had walked out and gone to live in a Hackney squat which he called a commune. Because how could Melissa talk to her, or to anyone really, without bursting into tears.

'OK,' said Lennie. 'OK, Mummy.' And he returned to bashing his little leather mittens together, for the sound. 'Pee-pall,' he said. 'Pee-pall.'

All the way there, Melissa had said, 'People, People, look!' Trying to rejoice, to pretend the ranks of 'BLiar' masks were funny. Now Lennie turned it into a siren: 'Pee-pall. Pee pall. Pee pall.'

'People,' said the dreadlocked girl, in an Irish accent. 'And have you ever seen so many?'

'I'm sure he hasn't,' said Melissa, wishing her voice wasn't so posh. 'It's marvellous, of course. The numbers. I mean, for the cause.'

The rainbow-haired girl had a thin, hard little body and scorch marks on her dungarees. Melissa wondered if she was in the circus. A fire eater.

The girl stared back at her, then laughed. 'Aye. It's off its own head,' said the girl. 'The numbers. The people. I mean, have you ever?'

'What numbers?' said Lennie, looking up through his little wire specs. 'One, two, three, four.'

The girl laughed again and squatted down so she was on Lennie's level. 'We're talking about the number of people,' she said. 'One, two, five... a thousand.'

'A million,' said Lennie. 'Trillion million.'

'I think you're maybe right about that, wee man,' said the girl. 'When I was a little girl in Ireland there weren't so many people in my whole county, I swear.' She looked up at Melissa and said, 'Sure, and have you seen the crowd from down here? The kid can't see a ting but hands and arms – it's crazy. You're a brave wee man, so you are.'

Lennie gazed at her. He was a mulish, stilted child, generally, a scowler at playgroup, but now, to Melissa's irrational irritation, he smiled and reached out a mitten curiously towards the rainbow girl's nose. There was a ring in it.

'Does it hurt?' he said.

The girl laughed. 'Naw,' she said. 'It's fine.' And she took a packet of biscuits out from her pocket, half-eaten.

'Do you want one?' she said, and Lennie reached out a mitten.

'No,' said Melissa, reflexively.

'It's alright,' said the girl, 'It's a Jammie Dodger. They're vegan. Jammie Dodgers are vegan.'

'Oh,' said Melissa. 'No. It's his teeth. You know. Sugar. Biscuits.'

'His teeth look grand to me,' said the girl.

They did. They were tiny and white, embedded in the pink heart of the biscuit, pulling strings of jam.

'Just the one,' said the girl, soothingly. 'A biscuit never did anyone any harm.'

'Where's Daddy?' said Lennie, crumbily. Melissa sighed.

'He'll be here soon,' said the rainbow girl.

'How do you know?' said Lennie.

'Your mammy phoned him, and he'll be on his way! You have to listen to your mammy.'

She smiled at Lennie, then up at Melissa. 'I heard you,' she said. 'Sorry.'

The rainbow hair was plaited in, you could see up close, dreadlocks of bright plastic. Under them, her head was small and pretty as a child's. Starry-eyed and guileless, like Lennie himself. Melissa smiled back, almost without meaning too. She thought she could take the girl's picture, maybe, bright against the grey and white cloud. Her camera was in the bottom of the pushchair. She should use it, really.

'I'm waiting for my man too,' said the girl. 'But there's an awful crowd.'

'Yes,' said Melissa.

'Your Daddy?' said Lennie

'Naw,' said the Irish girl, 'my boyfriend.' She winked at Lennie, and he ducked under his pouch, giggling. 'Except it's the other way round for me. He sent me the message. He sent me to the third tree from Achilles Way, and here we are.'

'Turd tree,' said Lennie, and the girl laughed. 'There's you mimicking my accent! Cheeky wee monkey.' And Lennie, after an anxious pause, laughed back.

'His dad was supposed to be here hours ago,' said Melissa. 'Maybe a bit optimistic.'

'Och, men,' said the girl. 'They always are,' said the girl. 'What about a biscuit for mammy?' She proffered the Jammie Dodgers. And Melissa, suddenly warmed, took one.

'Mind you,' said the girl. 'We're missing the speeches, hanging about here.'

'Do you want to hear them?' said Melissa surprised.

'I do, yeah,' said the Irish girl, 'I really do. Because you know, I'm here, but I want to know why I'm here, do you know what I'm saying? Tell you what I'm thinking, there are too many people here all with the same banner, and I'm not too sure what I want to put on my banner, if you follow?'

In the far centre of the park, the barking speaker stopped for a moment, and the crowd suddenly convulsed in applause.

'I mean,' said the Irish girl. '*Make Tea not War.* That's not my banner. I think we should bomb the bastards.'

'Iraq?' said Melissa, liking her.

The Irish girl laughed. 'No,' she said. 'Parliament.'

'I think,' said Melissa, 'I'm more on the tea side?'

The Irish girl giggled warmly. 'Och,' she said, 'that Blair. He went mad if you ask me. D'ye remember when he went to Kosovo? All those children, Ton-ee, Ton-ee? That's what did it, if you ask me. Something flipped in his head and now he wants to be Saint Tony of Iraq. Really. I think it's a fucking crusade.'

Melissa hadn't heard it put quite like that. She said, 'Yes, but are you sure bombing him is the answer?'

'Only language they understand,' said the girl. 'Church people. Trust me, I'm from Ireland.'

Melissa gave a great snort of laughter.

'Okay,' she said. 'I'll go with you. I'll plant the bomb.'

'Grand idea,' said the girl. 'They'd never suspect you. Open the doors right up.'

And they both laughed. 'Listen,' Melissa said to the Irish

girl. 'I'm going to take some photos. Would you mind my son a moment?'

'Sure,' said the girl. 'Grand idea.' And she squatted down by Lennie. 'Now, what else have I got in my pocket?'

Melissa pulled out the camera bag, screwed on the wide angle lens, and turned it out on the crowd, edging herself up against the trunk of the tree to get a better angle.

'There's a foothold round the other side,' said the girl. 'I was on it earlier. You'll get a better view.'

She was right. On the other side of the tree, facing away from the gate, there was a large bolus a couple of feet off the ground. If Melissa perched with her feet sideways on it, and her left arm clutching the scaly trunk, she was a clear yard above the crowd, and could click OK if she concentrated. She was concentrating. The light was dirty, and the raised white signs monotonous. It was the scale of the thing that was interesting. So many of them, with those flickering white billboards, like army ants, or ash. And the way they convulsed suddenly, in applause, like skin.

'There goes Mammy,' said the girl, to Lennie. 'Clicking away. Can you believe it? Does she do that for her job?'

'I did for a while,' said Melissa, slipping down the bolus to change the wide angle for the zoom, and to clip in a new film.

'You look professional, so you do,' said the girl. 'Now, see what we got, me and Lennie.'

It was a plastic bottle and a long, folded piece of wire, and for a moment Melissa worried it was a drug, one she hadn't heard of.

'Bubbles,' said the girl. 'I made the loop myself but you can never get them big enough.'

It wasn't a day for bubbles, but the ones the girl with rainbow hair blew for Lennie were so big they were enchanting. Bouncing snow globes, or fish bowls, comical and glamorous. They caught the half light and bounced and snapped on the trunk of the trees then out to the crowd. Melissa followed them with the zoom, caught them floating insouciantly, satirically, above the turned heads, breaking themselves on 'DON'T ATTACK IRAQ' signs, on the union bannerheads. Melissa pulled in the focus so that mouths and eyes and profiles coalesced against the smoky facelessness. People, people, as Lennie said.

The crowd was like grass, Melissa saw now, following the lines of the park like turf on a ruin: long furrows and crop circles. It was a miracle of gentleness. She pulled herself higher on her bolus perch, and twisted round to get a bubble running down a ley line of crowd, a sort of bowling run, ending in a singular Blair mask coming towards them. It was a dream shot.

There might be too many signs, thought Melissa, there might be too many people, even, and too many messages, but they were all right, they were all in the right. The consequence of today must be a change. Not the sort of change the Irish girl perhaps had in mind, or Luke, or the men in the green faces and peace signs, but a fudge of some sort. They'd send in some sort of token force, pull out a few token weapons, work something out. Luke could not be right with his vision of the apocalypse, any more than he was right about there being no weapons in Iraq. England wasn't a dictatorship, in the hands of one man. Look at England, the people of it, turning in slow gyres, enormous parts of an enormous clock. England had been here forever. They had elected a government. It was not about to start the eternal war for a lie. It was not possible to think it.

'Mummy,' cried Lennie, 'Look!' And Melissa swung back round the other side of the tree, camera still to her face, to snap her son's poreless, tilted, innocent profile against the crowd, and the Irish girl's profile, also significantly poreless and innocent, with that heavy head of rainbow hair.

'Blair,' said Lennie. 'Blair.' And there was the Blair mask Melissa had photographed, still coming towards them on its long legs, swinging through the crowd. Luke's long legs, Luke's swinging stride, Luke's long hand on the mask, tugging it up, off. Luke's warm, bright face full of love.

Melissa pulled her camera from her face, slipped from her perch, and saw the Irish girl tight in Luke's arms. She wrapped her legs around his torso like a child, her rainbow hair flung backwards in the last of the light. She said, 'I knew you'd come, I knew it!' And he said, 'I promised you, I promised.'

# Afterword: The World Protests, 15 February, 2003

## Laleh Khalili
SOAS, University of London

THE OVERWHELMING SENSATION EVOKED by Kate Clanchy's anxiously familiar story is of betrayal. I remember a great deal about that day, but perhaps because I anticipated the colossal betrayal ahead, my memories of it are tinged with brighter colours than hers. A great perfidy lies at the core of the story, the Janus-faced betrayal embodied in the wrenching personal rupture between Melissa and Luke, *and* the much more consequential global betrayal of the political class ignoring the public demonstrations on that day; the parliamentary pusillanimity and ultimately the sanguinary tragedy which was the invasion and its aftermath.

Because I anticipated the betrayal when I went on the march that clear, cold day in February 2003, what I remember is something else. The protest wasn't just in London, of course. And as my then-partner and our friends got on the train from Edinburgh to Glasgow to join the protest there, all I remember is a rambunctious joyous sense of commonality of purpose. What I remember from the demonstrations themselves is the awesome spectacle of a heaving, pulsating crowd, of city streets moving like a vast and mobile organism to a single rhythm.

Perhaps because I had no illusions about the craven geopolitics of the Bush and Blair administrations, for me that day of protest was something bigger, something more consequential: registering the extraordinary power of popular voice. For me, if there was any incredulity, it wasn't about the fact that the Blair administration chose not to listen to us, it was that there were so many people out there; that the opposition to war was so universal, so sincere (even if cynics like Ian McEwan make of that day something that can be mocked or dismissed). Because that day was not only about committed activists coming into the streets, but about the people who *ordinarily* minded their own business, the business of parish churches, of the quietist mosques, of 'Tories even'. But *that day* they didn't.

What I also remember with incredulity is that, even for those of us who studied the Middle East and who warned about the consequences of the US War on Iraq, the aftermath was far worse than anything we could have begun to imagine. It wasn't just the clumsily stage-managed invasion, the 'shock and awe', the theatrics of US Marines pulling down statues of Saddam Hussein (whilst being strategically cropped out of the picture so that it all seemed like some sort of spontaneous uprising), or all the pious pronouncements of 'serious' policy people against the naiveté of those of us who opposed the war, or even the daily valorisation of this or that military regiment engaged in whatever dubious heroics the press wanted us to believe.

What was horrifying was the piling of bodies upon bodies; the disbanding of institution after institution (not least the Iraqi Army); the razing of city upon city; the pillaging and plundering of Iraqi national assets, national memories, national infrastructures. The images that came out of Abu Ghraib, and the stories that followed about the interrogations and torture in Camp Nama and Camp Bucca and British-managed bases were bad enough. Then we heard about the random savagery of brutalised combatants. And we saw videos of beheadings. We saw walls built in formerly convivial cities to separate neighbourhoods declared one thing or another by instant experts on Iraq's sectarian makeup. Then, years later thanks to WikiLeaks, we saw videos taken from helicopter gunsights of innocent, unarmed civilians being slain (in one case, over a dozen people in a single mission, among them two Reuters journalists).[1] Then, even more years later, thanks to the Chilcott Report, we learned that a key piece of evidence about Saddam's chemical weapons capability provided to Blair and foreign secetary Jack Straw by MI6, allegedly from a new source 'with direct access', had actually been inspired by nothing more than watching a Nicholas Cage film.[2]

Over the next few years, Iraq became a laboratory in which a flailing US military tested its new doctrines of warfare, interrogation and intelligence-gathering. Names like Ramadi, Falluja, Najaf, Sadr City, Tal Afar, and Basra became not only markers on the map but metonyms for new ways of fighting counterinsurgency wars, for new tactics of population control, and for new strategies of divide and rule. If the Iraqi Ba'ath party had appealed to sectarian loyalties to manage popular revolt, conceptual fantasies like 'tribes' or monolithic sectarian communities with uniform political positions ended up becoming the premises on which the blueprints (and the constitution) for a new state were drawn up.

Iraq became a test-site for new weapons like drones and incendiaries, a battlefield proving ground for new covert operators; the Joint Special Operations Command, run by General Stanley McChrystal and responsible for pursuing al-Qa'ida militants, became famous for its particularly brutal brand of torture inflicted on Iraqi detainees.

What is left in the aftermath is not only a devastated landscape, littered with the nuclear pollutants from the depleted uranium weapons used so liberally, and fouled by the inevitable spillages of oil, but also hardened sectarian identities, divided and ethnically cleansed cities, and a population whose public health – physical and psychic – will likely take generations to recover.

Politically, the remnants of the disbanded Iraqi military went on to form the militarily-hardened kernel, not only of an

Iraqi resistance to occupation but of the brutal, brutalised and brutalising unconventional force that dubs itself the Islamic State in Iraq and al-Sham. If the strategists of that force are former Ba'athist, their Caliph, Abu Bakr al-Baghdadi, is a former prisoner who was detained in the JSOC-operated Camp Nama, and subjected to god knows what kind of torture and indignity.

Regional powers, struggling against one another for whatever residue of power was left after the great powers moved out, have used Iraq as a domain for their nasty proxy wars. Saudi Arabia and Qatar support one brutal faction; Bashar al-Assad's Syria supported another; the Turks tried to ally with some Iraqi Kurds, in order to pacify Turkish Kurds; the Iranian regime supported some of the worst people who came to power in the especially brutal Iraqi interior ministry. And in every instance of this tawdry patronage, a blowback is to be expected, if it hasn't already scorched all that lies in its path.

So why would I remember that cold crisp day of protests as anything but an abject failure, a damp squib, a gory and pathetic stillbirth?

Those marches have echoed through subsequent national security decisions of both the US and UK. Parliamentary and congressional votes for more intensive engagement in other Middle East wars and putting boots on the ground have been overshadowed or thwarted by memories of the march. Bush and Blair are perhaps the most hated heads of state in their respective countries (though Trump and Brexit seem to be softening the bitterest of the memories). The march led to organisational and dissident structures that mobilised in the UK around the bank failures of 2008; student fee revolts and other causes that had previously been abandoned following the fragmentation of the left in the UK under Blair.

There is a cold harshness to hindsight. We always look back and so often claim that we should have – even could have – seen the abject failures that were sure to follow a given action. My view of that moment is still coloured by the contingency, by the possibility that the exuberance of that day promised. Political movements begin in unanticipated ways, saturated with contradictions and potentialities of both success and failure. The marches on that cold, crisp day could have – even should have – gone in a different direction, leading to the hard tedious graft or organising. But as it stands, that day attested to one thing lucidly, unequivocally, coruscatingly: that a public emerged on the street; some hesitant, others with conviction, some even for the first time ever, and that the public declared that an unjust war should not be fought. That this moment of clarity was to be betrayed so cravenly says nothing about the joyous, raucous 'no' shouted throughout London and so many other cities of the world, on 15th February 2003.

## Notes

1. 12 July, 2007. See: https://www.theguardian.com/uk-news/2016/jul/06/
movie-plot-the-rock-inspired-mi6-sources-iraqi-weapons-claim-chilcot-report
2. https://collateralmurder.wikileaks.org/

# About the Authors

**Sandra Alland** is a Scotland-based writer and artist who has published and presented throughout the UK, Europe and North America. Recent highlights include *Feral Feminisms,* Disability Arts Online's Viewfinder Project, Malmo Queer Film Festival, Seattle Transgender Film Festival, and Comma's *Thought X* (2017). Sandra has published three books of poetry and a chapbook of short fiction, and is co-editor of *Stairs and Whispers: D/deaf and Disabled Poets Write Back* (Nine Arches, 2017). www.blissfultimes.ca

**Martyn Bedford** is the author of five novels for adults: *Acts of Revision*, which won the Yorkshire Post Best First Work Award, *Exit, Orange & Red*, *The Houdini Girl*, *Black Cat*, and *The Island of Lost Souls*. He is also the author of two novels for young adults: *Flip* (shortlisted for the Costa Children's Book Award, and winner of the Sheffield Children's Book Award, the Calderdale Book of the Year Award, the Bay Book Award and the Immanuel College Book Award) and *Never Ending* (2014). His first collection of short stories, *Letters Home*, is due from Comma later this year.

**Kate Clanchy**'s short story *The Not-Dead and the Saved* won the 2009 V. S. Pritchett Prize and BBC National Short Story Award. Her short story collection of the same name, published by Picador, was shortlisted for the Edge Hill Prize and described as 'literary hand-grenades…exactly what we need right now' by *The Guardian*. She also writes award-winning poetry, fiction, criticism and non-fiction and frequently writes and adapts for BBC Radio. She is currently at work on essays about her 28 years working in state schools: *The Book of School*.

**David Constantine** is an award-winning poet, translator, short story writer and novelist. His most recent collection of poetry was *Nine Fathom Deep* (2009). He is a translator of Hölderlin, Brecht, Goethe, Kleist, Michaux and Jaccottet. His short story collections include *Under the Dam* (2005), *The Shieling* (2009), and *Tea at the Midland* (2012), which won the Frank O'Connor International Short Story Award, and the title story of which won the BBC National Short Story Award (2010). His second novel *The Life-Writer* (2014) was one of *New York Times'* top 100 books of 2016, and in the same year a feature film based on 'In Another Country', titled *45 Years*, received an Oscar nomination for star Charlotte Rampling.

**Frank Cottrell-Boyce** is a children's writer and screenwriter. His film credits include *Welcome to Sarajevo*, *Hilary and Jackie*, *Code 46*, *24 Hour Party People* and *A Cock and Bull Story*. In 2004, his debut novel *Millions* won the Carnegie Medal and was shortlisted for The Guardian Children's Fiction Award. He has since published two more, *Framed* and *Cosmic*, both with Macmillan. He also writes for the theatre and was the scriptwriter of the highly acclaimed BBC film *God on Trial*. He has previously contributed stories to Comma's anthologies *Phobic*, *The Book of Liverpool*, *The New Uncanny*, and *When It Changed*.

**Stuart Evers'** first book, *Ten Stories About Smoking* (2011) won The London Book Award. He has since published a novel, *If This is Home* (2012), and a second collection of stories *Your Father Sends His Love* (2015). He regularly writes about books for *The Guardian*, *The Independent* and *The Observer*.

**Kit de Waal**'s debut novel, *My Name is Leon*, was a *Times* and international bestseller, and was shortlisted for the Costa First Novel Award, the Kerry Group Irish Novel of the Year and the British Book Awards Debut. Her prize-winning flash fiction and short stories appear in various anthologies. In 2016, she founded the Kit de Waal Scholarship at Birkbeck University.

**Maggie Gee** is the author of 11 novels, including *The White Family* (2002), shortlisted for the Orange Prize and the International IMPAC Dublin Literary Award, and most recently *My Driver* (2009), as well as a memoir, *My Animal Life*, and a collection of short stories, *The Blue* (2005). In 1982 she was selected by Granta as one of the original 20 'Best of Young British Novelists', and in 2004 became the first female Chair of the Council of the Royal Society of Literature.

**Michelle Green** is a British-Canadian writer living in Manchester. She has published one collection of poetry with Crocus Books, *Knee High Tales*, and one critically acclaimed collection of short fiction, *Jebel Marra*, based on her own experience as an aid worker in Darfur. She recently won a Julia Darling Travel Fellowship to develop her next book.

**Andy Hedgecock** is a writer, researcher and former co-editor of *Interzone*, Britain's leading SF magazine. He has written reviews, essays and non-fiction for 30 years for the likes of *The Morning Star*, *The Spectator* and *Time Out*.

**Laura Hird** is the author of collections: *Nail and Other Stories* (1997), *Hope and Other Urban Tales* (2006) and the novel *Born Free* (1999) which was nominated for the Whitbread and Orange prizes. A book based around her mother's letters, *Dear Laura*, was published by Canongate in 2007.

**Matthew Holness** won the Perrier Comedy Award in 2001 for *Garth Marenghi's Netherhead*, and has since appeared in *The Office*, *Casanova* and Ricky Gervais' *Cemetery Junction*. He was the creator and star of two Channel 4 comedy shows – *Garth Marenghi's Darkplace* and *Man to Man With Dean Learner* – and more recently has starred in the C4 series, *Free Agents*. This is his third short story for Comma; he is currently adapting his second 'Possum' (commissioned for *The New Uncanny*) into a feature film, starring Sean Harris.

**Juliet Jacques** is a journalist, critic and writer of short fiction. She has published two books: *Rayner Heppenstall: A Critical Study* (2007) and *Trans: A Memoir* (2015), and has published journalism on literature, film, art, music, politics, gender, sexuality and football. She documented her gender reassignment for *The Guardian* in a series entitled *A Transgender Journey*.

**Sara Maitland**'s first novel, *Daughters of Jerusalem* (1978) won the Somerset Maugham Award. Novels since have included *Three Times Table* (1990), *Home Truths* (1993) and *Brittle Joys* (1999). She is also the author of *The Book of Silence* (2010) and *Gossip from the Forrest* (2012). Her short story collections include *Telling Tales* (1983), *A Book of Spells* (1987), and most recently *Moss Witch* (Comma, 2013). Her short story 'Far North' was adapted for the screen by Asif Kapadia in 2007 and starred Sean Bean and Michelle Yeoh.

**Courttia Newland** is the author of seven books. His latest, *The Gospel According to Cane*, was published in 2013. He was nominated for the Edge Hill Prize, The Frank O'Connor award, and numerous others. His short stories have appeared in many anthologies and been broadcast on BBC Radio 4.

**Holly Pester** grew up in Warwickshire, close to the sites of the Midlands Revolts, and now lives in London. She is a poet with an interest in radical forms of storytelling and transmission such as gossip, magic, myth, lyric and fables, with published work responding to a feminist art archive (*Book Works*, 2015) and lullabies (*Test Centre*, 2016). She is a Lecturer in Creative Writing at the University of Essex.

**Joanna Quinn** is studying for a PhD in Creative Writing at Goldsmiths, University of London. Her work has been published in the *New Welsh Review*, the Bridport Prize anthology, and *Beta-Life* (Comma, 2014). In 2011 she was short-listed for the Arts Foundation Fellowship in Short Stories.

**Francesca Rhydderch**'s debut novel, *The Rice Paper Diaries* (2013) won the Wales Book of the Year Award 2014 for Fiction. She received a Literature Wales bursary to develop her short stories, which have been published in magazines and anthologies and broadcast on Radio 4. Other projects include a play in Welsh, *Cyfaill*, about iconic Welsh-language writer Kate Roberts, for which she was shortlisted for the Theatre Critics Wales Best Playwright Award 2014.

Grenadian **Jacob Ross** is a fellow of the Royal Society of Literature. His debut novel *Pynter Bender* was shortlisted for the Commonwealth Writers Regional Prize and chosen as one of the British Authors Clubs top three Best First Novels. His most recent novel *The Bone Readers* (Peepal Tree) won the inaugural Jhalak Prize for Book of the Year by a Writer of Colour.

Liverpool-born author **Alexei Sayle** is a comedian (with numerous TV appearances to his credit, including *The Young Ones*, *Comic Strip*, and *Alexei Sayle's Stuff*), novelist and a short story writer. His debut short story collection *Barcelona Plates* was published to widespread acclaim in 2000, and was followed by *The Dog Catcher* (2001), and the novels *Overtaken* (2003), *Weeping Women's Hotel* (2006), and *Mister Roberts* (2008). The two volumes of his autobiography are *Stalin Ate My Homework* (2010) and *Thatcher Stole My Trousers* (2016).

# About the Consultants

**Sally Alexander** is Emeritus Professor of Modern History at Goldsmiths University of London. Her books include *Becoming a Woman: and other essays in 19th and 20th century feminist history* (1994), and most recently *History and Psyche: Culture, Psychoanalysis, and the Past*, edited with Barbara Taylor (2012). She was an organiser of the first national UK Women's Liberation Movement conference held at Ruskin College, Oxford in 1970, was a member of several groups in the London Women's Liberation Workshop, and among other protests participated in the 1970 Miss World Demonstration.

**Laleh Khalili** is a professor of Middle East politics at SOAS, University of London, and the author of *Heroes and Martyrs of Palestine* (2006) and *Time in the Shadows: Confinement in Counterinsurgencies* (2012).

**Lyn Barlow** was a protester at Greenham Common from 1983 to 1987, then worked as a researcher for the *The New Statesman*, before studying at New Hall College, Cambridge. Her archives have been donated to the Women's Library, London Metropolitan University, and were drawn on by Jane & Louise Wilson in the Hayward Gallery's exhibition, *History Is Now: 7 Artists Take On Britain* (2015).

**Stephen Constantine**, born in Salford in 1947 to parents who believed in education but whose own schooling ended at age 14, was appointed in 1971 as a lecturer at Lancaster University and retired in 2010 as Professor of Modern British History, while retaining an active research interest in empire and migration.

**Elizabeth Crawford** is the author of *The Women's Suffrage Movement: a reference guide 1866-1928* (1998), *The Women's Suffrage Movement: a regional survey* (2013), *Enterprising Women: the Garretts and their circle* (2012), and *Campaigning for the Vote: Kate Parry Frye's Suffrage Diary* (2013). Website: www.womanandhersphere.com.

Dr. **John Drury** is Reader in Social Psychology at the University of Sussex. He has been carrying out research on crowd behaviour for over 25 years, and has published extensively on protests, social movements and collective action, behaviour in mass emergencies, and other crowd events. His research website is here: http://www.sussex.ac.uk/psychology/crowdsidentities/

Dr. **Ariel Hessayon** is a Senior Lecturer in the Department of History at Goldsmiths, University of London. He is the author of *'Gold tried in the fire': The prophet Theaurau John Tany and the English Revolution* (2007) and editor of several collections of essays. He has also written extensively on a variety of early modern topics: antiscripturism, antitrinitarianism, book burning, esotericism, communism, environmentalism, heresy, millenarianism, mysticism, and religious radicalism.

**Russ Hickman** grew up in a socialist family in a Tory heartland. Working in a number of management positions whilst raising six children, he found himself, like Tony Benn, became more left wing with age. He now enjoys Labour, union and other left-wing activism in retirement.

Dr. **Steve Hindle** is Director of Research at the Huntington Library in San Marino, California. Among other things he is the author of two essays on the Midland Rising: 'Imagining Insurrection' (*History Workshop Journal,* 2008) and 'Sir John Newdigate in the Court of Star Chamber', in *Popular Culture and Political Agency in Early Modern England and Ireland,* eds Braddick and Withington (2017).

ABOUT THE CONSULTANTS

**Avtar Singh Jouhl** was born in Jandiala Manjki, Punjab, India, and has lived and worked in Smethwick since 1958. As a trade unionist, he has spent most of his life campaigning against racism, and for equality in rights and opportunities, working with the Indian Workers' Association of Great Britain and the the Labour Party. In 1995, he chaired TUC Black Workers' Conference .

Dr. **Katrina Navickas** is Reader in History at the University of Hertfordshire. She researches the history of protest and democratic movements in Britain. Her latest book is *Protest and the Politics of Space and Place, 1789-1848* (2015).

**Gordon Pentland** is Reader in History at the University of Edinburgh. He has published extensively on the political and cultural history of Britain and Scotland since the French revolution, including a book on the Radical War, *Spirit of the Union: Popular Politics in Scotland, 1815-1820* (2011).

**Michael Randle** has been involved in peace work as an activist and academic since registering as a conscientious objector to military service in 1952. He was a member of the Aldermaston March Committee which organised the first Aldermaston March at Easter 1958. He has a PhD in Peace Studies from the University of Bradford.

**Stephen Reicher** is Wardlaw Professor of Psychology at the University of St. Andrews. He is a Fellow of the British Academy, a Fellow of the Royal Society of Edinburgh and a Fellow of the Academy of Social Sciences. For over 30 years he has been studying group and collective behavior, looking at hatred and solidarity, obedience and dissent, oppression and resistance.

**John Rees** is an activist, broadcaster and writer, as well as a national officer of the Stop the War Coalition, a spokesman for the People's Assembly Against Austerity, and founding member of Counterfire. He holds a doctorate on 'Leveller organisation and the dynamic of the English Revolution' from Goldsmiths, University of London, where he is currently a Visiting Research Fellow. His most recent books include *A People's History of London*, with Lindsey German (2012), and *The Leveller Revolution* (2016).

**Francis Salt** worked as a skilled fitter and acted as a Trade Union convenor, until he was injured and blinded in 1991. Since then he has undertaken M.Phil research into the work of the National League of the Blind, Ben Purse, and the Henshaw's Asylum, where his grandfather was a member and brush maker.

**Mark Stoyle** grew up in rural mid-Devon and worked for a time as a digger with Exeter Archaeology. He is currently Professor of Early Modern History at the University of Southampton, where he specialises in the history of the British Civil Wars. Professor Stoyle has written many books and articles on Tudor and Stuart history, including *The Black Legend of Prince Rupert's Dog: Witchcraft and Propaganda during the English Civil Wars* (2011).

Dr. **Em Temple-Malt** is Lecturer in Sociology and Criminology at Staffordshire University and co-director of Staffordshire University Crime and Society Research Group. Her current research interests are qualitative research methodologies, studying the everyday, relational lives of sexual minorities in this 'era of equality' and more recently using drama to help teens develop strategies to avoid unhealthy, abusive relationships.

**Ned Thomas** has had a varied career as writer and journalist, activist and social entrepreneur, magazine editor and publisher. He has taught at the universities of Salamanca, Moscow and Aberystwyth, where he founded the Mercator Institute for

Culture, Media and Languages of which he remains President. He has worked for twenty-five years in the field of European linguistic minorities and played an active part in the campaign for a TV channel in Welsh. Two of his publications have achieved a wider than academic resonance. *The Welsh Extremist – A Culture in Crisis* (1971) was influential in the 1970s New Left and in the Welsh language movement. His memoir *Bydoedd* was Welsh-language Book of the Year in 2011.

**David Waddington** is Professor of Communications and Co-Director of the Cultural, Communication and Computing Research Institute at Sheffield Hallam University, where he started out as a Postdoctoral Research Associate in March 1983. Since being appointed, he has continued to publish widely on the policing of public order, industrial relations in the coalfields, and the sociology of Britain's mining communities.

**Jane Whittle** is Professor of Rural History at Exeter University. Her research focuses on everyday life, society and economy in rural England between 1300 and 1750. She has published numerous books and articles on topics such as popular protest, wage labour, women's work, domestic material culture and rights to land.

Prof. **Adrian Randall** (University of Birmingham), and Dr. **Esmée Hanna** (Leeds Beckett University) also consulted on Andy Hedgecock's and Alexei Sayle's stories, respectively.

# Special Thanks

The publisher would like to thank the following, without whom this book would never have been possible: Dr. Peter Van Den Dungen (formerly of the University of Bradford), Tony Hobbs, Julie Evans, Dr. Ana Millar and Prof. Martyn Amos (MMU), Sarah Hunt, Alice Guthrie, Mandy Vere and Julie Callaghan (News from Nowhere Bookshop), Emma Gifford-Meade, and the filmmakers Humphry Trevelyan, Amanda Richardson, and Beeban Kidron.